The Vandervelde Documents

Richard Turner

ISBN 978-0-9930862-0-5

A CIP record for this book is available from the British Library

LLYFRAU CAMBRIA

Published in the United Kingdom in 2015 by Cambria Books, Wales, United Kingdom

"From now on humanity must live
as all life on earth must live:
on what the earth can provide us."

To Thelma.

For her unqualified support and help, despite her distaste for the subject matter.

CONTENTS

Prologue 2120

I am old; so old I forget the centuries unless I mark them. Slowly the thread gets thinner, and surely soon I will have no will to write. All effort becomes pointless; I am no longer relevant. I will die, perhaps soon, and the world will turn. I will be forgotten but for these scribbles, these electronic traces and marks on paper. I don't know how old I am or why I am different from other people. I don't even know my name so I call myself Vandervelde – from the open country.

This is my room, a few chairs, my table, my comms and its power source, and a trunk with the few things I've saved from all the phases of my life. Each of us has a room of our own and we all use the communal eating and washing areas.

I look up and see odd shaped joists of different sizes, holding up a rough looking ceiling. No doubt they are re-used from some building long forgotten by most people, but from a world I cannot forget. I can sort through the scenes as they are stacked in my memory, each with some symbol for me to retrieve them. It seems natural to me to organise my memories like this, but I have learnt that others do not. This space, these buildings and this small community are to me the physical traces of the birth of our Nation – flotsam left by the tides of history. It was 60 years ago but by a small neuroshift I can see it all so clearly.

Take this chair: Twm made it when he retreated to his cabin. It is an ancient type called Windsor – elegantly turned legs and thin whittled spindles set into a solid, shaped seat. He gave it to me later when he rebuilt his life in Cambria:

"Take it Van. It seems to mean more to you than it does to me. I was unhappy then."

“Yes, I can see that but I can also see love and gentleness in the work, and reflections of many other times which were good.”

The door is a simple wooden structure which opens onto a passage and as I walk down it to the dining hall I can see markers arranged in my mind - all those other passages, steps, corridors, tracks, roads, Transnets, portals and paths which lead to the other parts of my life. All that is but those of childhood. I have no memories of childhood and no marker for any memories.

Much has been lost but I’ve done what I can to preserve at least some of what I and the others have written during this long period of growth and collapse and re-growth. I feel sure this is the last chapter and I’m glad.

It’s a simple life now in these Islands; a hard one. All the good things in life we once had in abundance have each to be wrested from our meagre resources by hard work. For so many years before and after 44 we had so much stuff, so many things. All around us, afterwards, was the wreckage of the great civilizations of the 20th century. We had oil in huge tanks, steel in tangled heaps, timber, new forests everywhere, feral animals to hunt and eat.

With what we could re-use and with our accumulated knowledge and skill we built a new society and here we built a new Nation. It was a good one: Cambria - my great love; the thing I was most proud of. It still survives in some ways, like pools left as the flood ebbs away. And of course Cambria was just one; there were hundreds of Small Nations. How else could The Warden have been able to regulate human life? I have nothing to do with The Warden now, though some of the other elders are involved. I was manipulated, used. Was it a necessary evil? I will never know.

It, or they have set us this last great challenge. This is what the last century has been lurching towards – the final reckoning, for now we know that there are no more quick fixes. From now on humanity must live as all life on earth must live, on what the earth can provide us. We can take from it only what we can give back. Here, in this green, damp land, we share what the earth can provide and we can live in health and meet our needs, but we know, as no previous generation has known, that we can do no more than this. We cannot be greater in numbers or in wealth; if we grow we must also decline, but we will survive. We are, at last, learning how to live with our neighbours; we have learnt some wisdom, some sapience.

CHAPTER 1 2020 – 26

Sir Hector Grant (Air Vice Marshal rtd.) Memoires

Marlsburg, Britannica 2022

"Climate Change"; I'm sick of the sight and sound of it. Look at this. I ask you; how can they print such garbage?

"ARCTIC ICE HEADS FOR BRITANNICA"

Just because someone has seen a glacier somewhere near Iceland. Everywhere you look now it's 'Global Warming', 'Carbon Footprints', 'Sustainable Energy' and most people haven't got a clue. Amy and I disagree on this, but I've kept up with things since I retired. Nobody can deny our world is facing some hefty problems but I have grave doubts about some of the politicians who are vying for our votes. It seems clear to me that if we are to continue to improve life for all our burgeoning millions we have to ensure that everybody has a chance to develop. I can't see how that can happen if the lights start going out. Industry needs energy and it is absurd to think that we can simply switch to windmills and solar panels and all the other Green technologies everyone seems to be getting so excited about. It just won't work. Even if we cover every square kilometre of Britannica with wind turbines it wouldn't be enough and the cost would long ago have driven our industries abroad. I can think of no quicker way to send our great country into abject poverty than putting coal, gas, and nuclear power out of bounds.

Amy, my daughter, seems to think that we have to stop burning fossil fuel altogether. Don't get me wrong, I'm all for developing energy saving technology. Believe me I've nothing against Green technology per se, I just don't see the necessity for trying to do everything at once. Used sensibly our resources of coal, oil and gas could last for centuries. They, the Green lobby, say if we don't leave it in the ground the earth will fry, but where's the proof? We've had hot and cold periods in the past. We humans are amazingly resourceful when we've got our backs to the wall.

So I'm determined to enjoy my retirement – in fact I almost have a duty to do so. It would be a pretty poor show if the author of the "Grant Report into Armed Service Retirement" found himself climbing up the walls! My great regret is that Margaret and I could not be together. I can understand her dislike of service life, but how she could have fallen for that stupid man Dexter I will never understand. She said I was boring. I've not met anyone else who thinks that. I'm still close to Amy and the people I meet don't walk away in mid conversation like they do in the films. I've plenty of friends, some even from my days in the corridors of power. I still use the old pub in town that I used to go to when I was younger. To the locals I'm the same Hector Grant they've always known. I don't use my title except for formal occasions. I even took Tony (Blair – the one that used to be PM) in there once. That created a bit of a stir.

I had another visit from Amy recently, so I had to brush up my cooking skills. She always enjoys the meals I make. Not, I fear, because I am such a great cook, but because she hardly notices what she eats, and is always grateful not to have to do any cooking. Food is just fuel to her and a meal is more like a pastime, a way to lubricate social relations. She got her divorce last summer and she and Belle decided to move in with Margaret while she looked for jobs. I was a little hurt that she didn't want to live here, but also, I must confess, slightly relieved. What she said was that I was coping much better on my own, and I suppose she is right. I like to be able to do things in my own way. Margaret was all for the new life when she left me, but Dexter predictably turned out to be a dead loss, and now she is very bitter and angry. I'm sorry for her, but there's not much I can do about it – except to refrain from saying "I told you so"!

Amy and Ben used to live mostly in Germany, though they kept a flat in Sulis which they used when they were here.

It turned out that dear charming Ben was something of a gambler as well as a philanderer, and had clocked up some impressive debts. Amy was left custody of little Belle, the flat and a mortgage, so had to look for a job. Fortunately she had kept up with the latest research in her field, which was thin film technology, and started to look for jobs in engineering. Belle spends the school holidays with Margaret which has improved Margaret's mood, but it makes it hard for me to see as much of her as I would like.

Amy's great news was that she has a new job.

"It's so exciting Daddy. They are doing some amazing work on the next generation of graphene-like 2D materials."

"Where will you be based?"

"It will have to be in Redning where the labs are. I won't be doing anything too challenging at first, but they are growing fast and there is every prospect of promotion quite quickly."

"Sounds good. Have you decided where you want to live?"

"Give me a chance! I've hardly stopped for breath with this sudden rush of interviews I've had. I imagine I will rent somewhere in Redning to start with. Lucy has offered to put us up in Lyndain if I want to commute, but I don't want Belle to go to school there."

I didn't quite know what to say, and there was an uncomfortable silence.

"Ah . . . Lucy. How is your sister?"

"Oh sorry Daddy, I didn't mean to . . . Look, Lucy is as she is. She does still love you, you know. I wish . . . "

"As I've said before I am waiting. If she wants us to be close again she knows what to do."

"Oh for God's sake don't let's go over all that stuff again!

You can be so obstinate sometimes."

I did not reply. I have at least one daughter who truly loves me and I didn't wish to waste our time together quarrelling.

****

Dear Lord, not again! I really don't think I can stand another summer like 2020. We've had no rain now for six weeks. The poor little cottage has no air-con so I've been sleeping with all the windows open. Sleeping? More like just lying there in a pool of sweat worrying about intruders. Some days I just sit in the car with the engine on to run the air-con and read or sleep. Poor Bruce is really suffering. He lies stretched out panting on the stone floor. The river is dry again so he can't even cool off there. Last week when we hit 40 degrees I actually ran a bath of cold water for him. Some days we walk into town early so that we can get a seat in the only café with air-con. Understandably they don't let you stay for more than half an hour but it gives him a chance to cool off. Other days I just drive round with the air-con going. I can't do that for long either now that diesel is so expensive.

Talking of which I think our government has finally lost its marbles. It's very hard to get real information on this, but from what I hear from my old friend Tony it seems the coalition have handed over what is arguably the most important area of government policy – carbon emissions - to a non-elected body called Northern Resources Group. Tony has given up on Britannica altogether since Cherie died and has gone to live in the US. He still seems to be very popular over there and is still making a fortune on the lecture circuit. He has some connection with the US government's emissions policy, and tells me it is a lot more sensible than the European one.

Sometimes I lie awake at night wondering what sort of world Belle, my only my grandchild, will live in. I fear for her,

I really do.

Mollie

Brigstowe 2022

I've decided to keep some sort of a record of my life. I kept a few notes and things since I left school, so I'll start with them:

I'm still having to pinch myself. It seems only yesterday I was that earnest young student working for her finals in Grantabrig and desperate to do something about the climate. I'd read as much as I could about climate change and over-population, and it all pointed one way – we were heading for disaster. I made a firm decision – I would not have children. It's not fair to bring them into the world and then tell them the world is crap. The cold weather was back and people were saying "how can the world be getting hotter when we have such terrible cold weather." Now they seem to be getting the message.

I was heading for my finals and in a really weird place – in my head that is. It's like there were two things converging – my years doing the Bac at school – Life Sciences and Psychology - plus my years here. That was on one side and all the messy politics on the other. I had a real feeling of premonition - something really important is happening and I could be at the leading edge of it – not just me of course, there are lots of us all over the world.

Then we had one of those magical springs which dear old Britannica can turn up from time to time. The world seemed anything but crap when April arrived. How can anyone be depressed on a wonderful spring day? Even though I know it doesn't mean anything it's such a relief to see all the flowers coming out, the early butterflies and even the first of the migrant birds.

It all felt so normal. Even our lecturer, Dr. Hendrix, was less than his usual grumpy self. His subject was the reactive radicals in the atmosphere – not as boring as it sounds! In fact the whole Gaia thing is really trending since James Lovelock died. It's all "Global Life Systems" now. Look at the question of how the oceans maintain exactly the right amount of salt for instance. You can't explain it without biology. My special area of study is artificial photosynthesis, but there is masses of work going on in all aspects of biomimetics.

Some scientists think Lovelock was a fraud, but it seems to me he had some great ideas. It's not his fault he attracted a load of nutters. I was gobsmacked when Mari told me she had joined one of these groups. I think this one is "Sisters of Gaia". Mind you she's always been up for all sorts of alternative stuff. I just keep my head down and keep reading.

I had to opt out of a few gigs for a while. Our music is so intense that I couldn't do it justice when I was so preoccupied with formulae and the periodic table. It was a hard decision because our group "Sound Advice" is beginning to get noticed. One of my works even got over a thousand hits on MyLine. It seems that the music of sound is an idea with wings. Luckily for me they kept my seat warm. It keeps me grounded, working with my music friends. When we are on stage or even in the studio, it seems the most important thing in the world.

Hot summers are getting more common now, but the combination of hard winter/ warm spring and hot summer is still unusual so I remember that year well. It was 2020, two years ago. Luckily for me I had one of the old rooms in college, and old means 700 years old. It was in Old Court and had thick stone walls. If I kept the windows open and the blinds down I could keep the temperature down to 25 degrees which is tolerable. By then most people had stopped sunbathing. It doesn't seem clever any more to roast your skin and bring on the wrinkles.

I was excited about my work though – I was already thinking about doing a doctorate, when I stumbled on a bit of research which could really make a difference to the world. I had been mulling the problems of trying to mimic the natural process of photosynthesis. I'm almost sure I have discovered a new way of using cobalt oxide as a catalyst.

Then things really got interesting. Even cobalt oxide had to take a back seat for a while. It was after my last exam - dripping with sweat and trying to think clearly. When I closed my screen after the last essay I walked out into the hot sun feeling so happy and relaxed, I just wandered around singing to myself.

It was employers' day and Grantabrig was full of suits and IT nerds trying to recruit the best of us. Time was students used to queue up for jobs with the banks and big corporations, but there was a different feeling now. The mood had changed. Only the real corp-heads want to join a bank now. The big name here was Northern Resources Group. They seemed to be calling all the shots, and not just here but all over the world. I've still got the leaflet I picked up when I booked a place for a chat. *(see page 15)*

The next day I met someone called Rufus. He was older than me and really smooth. They were all casual there - not a suit in sight. Rufus was in shorts would you believe! He was even smoking! How retro can you get? I hope I didn't talk too fast – I was so excited. Anyway I went through the work I was doing and he went quiet.

"Mollie, we need to talk more. Can you come back at one? I'll get you some lunch – somewhere cool."

Of course my first thought was he was making a play. I'm not the best looker in the world, but I'm OK, and do get chatted up sometimes. He must have guessed what I was thinking because he then said:

“In case you were wondering, I’m very happily married. It’s strictly business, and by cool I mean with air-con.”

“Yes that kind of cool I could use, but I have to be back by 14.30”.

“OK, here at 13 then.”

Of course I was early - pretending to read all their screens. I thought we would be going to a pub or one of the cafes but we went to the Old Schools. It was sort of austere/grand if you know what I mean – white walls, oak timbers, very old, quiet, simple food well presented. I soon started to relax when Rufus put a glass of wine in front of me and started telling me about the work he was doing.

“We’re working on a global plan to curb carbon emissions”

“Bit late aren’t you? We should have been doing that 20 years ago.”

“Absolutely, couldn’t agree more. It is very late, but the public mood has changed. People are really frightened now and we think we can actually do something which is a lot more than cosmetic. Let me ask you this. If we can get emissions down to the right level how long do you think it would take for the warming effect to level off.”

“Oh come on.” (The glass was empty by then!) “You would have to get emissions down to something like 3 tonnes per head right across the world and even then we wouldn’t see much change for 30 years at least.”

“If I told you are target is 2 tonnes and within 20 years does that sound like something you would want to be part of?”

I was so surprised I actually stopped talking for a minute! My head was swirling.

“That sounds like big politics to me, and I don’t know

that much about politics and economics."

"Actually you've already shown me that you do, but I was thinking more of the chemistry, and I'm not really qualified to ask the right questions. I see from your CV that you are something of a polymath – musician, psychologist, chemist, biologist - it's people with a broad outlook we need. Would you be up for a meeting with one of our scientists to explore the possibilities?"

Did he have to ask!

Northern Resources Group – a Summary

The NRG Group (formerly Norde Handelsbank) is a non-profit making Non-Governmental Organisation. Its primary business is resource trading and it is funded by a sponsor list (see appendix 1) of National governments and by other NGOs.

Mission Statement

NRG is committed to the long term future of human civilisation throughout the world. Their commodity is the real wealth of the planet – its resources, the ecosystems which our societies need to flourish. That includes physical resources such as water, food, timber, metals, and the less tangible resources such as clean air, healthy seas, and even the air we breathe.

Structure:

In many ways NRG resembles the global corporations, but the group has no shareholders and does not make a profit. The head office is the former headquarters of Norde Handlesbank in Berlin, they also have offices in Japan, Canada, China, Britannica, the Netherlands, Madagascar and Brazil, and active groups in many other countries. There are three divisions within the company:

NRG Trading

NRGT is the only body now permitted to trade in commodities in the countries which support the parent body. Because any profit NRGT makes is returned to the sponsoring governments they can compete on very favourable terms with the private commodity exchanges.

NRG Innovation

NRGI is their research department which, because of their

constitution, is able to fund research looking well beyond the normal pay – back period for a commercial organisation.

NRG Society

This, the newest division set up in 2021 is concerned with human and animal behaviour and already has a remarkable track record in predicting how groups of people, and the animals they depend on for their well-being, will behave when confronted with the challenges which they anticipate the next 20 years.

The Council

The highest decision-making body is the NRG Council, a small group of top executives. Strategic decisions are made by the Council, but most executive decisions are made by an indeterminate number of small working groups, some international, and some local. They are supported by regional admin teams. In addition to the Chair, Vandervelde, the current members of the council are:

Voula Randriananta, (Madagascar). Horst Weber, (Germany). Yi Hua Chang, (China). Edmundo Almeida, (Brazil).

Vandervelde

Wohnung 3

Neustadtstraße 10

10178 Berlin

Look at them - like moths to a candle they rush towards the only comfort they know. Always it's more production, more consumption, more money, more jobs, more people more more more. Like laboratory animals they learn the buttons to press to get their fix. "More Jobs" is the best one, the people love that one. Can't you just see him there in the parliament, that well-dressed handsome man with his dark suit and neat tie, his hair carefully arranged, his righteous indignation carefully controlled, his text-book rhetoric delivered in resounding phrases. Oh yes, it all sounds good but what do those neat phrases actually mean? I'll tell you. This is what they mean:

"If you will be so sensible as to keep me in power, I will give you the comforts I know you want. You don't care what happens in ten years time so I'll make sure you get some goodies quite soon. It might not be next week or this year because I must be seen to be doing something about the mess, and I know many of you will not be fooled by instant gratification. What you really want is for me to solve the immediate problems (you will accept a little hardship for now, it makes you feel virtuous) and then bring back the good times: more jobs, more growth, more money in your pockets."

The horrible thing about this situation is that most of them actually do know it's all nonsense. They are not stupid these politicians even though they give that impression. They have intelligence but not wisdom.

You out there, you the people, you won't hear this because you don't want to but I shall say it anyway:

Business as usual will, before your children are old, lead to a world so toxic that most of us will die.

Berlin 2022

Haus der Handlesbank

I found those words in a little file in some personal folder I was about to delete. They were written at my lowest point when I had almost lost hope. Nobody but me has seen them, but somebody somewhere got the message.

It was the summer of 2020 which brought everyone to their senses. That was when the big changes started. I was on top of the world then, chairman of the Northern Resources Group (NRG) with more money available to me personally than the national output of a dozen or so countries. Money? I hardly noticed its loss when we changed the constitution. I had been around for too long. Personal consumption no longer interested me. Somebody – I didn't mark the name - asked me to write "a brief account of what NRG is and what we do" (link). Where do I start?

I suppose I should start with something about myself, because I am different from other people. The most obvious difference is that I seem to grow older very much slower. Over the years I have asked many people to describe how their memory works so I know that mine is different. It seems that the "others" – the rest of you, the "normal" people – seem unable to organise your memory systems in the way that I can. Against that it seems you all have clear memories of childhood, even of infancy, which I do not. Everyone except me and those like me, seems to know how old they are. We do not. I say "we" because I know there are others. This knowledge is in my memory, but I've never met any. Somehow I know that I am here, doing what I am doing, for a purpose, and recording these notes is part of that purpose.

Let's go back to the Autumn of 2020. It was bad enough in 2019 with the terrible winter: half of northern Europe froze for 6 weeks. Things eased off in April and it seemed at last Spring was coming but then the frost returned in May and the birds were dying in their nests. When it finally came in June the summer was warm, but it was too late by then for many of the crops. To everyone's relief the following winter was quite mild and spring came early. Out came all the barbecues and summer dresses and we all relaxed. June was hot right across Europe, and there were ominous signals from America of what was to come. The heat-wave in the Rockies broke all records and killed millions of birds and animals, but that was over there. Here, in Berlin hot summers were quite normal, but then July came and still the temperatures were rising. By the end of the month all records had been broken in every European country except the far north where they were below average. The emergency wards were full of heatstroke victims. August was slightly cooler but by then the water had run out. Every hotel in northern Caledonia, Scandinavia, arctic Russia, Alaska and Canada was full and we even saw refugee camps being set up.

That was when the governments turned to us, to the Northern Resources Group. In late 2020 we had a secret meeting with senior representatives of the governments of the G10, which then comprised: The European Union, Brazil, China, India, The USA, Russia, Australasia, The South East Asian Federation, Japan and the Federation of Central African States. At this crucial point in world affairs the then President of the USA, Wayne Shorter, once the most powerful man in the world, found he was without power in his own country - a country now so polarised by ideological and racial divisions - that he was forced to make a humiliating climb-down and withdraw from the negotiations. Russia too refused to take part, mainly because they controlled so many fossil fuel reserves which would lose much of their value if the plans under discussion came to fruition.

So it was that in November 2020 I found myself chairing a meeting of the NRG Council in Berlin. Those present included our most senior people from Germany, China, Madagascar, Brazil, Arabia and France. We use

International English (IE) for these meetings. Before us on our screens was the document we had received that day from the heads of the G8 (The G10 minus USA and Russia) joined by another 20 influential governments. There were a few introductory paragraphs but the gist of it was the simple message:

"Keep the Climate Change Index to plus 2"

The CCI is an internationally agreed way to measure climate change, and plus 2 was roughly equivalent to 2 degrees of warming. The general consensus was that +2 represented the current position. I'd thought for a while on how I would present this:

"My friends, if we accept this commission, these few words will mark the beginning of the biggest task any human organisation has ever undertaken. Beside it the ending of the Cold War looks like child's play, the Treaty of Rome a game of monopoly.

"We are talking here of a very rapid reduction in carbon emissions to near zero. There is to my knowledge only one mechanism which can hope to deliver such massive change so quickly, and that is 'Carbon Trading'. The proposal is to scrap the existing European scheme and introduce a new global one with much tougher penalties and a much higher price. Annual permits to issue one tonne of CO2 into the atmosphere will be auctioned. These permits will be traded on the commodity markets. The number issued will be reduced year by year until the required level is reached. The details are in the brief you have on your screens.

"Whatever we do will face formidable opposition. We will be blamed for the inevitable suffering that such rapid change will bring in its wake, but I believe we have no choice. Posterity will not forgive us if we are not brave enough to face this challenge. This is our chance or our nemesis. This is the Carbon Brief."

Mollie

Brigstowe

I was staying with Dad then, when l left Grantabrig. He's still self-employed doing commercial design. It brings in the money but he's getting bored of it. He gets very depressed about the future. It's funny – I find myself telling him that we CAN change things round, but when I start on the science he gets lost. Jamie was also there taking a break from Exeter where he's doing a multi-science degree. He seemed to spend most of his time in some basement with his friend Mark. He wouldn't tell the rest of us what he was up to. Mum got very cross with him for not studying.

As the results day drew nearer I knew I would be disappointed if I didn't get a 2:1, and I allowed myself a little secret squeezed-up ball of hope that I might hit the jackpot, so I was genuinely delighted when I was awarded a first class degree in Life Science.

I started that September with NRG. I didn't even have to move – they have an office here in Brigstowe. I've had several meetings with various people in the organisation, and last time actually met the big chief. He's called Vandervelde – just that or Van – and seems to be a bit of a mystery figure. Still, he's very pleasant and easy going. He's not particularly good-looking, has no airs and graces, but whatever company he's in you just sense that he is "the man" – charisma I guess. I asked one of the girls how old he was and she said nobody knows. He looks sort of early middle aged, and has a slight foreign accent of some kind.

Is this really me? Have I really gone straight from being a student to chatting on a level with possibly one of the most important men in the world?

******

Soon after I joined the Company I was told that Van wanted to see me. I'd made a small contribution to the new Carbon Trading scheme – they had used some out of date information on emissions from reaction chambers - so I assumed he wanted to talk to me about that. I was wrong.

"Mollie, come in; good to see you."

"And you Sir"

"Now that's the first thing you need to get right if you are going to be happy working here – don't ever call me Sir. I hate it. To everyone here I'm 'Van'."

"Oh...sorry S, I mean sorry Van. I've not been here for long as you probably know."

"Yes, Mollie, I know a lot about you. How's Dan? I liked his design for the Create Centre"

"What? You know Dad?"

"Not really, just showing off!" He laughed, and suddenly I felt relaxed and laughed too.

"Another thing you will find out about me is that I'm not very good at what is called "small talk" so let's get down to business. I'm putting together a small team to work here in Brigstowe and I want you to be part of it. I have set up a few similar teams around the world which will report directly to me. If you accept, your job will be constantly to question our decisions, to look for new ideas, different ways of doing things, new ways of thinking. From what I have read and seen of you I think you have the right kind of mind to do this. How do you feel about that?"

This was not what I expected. I was amazed that he had taken any notice of me. I'm not the sort of person who likes to be the centre of attention. I like being a good team member.

"Wow! Can you tell me who else will be in this group?"

"Not yet, but I don't think you will be disappointed. By all means take a bit of time to think about it, but keep it to yourself until the group is established OK?"

"Yes, thanks Van. It sounds like a wonderful opportunity. Perhaps I'm a bit too cautious sometimes. I'll contact you tomorrow."

Of course I accepted – who wouldn't?

******

I've met the most amazing man. He's got a lovely old-fashioned name – Eldred- and he's an artist. I didn't meet him at work of course – he hates anything to do with big organisations. He doesn't even have a comms. Can you believe it? If I want to get in touch with him I have to go and knock on his door or even WRITE A LETTER. I've almost forgotten how to do that it's so long since I last used paper.

I was wandering round the Haven at the week-end with my old friend Mari from school. We stopped to look at a stall selling what I can only describe as large "things" made of metal and plastic which didn't seem to have any function. Behind the stall was a man sitting hunched up reading a print book – one made of paper. He took no notice of us at all until I said:

"It's probably the wrong thing to ask, but what is this?"

"You're right, it is the wrong thing to ask!" He laughed and Mr. Moody disappeared. I noticed his eyes – dark and full of life; some laughter lines at the corners. He had a mass of black curly hair with a hint of grey, and brown skin. When he stood up those eyes were only slightly higher than mine, which made him about 170 cm.

"It's a device that tells people things about themselves."

"But ...ah I get you. I look at this and I think 'what if . . ."

He looked surprised – almost shocked for a moment. Then he grinned.

"Exactly. You've got me sussed already. Listen, these are just samples, and the prices are rental, not sale."

"OK, so what are they samples of?"

"Well, I know it sounds a bit old hat, but I do installations. Some are solid objects, some light, lasers, some sound."

"Sound – that's interesting. I do some work with sound myself."

"Anything I would have heard of?"

"It's possible. We're called 'Sound Advice'; heard of them?"

"I sure have. Fantastic. Look, this nice lady here has been waiting a while; I need to talk to her. Take one of these". He gave me one of those bits of card which people used to use for their comms details. Come and see my studio . . . please come."

"I promise – I'm intrigued."

I quickly scanned the card to my comms and we walked on.

****

Of course I went round to his studio. I felt a right fool just turning up there on my own. There was a hopelessly glam woman there who seemed to know Eldred really well. I almost left before getting past the door, but she pounced on me:

"ELDRED is this the Mollie you just 'happened to mention' yesterday? Oh sweetie, I'm so pleased to meet you. I'm Maisy; I suppose you could say I'm his aunt or cousin or something – I can't be bothered with all that family stuff.

Treat him nicely, he's a dear man, but watch his temper! OK OK I'm going. See you soon Moll."

I didn't much like the way she kissed him on the lips but Eldred really did seem pleased to see me.

It wasn't long before we were going around together and I started meeting more of his friends. According to Eldred they don't know what to make of me. He's met a few of my friends from work but I'm nervous about introducing him to Van – not that there's any urgency on that count. He's been away for weeks and is not planning to be in Britannica for a while yet.

******

How on earth did I end up getting engaged to be married? Is this some kind of cosmic April Fool's Day? Didn't I make a vow not to have children? El thinks that's all nonsense.

"Do whatever Nature tells you to do Mollie. Even if burning all this coal and stuff has changed the climate there's nothing we can do about it. If there are too many people then one day a whole lot of us are going to die – that's how things are. The balance will be restored as it always has been in the past.

Just think of it all as our life. This is where we are now. Look for the beauty in our lives. It'll change soon enough. Bring on the catastrophe then we'll see what we're really made of."

And this is the man I'm going to marry! I must be mad. I am mad – with happiness! It will be in July. We decided if we were going to actually do the wedding thing then we'd do it properly with a marquee and Sound Advice are booked to play – without me, though I don't think I can resist sitting in for one number! It could be their last gig. I can't find the time to practise now, and one of the others has got a demanding job too. Perhaps it was just a student thing. I shall miss it.

It seems Eldred hasn't got much family. His dad long ago upped sticks and went back to Jamaica. I've met his mum – she's a nice lady but a bit boring. She's a native Brigstolian and there are a few aunts and cousins. It's a bit sad really. I would hate not to have my family, they're great. Mum and dad divorced ages ago but they're still friends and we often do things together. I used to have eight grandparents but there are only four now. Dad's father died a long time ago, but his mum is still going strong and both my mum's parents are still alive.

The only one I'm not sure about is my brother Jamie. He can be such a pain sometimes.

So there will be a fair few step parents, aunts, cousins, grandparents, nieces and what have you on my side to make up the numbers. When we heard that the CREATE Centre had started to do weddings (or handfastings as some now prefer) we knew that was for us. Create were pioneers of alt tech living back in the 1990s, From eco houses and permaculture to Smarthus and 3d gardening they are still breaking new ground. Eldred knows several of the people involved so they are pulling out the stops for us. I keep thinking really corny things like "This will be the best day of my life!"

Sir Hector Grant

Marlsburg

My poor sister Isobel finally lost her battle against cancer. Amy came with me to the funeral which thank goodness was in a cool chapel. I hadn't dared ask her if Lucy was coming, and I couldn't help looking back a few times to see if anyone had come in late, but she didn't come. When the girls were small they had loved spending time with their Aunty Izi, but . . . I really do not want to write about these things at a time like this.

Amy and Isobel were very close, and her death, though expected, affected Amy badly. As it turned out though, Iz had a big surprise for us – she had left a lot of money. I got enough to get this old cottage better insulated. Lucy had a substantial legacy too, but the real surprise was that most of it went to her favourite niece - Amy - with the instruction: "Do something exciting with it". Amy doesn't know whether to laugh or cry. She misses Iz dreadfully, but it seems the job in Redning was not what she hoped – she's still doing boring lab work – so perhaps this legacy will give her a the chance to do something really different.

****

I've given a lot of thought recently to Amy's legacy and I've had an idea. I'm taking her to see my old friend Patrick who retired from the RAF much earlier than I did, and I'm glad to say has proved a good example of what can be achieved by ex-servicemen. He inherited the old family farm on the downs near Ramsburg a few years ago and has adapted one of the barns to what he hopes will be his new business. He could see the way the wind was blowing in Air travel (pardon the pun) and I have a hunch that this could be an opening for Amy.

When I got to Margaret's house in Bourne I stopped outside and sounded the horn as I usually do. I did not have long to wait before Amy appeared looking neater than usual. She and clothes don't get on poor dear. She's always buying new things and then sending them to a charity shop. Mostly she wears the same jeans and sweater, but today she'd evidently made an effort – smart new skirt and top.

Bruce was banging his tail slowly on the floor at the back of the car with his eyes fixed firmly on the front door. As soon as he saw her he leapt up and danced round in circles until she let him out.

"Hello Bruce you lovely man. Steady, woa – down Bruce. Hello Daddy, lovely to see you."

She finally managed to subdue the dog, get him back in the car and get into the passenger seat.

"Have you got your wellies? It might be muddy." She went to fetch them, much to Bruce's consternation. Five minutes later she was strapped in beside me and we were on our way.

"So, what's this mystery outing then?"

"Well, I want you to meet an old friend from my RAF days. You haven't met him before because he was until recently serving abroad, but he inherited the family farm at Downend a few years ago and has all sorts of ideas about what to do with the buildings."

"Sounds interesting."

There was a pause. We were passing one of the racing stables and could see the string coming in from their morning ride.

"Actually I've something to tell you Daddy. I've given up my job."

"Oh. . . well, I'm not surprised. I had the feeling you

might have left soon anyway even if you hadn't had the legacy."

"It was holding me back. I had lots of ideas but whenever I talked about them with the higher-ups I got the 'all in good time' spiel - patronising bastards."

"Funnily enough that fits in rather well with today's outing – the job, not the bastards".

Downend is not far from Marlsburg and we were soon making our way gingerly down a muddy lane and into the even muddier farmyard. When the drought finally gave up in September last year it hardly stopped raining all winter. The floods weren't as bad as 14 but bad enough. Patrick was there to meet us and soon we were edging past piles of building materials and temporary polythene doorways until we reached the warm haven of the farm kitchen. There was a huge old AGA cooker with a kettle steaming on it. Amy was delighted.

"Gosh I haven't seen one of those for ages. Nice to meet you Patrick"

"And you Amy. Ah, the old AGA – yes, but I'm afraid it will have to go. There's no way we can bring it up to current energy standards."

"Well, I suppose they must cost a fortune to keep going all the time. It's technology left over from the 1920s really isn't it?"

"I guess you're right. I hadn't really thought about it like that. Hector tells me you have a degree in Chemistry. What's your area?"

"Materials, mostly polymers and thin films."

"Really? How exciting. As you will see, I have quite an interest in that area too."

We had some excellent coffee while we talked, but

Patrick was obviously impatient to show us something outside, so we got back into the rubber boots and went out again. Back in the 20 hundreds Patrick's parents had built a huge single span barn to house their animals in winter. It was beginning to look tired and shabby and the huge doors squealed and grunted as we slowly responded to the hydraulics and inched open.

I had some idea of what to expect, but Amy was rendered speechless. The entire barn was filled with what could only be an airship, but quite unlike the old Zeppelin type. It was a delta shape – a bit like the old Vulcan bombers from my early RAF days – a similar shape but much bigger. It loomed over us like some alien spacecraft in a B film.

"Wow – fantastic. It's some sort of airship isn't it?"

"Yes it's what I hope will be part of a new future for Lighter-Than-Air travel. It's a hybrid – it has powerful engines so can move around quite quickly."

****

I didn't hear much from her or Patrick for a couple of months, but then Amy buzzed me on my new comms device and said she had something to talk over.

"Daddy, you'll be pleased to know that introducing me to Patrick was one of your better ideas."

"Ah – I thought it might be fruitful. I'll bet you've been swotting up on LTA flight now?"

"I have, but rather more than that. Do you remember the message with aunt Isobel's legacy? Well, after our day with Patrick I couldn't think of anything more exciting than getting into the Airship business. I made him an offer for the whole business, and, subject to certain conditions, he's accepted!"

"That's my girl! Tell me all about it."

"Actually I was wondering if you would help me go through the contract and make sure I've got the terms right?"

I'm no lawyer, but she just wanted another opinion. Later that same day she dumped a pile of documents in front of me.

"There's no mention of the barn or the farm here. Are you planning to set up somewhere else?"

"Yes, I talked it all through with Patrick and we decided that the farm buildings, big as they are, would not allow for much expansion. As you know there's a lot of interest in LTA flight now and since the long term plan is for the whole business to be carbon neutral, we can get finance on very good terms. I've negotiated for the purchase of a large industrial area outside Swinsdun, subject to contract."

"Amy – what are you playing at? You've never run even a tiny business before and now you're proposing to borrow huge amounts of money and go straight in at the deep end."

"I know, it's a risk, but I certainly wouldn't be doing anything this ambitious if it weren't for these Carbon Trading regulations."

"Yes, I've followed the news too. It seems oil and gas are going to double in price every few years, but that will affect you too. What about all the set-up costs? Machinery, buildings and so on. Surely the hybrid craft have hefty engines don't they? That's more fossil fuel costs."

"All costed out. The thing is, I may not have much experience at running a business – well, as you say, none really - but I'm a good listener and there are plenty of consultants jumping on this bandwagon who can give me all the advice I need. You'd be amazed how much money is coming in from the carbon permits: there are just so many schemes offering help to this kind of business. Even the bank loan is at two percent less than the normal rate."

"Huh, I've heard all this before – banks falling over themselves to lend money they don't own. Oh I don't know Amy. I'm glad, of course I am, that you are well on the way to a career in aviation, but I can't help worrying. You're a parent too – you know what it's like."

"Oh go on you old softie". She gave me a hug, and I tried to stop worrying.

Brother Ulm

There are six of us elders in the Fellowship of the Trees. Four of us have accepted the call to work outside in the world. Brother Fagus, Brother Quercus, Brother Fraxinus and I all have names and status within the worlds of business and government. Brother Quercus has a special mission and he does not know the rest of us. Sister Tilia and Sister Acer both live and work in the Hub.

We four can freely move around in the society of normal humans, and part of my mission is to observe and report on Brother Quercus, his colleagues, friends and lovers. Of course he does not know this. He could not have done his work encumbered by the load we carry. At his own request, his memory was adjusted.

All so long ago: we were younger then, but already adults. I've tried to recall the time of building, when the Hub was created, but the tags are corrupted. It seemed natural then to divide the work on gender lines with the two women remaining at the Hub and us four men working on the outside. It is hard being amongst these people, working with them and yet knowing that we are not of them. It is even harder perhaps for Tilia and Acer to leave the world and take on the huge responsibility of the machine. Of course in those days it was not much more than a bean counter, but still, when we all joined hands and made the link it was powerful enough to make those changes to our memory systems which had been decided. All three of them, Quercus, Acer and Tilia have no memories before the moment we disengaged our hands and began our great work.

CHAPTER 2 2026 – 31

Vandervelde

The impact of the Carbon Brief was astonishing. Within a few years of its launch the price of anything dependent on fossil fuel was rising rapidly and money was flooding into any and every scheme, crackpot or otherwise, which was sustainable. As expected, attacks were coming in from all sides. I was spending far too much of my time travelling – Germany, Britannica, Rotterdam, Japan, Brazil, China, Madagascar. Everywhere there was disruption. The big corporations hated us, and some industries were facing melt-down – none more so than air travel. As soon as the aircraft industry permits hit the market they started a rapid rise, and the cost of Heavier Than Air (HTA) flight rose steeply. Millions of Euros was pouring into Lighter Than Air (LTA) flight and the NRG board decided it would be a good time to look at the possibility of buying an LTA craft to act as a mobile base.

That's how I came to meet Amy Grant.

People sometimes ask me how many wives I've had. It's a question I can usually get round by claiming to have very little recollection of my early life. There is some truth in this, and I can honestly say that I don't know how old I am, but I have tagged all the women I have lived with. For many years I lived in a state of near celibacy. That changed in 1971 when I met Katerina. My time with her was mercifully brief, but it taught me a great deal about relationships – stuff I had steered clear of until then. Since then I have had just two serious relationships before meeting Amy.

The company, Airlift Ltd. was based in southern Britannica – Swinsdun, then a rapidly developing centre for research and development in sustainable technology. I travelled by rail on a fast sleeper, stopping for a couple of hours in Paris and then Lyndain where I had to change to an overcrowded Britannic train.

It was one of the hot years and the drought in Britannica had been going on for 6 weeks - though the highest temperatures were still comfortable compared to continental Europe. The train was hot as well as crowded and I was very glad when we arrived at the old home of rail manufacturing. I was told the CEO A G Grant would meet me at the station, so I was surprised when a rather unassuming looking woman came towards me. Her hair was short and neat and she was wearing a baggy shirt and rather unflattering trousers. I hid my surprise, made the usual greeting noises as we shook hands and followed her to the anonymous car waiting, with a driver, in the little car-park outside the station. She was silent until we were in the car. Then she surprised me:

“I have to say I have some reservations about your company Mr. Vandervelde”

“So do I. I often feel we must seem like some secret cabal with far too much power.” To my relief she then laughed, and her face came alive.

“Couldn’t have put it better myself”

“The fact is Ms Grant we only do what governments all over the world pay us to do. Because we are not directly accountable we can do what has to be done.”

You couldn’t miss the factory. A good proportion of the sky above it was blocked out by one of their enormous CN (carbon neutral) liners. I was suitably impressed and wished I had time to see round that too, but I had to be back in Berlin the next day.

We came to the gate and a voice asked us to say our names:

“Amy Grant”

“Thank you Ms Grant, you may proceed. Please say your name.”

"Vandervelde"

"We do not know your face Sir, are you a visitor?"

"Yes"

"We do not recognise the response. Are you a visitor" Amy wrote 'Say I am' on her comms screen.

"I am"

"Please say your name"

"Vandervelde"

"Thank you Mr Vandervelde. Please look directly at the screen. Thank you, now please place your palm where indicated. Thank you. Please enter your code" Amy showed me some letters and numbers on her comms.

"Please enter the code. Thank you. Enjoy your visit Mr Vandervelde"

"Thank you gatekeeper."

I was pleased that they had installed the most modern security systems, and we walked across a stretch of tarmac made sticky by the heat. It was wonderful to get into the elegant, spacious and above all cool offices. She told me about all the photo-voltaic (pv) collectors they have on the buildings and on the airships which are tethered there - evidently quite enough to run a full air conditioning system.

"Have you always worked in aviation Ms Grant?"

"No, I graduated in Chemistry, but an old friend of my father's was making a prototype airship in his farmyard. He took me for a ride in it and I was hooked. My favourite aunt had just died and left me a pretty substantial chunk of money with the instruction to 'use it for something exciting'. Buying a prototype airship seemed exciting enough."

By then we had arrived at her workspace. Amy's was the same size as all the other private spaces in the admin area.

Like most manufacturing organisations now, Airlift was moving towards an integrated staff structure. She explained how their version worked as we walked down a series of long corridors, through more security and into the main assembly space. It was surprisingly quiet; small groups were working with huge robot machines which creaked and clunked softly as they moved quickly and gracefully round the assembly areas. The staff were doing the things that humans do better: making value judgments, watching for anomalies, adjusting the programming. As we watched, a machine was assembling one of the 2 metre diameter engines used in the biggest ships.

"This new model is something we are quite proud of Mr – oh I can't get my tongue round all those syllables, what do people call you?"

"Mostly just 'Van'. I'm quite excited about this too since I will probably spend a lot of time living in the craft. There are a number of things I haven't fully understood – perhaps because some of the information is too secret. There seems to be a gap in the public data on the new gas –HX. Can you explain to me in layman's terms why I should feel safe?"

"I find it difficult to think of you as a layman, but I'll try."

"Amy, I'm ashamed to admit that the world of numbers – mathematics – is largely closed to me. I know it is hard to explain scientific concepts without using the language of figures, but please try."

"Well, as you probably know the development of LTA craft has been held back for half a century by the very limited and expensive supply of helium and the incendiary qualities of hydrogen. There was nothing the industry could do to increase the availability of helium so we looked at other light gasses. Nothing came near to hydrogen in terms of availability – three quarters of all the water on earth is plentiful by anyone's standards. After many years of research, one of our rivals, HAS (Humbert Air Systems) in

America patented a mixture of gasses which is inert. Our own laboratories believed they could do better, and we now have our own patent gas called HX. It is heavier than hydrogen but can be manufactured very cheaply, and it has the same fire properties as nitrogen. We do use some helium which is stored in highly pressurized containers. When the craft needs to rise the system releases helium into the 10 buoyancy balloons contained within the main envelope. As the helium is decompressed the tanks become much lighter, and the balloons combined with the main HX gas envelopes allow the craft to rise. Water is used to trim the craft when under way."

Her eyes sparkled as she described the process. Here was a very different person from the one I had first met. I was discovering that her awkward manner disguised a person driven by a passion for science and by anger at what she calls 'sloppy thought'.

"Apart from your mysterious gas I understand that, and I'll trust you on the gas." She looked alarmed.

"Oh, er I'm boring you aren't I?"

"Absolutely not. If I gave that impression I apologise. It was not my intention."

"You . . . well, never mind." She paused. We continued walking.

"These people get so involved with the machines. You wouldn't believe some of the messages they leave on them. What I find so exciting is that everything we do is research based, and right at the front is research on what motivates people. Physics and Chemistry are the servants of psychology."

"Interesting – so does that mean you look at personality types before qualifications?"

"To a certain extent. We can quickly spot if someone is claiming to be an expert in a subject which doesn't match their psychological profile. That could of course be an indication of an unusual personality type and we are always looking out for that kind of person. I don't like the jargon, but we look for people who can 'think outside the box.'"

I knew that they had worked out a way to move people and goods to and from the ship when tethered at height, so she took me to another workshop where we were confronted by a fat cylinder with rounded ends suspended upright on a cable which was in turn held by a gantry.

"This is our smallest transit pod."

Facing us was a hatch with a recessed catch. She opened it and we stepped inside. There were four seats, each with a monitor and some controls, which she briefly explained. I sat in one of the seats to see what if felt like. At least on the ground it felt safe! Amy took the seat opposite and we smiled at each other briefly.

"You can control what you see of the view outside with this button . . . some keep this firmly shut."

"I can well imagine!"

"Yes, it's a bit scary until you get used to it. This is an emergency switch and with these you can call ground or call air. The cable is actually a highly complex bit of engineering. It's the only link with the ground when the ship is tethered – even at full height."

"Um . . . I . . . er . . ."

"Oh don't worry it's been tested to destruction. This cable can even survive a hurricane. What makes it even more extraordinary is that there are two main cables inside the sheath, because there are two pods which can safely pass each other on the cable so that the weight of the down pod does most of the work lifting the up pod."

"So, in principle, similar to the old ski lifts?"

"I never saw one, but I think so, yes. I have to admit, er, Van, that there are some people who refuse to use these. They must restrict their LTA travel to places where the ships are tethered much closer to the ground. With this cable we can station a craft up to 600 metres."

"Good grief- up in the clouds."

"Yes, even above them sometimes. Now for the gondola: shall we? We have a TX model here – similar to the one you are interested in."

It looked a bit like an aerodynamic bus with windows all round and two doors. It was about 20 metres long and 8 wide. We entered a small reception area and I sat in the main control seat. In front of me was an array of screens with controls below each one – nothing like the traditional aircraft cabin. It looked quite simple.

"That door leads to the living area and here is the pilot's cabin – we call it the Bridge. Most of the work is done by the automatic systems, but one member of the crew must be in attendance all the time to monitor the system."

"So how many crew would we need for a long flight?"

"You will never need more than two. Our systems really are very efficient."

"Good, now, lead me to the bedrooms."

"Well, er . . . The only bedrooms as such are the two in the apartment. The crew and passengers have cabins; this is a typical one."

I wondered if my feeble joke had caused offence. I hoped not because I was beginning to like this lady. Like everything else on the ship the cabin was build of very light-weight materials: a fold-away bed, table, wardrobe, storage and a tiny kitchenette. An internal door led to a very compact shower and toilet unit.

"You asked about waste. We did a lot of research on this, and found a firm in Sweden making a total water and waste system. The solid waste is separated and dried ready for use on the land when we descend. The liquid goes through a natural process which removes all the pathogens. It comes out as pure water. The only slight losses are from perspiration and evaporation when water is heated. This small percentage can easily be made up when the craft docks."

She drew some water from the basin into a plastic beaker, drank some and handed it to me. Our eyes met.

Here I must insert a pause. 'Our eyes met over a beaker of water' - really? Not really; life seldom fits such clichés. Why then do I remember this so clearly? Here I was in the company of a woman I found difficult; someone not obviously attractive, but clearly quite special. If she hadn't done what she did next I think I would probably have forgotten about her. She touched my arm.

I tried not to show how disturbed I was by this gesture and we continued to talk about the ship and the company she was so proud of.

" Van, I'm impressed. I've thrown all sorts of stuff at you and you've taken it all in your stride. Whether or not you want to buy the Condor, I hope we will keep in touch."

Letters from Amy Grant 2026

E-letter address

The Old Post Office, Bourne St George

Britannica

Dear Van,

So, you decided to buy the Condor. With my Airlift hat on I'm delighted to have sold another of our XT9 units, but with my Amy hat on I'm nervous. What if you don't really like it when you take possession? I prowl round the production shed trying to play the serious boss checking all the details. The production crew seem to smile a lot. I think they might have guessed!

I told you about Belle didn't I? She was only 5 when my parents divorced. This old house in the high street was my parents' home, and Belle and I moved back in with Ma when my parents divorced. I was never married to Ben, her father, and we had already split up a few years earlier. She's 10 now and it's actually helped Ma a lot having Belle here, but I worry that I don't see enough of her. I don't want her to become dependent on her Grandma. Since I met you I've been thinking a lot about how I would like to live in the future, and have made a resolution to allow myself more leisure time. The trouble is I get bored so easily when I am not at work. I have to force myself to sit still!

You asked if I could get away for a weekend in Berlin. Actually it could work out rather well. In two weeks time, if all goes to plan, the Condor will be ready. By co-incidence we have another order from Germany finishing at the same time. The client is in Magdeburg so I could quite easily justify a trip to Berlin as well.

I've so many things I want to ask you. You said something about being an "elder". Is this some sort of title, or are you older (a lot!) than you look? Sometimes I think you are not much older than me, but then you say something about times before I was born as if you were quite old then. I don't care if you are even 20 years older – you have a great mind, and a pretty good body too! I can't imagine ever being bored in your company.

Just one more question and then I will close the screen and help mum with the meal. I've heard you speaking German and you sound very fluent, and when you speak English you have a very slight accent of some sort. You have a Dutch name, but you don't sound Dutch. Where do you come from originally?

Your friend

Amy

Tuesday

E-letter address:

Airlift Ltd. Swinsdun

Britannica

Dear Van,

I can't pretend your letter wasn't a shock, and I can't tell you how many times I've edited this. I still can't quite believe it. One minute I'm proud to be, what shall I say, a friend, of someone so extraordinary, and then I get waves of panic - am I seriously thinking about a life with a man who is well over 100 years old? In your letter you say:

"I must tell you that if we still together in 20 years time I will still look much the same."

So I could end up with a what ...partner? husband?..freak? who looks younger than I do? I start life with an older man and end up with a toyboy?

Wednesday

It was a bad day yesterday. I'd hardly slept the night before and all these dreadful thoughts kept going through my mind. By the end of the day I had decided that we should stay as colleagues. I had a few glasses – well more than a few actually, and then slept, (passed out) for 8 hours.

Now things are much clearer even though filtered through a hangover. The fact is I've had a difficult time with relationships. Most of the men I meet – mostly through business – seem dull or immature. I had a feeling about you the moment I met you, and now I feel sure that my gut instinct was right.

Van, you've been very straight with me; done your best to put me off, but if that was your intention then you've failed. You are amazing and I don't want to go back to life without you. Please let me know by message that our date in Berlin is still on!

Your perplexed

Amy

Sir Hector Grant

Marlsburg

The day started well. It was June and the early dawn must have woken me. I was up just before the sun hit the tops of the trees, but instead of taking my time with a leisurely breakfast – porridge and fruit – I gathered up my fishing gear and took the short walk to my favourite spot on the river. I did my best to creep slowly into sight of it, but not carefully enough to avoid flushing a pair of mallards who flew off quacking angrily in a cloud of spray. This slight disappointment was countered a while later when a dipper bobbed up onto a rock. The water was high after the massive rainfall we'd had last month, but now we were in a high pressure phase and today would be hot.

Using a 2.4m rod with a 4-weight line, I placed my first fly, a Dry Olive, just upstream of a favourite pool and watched it float down. The cast had been a bit clumsy, and although I could see fish jumping a little further off, my next few casts were unsuccessful. I decided to take my time, and my patience was eventually rewarded with a good sized Grayling.

My satisfaction was complete when, just as I was leaving, I saw a Kingfisher flash past. When, hungry and happy, I began a late breakfast, my comms buzzed. It was Amy.

"Daddy I want you to meet someone special. Can we come for lunch?"

I must admit my first thought was unworthy. She's not had much luck with men, and I feared another charming wastrel. Then I had another thought – perhaps it's a woman? I really have very little idea about Amy's sexuality.

"Goodness – male or female?" (I was proud of this touch of modernity!) She laughed

"Oh male. He's an amazing character, quite famous. I expect you have heard of the Northern Resources Group?"

"I have indeed – that awful quango with far too much power. Is he involved with them then?"

"You could say that." She laughed again. She sounded happy. "It's unlikely you will have heard of him because he keeps a low profile, but he's the Chairman!"

"Oh my goodness I will have to mind what I say then. How on earth did you meet him?"

"He's buying one of our XT9s. He plans to live in it and use it as a mobile office."

"Good Heavens. What an extraordinary idea."

"Anyway, are you OK with this? I think you'll like him." There was a pause. "He's older than me – quite a lot older."

The thought of losing touch with Amy as well as Lucy was too much to bear. If this man is really going to make her happy then how can I dislike him?

"To tell you the truth I was beginning to think that you would never find a man your age to suit you. If he's right for you then I shall be happy. Twelve o'clock OK?"

"Daddy, you're wonderful. See you then."

Of course I was nervous when the time came, and kept looking out of the window. I should have watched Bruce. He started wagging his tail long before the car turned into the drive. My first impression of her companion was neutral - average height and build, brown hair with a hint of grey above a rather weather-beaten face. His bearing was upright and confident and his walk brisk. I didn't notice his clothes. As usual Bruce made a great fuss and it was a few minutes before Amy could do the honours.

"Daddy, this is Van" I extended a hand.

"Very pleased to meet you. I'm Hector."

"Ah, Hector, I must admit I've been quite nervous about this meeting. I'm not very adept at social stuff. Thank you so much for this . . . this occasion, these convivial surroundings."

"You are most welcome, but Amy tells me you move in very exalted circles – Chairman of NRG. You must meet all sorts of statesmen and captains of industry."

"Oh, yes I do. I can deal with them – I've had lots of practice - but with personal relationships I'm much less confident. I think what drew me to Amy was the sense that she has the same difficulty."

Well, that was a good start. He seemed quite modest. One thing did strike me – I found it really difficult to guess his age. There was something about him which suggested a lifetime of experience, but he certainly looked younger than me. I found he was not very adept at small talk, so I left Amy showing him round the garden and the river while I prepared the lunch. I didn't want to give the impression that I was treating him like royalty so had made a modest meal of my homemade pea soup, bread and salad with a shop bought sweet for afters, and a bottle of Chilean wine. They seemed happy with this and we chatted about fishing (of which he knew little) and freshwater management, of which he was surprisingly knowledgeable. He knew about the work I had done not only on the Grant Report but also my work with the Water for All charity. From water the discussion moved on to climate change. Here I was out of my depth.

All I knew was that I didn't like what I was hearing.

Vandervelde

Maiden flight of the Condor

Affairs of state seldom cause me to lose sleep, but this was different - personal. I was in Brigstowe, staying with Mollie and Eldred. I woke ridiculously early and couldn't get back to sleep, so I was kicking my heels in their kitchen drinking tea and eating what I could find in the fridge. I was actually excited, and it's not often in my long life I have admitted that. NRG were taking delivery of the Condor, and of course Amy would be there in her official capacity.

I think our 'date' in Berlin went well. I certainly enjoyed it and I'm fairly sure Amy did too – I find it so difficult to judge such things. At any rate I am hoping she will still be keen on sharing that little apartment on the Condor.

I thought our lunch with her father went quite well too. I wasn't sure we would get on at first, but found I warmed to him. He seems very conventional at first but he's clearly a thinker and we had quite a good exchange of views. I look forward to meeting him again.

Edmundo Almeida, our council member from Brazil, was in Britannica on a visit, and asked if he could come. I arranged to meet him at the site in Swinsdun. The launch ceremony was at 14:00, and I asked Mollie too. At that time she had not met Amy and was determined to find out what sort of woman had captivated her 'stony-hearted' boss. I was nervous about this too. I've known Mollie for a lot longer than Amy.

I can't honestly say that the Condor is beautiful. Only the very fastest of the hybrids can look remotely sleek, and Condor is not fast. There is something of the inflatable toy aircraft about many of the designs, but Condor is different. The envelope on this craft is shaped like one of the old delta winged bombers of the cold war. The upper surface of the "wing" is covered in solar panels which provide enough power, when above the clouds, for the ship to travel for an unlimited time. Manoeuvrability comes from the four motors – two electric and two large hydrogen powered units. They are all independently moveable so we can move (relatively) fast just above the ground if necessary and turn quickly too.

At the appointed time we shook hands all round and Amy introduced us to the key people on her team. I introduced her to Edmundo, and lastly to Mollie.

It was an awkward moment. Mollie tends to talk too much when embarrassed and Amy too little, but Edmundo smoothed things over by introducing them.

"Mollie, this is the first time you meet Amy?"

"Yes it is. I've heard so much about you and Airlift; it's great to meet you and the team."

"Thank you Mollie, my pleasure. Come, let me show you all round. The experience of entering the ship is very different when tethered at ground level to when on air station. Here it is like entering an aeroplane – please, follow me. If we were tethered above the clouds you would now be getting into that thing over there, the pod."

As we walked up the steps to the gondola I had a strange feeling – almost as if I was being watched. I stopped, looked around, shrugged and continued. As soon as I had tagged it, the feeling was gone, and I entered the gondola unperturbed. This time it was in position in the shadow of the great wing only six metres above us.

"Amy – I've just realized that we will seldom see direct sunlight. Do your crews find that a problem."

"Not at all. It is an advantage. You will find light levels above 600 metres are very high. You will be glad of the shade."

I couldn't help smiling when I saw the cabins with flowers and pictures, rugs, cushions and a few carefully chosen ornaments - details that made such a difference to the feeling of the cabins compared to the utilitarian look I had seen before. I hung back a little and Amy joined me.

"Well Van, do you like your new home?"

"I love it, but how do you feel about it?"

"Van I . . . Oh yes, I do so want this." He face relaxed and she laughed. "I'm sorry, I'm not very good at things like this. Look, we'll talk later. I have to get the show on the road."

She moved hastily forward to address the whole group.

"Ladies and Gentlemen, I must now ask you to take your seats. As in an aeroplane we have certain safety precautions for take-off and landing, although for vertical take-off, which is what we shall do today, you will not need to fasten seat belts."

We moved, as instructed, to the saloon area where there are a dozen or so comfortable arm chairs facing the large elliptical windows. The actual take off was so gentle we hardly noticed it. What a strange feeling seeing the ground recede as we rose smoothly and silently to our cruising height. Even when the two electric motors cut in we heard very little. We could see them above us, one on each side, and as the ship began to move forwards we could see them moving, tilting a little as the computer made adjustments to keep us at a steady height and course.

Amy's voice came over the hidden speakers:

"Now, you are free to explore the ship at your leisure. You will be able to follow our course on the screens, and we will meet back here in two hours for the descent. Enjoy the flight"

As she walked out she caught my eye and after a few minutes I followed her. It's not that our relationship was secret, but this occasion was not about us but about the ship and its purpose. We had arranged earlier to meet in the apartment area. As I opened the door marked "Private, staff only" She turned round to greet me and grinned.

"Hello you, welcome home!" I knew then that we would be happy on this ship.

Sir Hector Grant

Marlsburg

There have been some extraordinary changes in my life since I last wrote in this diary? memoire? – I'm not sure what to call it. We were lucky here that the Great Flood of 28 didn't affect us too badly. The Kennet of course burst its banks and most of my garden was underwater for 10 days or so, but very few houses were affected. That was far from the case elsewhere. In a national emergency it is the job of the armed forces to give the maximum physical assistance, and so great was the need for extra manpower that even the old duffers like me were called up. I was pleased to be asked to help organise the refugee centre in Marlsburg, and spent an exhausting but satisfying two weeks helping the area assigned to us, which was Stane: not a place I would normally have visited, but I found much to admire in their town, even a few pleasant buildings.

Indeed there was hardly a town in Southern Britannica which didn't offer some kind of hospitality for all the refugees from Lyndain and the Midlands. There is even talk now of parts of the Isis Valley being abandoned permanently.

For me though, the cure, as prescribed by Van and his cohorts in NRG, was worse than the disease. After our first meeting I spent a while walking and thinking.

Did I like him? Yes I did.

Was he good for Amy? For Belle? - probably not.

There's no denying he has charisma. You immediately sense a piercing intellect. Even though what he was saying was so radical as to be almost incredible, you can't help feeling that he may be right.

If he is right, where does that leave me? My whole career has been about life and death. I've thought long and hard about our world and where it is going. Now it feels as if a great gulf is opening up under me. How could I be wrong when my friends in the government all tend to see things in the same way? We couldn't all be wrong surely?

Whether Amy could see this I don't know, but even as I was swept along by his – Van's - confident manner I couldn't help feeling that there was something more than odd about him – something almost un-human. He claims to have no knowledge of his age or his childhood. That suggests a major trauma, but everything he says is completely logical. He clearly feels strongly about his work but you never see emotion overcoming logic. His anger is controlled. What if his feelings for Amy are controlled too?

****

Of course I've been following the business news avidly since Van told me about his Carbon Trading initiative, and I've been astonished at how quickly things are changing. Every day there are reports of new technologies being developed. Anything that saves fossil fuel can get a start-up grant, and places like Grantabrig, with its concentration of high tech business and research, are assigning lab space by lottery. No sooner had they built an international airport there than the old Heavier than Air craft became uneconomical to run. Undeterred, they created several airship stations and turned over the big runway to yet more industry. Of course the RAF will continue to use jets, but even they are now looking at much more fuel efficient ways of protecting us.

Good news of a sort I suppose, but there are also some terrible stories of hardship. Whole industries employing thousands have suddenly found their order books empty. Those of us who are old enough to remember it are making comparisons with the days of Margaret Thatcher and the miner's strike. I felt then that although there was certainly a case for reining in the Unions, Thatcher's solution was far too draconian, and in the end probably made things worse. I tend to feel the same about NRG.

I must admit though I was pleased when Van turned up on my doorstep again last week. I've had a few problems with my health lately and Amy must have sensed that all was not well despite my protestations. She tried to grill me about it on the comms, but I kept quiet.

"Are you around next week?"

"Of course, where would I go?"

"How about I come over on Wednesday?"

"OK, lunch?"

"That would be good. See you around 12 then."

"I shall look forward to it."

So, when the time came I was expecting her on her own, and was amazed to see Van with her. I just stopped myself from saying something sarcastic about not being at death's door just yet, and was glad that I did. He seemed genuinely pleased to see me.

"Hector, it's good to see you again. When Amy said she was coming to see you I realised that I didn't really need to rush off to Brigstowe again and we had a nice late breakfast at the hotel and a stroll on the downs before coming here. It was lovely then" He was looking ruefully at the black clouds on the horizon.

"Well, I'm very pleased to see both of you. Come on in before that cloud hits us."

We went through all the usual stuff about how we were and the weather, but I could see Amy was distracted. She was nervy, excited perhaps.

"Amy love you look as if you have something on your mind."

"Ha ha" – nervous laugh – "Actually it's more on my body. Oh Daddy, I can't not tell you – I'm pregnant!"

"Oh my, Oh Amy how wonderful. Are you feeling OK? Not sick or anything?"

"Well actually I have been sick a few times but they tell me that's normal."

So, I was to be a grandfather again. I felt absurdly happy - to the extent of embarrassing Amy by shedding a tear! Van was the soul of tact and kept in the background. Actually I was pleased to see him too because I wanted to ask him about something that was puzzling me. When we had eaten, drunk coffee and I had sidestepped another grilling by Amy about my ailments, I asked Van if he could explain the difference between the 'Smart Grid' and 'The Internet of Things', both of which had been in the news lately.

"Hm . . . well I suppose you could say that they are both about a two-way flow of data."

"That's another thing, why use a plural word like data when you could just use the common 'information'.

"Ah, that's a thorny issue – why we use jargon. The two words 'information' and 'data' are not synonymous, but let's stick to information for now. I assume you have a smart meter?"

"Yes. It's supposed to help me buy electricity at the best price but it doesn't seem to have made much difference."

"That's probably because you don't have any generating resources or any big batteries. Your home is not what they call a "connected home".

"Perish the thought. It's connected to the ground and that's good enough for me." He laughed dutifully.

"The Smart Grid can now tap into any form of storage or generation in any building with the right connections and buy electricity from them when the solar or wind supplies are down. If for example there was enough head of water in your little river and you had installed a water turbine, you could sell the power from that back to the grid at times when the wind turbines were down. It also gives you the ability to automatically buy power when it is cheap, and you can set your appliances not to come on at peak times when power is expensive.

The "Internet of Things" is about the same process but with information flowing in both directions. Nearly all electrical appliances now have sensors built in which can transmit data to the Net. The owner of a Connected Home could, for example, set their automation to re-order food supplies when the food store tells the Net something is running out.

"All this has been going for some years now, but we still have two huge networks of cables – one for data and one for power. I have a meeting next week with an entrepreneur who claims he has developed a material which can transmit data and power together. Think of the massive savings we could make if or when that becomes reality."

"Ye Gods, the mind boggles. All I can see for us old'uns is life getting more and more complicated and difficult. Don't you feel that sometimes?"

"I certainly do. I often feel I'm on a conveyor belt which keeps getting faster and I can't get off. If only we could have done all this twenty years earlier we would be in a much better position now, but that's down to human nature. It is extraordinary and depressing how resistant most people are to this kind of change. All they want is for things to carry on in their comfortable fashion. How hard it is to grasp this paradoxical truth: it is that very reluctance to 'rock the boat' that is forcing us to change. If we do not make positive changes very rapidly then catastrophic change will be forced upon us – and all because we want to stay as we are."

He was in lecture mode again, and just getting into his stride, but he checked himself.

"Ah, here I go again. Sorry . . . er, look Hector, I'll leave one of our leaflets for you to have a look at later. (See page 59)

"It's very hard; unfortunately for you – well for all of us really – the status quo is not an option, and by some quirk of fate I have become the agent of change. The mantle has fallen on NRG and I am the hated face of NRG."

We sat in silence for a few moments.

"Well, you're not hated here."

"Thank you Hector, that means a lot to me."

I almost felt sorry for him.

*Carbon Trading in a Nutshell:

The NRG position

Basics:

A carbon trading scheme is one in which a government issues permits to emit a unit (normally one tonne) of carbon dioxide into the atmosphere. At the start of the scheme the number of permits will be calculated according to the current rates of emission. They can be given away, auctioned or sold at a fixed price. The number issued will then reduce steadily until the required national emission rate is reached.

The permits can be traded in the markets so that high emitters can buy surplus permits from low emitters. The market value of each permit will depend on the degree of enforcement and the number issued.

The largest scheme in 2018 was the EU Phase Three which began in 2013. However, too many permits had been issued, too many of them for nothing, and there was no real will to enforce them, so the price was too low to have a significant effect.

The involvement of NRG

The imposition of a scheme tough enough to bring down emissions rapidly would inevitably lead to severe economic disruption, and the democratic leaders were too afraid of being voted out. As a last resort they turned to us with the usual stipulation: deniability.

Before we even started we laid down some conditions. The G8 governments – that's the old G10 minus America and Russia – must agree to enforce the permits. That's to say there had to be severe penalties for illegal emissions and an enforcement structure.

When we took over, the price of a permit to emit one tonne of carbon was 10 Euros. The figures were clear. The global average per capita emissions in 2015 were around nine tonnes, but with huge differences between Australia at one end and Madagascar at the other. With a world population of around eight billion there was then around 450ppm (parts per million) of C02 in the atmosphere. Estimates had shown that a 500ppm concentration would have a 99 percent chance of leading to a two degree rise in global temperature and a 44 percent chance of a three degree rise – the level agreed to be catastrophic.

Our target was an average two tonnes per capita by the end of 2035. Since the current big emitters led by the USA were then on around 20 tonnes pc, there was a long way to go. To achieve this with carbon trading as the main "weapon" we would need the carbon price to rise fairly rapidly to at least 40 Euros per tonne.

With the leaders of the G8 behind us we had the credibility to set compulsory emissions limits for every kind of manufacturing process. These limits started at present levels and reduced each year. This meant that anyone wishing to invest in any of the rapidly developing low carbon technologies had a market which could be quantified for the next ten years. They could see for example that within four years coal fired power stations would be so expensive to run that carbon capture and storage would become a viable proposition. The emissions cost of cement production would double the price of concrete within two years, so alternative materials became a priority.

To complete the picture we set a similar sliding scale of carbon tax debits and credits on finished products.

Mollie

This is our new house. Can you believe it? Me a married woman? It's a bit of a mess at the moment. We only moved in last week but already it feels like home, and we have our own garden. We were so lucky to find this place; it's only a small terrace but it's in Mountpellier, only a short walk from the shops and we have friends in the next street.

The marriage was great; all the Brigstowe crew in force, but the guest of honour was Eldred's Dad Errol! It turned out he was already thinking of coming back here for a while, so when he got the invite he brought forward his plans. He is just such a lovely man, and that Jamaican accent with his deep voice...and Oh you should hear him laugh! We'd both bought special clothes for the occasion – mine a soft clingy knee length frock in burgundy, his a lightweight suit also in burgundy. Eldred asked Maisie to be his 'best woman', but when Errol turned up she was all over him and insisted that he take her place. Now that I know her better I like Maisie, but you can have too much of her. She's a very dominant presence; still, always cheerful, I'll say that for her.

I did cry - once. It was when both my parents hugged me together and it really hit me that Jamie wasn't there. He hadn't turned up for his sister's wedding! Arrogant little bastard I'll have words to say to him when we next meet. How can he say his business meetings are too important to miss?

Another surprise guest was Rufus. He'd travelled all the way from Berlin! He said he had some urgent business here, but I'm not sure that wasn't just an excuse. He was still in Britain when we got back from our honeymoon. (I won't go on about how lovely it all was; just take it from me it was the best!) I felt very refreshed and up for anything when I got back to the office and it wasn't long before I had a call from Rufus.

"Mollie – good to see you again. I hear the honeymoon went well?"

"Oh it was wonderful; we had such a good time." I paused "but I'm sure you didn't get me here to talk about my honeymoon – let's have it." He laughed.

"You're right of course. I've just been landed with a project which I'm struggling with. Have you come across the "Educate the Girls Foundation"?

"Of course, they've been around for a while."

"Right, well to be honest they are having a hard time. There is still a strong link between the countries with the highest population growth and those with the lowest figures for women's education. Needless to say it also links to poverty. It's been clear for a long time that the quickest way to drag a country out of the population/poverty trap is to educate the girls, but there are still powerful cultural and religious barriers against sexual equality. The Foundation has done its best, but they have no real power, so they have approached us – NRG Society that is."

"I don't know how these people expect us to solve all the problems of the world. I'd have thought we had enough to do already."

"You're right of course, and my small team at NRGS is pushed to the limit. We are recruiting continuously but as you will remember, our recruitment procedures take up a lot of senior work time." He paused, and I realised he was looking tired. His hair was mostly grey now and was receding, but he had great dress sense and still looked very youthful and fit – in all senses!

"I want you to take this one on Mollie. I'll be there for help and support but I just don't have the time to give it my best."

"But what about Van? Have you spoken to him? I can't just take on a big new area of work without his approval."

"It was Van who suggested I approach you."

"Oh, he would!" I laughed. It was a daunting project but I felt quite flattered that these two important older men had that much trust in me, even though I had only been here for a few years.

"What can I say? I'll have to have some more staff. Can you fix that too?"

"I'll do my best. I have one good contact for you and one member of staff I took the liberty of sounding out. The contact is Voula Randriananta from Madagascar."

"Oh yes, She's one of the Council isn't she?"

"Yup and she's here now in Lyndain. The staff member is Eduard Villiers. He spent 5 years with MSF before joining NRG so he's well used to . . . "

"Hold on, what's MSF?"

"Oh sorry, Medicins Sans Frontieres. Yes, so he's well used to dealing with tribal elders. ETG have . . . er . . . Educate the Girls?"

"OK I got that one." We both laughed.

"They've identified six target countries that have the worst records for female education, but they are having great difficulty getting to the decision makers in those countries. Frankly I think they are talking to the wrong people – mostly men. What I want your team to do is to get out there at ground level and find the women who could move this forwards."

I immediately saw myself bumping down some dusty road to a remote village and being welcomed by a bunch of laughing black women. It sounded a lot more fun than Carbon Trading, though I suppose my team will still have to keep working on that too.

Rufus took me briefly through the project and we planned what staff I would need and where they would be based.

Vandervelde

Britannica

It's been a difficult year 2030. Amy lost the baby. She miscarried. I don't know how to console her. I long to be a parent. That is I would love to be able to bring up a child of my own with its mother in a stable relationship. I may well be a father in absentia – who knows. I might even have BEEN a father; some child might have lived its whole life without me knowing; dreadful thought.

The doctors tell us there is no reason why Amy should not be able to conceive again – she brought Belle into the world without any problems. So, there is still some hope.

My first meeting with Belle was not a good start. She seemed very shy, and had clearly been told to be polite so when I said "Hello Belle, I'm very pleased to meet you" she extended her hand and said:

"How do you do Mr Vandervelde."

"I'm very well thank you Belle. Please call me Van; all my friends do."

"But I'm not your friend. You're Ma's friend."

"Yes, but I want us to be friends too. Would you like that?"

"I don't know."

I think I need to learn more about children.

The Carbon initiative has been more successful than I

feared, and the storm of opposition from the corporations which seemed to be brewing has subsided sooner than I expected. We must be doing something right.

One big change has crept up on me: I seem to be spending a lot more time in Britannica than I used to. In many ways Britannica is a ridiculous country. For a start it's hard to define because the collection of islands known as the Britannic Isles is in theory three sovereign nations. Two are relatively easy to define: The Hibernian Federation and Caledonia. The third nation is made up of three crypto nations: Anglesland, Cymru and Vannin. If ever there was an odd amalgam it's these three. Anglesland is by far the most powerful and populous of all the Britannic nations and Vannin, a little island between Caledonia and Hibernia by far the smallest. Cymru and Anglesland have it seems fought each other for centuries and still maintain an intense rivalry. Add to all this a climate which was never predictable and is now so unstable that it's sometimes difficult to tell which season you are in.

It's difficult to believe that this odd mixture was for several centuries the most powerful nation on earth, and was the birthplace of the first industrial revolution.

So, within not much more than a year I find myself thinking that perhaps I will become Britannic, and perhaps even a married man again. Both these are very much intertwined with the whole idea of the Condor. What started as a convenience, a way to rationalize my very mobile life, has become an emotional focus, it's where I keep my sense of "home", and it's made me realize that for many years I have been suppressing this basic human urge – call it "nestbuilding". I've derived a great deal of pleasure from the many places I've lived in or stayed in. I still love going to those places, especially my little apartment in Berlin, but now wherever I am I find myself thinking constantly about the Condor, and worrying about Amy.

Mollie

The ETG project is well under way now. I had a fascinating trip to Africa. Van wanted to take the Condor to Madagascar so I hitched a ride. No meetings for three days! Bliss! And it's so peaceful drifting along above the clouds with just the gentle hum of the motors and the chatter on our screens. I got so much work done. It took three days to get to Tana (That's what the old Madagascar hands call the capital Antananarivo. Like so many Malagasy names it seems to have too many syllables!) Van dropped me off at the air station where Voula was waiting. He had to go somewhere down south. In fact I didn't see much of him during the trip. He stayed in his apartment most of the time – strange man!

I spent a day with Voula in her nice little house covered in bougainvillea at the top of one of the hills in the huge sprawling city. Then we both, (plus one of her staff) were back to the air station and on a commercial LTA on the long trip across the continent to Senegal. Here we had a chaotic meeting with a bunch of amazing women all shouting at once in a mixture of French and Wolof. They insisted in all coming to see me off with great protestations of undying friendship. It was overpowering; just so lovely. I was shattered and slept a lot of the trip back to the airhub at Gravesham.

I so feel for Van and Amy. Poor Amy – to go through all the pain of a birth knowing the baby can't survive.

I had only been back a few days when I got this paper letter from Voula. She writes just how she speaks in English, so all I've done is add a couple of notes to the more obscure expressions. I really think we will be able to make some progress now. I love to think of all those little girls in their neat uniforms on their rough benches in the tin and mud-brick schools. They are just so keen to learn. It's fantastic.

Letter from Voula

4356 Antananarivo

Madagascar

19 November 2030

Ma Chere Mollie,

Please forgive my imperfect English. I fear I am too old to learn well. Tant pis – I continue the struggle.

I write about the project "Educate the Girls" with which you asked me to help. As you know, we looked for the statistic on big population growth and all other things such as income, land area, food provision, climate and so, and we found one element outstanding: the elevation (education) of girls. There was strong linking between those countries which had the big birth rate and those which had the low teaching level for the girls.

How to get these countries to teach the girls at the same level as the boys? We can not simply tell the leaders, who are always men of course, that they must elevate girls at the same as boys. It is necessary that the reply to this problem comes from the countries themselves. We therefore invited women from these countries: Sierra Leone, Pakistan, Senegal, Mali , Afganistan, Yemen, to a meeting in Cairo in the month past. It is interesting for me because Madagascar is not one of these countries. We have different religion and different peoples to other countries in Africa and we teach our girls just as high as our boys. Nevertheless we still have big birth rate, but it is less now. The Madagascar population still grows but since 2020, less quick.

All these women want with passion to elevate the girls so we tell them:

"You have behind you the NRG. We will give you all support. You stay as guests of us in this comfortable place, we give you people to research for you and write for you what you decide, you have IT systems for use, even we give you places to pray – everything to help." (One lady, who I do not mention the name, ask for nice young men!) This we say is your task: (official words)

'To devise a mechanism which will induce all countries to educate girls to the same level as boys'

When I tell them this there is great noise. Mme Toure from Senegal say in French (I translate to English) "It is our history, the history of the Mandinka and Wolof peoples. Always for hundreds of years the rights go from the man to the man. The women is not considered until the years 1960. " There is much talk about how dreadful the men are; much shouting but also much laughter.

Anyway, in one word like a hundred, (to cut a long story short) we agree that the only way to change these men is to give them some benefit, some personal reason to allow girls into knowledge. So, we propose the following:

In all countries with lower elevation for girls than for boys, there is a bonus or prize given by the state to the father of every girl who will complete 5 years at school.

We now put this to the General Council of the GRN (Groupe des Ressources du Nord) and expect for the detailed plans to be organized by a Working Group.

I look forward to telling you more about this when we are meeting.

Your friend

Voula

So here I am, back in Brigstowe with a huge pile of virtual papers in my virtual in-tray. Never mind; work is good.

Home is not so good. It's Jamie that's the main problem. Success is bad for him. He'd already had things a bit too easy in his life and now he's a media darling – the handsome sharp young executive transforming our lives. We're drifting apart. We just can't seem to re-create that old easy love/friendship we used to have. I had a call from him last week.

Comms transcript:

"Mollie – how are you? It's me."

"Hiya Jamie –where are you – I don't recognise the room."

"I'm in Britannica – look. Did you get that?"

"Yes, very grand. What is it?"

"It's a house we're going to buy. We're selling the old flat in Brigstowe and moving to Cymru near the factory. We've found this fantastic old place right in the centre of town but with its own grounds. It's like a little oasis of green."

"Have you bought it then?"

"Not yet but we've agreed a price."

"Well done you. What about the place in France?"

"Oh we're keeping that. I'm likely to be spending quite a bit of time over there so we need 2 homes."

"Need – come on, just admit it you're stinking rich. "

"Ok, but honestly it doesn't feel like it half the time - you should see my outgoings"

"I'm crying for you. When do we see you? Why didn't ou come to the wedding? . . . Never mind, come and meet Eldred."

"Are you still in York Road?"

"Yes, but Eldred's got a big studio in the haven with lots of space. Let's meet up there – it's on Spike Island. How about tomorrow?"

"Hm, yes actually that would work out well. It's just me though, Fay and the brats are still in France."

"OK see you at 12.30 ish"

[end of transcript]

I told Eldred that Jamie was coming and he seemed a bit nervous. He knows how important Jamie is to me and I think he wants to make a good impression – whatever that is in Eldred terms!

I managed to get him to stop work just in time to clean up and he appeared soon after 12 with his hair smoothed down with water, a slightly newer pair of canvas trousers and one of his baggy pullovers.

Jamie was all understated designer fashion – a really elegant dove grey jacket, the new style denims just washed enough not to look too new, a really beautiful silk shirt, shoes of leather so fine they glowed, a chunky steel mini-com on his wrist and a platinum wedding ring.

"Hi Eldred, very pleased to meet you."

"Hello Jamie. So this is Mollie's little brother. I'm impressed. I hear you're quite a big noise in the world of business."

"On no, I'm quite a minor player really, but the business is moving very fast. We've just done a refinance package for a couple of mil."

"Oh? What's a mil when it's at home?"

"Sorry – million Euros."

"Good grief – all that money stuff is a mystery to me. As long as my work sells to your friends in the city for enough to keep a roof over my head then I'm happy."

"They're not really my friends Eldred. I just make things, but we do need financiers to provide us with capital, and now, thanks to Mollie's lot we need analysts to tell us when to buy and sell carbon permits. You wouldn't believe how difficult it is charting a path through all these regulations and restrictions."

I wasn't going to let that pass:

"Oh come on Jamie – you know as well as I do how important these regs are."

"Yes of course Moll, but them being necessary doesn't make them any easier."

Eldred added:

"Well, I'm afraid I don't even try to follow all the stuff which Moll and this Van character are doing. I agree with you as far as regulations are concerned, but it seems to me that business people and corporation bosses hate regulations which prevent them from making massive profits, but are all in favour when it comes to keeping the rest of us in our place."

Jamie was looking annoyed but held his hands up, palms out –

"OK, OK, let's talk about something else shall we? Eldred – tell me about your work, I'm intrigued."

"Well I'll try, but I'm not sure you'll like it."

"I don't think whether I like it or not is relevant. I'm sure you wouldn't want to devote all your energy to preaching to the converted."

"Ha, you're right. Let's all go next door and I'll show you the latest stuff."

"Lead on".

I breathed a sigh of relief. There was real tension in the air between them. It would be awful if the two most important men in my life could not get on. Eldred seemed to have a knack of pressing the wrong buttons as far as Jamie was concerned. What he said next didn't help much either:

"What you have to understand is that for the last 20 years or so the Art mainstream has moved away from the creation of quote 'beautiful objects to delight the eye' unquote. Most artists now see their role as being to light up people's perception. To awaken dormant areas of the brain and make new connections."

"What you need to understand is that most of us have been aware of that for at least as long."

Again I felt I had to smooth things over.

"You may be aware Jamie, but I think you underestimate the power of ignorance. Look around you – not here, but in general – and you still see, hear and touch all sorts of artefacts which leave the brain totally untroubled. Don't you think the artist's job is to stir us up?"

"Of course, that's what I'm saying – Eldred, just because I'm involved in commerce doesn't mean I don't appreciate art."

Eldred was getting agitated, waving his arms around and raising his voice:

"APPRECIATE – God I hate that word. You don't have to 'appreciate' art. Art is at the centre of human life. Sure, commerce has given us lots of toys to play with and kept us entertained, but what is the latest comms unit compared to the works of Shakepeare?"

It got worse. I can't repeat some of the things they said.

****

Nearly a week and still no word from Jamie. Every time I think of that dreadful afternoon my heart sinks. I hardly slept at all that night. Eldred has been dancing round me trying to get me to cheer up, but I'm still very bitter with him for saying all those awful things. What makes me feel even worse is the thought that it was all about me – that they were nothing more than two males fighting over a female. I can only hope they've both got enough intelligence to realise how stupid, how 'old brain' such behaviour is. They don't have to be friends. All I want is for them to be 'nice' to each other.

Every day I think 'surely today he will ring me and say how sorry he is' but every day I'm disappointed. The longer it goes on the harder it will be to mend. Eldred says:

"All he has to do is apologise to you and I will be nice to him as you ask. If he can't be bothered, even for his beloved sister then he's not worth all these tears."

"Oh shut up – what do you know about it. He's my flesh and blood. We did everything together when we were little. How can you speak of him like that? You think he's a poser? Well so are you – you and your 'arty' clothes and your 'arty' friends."

Then the tears came again. I sobbed until I was exhausted. He tried to console me and eventually we hugged and made up, but the scar was there.

****

He did ring eventually. Just when I have given up and made a resolution to get on with my life. He spoke on the comms as if nothing had happened, but I could see from his body language that he had changed. There was no going back. He would still be there for me, but he would have nothing to do with my husband. I had made my choice. If that was the sort of person I wanted to spend my life with then so be it. I was welcome to come and see him but he would not come to see me.

What was I supposed to say to that? My life was with Eldred now. I told him to fuck off.

****

It was only a few weeks after that when I missed my period. We hadn't been trying particularly, but then I suppose we hadn't been trying very hard not to either. A trip to the doctor soon confirmed my suspicions – I was pregnant! There's another resolution down the drain. Actually I gave up on the "no children" thing ages ago. Now that I'm in the thick of the action the future doesn't look so bad. I'm coming to the conclusion anyway that you don't solve political problems by voluntary individual effort. "You shouldn't do that" is a pretty useless tool for human development.

The pregnancy went as well as can be expected and Magnus was born a little late on 3 September 2030. Eldred was delighted at first and made a great fuss of him, but after a few weeks he got bored.

"Come on little man, when are you going to say something other than 'EEE'. You get off to work liebling, he'll be fine here." Here was in his day cot in the studio.

"Don't forget.."

"Mollie – go; I know what to do."

He really meant it too, but when he gets focussed on his current work the rest of the world fades away. It was lucky that Magnus had a good pair of lungs and could yell hard enough to break through to him. We carried on like that for a few weeks but I knew it wasn't going to work so decided I would use the crèche facility at 'The Temple'. It's free and in many ways far better than Eldred, but I did so want Magnus to grow up with his father. Perhaps when he can talk it will be better.

Van of course was oblivious to such things. He buzzed my screen recently:

"Mollie – please meet me at our Rotterdam office as quickly as possible. I've some urgent work for you."

Typical – What does he think I'm doing? Knitting?

I suppose he thinks we can stop working on ETG now and move on to the next big idea. I knew it would be pointless to mention Magnus so I rang Mum and got her to pick him up. She can look after him tonight and I'll go over there to collect him when I get back.

What a day! I was met at the airport by Anneka with one of the new silent electric cars. "Why the urgency" I asked her.

"Oh we've just had the latest figures on food shortages. The situation is urgent in the sense that people are dying, but it will take more than a few days of discussion to solve that one."

"Ye Gods. Typical Van. I never learn. Next time he does this I will refuse."

"Well Mollie you know as much about our great leader as we do. Perhaps we just have to learn to live with it?"

When I arrived he wasn't even there, but he left a memo for me and a space to put my screen. When I opened it up I found all these documents.

I CAN'T DO ALL THIS. IT'S TOO MUCH. HE'LL HAVE TO FIND SOMBODY ELSE.

Document Folder: M. Edmundson

WHO: Pathogen Resistance levels 2030

MRSA pathogens now widespread with mortality levels rising rapidly in some countries. With the re-appearance of Ebola haemorrhagic fever the Emergency Isolation Units (which eventually enabled the 2015 outbreak to be controlled) have now been established in all areas of high population density.

In addition to bacterial and viral infections there is a type of pathogen recently discovered with attributes of both virus and bacteria.

Antibiotics:

It is now clear that the blanket use of antibiotics from the 1950s to the tens not only contributed directly to the spread of resistant strains of bacteria, but was one of the main contributors to the epidemic of auto-immune diseases in the first few decades of this century. The steep decline in the effectiveness of these drugs led to the revival of isolation as a first barrier against infection.

Nevertheless, there is still a place for effective antibiotics, and recent discoveries by the WHO research teams have identified several potential new anti-viral and antibacterial substances. Crocodiles for example were known to be able to recover quickly from substantial injuries, and a serum has been developed from this source which is highly effective against necrotic bacteria. Other areas of research were plant pathogens, animal dung, bee propolis (a resinous substance used in the construction of bee's nests) and many kinds of parasite who are able to protect their hosts.

Resistance in Humans:

Twentieth Century research into the genetic characteristics of certain Northern European populations had shown inherited resistance to bubonic plague. The research was abandoned before the sequencing of the human genome, but has recently been resumed under the leadership of Nils Stromberg in Sweden. His team now has a large data base of DNA and have been able to identify thousands of individual genes which might have protected their carriers from one of the thousands of diseases. Data samples are so large that the team has been unable so far to identify any consistent lines of enquiry.

Recommendations:

- *Strict quarantine measures to be enforced in all countries where possible.*
- *Travel from any area with infectious disease to be subject to increased bio-security checks*
- *Travel to or from any area with type D virus identified to be forbidden*
- *New research facilities to be set up with increased funding from member countries*
- *NRG be requested to re-examine the data on resistant DNA in humans.*

NRG Notes on Food Production 2030

Ongoing situation:

Endemic food shortages in 'third world' countries

Recent Situation:

Food shortages in high population countries in the 'developed' world.

Densely populated countries like the Netherlands, Japan, Belgium and Britannica have relied on contracts with supplier countries that need tradable currency. Until the twenties, air freight was quick and cheap and the buying power of these countries kept the prices low. Elites in the provider countries controlled what was produced and profited from the system. The effects on the end producers were mitigated by 'fair trade' deals, but these were killed by the economic downturn in the late tens, when China began using its huge cash surpluses to buy up the land where their food was produced. Food prices have increased by an average of 20% per annum since 2020, and are now rapidly approaching a hyper-inflation situation.

Involvement of NRG

In 2029 NRG Innovation was asked to take on food production. The terms of our contract were the same as those for carbon trading and all the other measures necessary to prevent ultimate catastrophe – deniable power.

The NRG sponsor governments had not only to produce enough food, but produce it within range of the consumers. The huge demand for meat and dairy products meant that not only were we turning over huge areas of productive food-producing land to animal husbandry (thereby reducing its output to a tenth of its potential) we were also losing even more of the vital ecosystems - forests, marshes, etc. - which the planet desperately needed to survive.

The Model

The NRG research department looked at all countries who were self-sufficient in food and found the closest model to the current situation was Cuba. - not the modern integrated part of the Caribbean States, but the old Castro fiefdom, the one that suddenly lost its food supply when the USSR collapsed. Facing starvation the then communist government encouraged every scrap of land to be turned over to horticulture. It was highly labour intensive but successful.

Typical developed country scenario

Productive land around the cities was partly devoted to leisure - horses mostly - and partly to high-tech agriculture. Between 30 and 70% of food was imported by air: high capacity transport jets would load up in the sub-tropics and unload straight into road transport. The food was on the supermarket shelves within hours. The energy cost was enormous. By the late twenties when carbon trading began to kick in, this system had largely broken down both because of the spiralling costs of air transport and of artificial fertilizers. However, there was no consistent system on hand to replace it

NRG Proposal: developed countries

To requisition all productive land within 30 miles of the cities for intensive horticulture. Any shortfall in fertility to be made up for by the use of human sewage.

NRG Proposal: developing countries

The biggest problem for the third world food exporters was that many of the crops they had been producing for export were not accepted as human food by the local population. A further massive problem was the shortage of irrigation water. It was clear that there was sufficient fertile land in the tropics to feed even inflated populations, but great cultural hurdles to overcome. Carbon trading has already dismantled many of the trade imbalances. We propose that incentives directed towards the education and empowerment of women should be given even higher priority, and greater resources must be put into alternative crops, so that these can be made available simply and cheaply.

2030 Britannic Food Standards Act:

Draft directive

Primary objective:

To ensure that the whole population has access to foods of a high nutritional value at prices they can afford

Method:

We used the well-established Glycaemic Index to classify foods into 3 classes:

A : Foods subject to the least amount of processing, and with low Glycaemic Index, ie high fibre, low salt, low fat and low sugar. Examples are green vegetables, whole grains, lean meat, pulses.

B: Foods prepared and packaged from A-food ingredients. Examples are low GI ready-meals, whole grain breakfast cereals, low fat meat products.

C: Prepared foods designed to satisfy a craving for calories. These have high fat, sugar and/or salt levels and are made from high GI and highly processed ingredients.

Proposal

The current regulatory mechanism is ineffective because it does not prevent C class foods from being cheaper than B or A class.

We therefore propose legislation to ensure that A class foods are available at a lower price than C class foods. We looked at two ways of achieving this:

Under a taxation regime: tax would be levied on a list of High GI foodstuffs including: white flour, corn syrup, white sugar, salt, potato flour, butter, vegetable oil, animal fat. The resulting income could be then used to subsidise the production of Low GI foods.

Under a voucher scheme: legislation would be introduced in which a proscribed list of ingredients would only be available to the food suppliers on the production of vouchers for the relevant class. The Foods Standards authority would decide on the quantities of these ingredients which would be compatible with a healthy diet and auction vouchers accordingly. A market in vouchers would be created so that food companies could buy enough vouchers to produce, for example, very attractive cakes, but the retail price of these would be correspondingly high.

Companies producing low GI foods B class foods such as wholemeal bread would have a distinct price advantage and could expand production accordingly.

Vandervelde

Downend

This is our new house – new to us that is. It was built in 1790 in a style called Georgian – quite plain with pleasing proportions. In its heyday it had 12 rooms on three floors, and a beautiful slate roof. It is in a fairly remote spot with a large garden with lots of mature trees and a range of outbuildings. Amy tells me this is where her business started. It was a friend of her father's who had built an airship in his barn. Amy had just got an unexpected legacy and, despite having no previous business experience, bought the stock and goodwill of the business but not the premises. I'm still amazed at her temerity and proud of her for following her instinct. I can see why she suggested Downend as our base in Britannica.

The land beyond the garden is chalk downland which for many years was used for intensive cereal crops. At its peak this was highly mechanized with huge gps-guided machines. That element of our food production collapsed when carbon trading took off and the land is now used mainly for grazing. Looking over our boundary I can see just two fields, each of several hundred acres, and both dotted with hundreds of sheep.

Now all that is left of the house is the walls, for it was gutted by fire four years ago. Poor Patrick, Hector's friend, had been the victim of some insurance fraud which left him without proper cover. He and his partner tried for years to get enough money to restore the house but in the end decided to cut their losses and sell. I offered them considerably more than they would have got on the open market because it was exactly what we were looking for.

Several of the outbuildings were in good condition so we have created a temporary home in a barn – not the aircraft hanger, a smaller, older one. Work has already begun on the restoration programme, and my brief to the architect was a tough one – restore the appearance and character of an 18th century house but make it carbon neutral. With the price of carbon permits now near €60, this is essential.

******

It's raining again. It began on Christmas Eve 2027 and rained solidly for a week all over Europe. Then it turned cold for a while but soon the rain was back. In southern Europe they have had fantastic storms and terrible floods. Everyone is saying it is worse than 2014. A massive amount of money went into flood defences after that terrible winter, but again, faced with rising sea levels, overflowing aquifers and record rainfall, no amount of flood defences can protect low lying areas. At least this time the evacuation plans went smoothly.

It just goes on and on. On the ground they have not seen the sun for six weeks, and up here we have not seen the ground. Some days it stays cold and dry, but mostly it rains. Dear Lord when will it end?

There's now a mood of panic amongst the EU governments. Nobody is in any doubt that climate change is upon us and will get worse before any changes we make will take effect. Yet if we do not make these changes it will become catastrophic within this century.

The Hub

The days didn't change much, and as far as she knew it had always been like this. Until recently, one day had been very much like the one before or the one after. Sister Tilia had always lived in the Hub, and so, she believed, had her mother. Her father was not important.

When she needed a man, one would be provided. They were all similar - beautiful, well formed, strong and tall: good breeding stock. The one child she had been allowed had been a boy so she had passed him on to the Nurturers. She still occasionally recalled the tag and felt an echo of the terrible pain of loss, but her life was dedicated to service and there was satisfaction enough in that. Family was baggage - she had no need of it. Once, countless years ago, before she had even heard of the Fellowship of the Trees, another person had filled her consciousness and made her body ache. For months her every waking moment was filled with thoughts of Alene, and when, finally and inevitably they had to part, her grief was degrading, and her conduct was noted. It had taken her years to re-train her mind, but the Minders had cared for her. They helped her to rebuild her inner power and led her on the path which had brought her, many years later, to the Hub, and her present exalted position. She was now Sister Tilia, one of the Fellowship of the Trees. She was never told what had happened to Alene, and did not want to know.

There were five of them in her work group, her comrades. They had all learnt how to be friends, and she shared a special friendship, what they called a "Mateship" with one of them. Years ago, when Calan was younger they had been encouraged to copulate, but there was no issue, and in the end they both preferred to use the companions provided by the Minders. Two of the others, Ciri and Pento had also formed a mateship and Colis had a mate in one of the other groups.

There were different skills to be learnt from each kind of

friendship. When they were together as a group they treated each other equally, and would talk about the surface of their lives. With their special friends, their Mates, they could discuss deeper, more emotional issues, and help each other to a fuller understanding of their lives in Gaia.

The day had started well. Tilia shared a room with Calan, and normally they would put away their bedsheets when the call sounded, but today she had been in a strange mood when she woke. It was always hot here, but the night had been unusually hot and Calan was lying naked on his bed. Despite his age and gray hair, his body was still trim and muscular, and suddenly she wanted him. Quietly, naked and on bare feet she stepped over to him. He was on his side, facing away from her, his chest gently rising and falling with his breathing. She leaned over and gently brushed her nipples along his back. His breathing changed and slowly he rolled over, eyes still closed. She again moved over him, letting her breasts brush his chest. He groaned and she could see his penis stirring.

"Tilia. We are not supposed to do this." She said nothing but climbed on top of him.

"Oh God, you are such a bad lady."

"I know, sorry. Oh yes . . . ahh." He was inside her and they were remembering times in the past as they moved together. It was good, perhaps not quite as good as the old times, but there was no guilt. A good way to start the day.

Half an hour later they met up with Colis and her special friend at the refectory where they had the first meal of the day. Tilia could not remember a time when this hadn't been the same – a carefully balanced mix of plant protein in a choice of three flavours, essential carbohydrate with fresh fruit and a dark stimulant drink. All their food was grown in the compound, and it always tasted fresh and wholesome. As they sat down Colis looked tired.

"Why the droopy shoulders Colis?" Tilia asked her.

"I had to volunteer for an extra shift. There's so much new work on pathogen resistance the labs can't cope, and the new STC staff haven't arrived yet."

"Oh, are these Short Termers then?"

"Fraid so. They will all no doubt disappear when things calm down, but in the meantime we can make the most of them."

"Good. When are they due; have you seen any images of them?" This was Tilia

"Tomorrow I hope, and yes we've seen pictures and it looks as if several of them are potential breeders. Fredo here," she nodded at her special friend "has been particularly interested in one of the females."

"Well why not" said Fredo "It's good to have a change." Calan said:

"I hope we will get a look in too, though how we're going to find the time I don't know. Our labs too are under massive pressure to get all the doses out to the destinations on time."

"Well, let's hope we get some more free time when it's all over. I could really do with a couple of weeks on the Island - it's ages since I went to Beach 2"

"Oh, the Island! I prefer the Mountain, if feels more real to me. Which one's Beach 2 Colis?"

"Oh, you know, on the East side of the Island where the big waves are." Tilia nodded, stood up and said:

"Well Colis, don't forget to reserve the space in good time. Beach 2 is particularly greedy on processor time."

CHAPTER 3 2031 – 38

Sir Hector Grant

Marlsburg

Until recently I had been enjoying my retirement. I've lived longer already than both my parents, and unless my mind goes I shall always remember how harrowing their last years were. The old National Health Service always seemed in such a muddle. Thank goodness the new Health Partnerships work so much better. Nobody worries now about things like arthritic hips, hernias, cataracts and so on. We just get them replaced. Even most cancers are now routinely treated, but of course there are far less of them, thanks to the huge resources going into primary health care now.

So, even at 83 I can still do most of the ordinary things, but no health service on earth can cure heartache. My poor Amy lost her baby, and it seems very unlikely now that she will try again. Margaret, the woman I still think of as my wife, now no longer recognizes me. She even gave me a friendly greeting the other day, thinking I was a neighbour! Funnily enough this has enabled me to do more to help her. She now sees me as some sort of friend.

As for Lucy, well I've not heard anything for years. I've stopped thinking about her – almost.

I've tried to think kindly of Vandervelde, but I can't pretend that this business of Amy losing her child has not put even more strain on our relationship. Even if she were to leave him, it is too late now for Amy to attempt another pregnancy. He tries too hard with Belle – I really don't think he has a clue about young people. It's all work, work, work with him. He is so good at getting the rich and powerful to dance to his tune that he forgets to switch off the 'power' button when he comes home. She never complains but I know Amy feels lonely stuck in that big old house up the road. She much prefers being in the airship, but so often Van has important guests on board and she has to stay behind.

Belle is my great consolation, but since she went to university in Caledonia I only see her on occasional visits when she divides her time between Margaret and me.

******

Life gets more and more difficult, and most of it is down to my "son in law". I walked into town the other day and suddenly needed a pee – not an uncommon fate for us oldies. The old public toilet I've used for years was shut and there was a notice outside saying that it was being converted to a composting toilet because they couldn't afford to run the heating, lighting and pumps which used to make the necessities of life a bit more comfortable. Even when you find a decent toilet that's open, there's no water to wash your hands with. We have to use that gel cleanser stuff which just dries off leaving your hands just as dirty as they were before.

You can't get 'next day' delivery any more. It's evidently too expensive to carry goods against deadlines. You now have to wait until transport is available. I managed to save up enough fuel to drive to Swinsdun the other day with a long shopping list. It was February and quite cold so I was looking forward to going to one of the big stores where at least I could potter around in the warm. Some of the changes have been in force for a while now. Most of the shops have converted to "interactive showrooms" where you can see and handle what is available and negotiate a delivery deal. It's rare now for any of the larger businesses to offer goods to take away. So, I chatted to a few of the assistants about various bits of kit I would like but can't afford and then I decided I would go for a bite to eat in the café which was two floors up. I had heard that the lifts had gone, but was not expecting to have to climb all those stairs unaided. The escalator was still there but apparently inactive. There was a nice young lady there to explain.

“I’m sorry Sir, you will have to wait a few minutes until there are more people ready to come down. When the track registers enough weight going down it will start moving, but there always have to be more people coming down than going up to make it work.”

“But what if you get here early in the day and there is nobody upstairs?”

“Well I’m afraid you would have to use the fixed stair. We do have staff who can help you.”

“Good grief I don’t want someone pushing me upstairs – not yet at least!”

Later Amy told me that there are special schemes now for people to donate unused carbon permits to help the less mobile. I should be grateful for small mercies I suppose but I still have some pride and dignity left and I don’t wish to be treated like an invalid.

Mind you, I’m not sure I shall want to eat anything in the café now that the government are bringing in these new food standards. I won’t be able to afford my mid-morning treat anymore – good coffee with a sticky cake. The coffee falls foul of the carbon taxes on imports and the cake is classified as a “Class C” food. There are only so many vouchers issued for foods which are high in fat and sugar and the bakers have to bid for them.

If, on the other hand, I was feeling virtuous, I could have one of the new coffee substitutes made from locally grown ingredients, and a “no sugar” carrot cake. These are made with local ingredients which are low on the “Glycemic Index”.

I can just hear Amy saying “Oh stop playing the old duffer! You don’t really want to go back to all that junk food do you?” Of course she’s right. It is good to see so many more people looking fit these days, but at my age I really don’t see why I should have to pay so much for something I have been enjoying for many years and which has never done me any harm. At least with the old system you weren't eating stuff grown from human shit. I can still hardly believe that we are now recycling our own sewage. I find myself sniffing my food before eating it. Now that is old duffer behaviour!

I suppose I do more or less support what governments all over the world seem to be doing these days. They have frightened us all into submission, but I don't feel I "own" our governments any more. The parties in power change around like musical chairs, whoever happens to be in power, there never seems to be much opposition, and that always makes me suspicious. I'm sure it's still Van in the background pulling the strings.

******

You can't get to 83 without thinking about death, and it's been a lot on my mind lately. I was recently diagnosed with prostate cancer. Surprisingly for someone of my vintage the doctors don't seem particularly concerned for me, but if, as they say, I am unlikely to die from cancer at my age, what am I likely to die of? Well, there is one big killer which has been little considered until recently but is now gaining a lot more credibility: old age; in other words the natural decay and disintegration of the body.

I've never been one for sweeping things under the carpet. What's the point of pretending? I long ago passed the Britannic average life expectancy, and statistically have a mere 7.6 years of life remaining. Being brutally honest with myself I don't think I will last that long. I've kept physically active but I no longer feel safe making quick movements. I get a lot of aches and pains and I get out of breath far too quickly.

There's been a lot of talk in the last few years about "The Good Death". Of course we all want a good death, but I still think asking your nearest and dearest to help you die is outrageous. We put enough burden on them as it is. I can't stand all that maudlin stuff about planning the moment of death with your favourite music playing and everyone trying to look cheerful: horrible! No, I think Dylan Thomas had it nearly right when I was a lad: "Do not go gentle into that good night" - though I'm not sure about the next bit: "Rage rage against the dying of the light" as he so memorably put it. My philosophy is to let nature take its course. I'm not afraid of death, but I am afraid of pain so I've just one request to my daughters, which I have written down and asked them to witness: "keep me from severe pain".

Vandervelde - Crisis Planning

above Gravesham

Amy is not with me on this trip. It's now 6 years since the miscarriage but she hasn't really recovered. I am almost certain that I am not destined for parenthood. I've not had the courage to tell Amy yet, but I've been to several clinics. One was completely baffled by my DNA. Another said they couldn't see anything wrong with me - "Perfectly normal for a man your age Mr Vandervelde." I hadn't told them about my age. Two of them made similar diagnoses: the strange configuration of my genome that has so dramatically slowed the ageing process has interfered with the mechanism by which the sperm combines with the ovum. The foetus never stood a chance.

Not for the first time I cursed my fate. Work is what keeps me going.

I've been asked by the Britannic government to go to a secret meeting in Lyndain. They were reluctant to say what it was about or who would be there. I would much rather have stayed in the ship above the rain, but it was clear my attendance was "required".

There had been a lot of up-beat talk in the Net recently about the "Transition to a Sustainable Economy" so I was surprised to find the mood was sombre when I arrived at the building in Blackhall. There were there some high level people from 5 different countries, and none of them looked as if they'd had good news. The Chairman was a woman, Helen McGuire, a senior member of the Brit coalition, and she wasted no time in getting down to business. She spoke in English and I could see several of the people round the table wearing translation phones.

"Ladies and Gentlemen, thank you all for coming. I have been asked to chair this meeting because for various reasons of timing and convenience it is happening here in Lyndain, but I do so on behalf of the Council of Europe.

We meet at a time of rapid change. We have all seen the old familiar economics of growth and consumerism crumbling beneath our feet and our governments have risen to meet the challenge. We are well on the way to creating a more stable world system, but, and this is the reason for this meeting, all of us in this room are aware of the dangers we face if we fail. We've made huge changes to our way of life, but they have come too late. Whatever we do short of re-engineering the planet, we are too late now to affect the climate changes already happening, or those we expect in the next few decades. Climate chaos will get even worse, and we are so constrained by resource limits that we cannot be sure we will be able to manage the effects of this.

All our nations for many years have had crisis plans in place, but have struggled to adapt those plans to the rapid changes around us. We in Britannica have separate plans for war, for famine, for epidemics and particularly for floods since the recent partial inundation of our capital. However, what we and most of you here do not have is a combined plan; a plan for how to cope with all these catastrophes happening at once.

Not only do we have to urgently update our plans but we

have to have a much greater degree of co-ordination across national boundaries. At this meeting we can only hope to agree a basic framework for a co-ordinated international response to system failure. The most important element of this is the timing. What is our first response? What will trigger that response?

If you look at the screen behind me you will see the main headings which we wish to discuss today. -

- Movement Restrictions – disease, civil disturbance
- First response teams – flood, earthquake
- Martial law – civil disturbance, armed conflict
- Secure Centres of government - civil disturbance, armed conflict
- Emergency Storage – famine, extreme cold

To help us in deciding on priorities, we have put together a number of possible scenarios, as you can see behind me.

1. An epidemic with above 10% mortality. The outbreaks are localized but effect many countries simultaneously.
2. A regional natural disaster – floods, earthquake, fire, drought, extreme cold, all with high mortality.
3. Destitution caused by collapse of the economy
4. Regional conflict with high mortality
5. Civil unrest with high mortality
6. And lastly, any combination of the above or all of them at once.

That is all I have to say for the moment. We will reconvene after the discussion groups.

There was a curious air of detachment in the room. We were looking at scenes of dreadful misery as if they were far removed from our lives. At this level perhaps they were. Perhaps none of these people believed that they personally would be affected, but I doubted this. We knew it was personal but could not act effectively unless we detached ourselves from our emotions. The discussion was long and sometimes heated, but eventually there was agreement on the shape a co-ordinated response would take.

NRG Britannica was to play an essential role in the Britannic response and I was asked to set up another work group to look especially at the detailed parts of the plan which the government wished to distance itself from. I knew I could not lead this group – I needed to focus on the so called 'Transition' in the hope that these measures would not be needed. Who could I spare for this work?

It was a weary journey on crowded trains to get to the ground station at Gravesham, thinking all the time about how NRG could respond. I knew who I wanted to lead this group, but would she agree?

******

Midsummer. This is when I really love being in this ship. Every year I make this promise to myself that I will try to see the dawn on the shortest day. Since living in the airship I have been able to see the sun rise too, unless the cloud is too high for us to get above it.

Today is perfect. Below me there are just a few lights showing in the town, and even fewer out in the country. Ten years ago you would have seen several megawatts of energy being burnt to light up streets with nobody in them. It was supposed to deter crime, but actually made things easier for the burglars. Away to the south are the Hamtun downs. To the west are the round bare hills of the wolds, with all above a deep blue-black dotted with millions of stars and the great drift of the milky way.

What was, half an hour ago, a faint glow above Lyndain has now been dimmed by the orange glow of the dawn. If I look west I see the sun striking to tops of the hills and slowly moving down them.

I remember some years ago - 2020 perhaps - watching the dawn from the South Downs and seeing the rising sun catching the tops of all the pylons which used to carry power on the grid. What a symbol they were of our lust for electrical power. In their commanding ugliness they seemed to say "You want the power, this is what it looks like".

Now they have all gone and the sunlight, moving down from the hills and across the Isis valley shows up a dense patchwork of horticulture and silviculture. Soon thousands of people will be starting work in this landscape and so productive is their labour that 70 percent of Lyndain's food comes from within 50 miles of the city.

Thinking about the Power Net reminds me of a conversation I had with Mollie recently. It was at the end of a long day of meetings in the "The Temple" as we called the old Lloyds Building in Brigstowe. We were sitting in two easy chairs having a drink and saying very little. I asked about her Brigstowe-based family.

"Oh yes, Brigstolian I am" – slipping easily into the local speech. Both her parents still live here though with different partners. To my surprise she mentioned a brother.

I said I didn't know she had one, but she seemed very reluctant to talk about him, just saying that he had moved away. His name is Jamie, and I thought I recognized the name so looked it up on my screen. It seems he is actually "Sir James" and MD of Cable Networks Ltd. Far from being proud, Mollie was critical of his desire for the trappings of status.

She quickly changed the subject and asked me if I had siblings. I parried that one but she was clearly unhappy and got up to leave.

"Van, I must go. Jamie is Jamie; let's just leave it at that please."

She left me feeling puzzled and uncomfortable. I decided to find out more about this mysterious brother. It wasn't difficult. It seems he was one of the main movers behind the "Smart Grid".

Mollie

I NEED TO WRITE THIS DOWN NOW. I've told Van but it doesn't seem to register. Now Eldred is threatening to leave me. I have to make a stand or I will be carried off to some secure ward tied to a trolley. These are the projects I currently have teams working on:

Educate the Girls

Food and Water supplies

Pathogen resistance

They are all global in scope and all urgent. Now he wants me to take on Crisis Planning. I simply can't do it. As things are I hardly see my poor children. Eldred is a good parent when there are other adults around but hopeless on his own. I've now reached the stage where I fret about Jamie to take my mind off work! I will write an official letter to him - Vandervelde.

Letter from Mollie Edmundson

20 York Road

Montpellier

Brigstowe BG2...

Dear Van,

Attached to this personal letter you will find my official letter explaining why I do not think I am the right person for the Crisis Planning job. I feel I ought to explain to you candidly why I was rather abrupt with you last week, and the personal reasons behind my decision.

Both have to do with Eldred. I knew almost as soon as I saw him that life with him, especially through such a critical period in our history, would not be easy. As you know I have struggled with shyness all my life. It's hard for me to be assertive – much easier to pull back and let others do the talking. I don't admire this characteristic in myself and I don't admire it in other people either. I have always been drawn to self-confident even flamboyant people, especially the men in my life. My father, as you know, is an extrovert; a cheerful talkative person with plenty of self-confidence and style, and a sharp intelligence. On the face of it Eldred and Dad don't seem very similar at all – the moody, scruffy, angry artist railing against modern comms and the cheerful optimist. The outward show doesn't tell the whole story. They are both artists of course, and they are both thinkers. Dad can be very angry and depressed sometimes and Eldred is fantastic company when things are going right for him.

Eldred has never understood my relationship with you, and he couldn't stand the idea of me becoming a sort of civil servant making horrible plans for disasters. He sees disaster as an inevitable part of life; part of the creative process. He loves storms and floods. Power cuts energize him. Although I was looking forward to getting into crisis management, part of me knew that it was almost a lazy option for me - tapping into my love of order. Eldred has shown me that we are most truly ourselves when we push ourselves outside our comfort zones.

Jamie and I were very close when we were growing up. Although nearly 2 years younger, he was always the dominant one, the extrovert. He would take delight in goading me out of my shell; mentally and physically teasing me until I got into a temper. Even as a child he had a great sense of style, and in his teens he always had to have the latest fashion in clothes and gadgets. His wretched girl friends would come crying to me when he went moody on them. They thought they were in love but I had no patience with them. He was always there for me when I needed him.

Jamie didn't excel at school – he had too many interests; too volatile to work at his chosen subjects. Surprisingly he started a multi-science degree at Exchester, but when he and a friend – the now famous Mike Fuller - invented that thread (the material which enables power lines to carry so much information) he dropped out and formed his own company. It just took off. One minute he was my kid brother the next he was all over the net. There were pictures of him everywhere – always well dressed, always charming. We found ourselves drifting apart. We couldn't quite re-create that old easy love/friendship we used to have.

Things really fell apart when I introduced him to Eldred. The details are still too painful for me to recount here. Suffice to say that they had an almighty row. I, of course sided with Eldred. I was in love and I didn't like this new fashion icon and comms star that Jamie had become. I've regretted so many times what I said then, and tried hard to make amends but he won't talk to me. I haven't seen him for years.

So that's it; the great sadness in my life. I feel sure he will eventually come round, but I must move on and stop thinking about him.

Change of subject: I'm really glad you met Judith. She's a dear friend. If she wasn't so involved with the elections in Caerdydd I'd suggest we find a place for her here. She is so full of energy it makes me feel tired sometimes.

The children are a great compensation. Magnus and Cassandra send kisses to their "Uncle Van"

Kind regards

Mollie

Vandervelde

The Transport Brief

Even the so called “petrol heads” of the twenty-tens knew that the automobile was a ridiculously wasteful way of getting around, but four or five generations of us had grown up using this as our main means of transport. Not only was the car “essential” to how we lived, it carried a huge emotional charge: our cars were our second homes, part of that private space which became increasingly important to so called “western” cultures. No elected government could introduce the changes needed with any hope of being re-elected. This was where we came in. We faced two enormous challenges: find a system which cut carbon emissions by a factor of four, and sell the idea to the people.

It was at this point that Twm Pritchard appeared. We were in the Condor moored above Ystwyth when my screen buzzed with a message from the air-station below.

“There’s a young man here who insists he has to speak to you. There’s no data on him at all.”

“What’s it about?”

“He says he can cut our transport carbon costs by 70 percent.”

“Is that him there by your desk?”

“Yes, do you want to speak to him?”

“No, I want to meet him. See if he can cope with the transit pod.” Nearly every day we get someone turning up with all sorts of crazy ideas, but I had a hunch about this young man. He did look odd, but not in a swivel-eyed sense. If he could cope with the 15 minute ascent in a tiny pod swaying on its cable then at least we would know he had determination.

When he finally arrived in my work room he looked pale and sweaty. He prowled around looking at all the comms and ignored my first request to be seated, launching instead into a disconnected diatribe about starting from zero: our feet. He had a distinctive accent which I was beginning to recognize as that of a native Cymraeg speaker from the Ystwyth area.

"Look, you have to start at zero - just feet, - no cars, trains, trucks, bicycles or even horses and carts. Then look at the figures– where do we go, how often, how far and for why."

"Mr Pritchard, please sit down. I do want to hear what you have to say, but you're making me uncomfortable striding about like this".

"Ah I'm sorry. It's getting to me, all the stuff going round in my head. I can scarcely believe I'm here speaking to you at last."

"OK, so we start from basics, as you say: feet. We know that walking on two legs is highly inefficient. It uses nearly as much energy going downhill as it does going up, and even running can only attain speeds of up to 26mph for very short periods. We have of course looked at the travel statistics and they confirm what we knew anyway, that most journeys were unnecessary and wasteful. The problem is we have a strict brief: travel for pleasure must remain a priority, so as well as looking at the greatest productivity, we have to look at how to get the most pleasure from the least input of energy."

"Well I can cope with that. My system is very flexible."

"You have a system already?"

"Of course. Look, walking - too much friction with the ground is the problem. How to reduce friction? This is where mechanics come in. Two groups of devices: revolving devices - wheels, rollers etc. OR low-friction surfaces - water, air, skis or mag-lev. If all we want to do is move our bodies around, then bicycles and skis are the most efficient. They both use gravity and forward momentum to boost the output from the same input of muscle energy. If everyone used bicycles or skis for short distance travel we could make massive energy savings."

"Mr Pritchard, why are you telling me this? It's been common knowledge for a lot longer than you have been alive, and for almost as long the transport experts have been trying to encourage or even force people to use their legs, but why should they exhaust themselves when cheap easy alternatives are available?"

"I know, I know. I did say 'if all you want to do'. The point is we need to do a hell of a lot more than that – moving goods, pleasure trips and so on. You are using low friction when you travel in this ship, but what about on land? Sealskin. That's the answer".

"You've lost me"

"It's what arctic skiers used to stop the skis sliding backwards. Sealskin has very low friction in one direction and very high in the reverse. We could use the same system for tracked transport. Look at a dog-sleigh team. They use high friction for the locomotive – the dogs' legs – and very low friction for the carriages – the sledges."

"Interesting idea, but in that case why did we give up pulling barges along canals? Wait, I know what you're going to say - that the railways could exploit fossil fuel more effectively"

"Exactly, canals were very expensive to build and maintain because the surface has to be level. They were also very slow – water friction increases with speed and it takes as much energy to stop moving as it does to go forwards. Air as a surface doesn't need to be level but the carbon cost of HTA transport was much too high – as you know of course."

"Mr Pritchard, Twm, I'm not sure you understand what our brief is. We are required look in detail at what we use transport for – 'what do we need' and 'what do we want?' We need to transport people, and goods to trade, but we want a whole list of things including speed and excitement. Our brief is offer all these, but to see them all as 'demand' would not save enough energy, so we will have to have some kind of regulation to ensure that transport essentials have first call on available power."

"No no, not regulation! That's totally the wrong word. Permits – vouchers, that's what we should use. An extension of your carbon trading scheme would work."

"Yes, but that is strictly regulated. If we didn't enforce the terms of the vouchers the whole scheme would collapse. Twm, you're striding about again."

"Sorry sorry," He perched on the edge of his chair. "but the principle of vouchers is one of trade. It taps into a uniquely human ability - trading something you have too much of for something which is in surplus somewhere else. We say to the public – look, we do not have enough energy to do all the things we want so we are going to create a market in personal carbon credits. Everyone will have the same allowance, but anyone can increase their credits by sending power to the grid or by buying unused credits from someone else.

In the same way that companies can gain credits by exporting power, individuals can gain by using their muscles. Suppose we set up "gyms" where people could go to exercise, but where every calorie of energy they expend on the machines goes straight to the grid and adds to their carbon credits? Maybe we could even get power from sports events?"

"Wow – let's backtrack a little. You said you had a plan."

"Yes, I've got some drawings here. This is what the basic module might look like."

"Hm, looks like one of those old Pedalec things."

"Ah but those things could only go for about 20 miles.

These can go for hundreds without being recharged!"

"How, by magic?"

"Ha . . . no, I do know a little about the laws of physics. No, they link into a track system which pulls them along until they get to the nearest track station where they leave the track and carry on under their own steam . . . so to speak"

"Are you suggesting that we do away with the rail network?"

"No, not all of it. Keep the land and replace the rails and locomotives with a much more efficient system which can pull these modules."

"I was afraid that's what you had in mind."

I felt again that sudden flash of foresight. For a second I had a glimpse of these vehicles flying along a track in a long string. They had a distinctive smell – slightly metallic.

It all sounded off the wall, but the more he spoke the more I could see the sense in what he was saying. Pacing up and down, waving his hands around, breaking into Cymraeg, whispering, shouting, it was not long before he lost me in technicalities. It transpired that he was not a scientist by training, had never been to a university, and had educated himself on the Net. I could see that my hunch was right – here was someone who would never think in conventional patterns. With every soaring flight of inspiration, Twm was carving out a space for himself on my team.

He joined at a time when we had already concluded that neither of our current systems – road and rail - was capable of fulfilling our brief. My heart sank at the thought of the mega billions a system like his would cost to set up, and it wouldn't be much use if it was just one country – the whole world would have to be convinced by Twm's idea.

Unfortunately his logic was compelling. We simply couldn't afford to go on burning fossil fuels in the way we were. Apparently such ideas had been circulating on the Net for some time but had never reached the mainstream.

******

Thus it was that we began planning the biggest change in people's personal lives for 100 years: nothing less than the demise of the automobile. We would still have horseless carriages, but the motive power would no longer be fully controlled by the driver. One of the great personal freedoms of the 20th and 21st centuries would be lost. Enormous and powerful industries would find themselves in a different business. We would be up against the most powerful corporations, the most fiercely defended vested interests. This would be the biggest test that NRG had ever faced.

If we failed then all our achievements of the last 20 years would be lost.

The story of how the great corporations lost their power has been told in many books, but the role played by NRG has been much exaggerated. We have been portrayed as a sinister secret society of Stalinists intent on creating a Big Brother state. In truth our power came from the governments who paid us, and the most important of these was the EU.

It's difficult to remember now how corporate the European Union was even 20 years ago. The anarchists and fringe left hated it of course, but so did the conservative fringes. "Brussels" became synonymous with bureaucratic control, economic conservatism, and a close relationship with "big business". It was seen as a businessman's club, managed by cautious hard working Germany, yet it was in Germany that what was then called "Green" politics had its power base, and it was the German politician Eberhardt Merkel, son of the first female Chancellor who brought the politics of no-growth into the European mainstream in 2020. Because our carbon trading scheme was based on the old EU one, it was natural for the German government to be the first to support the "Transnet" scheme openly.

It took two years of constant negotiation before we could be confident that it would work, but even then we couldn't find a single country willing to pilot the scheme –even though we had secured massive financial backing. Then in 2034 there was a general election here in Britannica and for the first time the Green Party became the largest in the Anglo-Cymric Parliament. Almost their first act was to issue this statement:

Britannic Government Press Release

The people have voted for change and with the support of the Cymric Assembly we are proud to announce that we have offered our support for the proposed TRANSNET system. We should not forget that the Transnet concept originated in Britannica and that the Britannic arm of NRG did most of the work on the scheme. Rail transport, like many of the other technologies which mould our lives now, originated here and we are convinced that yet again we can show the world that this small group of Nations can take the lead. In this we have the unequivocal support of the government of the Caledonian Republic. The Hibernian Federation will not oppose the scheme but the government in Stormont prefers to wait for the first phase to be on the ground before joining.

******

So, at last we had the green light. Britannica would be the pilot. With Caledonia at the forefront we looked at the main arterial lines out of Lyndain and decided to make the Lyndain to South Cymru line the northern limit for the last third. The Lyndain to West Caledonia was to be the first and the East Coast to be second.

The disruption was appalling and created a lot of ill feeling - slightly moderated by the thousands of well paid jobs we were creating to speed the transformation. By the end of the summer all the track on the closed part will have been changed and half of the rolling stock adapted. The locomotives, many of which were nearing the end of their lives anyway, have all been scrapped and will be replaced with the new ones already under construction.

The new powers which were brought in across the G10 enabled the governments to put certain industries on what used to be called a 'war footing'. With remarkable ingenuity, engineers in the big three European motor companies – General Motoren, Union Peugeot/Citroen and Svenka Volvo AB, have adapted their truck and van production lines to produce a limited range of vehicles capable of running on both old and new rails. These have been used to boost the capacity of the remaining rail network and to run a service of sorts on the new transtrack. Some parts of their manufacturing have been completely converted to build the new Very Low Friction (VLF) locomotive carriages. These use the same principle as mag-lev trains, but without the levitation. The electromagnetic field will only pull the powered carriages – locomotives. The rest of the work is done by the VLF surfaces. We were ready for the next publication. (see page 113).

With the pent-up desperation of the millions struggling to get around the country, the take-up was phenomenal. Within days the waiting list had stretched to 6 months. Even with all the resources we were pouring in to the new factories we couldn't make enough. It was time for some outsourcing again. We offered huge incentives to small engineering firms to adapt existing cars. Out came the engines, in went the electric motors and batteries. The wiring was replaced by the standard guidance loom and the retractable VLF shoes were fitted underneath.

We never intended to create collectors pieces, but we reckoned without our species' innate love for personalised devices. Soon these odd looking contraptions were fetching higher prices than the much more efficient purpose built models. The modified ones got called 'Mods' or m-cars to distinguish them from the more efficient but duller e-cars.

Britannic Govt Publications 2036

TRANSPORT FOR THE FUTURE

The new system explained.

Carbon Credits

From today everyone in Britannica will have a new kind of money to spend: Carbon Credits. To access your Carbon Bank log on to britgov.net and download the software. One carbon credit gives you the right to emit 1 kilo of CO2 into the atmosphere. We all know that carbon emissions have to reduce substantially if our grandchildren are to have any future at all. Here in Britannica we've made great progress. From a high of 14 tonnes per person in 2020 we are down to 8 but we still have a long way to go and progress in the last few years has slowed.

You have now in your carbon bank 5000 units which are valid for one year. In a few days you will receive your carbon card which will enable you to spend the credits on any of the devices which use energy and are equipped with the card readers.

The Carbon Exchange.

Your credits are worth money. If you register with the Personal Carbon Exchange at the britgov portal you will be able to see what their current value is, and you are free to buy and sell a limited number of units per week.

Some of your credits will be used automatically by your home appliances, and if you can generate energy you will be able to increase your stock at the carbon bank. If for example you have solar collectors, instead of being paid in cash when you sell to the grid you will receive carbon credits. If you have an exercise machine connected you can gain credits by pedalling or rowing. It has been calculated that one hour of cycling at a "speed" of 20 kph will generate 0.5 credits.

Transnet

Most of us will use our credits on the new transport system. During the next two years the whole of Britannica's road and rail system will be changed! All the rail track will be changed to VLF (very low friction) and thousands of miles of roads will be changed. One lane of all our motorways will be converted to VLF track. From January 2038 you will need a special licence to drive a vehicle which is not powered by electric motors.

What happens to your car

In future your personal vehicle will be able to travel up to 25 kilometres on its own battery, but for longer journeys it will link into the Transnet. You will have two options for your existing vehicle:

Trade it in for a new Transnet e-car

Have it adapted to run on the system.

In each case there are grants of up to £5000 available to help you to adapt to the new system. Once the system is complete there will be a Transnet charging point within 25 kilometres of every house and an access station within 40 kilometres of every house. Each charge is paid for in carbon credits and all journeys on the network will be paid for in the same way.

How it will work – examples:

1 You wish to travel from your home to do some shopping in the nearest large town which is 20 kilometres away. Your vehicle will be charged at your home charge station and will

easily take you to the town at around 50 kph. When you arrive you plug into a charge station, pay with your carbon card and walk to your destination(s) in the town. A short time later* your vehicle will be ready for the return trip.

2 You and your family wish to visit a friend in another part of the country. You look on the Net to see where your nearest link station is and travel there in your vehicle. When you arrive you enter your destination at the link console and your card will be debited with the carbon cost of your journey. Because the system is so efficient this will be less than half the carbon cost of the same journey driving along a road. You then drive onto a waiting lane. When the next locomotive is due you will be told to drive onto the acceleration lane where your vehicle will lock on to the locomotive link and rapidly accelerate up to 150kph. Your motor is switched off and you sit back and enjoy the journey. When you reach your destination station the track will automatically eject your vehicle and you will drive on to your destination under your own power.

3 You wish to transport some bulky packages to the other end of the country. First you need to hire one or more standard goods modules (containers). Some of these will be self-powered and available at most charge points, others will only be available at the Transtations and will need to be towed to the waiting lane by your self-powered e-car.

4. You are going on holiday and have saved enough carbon credits to use a self-drive camper (not yet available) or another large vehicle. Your comms tells you there is one 5k away so you book it, grab a basic pedal assisted e-car, drive to where the camper is and exchange it for the camper which you drive back home, load up and set off a second time for the station.

*see charging times on reverse

Once the last third of the railway was dealt with we had a fantastic track network with thousands more stations, but a dwindling number of trains capable of using it, all carrying desperately overcrowded passengers at exorbitant cost. It was time to roll out the next phase. By then we knew we could not finance the production of so many vehicles for hire. They would have to be sold, and that meant a marketing campaign. This is how we advertised the first of the changes:

Britannic Govt. Publications

A New Kind of Vehicle

Be the first to take up the challenge!

From April 2037 the government is offering a £5000 bonus to everyone who scraps an internal combustion engine automobile for one of the new electric Transnet Cars.

Even better you can save another £2000 by opting for the A version with a limited choice of optional extras.

These new vehicles have a range of just 20 miles, but DON'T PANIC! 90% of the population will easily be able to get to one of the 20,000 new Transnet stations, and there all you have to do is tap in your destination, sit back and let the track take the strain. As your vehicle is whisked along at 120 kph it will be charging ready for you to drive to your final destination from the end station.

Longer range higher speed vehicles will be available for those living too far from the nearest Transnet station, and there is a special finance package for these too.

THIS IS YOUR FUTURE:

DON'T GET LEFT BEHIND

Letter from Twm Pritchard

International Letter

Sender Twm Pritchard

Coed Las

Dear Van,

I hate this compulsory letter style. Rules, rules – why does everything have to be so corporate? I can't believe this monstrous bureaucracy is what you really want. What happened to those whisky fuelled nights we used to spend working on Transnet? Those great discussions about wilderness; the long rides through the forest?

The only thing wild round here now is me. I rant and rave but nobody takes any notice. They're all too busy storing up carbon credits. Did you know that we had to give up our horses – all except Jasper who is too old even for petfood? I really don't feel comfortable at Pritchard Enterprises now. Would you believe we have a revolting great wire fence round the whole compound? We even have guards. Every scrap of paper I write on is taken away to be archived, and my screen keeps telling me what I can and cannot save. I know things are tight Van but it seems to me sometimes that we have exchanged a culture of waste and greed for one of secrecy and control.

OK, rant over. I know you have to do all these things.

How are you anyway? Still as young as ever no doubt. Do you actually enjoy all that power?

I was very pleased to hear about Downend – pity it's not in Cymru, but I guess Wiltunshire is better than Suthrig anyway. In fact the reason I'm writing is that I have a trip planned which will bring me within range of your house.

Could I hitch my cable to your charging post – ie come and visit? The possible dates are July 5 to 8.

Yours sincerely (bah)

Twm

Vandervelde

At Downend

I'm proud of this house. Work began on it nearly nine years ago, and I'm glad to say that the systems we chose are still working perfectly. The outer shell is that of a Georgian Manor House. Only the windows look different – each a single sheet of multi-glass in a simple frame. Even in 2020 the use of fossil fuel for domestic heating was on its way out, and I knew that the 'smart grid' was then in development so was able to buy all the new devices which would make full use of it.

Take this cup of coffee on my desk: it uses hot water from the HH supply which is kept at 99 degrees. The much larger capacity H supply is at 55 degrees and the C is at one degree. The heaters and coolers for these draw power from the net only when it is efficient to do so – at periods when demand is stable and the power sources – solar, wind, tide, hydro etc – are operating fully.

In addition to the huge national pumped-water power storage reservoirs, every house has some form of storage depending on location and cost, and most can also generate. We have both lithiuim ion micro-batteries, and pumped water. The reservoir can only deliver power for about six hours but the batteries can last for days. The net will automatically charge up our storage when power is cheap and will buy from us when the national generating capacity is low. We also have a water turbine so we are net generators to the system.

The beauty of this system is that being modular it integrates local and national. Any part of the power output side of the Net can be shut down at any time without loss to individual houses and businesses: they simply switch to their local systems. This doesn't apply to the Info Net which is programmed to be always on. Since it became fully operational in 29 there have been some periods when the Power Net has been down for several days, and in a few cases some people ran out of power, but these areas now have better storage and the main problem now is the big demand for highly trained engineers to maintain all these systems.

Insulating old houses like this used to be a big problem, but since the development of ultra insulation we have been able to achieve a u value of less than 0.1 using a continuous moulded 50mm layer covering the inside of the building. The only openings are for the doors and windows and these are air-lock sealed and multi-glazed. The insulation has a rigid surface which can be painted and onto which frameworks can be fixed. Underfloor heating and stone or board floors can be laid on top of the floor layer.

So we have no difficulty in keeping warm in winter and cool in summer. Of course the same could be said for 20th century houses with efficient oil heating and air conditioning, and long ago builders realised that there was a deep human need for a fire, for flames, a source of radiant heat and a focus for the main room. We had to accept that in our genes we were still hunter-gatherers, and the open fire used to be essential to our survival. Although chimneys, fires and stoves had made a big comeback in the 90s and 10s, we could no longer afford to have big holes in our roofs. All our buildings are now air-tight and fresh air is supplied by heat-recovery ventilation. We do have radiant heat though.

For example, I've set the temperature in the sitting room lower than is really comfortable. I walk in and sit down. The wall opposite is made of a dark, matt composite material. I speak to it:

"Light the fire"

There in front of me is a 3d image of a log fire and already I can feel the warmth coming towards me. If it burns too low I tell it to put some more 'fuel' on. I ask another question.

"What's the news?"

Above it a screen lights up and I can chose the items I want to see by using voice commands.

Some of us can remember the times when there were all sorts of different screens, some called 'televisions', some 'phones', some 'computers', 'cinemas', 'tablets', 'games consoles' and so on. Here at Downend we get all our information (as well as our power) from the Net, and we have three kinds of screen – worktables, communicators and entertainment. The underlying technology is the same but they have different controls. The worktables use voice, touch and gesture commands, the communicators use voice and touch, and the entertainment screens on our system use voice only, though they can be configured to accept touch commands if required.

If I have some work to do I sit at my worktable and activate the parts I need by running my hands over them. We can speak to them and they speak back, or we can communicate with them using gestures and signs; stroke them, hit them, even type on them if, like me, you like typing.

I see I wrote that I am at my 'desk'; an old and re-assuring word, and in many ways a modern worktable is more like the traditional wooden desk than the messy mix of keyboard, mouse, screen, cables, bits of paper that used to clutter the surfaces we worked on. I sit at something which looks like a table. If I have any physical, paper documents to look at I can spread them on the table, and if I have someone to talk to formally I can sit them the other side of the table. Paper however, is an expensive luxury so mostly I tilt the table towards me so that I can easily bring up all the images and information I need.

Today I have to read some online documents and suggest amendments. I bring up a virtual qwerty keyboard and type in the amendments. Once saved these will be committed to archive paper at the office in Berlin.

If I had better musical skills I could play music on the screen, but I usually relax with a game of chess in 3d.

Visit from Twm

I played some chess recently with Twm who came on a visit. There he was in the porch, hair flying around, crumpled shirt and baggy trousers. He seemed ill at ease at first. Twm feels that the modern world has no place for people like him. I wish I could have been more re-assuring, but more and more these days I have a knot of worry in my stomach. I got the Penderyn whisky out, and we sat in the kitchen talking about the time we first met.

"Ah diw, that elevator. I'm dwli for heights Van – anything above roof height and I feel queer. Every time the damn things swayed around I thought I was going to die. It took me ten minutes to get some colour back before I came in to see you."

"Yes, that was something of a test. I saw you on the entrance camera and thought you looked a bit, er, eccentric."

"Eccentric? Well I suppose I can live with that. I was surprised you asked to see me."

"Well, I had a hunch, and I thought if you could manage the pod it would show you had determination at least."

"Ha – little do you know how close I was to walking out.

It's a good thing there aren't microphones in that horrible pod – I was cursing you every which way."

"Oh but there are!" We both burst out laughing.

"Well, well, diw diw, we've come a long way since those days, but to be honest Van, if I could wave a magic wand and half the people on this planet disappeared I wouldn't give a toss. Ffion has the kids most of the time now – I hardly see them, and when I do I don't know what to say to them. They seem to live in a world which has no use for people like me."

"Well, there'll always be a place for you in NRG"

"I know that Van and a bit of me is grateful, but for fuck's sake where's the joy? Where's the freedom? You've got everything wrapped up so tight now."

"Yes . . . you're right of course and I don't like it either. I long for the days when we could ride over the mountains or wander over the downs, fly off on holiday, cook huge steaks on a Barbecue . . . all those things, but even with everything we've achieved . . . I . . . Listen Twm, do you value our friendship enough to keep things I tell you quiet?"

"Fuck you elder man. Who do you think I am? Some sort of village gossip? You should know by now that I will only pass things on if you tell me to."

"OK, sorry, sorry . . . I get so paranoid sometimes. Put it down to old age. The thing is, as far as the public goes NRG is doing a great job . . . no, on second thoughts I'll tell you later. Let me show you the garden."

I'd had another of my funny turns – a flash of unease, a fraction of a second of something that felt like the future. As before it soon passed. It had stopped raining so we put on what Twm would call "seaboots" and strolled round the garden. It smelt damp and clean – like a knife after cutting a lemon. Here I was sure we would not be overheard. Paranoid? Probably.

"So, We've succeeded in bringing carbon emissions down to the target level; the population has stabilised; we have enough food and water and so on, and yet..... we are living on the edge of a precipice. We've set up barriers and we can keep within them, but we are all pressing up on those barriers."

"Van you old bastard come here" He gave me a big hug. It felt good. "It doesn't take much to guess that. We're not going to be really safe until there are less people are we?"

"Well, either that or even more equal distribution of resources, which means a very dull and controlled life for everybody for at least a generation. If I were in your position Twm I would stay away from the cities."

"Seriously? You think it's that close?"

"I really don't know. It's just a gut feeling, but I've learnt over the last 100 years or so to take note of my gut feelings. They haven't always been right, but they always mean something" We returned to the house in silence, each with our sombre thoughts. I could see Twm was pre-occupied.

"What is it Twm?"

"Ah, sorry. I'm not sure if I should tell you this. It sounds trivial."

"Well that would be a change from transport"

"Yes . . . well . . . the thing is, someone came to see me recently. It was a man of about your age – in fact he looked a bit like you. He was very polite and had evidently done his homework – he knew all about my family and seemed to know some stuff about transport which I thought was secret.

I don't remember his name, and I can't really remember what we talked about. I do remember shaking his hand and thinking it felt a bit odd, and then I remember him saying 'It would be better if you didn't tell Vandervelde about this.' I wasn't going to tell you but when you said the cities might not be safe, and that even you were worried, I had a sudden feeling that this man might have been important. I'm quite concerned that I seem to have had a memory lapse. Must be old age come calling. Anyway – that's it – not much really."

"Hm, thank you for telling me Twm. It could be important, though I can't see at the moment why it should be."

"Oh well then, enough of this gloomy talk – pass the Penderyn."

"Now you're talking – Iechyd Dda!"

"And 'prost' to you too."

Letter from Judith Evans

International Letter

Sender: Judith Evans

5 District 2

Caerdydd CF1 9LX

Dear Van,

I was appalled by your recent gloomy letter.

It's ridiculous. You should be very proud of what you have achieved. It really is extraordinary how far we have moved in such a relatively short time. Have you forgotten how pessimistic we all were back in the twenties? We were convinced that total catastrophe was just around the corner. Things happened so fast. I know you deny it, but I still suspect that someone in your organisation hit the panic button. The response was so co-ordinated I can't help seeing your hand in it. You always believed that those in power would not act until the threat was no longer decades away, but years, even months away. How right you were.

You may well be right too about just how precarious our present stability is. Most of us are happy to believe that the catastrophe has been averted; the urgency has gone. Nobody wants a return the age of greed, we are just grateful that a measure of democracy has been restored.

It is certainly worrying that the amazingly rapid de-salination programme is already pushing power demand to its limits. You seemed so convinced just a few years ago that our clean energy supply was more than adequate. I suppose it's inevitable that until the population graph goes from stable to reducing we will have periods of belt-tightening, but just think – we've stopped burning fossil fuel! Isn't that astonishing? All those precious hydrocarbons now being used for food and materials! Surely it can't be long before extraction rates start going down?

And who would have believed that "democratic" governments could have introduced food rationing so successfully? In 20 years we've all gone from treating real meat as our birthright to regarding it as a real luxury.

Yes it's very disappointing that there are still pockets of starvation, and it's tough that food rations have had to be cut again, but look how healthy people are now. Surely these food riots can be contained? I can't believe things are as tight as your last letter implied – you have seen so much more of life than any of us that you can always anticipate the worst outcomes.

Rhys has got very gloomy lately. He hates all these restrictions and rules. I tell him he's shortening his life by looking on the black side. I suppose a consideration like that doesn't cut much ice with you! Anyway he sends his regards.

My dear Van; I have such confidence in the sheer intelligence of NRG that I truly believe you will start to see that longed for downturn in the census figures very soon.

With great affection

Yours sincerely

Judith

Mollie

I can't sleep. I feel sick. My head aches. I don't think I can take much more worry. I used to love my job but in the last few years it's got so intense. I'm working far too many hours and still I can't get on top of things. Van is no help. He seems indestructible. Even though he was up to his ears in the new transport scheme, when he got my letter he immediately started a big re-organisation to take some of the pressure off. All very well but I can't just abandon things in mid-stream. Eldred's not much use either. He doesn't talk about leaving me, but he's on another pet scheme now – setting up some sort of time capsule where images and sounds play indefinitely without repeating themselves. I give up. I used to try to appreciate – oh God I can't say that can I? Let's say 'try to understand' his works, (which is closer to the truth) but I just haven't the energy now.

Magnus is sweet. He's 10 now and always trying to help – be the man about the house. He's quite tall and strong for his age and I guess it won't be long before it really does feel like he is playing that role . . . ye Gods, how can I say that? Oh Eldred, where are we going?

What is so galling is that the media are now singing our praises! For so many years we had to fight them tooth and nail, and now we can do no wrong. They've even come round to the Transnet – at least the more liberal of them. So why am I complaining? Well I hope this never becomes public knowledge. I'm not supposed to say these things, let alone write them down. The fact is we are dreadfully overstretched.

I'm working with a group from India on water supplies. They tell me that Andhra Pradesh and Tamil Nadu were only saved from a catastrophic drought last year by the massive storms and flooding they had this year. They are rushing to install huge de-sal plants, but the solar power stations to run them are only just coming on stream and with a lot of problems too. It looks very likely that they will be opening de-sal plants which will have to stand unused until they can get enough power.

It's now looking almost certain that some of our targets will not be met. There are now very few places in the world where the birth rate is still rising, but even with a stable birth rate the populations go on growing. We had hoped to see the first signs of a decline in birth rate this year, but if anything we are looking at a slight increase. We've had three crisis Netmeets in the last month, but there's not much more we can do except keep our fingers crossed.

Then there's Judith. It's only a few years since we first met but I think of her as one of my best friends. Of course she is younger than me so I suppose it's inevitable that her priorities will be different as we get older. She seems to be getting quite pally with Van which I suppose is a good thing, but she doesn't seem to have so much time for me. It's weeks since we last got together over a bottle of wine.

The big four o is looming. Forty is a good age; it's the peak of adulthood. You're young enough to do (nearly) all the things you could when you were a spotty youth but you have some standing in the world.

<u>Resolutions:</u>

- I will not go into my fifth decade with my personal life in a mess.
- Eldred and I will do more things together.
- Judith will spend more time with me.
- Cassandra will do better at school.
- I will do more music.

Then there is the big one. The one I have been pushing behind me all these years: Jamie.

Some years ago when I was going through a bad patch, I found a good way to get on top of worry. You have to see worry as fear, and you have to really find out what you are afraid of: stare the beast in the eye. What, you ask yourself, is the worst thing that can happen? What can you do to prevent it happening? This works well with many of the problems I grapple with in NRG – at least it does if the problem can be localised:

"What's the worst that can happen if Andhra Pradesh runs out of water?"

"Some of the citizens of Andhra Pradesh will die."

To be brutally honest I can live with that. Their problems are too far away. The technique doesn't work at all with a problem like Jamie.

"What's the worst that can happen?"

"The situation will continue".

No, even that's not the worst. The worst would be that Jamie dies without making contact with me, or even worse, dies cursing me. Is that what I'm afraid of? Is it possible that he feels the same? These thoughts keep going round and round in my head. I can't leave it alone and keep searching out what he's doing on the Net. I've followed his career - cringed on the few times he's hit the PopNet - even the French versions once. I've felt proud when he is praised for his latest break-through. I even managed to read an article about his and Fay's home life which *really* made me cringe.

Now though there is something odd happening. For the last two years there has been hardly anything about him in the media. I subscribe to a couple of forums that discuss the doings of people like Jamie and there have been curious hints that he has got involved with some religious group. Jamie? Religion? Doesn't sound like my little brother. It sounded more like that group that Mia used to belong to – "The Sisters of Gaia". There was a trivialised media story about Jamie and a group called "Fellowship of the Trees". Jamie was insisting that he did not 'belong' to the group and that in any case the Gaia hypothesis was based on good science. The Fellowship were simply trying to promote the concept of the self-regulating biosphere. He came over as a bit arrogant, but not the raving hippie they were trying to suggest.

It always upsets me to see him on the Net, but I can't stop myself looking for stories about him.

The Hub

The years rolled on and nothing much changed. It was a comfortable life. They were never too hot or too cold, never hungry or thirsty, seldom without sexual pleasure, and never short of friends. If they ever wondered what life was like out there in the world they watched, it was always with the knowledge of all the dangers which confronted the millions out there - always struggling to eat, to find shelter, to avoid pain, to repel those who would take away the little that they had, and of course to find love.

Sister Acer was staring at the Globe, standing on the walkway around it as it slowly moved round in front of her, a huge holographic image - the display area for the Warden. She could see the clouds drifting slowly across as day followed night. Week by week it would shift slightly on its axis as the seasons turned and the plants, the trees, and the vegetation changed colour.

She narrowed her gaze, focussing tightly on a small area of Europe where she could see rain showers brushing across the green fields and forests, and sunshine following to light up the flowers and trees. She narrowed her focus still further and saw a group of people running from the rain and laughing.

"They are getting wet" she thought "why are they laughing?" She could, if she took her vacation in the

Mountain, experience rain, but it was cold and nasty – not something to laugh at. Not many tried it. There must be something wrong with the programme. She would ask Simon about it; he was the one who knew all about the Mountain. There must be something about "real" rain in the outside world which made people enjoy it, laugh about it.

Acer was not really supposed to be watching the Globe, but she was an elder, one of the Fellowship of the Trees, so she was hardly going to be in correction because she spent the odd half hour away from her primary duties. She could always log it as 'research'.

She had no Mate at present. The last one had died some years ago. Most nights she preferred to sleep alone. At first, after Eled died, she had got quite excited about the new partners she could call up, but none of them quite filled the need in her for . . . well, for what? She was no longer sure what it was she was looking for. Love perhaps? Surely not. Love was dangerous; it made people miserable – they lost their command, their control on life. No, she was beginning to think, to fear even, that the state of mind she wanted to attain was something which could seriously damage her work, her leisure, even threaten her life. She felt its presence hovering just outside her vision. It was there whenever she thought about a different kind of life, whenever she spent too long on the Globe, or got too close to one of her partners.

"I want danger." There, she had admitted it. "I want to live like the Brothers out there, even if it causes me pain. Pain, yes, pain, pain, pain - I WANT TO HURT!"

CHAPTER 4 2039 -44

The Hub

They were both shocked, Tilia and Calan.

"I'm so glad it was me who found her: poor Acer, scarred and bleeding. Whatever would have happened to her if one of the Minders had found her?"

"Surely not much different" said Calan. "She would perhaps have been put on a more direct route to Correction. You made her feel better about it I suppose"

"I hope so, but I still don't understand why she did these things to herself. Why would anyone want to cause themselves so much pain?"

"I have heard of this on the outside. I think it is to do with body chemistry. Physical pain can block certain chemical pathways which cause mental suffering."

"Well . . . all I can say is thank the Fellowship we have the Minders. It must be dreadful to feel like that. I wonder how long Acer will be in Correction. I'll have to take on her portfolio while she's away, and there is a major problem brewing."

"What, the waste plants?"

"How do you know about that? Oh never mind. No it's the new tunnels. It's getting more and more difficult to find places for the stone and rubble. Our outside contractors are demanding more money."

the Warden had decided that they needed more space so that they could accommodate the extra workers which would be needed for the big event. Most of them would be here, at the Hub, but the Spokes in the other countries also needed help. Only the Fellowship knew the nature of the event they were preparing for, but all the staff knew it was something important. Until now they had always managed to find ways not only to move their waste products outside, but to incorporate them into the waste management of the host country. Now they would have to take some risks and offer more protection to the contractors.

Vandervelde - Nemesis

I'm worried about Amy. Since Hector died she's been very withdrawn. It feels as if somehow she blames me, but I grew to be very fond of him and was genuinely sorry to lose him. She was very unemotional at the funeral:

"Van, I need to look after Lucy. You'll have to manage Mummy. She seems to think you are some sort of nephew."

"Of course. You do what you have to do, but I would like to speak to Lucy later."

I found Margaret Grant sitting staring into space. She looked frail but quite healthy. What a horrible irony it is that Hector, who had a very active mind right until the end, should be the one to die first.

"Hello Margaret, would you like to come with me?"

"Thank you young man. You can take me to Marks and Sparks. I do so need a new jumper"

"Well perhaps later. We need to go to the church first."

"Yes, we will go and see that nice young vicar". The last time the church had a vicar, at least according to Amy, was nearly 20 years ago. For a long time now it has been a community centre. Hector had done some volunteering there and Amy had arranged a simple funeral "service" for him at which she would officiate. She had already licensed a burial plot in the garden of his old cottage.

Margaret seemed to retreat into whatever was going on inside her head. She sat upright and unemotional throughout the ceremony which, to Amy's great credit even I found very moving. As we were walking out she suddenly became very distressed. Her body seemed to lose all its strength and I had to support her and try to get her away to somewhere quieter where her shouts of anger and grief would be less upsetting to the other guests.

It was a gruelling day, but lightened by the memory of the short speech that Lucy gave. I met her for the first time at the church – a rather stern looking lady, thin, with smart grey hair and a gaunt looking face.

"For a shamefully long period of my life I thought of my father Hector as a stubborn high minded arrogant man. On almost all counts I was wrong, and it is a cause of desperate sadness to me that we lost so much time, time we could have spent together. I have absolutely no wish to go into the complicated causes of our original quarrel – from this distance it seems petty beyond belief. Our lives diverged – mine into my work as a doctor, his into his holy RAF. How I hated all that services stuff. I....sorry, sorry I didn't mean to get into all that again."

There was a pause while she dabbed her eyes.

"Look, I can't talk about all that. All I want to say really is that one of the most important and moving days of my life was the day he and I came together again. It was Dad who broke the vicious circle, and I can guess how hard it was for him to say sorry to the daughter who had treated him so badly. Thanks to that day we have both been able to enjoy a few years of love and free exchange of ideas. Thank goodness he went to his grave knowing we had forgiven each other. I shall miss him dreadfully."

I found later that Amy had written an account of Hector's last days. This is it:

"I shall never forget this date: 12 January 2043. I had a call from Daddy to say he was not feeling too good. He didn't sound too bad on the phone, but he does tend to play thing down a bit so I was concerned. He was 88 after all.

When I got there I could see he was very sick.

"Oh don't fuss Amy, I'm sure once I can get some antibiotics I'll be OK."

"But Daddy, there is no way someone your age would be given antibiotics – they're like gold dust these days. Have you looked at your health checker."

"What? Oh that gadget thing. I keep forgetting to wear it. It's in the drawer over there." It wasn't even switched on.

"Oh my God look – it's flashing red. Oh Daddy I can't bear it; you'll have to go into isolation, and now I've been in contact with you I will too"

"What are you talking ..." He went into a violent coughing fit. "..talking about Amy. It's just some bug I've picked up."

"Oh shut up! Oh hell why does it have to be like this? Look, stay there. Don't move. I'm going outside to call the... Oh NO! they're here already."

There was a flashing red light outside and a heavy knock on the door. Standing there was a figure from a nightmare – a man in full isolation rig with a menacing looking face-mask.

"This way, please Madam."

"Wait, it's my father, he's..."

"Ok, my colleague will bring him. Don't worry you will both

be very well looked after, but you must come right now."

A few minutes later we were in the Medicar and men were sealing up the house with warning signs. It took half an hour to get to the isolation centre – a place hidden in a fold of the downs, high up and with nothing but grass and sheep round it. Of course the standard of care was excellent, but nobody made any pretence that Daddy would get better. This was where he would die. It was so hard for me to try to show a cheerful face. In the end, as he got weaker, he accepted his fate calmly and spent his last few days trying to make me feel better about it.

I didn't much care what happened to me then. If I got sick I would probably recover, but it could take weeks stuck in here with just my memories. After doing not much more than cry for 3 or 4 days I realised that I was hungry. There had been a string of messages from Van which I had hardly bothered to reply to, but now I sent him a proper loving reply. A week later I was released, just in time for the funeral. It turned out that the virus which had killed my father was one which was not considered dangerous to healthy adults – only to the young and very old."

Letter from Anders Fuller

International Letter: Secure Service

Sender Anders Fuller

US Federal Headquarters

1 May 2038

Dear Van,

Hell I can't get used to this formal stuff, but I guess it feels about right for what I want to say to you. I have to tell you this great country is falling apart. All my work here has been for nothing.

Do you remember the group I told you about: "Christ's Kingdom of America"? It seems they had gotten a lot more powerful than I thought and have groups not just in Alabama but right across the south. We had to set up a conference with their leaders to discuss their demands. It was a farce; a shouting match. Now they've made a "unilateral declaration of independence". Can you believe it, a bunch of crazy preachers and shock jocks setting up a so-called "Holy Nation"?

As if that wasn't enough we've just heard that the new governor of Texas, Juan Rodrigues Cordoban, has declared April 25th to be "El dia Hispanica". Evidently the number of Spanish speakers in Texas officially passed the English speakers on that day. He's planning on re-naming the State and declaring Spanish the first language.

I'm seriously thinking about getting out of Washington and heading north. It seems like the more federal troops we have protecting us the less safe we feel. I feel I want to be where our history is, the original America of the Declaration of Independence.

As you know, Judy has taken Jonas and Michael up to Maine where her parents are. I still have a few cousins up there so I'm more and more tempted to ditch my job here and find somewhere nearer to them. I used to hate the winters up there but Vermont has just had its first winter with no snow, and Washington had no rain at all this year.

Wish me luck buddy.

Yours truly

Anders

Vandervelde - The Trees

The priority channel on my comms buzzed: it was Mollie, and if she wanted to see me it was important. We were in The Temple in Brigstowe.

"Van – you need to see this."

"OK, just let me clear these docs." I moved my hands over the screen, saving, linking, prioritising, docking.

"It's from Tupac" He was in charge of one of our regional centres for protein production. Some months ago one of the protein plants in central Asia had been destroyed by a totally unknown and very virulent virus. It had been sealed off and everything possible was being done to identify the virus, known as TFP7. We had experienced problems like this before and were not unduly concerned.

"It just says 100 hectares of forest in Pakistan infected with previously unknown virus. Initial analysis suggests identical to TFP7"

I felt a crawling sensation up the back of my neck. Neither of us said anything. If confirmed this could be the news we had all been dreading for decades: a pathogen which could travel hundreds of miles and leap species.

"Forest? Are you sure?"

"Tupac has never been known to deliver inaccurate data." Her face was white, making her freckles show up like spots. The room was silent. I sat down and tried to collect my thoughts. TFP7 as far as we could tell, attacks the growth mechanism of the fungi we use to produce edible protein. If it was now attacking trees there were a number of possible explanations, all equally improbable.

- Some had escaped from the protein plant and spread by the wind to land in Pakistan where it was attacking fungi living in the trees.

- The organism which had mutated into TFP7 also existed in other parts of the world and had made an exactly parallel mutation
- Someone had deliberately spread the virus

It may seem odd but there were a few mad doomsday cults around who would do almost anything to reduce the human population, even if it meant suicide.

"Van – we've got to do it" Neither of us moved. I stood up.

"Yes, you're right, give the order."

Quietly, without fuss, a series of events was put in motion.

Every country in the world has a biohazard emergency plan, and the government in Pakistan was one of our closest collaborators. A 100km zone was established round the contaminated area. Fortunately the forest was, in Pakistani terms, lightly populated. The army, in isolation suits, moved in, collected what they hoped was every one of the few thousand people living there, and put the villagers and themselves through the zero plus decontamination plan, emerging as naked and hairless as the day they were born.

Then the big fire drones moved in and the area was totally destroyed by fire.

Letter from Yi Hua Chang

International Letter Secure Service

Sender Li Hua Chang

Hangzhou China

Dear Van,

I have delayed writing to you until I had checked all our figures again and asked our scientists to look again at the genetic material. I am now in no doubt that what I have to tell you is accurate.

You may remember we had an outbreak of a previously unknown infection in Gansu province last year. The symptoms were similar to previously identified plague-type infections: a sudden onset of headache, nausea, dizziness followed by rapid deterioration of all bodily functions. Of the 38 people infected only two have survived. Both are severely disabled.

By great good fortune the area affected was remote and we managed to isolate it. Since then we have been running exhaustive tests on the pathogen involved. It appears to be a symbiosis of bacterial and viral cells. The vector in this case was an insect – a fly which is common all over China but which has not caused anything similar anywhere else.

We took samples of the pathogen from both the victims and the vectors, and began a long series of experiments with them. The details are in the attached annex 1, but I can summarise the results quite quickly:

I believe what we are dealing with is the ultimate "super-bug" as you would call it. It is capable of very rapid adaptation to both vector and host. It can lay dormant for long periods and can then reproduce with startling speed. We can damage the bacterial component with antibiotics but the viral component is capable of . . . here I am searching for a word . . . let me say 'seducing' other bacteria to work for it.

Why, you may ask, if this agent is so deadly have we not seen a massive epidemic? I believe the answer is both slightly re-assuring and also very sinister. We believe that this agent is already widespread and that it will strike in many different places with devastating results. The only re-assurance is that the infective period is very short. If an attack can be isolated the agent will change and go into dormancy again.

The two survivors can also offer us some consolation. The tests on them are far from complete, but I have sent the results and our conclusions (annex 2) to you via the double S channel.

These are hard times my friend and sometimes I wish we were not as we are.

Yours sincerely

Li

Vandervelde - Waiting

We are waiting. No further outbreaks of either the Pakistan or Chinese infections have been confirmed, but I am consumed by fear and sorrow. So few of us really know how stretched our systems are. This is our great success but also our greatest failure.

I can't stop thinking about these flashes I've been getting. I'm convinced, though I don't know why, that they are linked in some way to Twm's mysterious visitor. I feel my mind is being manipulated, and I'm almost sure that is what happened to Twm. I can re-run these episodes clearly and each time I feel a sense of being connected to something much bigger than me; bigger than all of us.

I have them clearly tagged. The first was during one of our Council meetings. I had a sudden feeling of being watched. Then again when I entered Condor for the first time. The next was different; it was when Twm was telling me about his transport ideas and I had a brief vision of how it might look. I think there was a gap then. The next tag I recorded was years later when Twm came to Downend. Again the sensation was of being overheard.

If I am to be facing a crisis, and I'm almost sure this is what is coming, then I need to be at my mental best. I must clear my mind of these fruitless speculations and be ready. I must walk, high on the hill, put my boots on and begin to trudge. It's cool and misty but the sun is just breaking through and I can see all over the valley. On the other side is a huge expanse of ancient chalk grassland dotted with an astonishing variety of wild flowers. There are no fences in sight but over to my left is a small herd of longhorn cattle, kept semi-wild, mainly to preserve the downland. It's heartbreakingly beautiful and a great testament to the work of the conservation societies. This walk, even in bad weather, has seldom failed to raise my spirits, but this morning I am close to tears. The sorrow is not for the landscape. Nature, when the human footprint is light, will always be beautiful. What distresses me most when I have a chance to think about it is that we humans might be about to lose our sense of purpose, our culture. This amazing edifice, this system of interlocking societies, this striving for knowledge and beauty – has it all been for nothing? Is it possible that it will all be swept away?

I still have hope, but I really don't see what more we can do. There is no more slack in the system. Mollie and a few of the others are here with us, and when I got back from my walk she was waiting for me – pale, drawn: I feel guilty – it is my fault that her life has got so tough.

"Look at this Van – 10 new de-salination plants have come online in the last month and the power demands are going haywire. "

"Let me see. Hm . . . does this mean that we have virtually no spare capacity? Surely the power plants can't all be running at 90 percent?"

"They are – pretty impressive in one way, but it means we'll have to put some drastic restrictions in place right now." Her comms buzzed and she hurried out without a word.

I turned back to my screen to try to work out why all last week's production at one of our biggest protein plants has been recalled. The cultured cheese has been affecting people's speech. It's certainly not a virus thank goodness, and doesn't seem to be bacterial. We are afraid it might be similar to the prion which caused mad cow disease.

Later the same day she took me aside again:

"Van I've had the most strange message. It's supposed to be from my brother but there's no address and no signature. It's hand written on paper."

Mollie you are in danger. The Warden is watching you. Vandervelde is one of them. Don't trust him. He will

> *say he knows nothing but they have a plan. The Fellowship of the Trees know about it. Millions of us will die.*

I stared at it, scarcely seeing the laborious hand-writing. I had a wave of nausea and sat down quickly.

"Van. Are you OK?"

I put up my hands. "It's such a shock. You don't believe this do you?"

"No, of course not – I wouldn't have shown it to you if I did."

"Oh Mollie, what is happening to us." We were both tearful and moved to hug each other. She kissed me. For a moment we clung together, despair and arousal mixed, and I knew that if I did not pull away now I would not be able to resist. I didn't dare even to begin to think about the implications of it.

"Sorry . . . that shouldn't have happened." We both turned away and sat silently.

"We need to concentrate. Are you sure this is Jamie's writing?"

"Well it certainly looks like it, but I don't know anything about handwriting."

"Do you have a sample which you know is his?"

"I doubt it. I told you we haven't communicated at all for years."

We were too exhausted to think any more. I was in despair. What I hadn't admitted to Mollie was that I had been having a terrible dream, a dream of people dying, hundreds, thousands of them. I dreaded going to sleep and lay awake staring at the ceiling in Downend, with Amy sleeping quietly beside me. If I did manage a few hours it would only be to wake with the dreadful knowledge that all the people dying knew I had done it. It was all my fault. I could see and hear their screams and insults, and it took minutes for the dreadful visions to fade – fade into another day of worry and overwork. Why has it come to this?

The Hub

Nobody could remember a time when there had been so much activity. There was an intense air of controlled excitement with so many new staff, and work stations in every available bit of space – even in the corridors. It was quiet; people walked purposefully and spoke in low voices.

Acer, fully recovered from her lapse, was so busy coping with the demands of all these people she had no time to think about her feelings. Emotion was a luxury they could not afford. The power of the Hub was growing. They all sensed it.

With Adjustment Day now so close, Tilia had been assigned to the most important player out there - NRG, and in particular their man Vandervelde. She had been plotting his moves on the Globe, and had gained valuable information from Brother Ulm who had also been watching him.

She settled at her work table and joined the Warden. First she checked the incoming data stream for Britannica. She chose "thought profiles" and saw in diagram form a hundred or so of the issues that were motivating the peoples of Britannica at that moment. Van himself was filled with negative thought streams. She wondered if they had made a bad play. They needed him to be in good mind.

After some time spent studying the flow of information, she made her selection and sent it to be played. If her selection was sapient enough it would go through and she would be able to watch the scenario being played out in the data web that was her region. If there were flaws in her thinking the Warden would reject it and she would have to start again.

There were no flaws. It was time.

Brother Ulm

It is time. My work in Britannica is coming to an end. For so long I have lived with these people, watching, always watching. Only to Sir James and Mr Pritchard have I spoken directly. The others I have helped without their knowledge, though Vandervelde, being a Sapient himself, has several times felt the Fellowship energy. He suspects, but perhaps that was inevitable. Sir James has been very useful but even he knows little. Now it will begin and even the most far-seeing Sapient cannot tell how it will end. We always knew that we were not all immune. Most of the Fellowship are safe, but the resistance we have carried for centuries is imperfect, so it is possible that some of us may die. That is of no importance and will not affect the mission.

******

This I did not expect. It is me. I am called to sacrifice. I can feel it starting. I am to leave this human life and become part of the great Mother, the planet Earth. I am prepared. It will not be painful, but when the time comes I know that all the impulses that give me thoughts, emotions, memories and sensations, all will be switched off and then I will cease to exist. What remains will be a collection of molecules, most of which will become food for a host of other living things. I will become a tiny part of Gaia, the greatest of all known living things, and if our work succeeds we will have played our part in preventing the plague of human life from fatally contaminating her.

We in the Fellowship of the Trees are servants of Gaia, the great Mother whose heartbeats are the rhythms of the seasons, the ebb and flow of life, the rise and fall of populations, the pulse of generation succeeding generation. Her own life is measured in a much slower rhythm – that of entropy, the slow decay of energy which will see our sun die and other suns be born. What right do we naked apes have to cut short that life? I am glad to my heart that I go to my place in the cycle of life in the knowledge that we have given Her a space to breathe again. It is a small space but those who come after me will continue the work.

Now the effects are beginning. I feel sick. Soon the pain will begin, but I have my syringe. *Oh dear Mother it is fast. Why could you not spare me*?

The story continues in Book 2

"The Phoenix Nation"

Glossary

Comms - universal communications device. Almost everyone carries a device like a 2015 smart phone which is their only means of communicating with others - by video, voice or text.

Transnet - the track element of the 2036 transport system, including the stations and control systems.

Ek (e-car), the mobile part of the Transnet system. These are various kinds of vehicle module which can link to the Transnet.

The Net – combined power and information grid

Netmeet – Online meeting

Place names:

Most of the action in the book takes place in a fictionalised version of Britain. To keep a fictional distance from the real places in Britain, all the English language place names have been replaced with Welsh, Anglo-Saxon, Latin or on occasion made-up versions of the name.

Anglesland – England

Blackhall - Whitehall

Brigstowe - Bristol

Caerdydd - Cardiff

Caledonia – Scotland

Gravesham - Gravesham

Hibernia - Ireland

Lyndain – London

Swinsdun - Swindon

Marlsburg – Malborough

Suthrig - Sussex

Vannin – Isle of Man

Wiltunshire - Wiltshire

Ystwyth - Aberystwyth

Welsh (Cymraeg) words

Croeso - Welcome

Duw - God

Yn wir - indeed, in truth

Meibion - boys

Cyngor - council

Shwd mae/shw mae - how are you?

Pennaeth - colonel (approx)

Dwli - mad, dull, stupid

Iechyd da - good health

Cornish Words

Kernowek – Cornish person

"As long as they were sane and healthy they got the white suits and set off in the white vans."

CONTENTS

Prologue 2120

I am old. Not just old but so old that the memories stacked up in my head - all waiting there, each with its tag - stretch back so far I can't even remember which century they reside in. Here in this green damp land on the edge of Europe we have enough for our small community in a small nation. Enough but no more, and for what we have we work hard, even us old ones.

It's a hundred years since I began collecting all these documents - some on paper, some audio and some on embedded archives; even a printed book. Sometimes, looking round my simple room here, some detail like the reused oak timbers in the roof, or a smell - petrol for example: there's a nostalgic one - any of these can call up a memory. Walking down the long corridor to the refectory brings back memories of roads, transnets, sea routes, even that great silent luminous space outside the airship.

What abundance we had then - all those things, that stuff as we used to call it, but even more astonishing looking back were the hidden services, all those bits of electronic trickery which made our lives so easy.

What a price we paid. Somehow we fought back from the chaos of 44, and here we built a new nation. It still survives in some ways, like pools left as the tide ebbs away. And of course all over the world there were hundreds of Small Nations. How else could the Warden have been able to regulate human life? I could have been part of all that - they were my fellow Elders after all. Not for me. I wanted nothing to do with it.

Here in the real world, the world of trees and grass and

stone, water and sky, and all the impossibly various living things, here we have at last learnt our place. We are a species like all the others, and to continue we have had to learn how to live with all the others. We've gained some sapience.

CHAPTER 1 2044 – 48

Vandervelde: Flight

22 July 2045.

I am alone; only my communicator and the wind. It's cool up here and my tent is tiny. It is part of one of the standard emergency kits we put together for key NRG staff last year. Everything is ultra-lightweight – rucksack, low-vis insulated tent, sleeping bag, thermal shield, low-vis all weather suit, ready-heat meals, water-pur, stun-spray, all-tool kit - all the boys toys plus a few NRG specials. It's early – four am and the sun is rising over the rough downland behind me. I've heated some coffee and eaten a high nutrition bar. I am ready to face the day. I am still alive.

We were at Downend when Amy got sick. It was over very quickly. Men in isolation suits took her body up to the beacon and burnt it. It was lucky for Hector, her father, that he did not live to see it. I did not go but I could see the smoke from the house. With it went the happiest part of my life. I'm so glad now that I never told her about my fertility problem. She always had the hope that the next time it would all be fine. I made sure there would not be a next time. I could not put her though all that heartbreak again.

Happiness is a distant dream. It is enough that I am alive, healthy and fit. I will have to struggle on, and there is a certain comfort to be had from the knowledge that my terrible dreams and visions have not been madness. I am an Elder. I see things differently. For some time now – a year or more – I have known in my heart that there was some kind of canker in our shiny new world. We were so close to success. By we, I mean NRG, the Northern Resource Group, the global organisation of which I was Chair. NRG is or was (Does it still exist?) a Quasi Autonomous Non-Governmental Organisation – a quango if ever there was one. It still amazes me when I think what we managed to achieve in so short a time. With the secret permission of our sponsoring governments, we by-passed the whole pseudo-democratic apparatus which had ensured the triumph of short-term 'business as usual' and which very nearly cost us the planet. Our brief was nothing less than to bring down carbon dioxide emissions to near zero in 10 years. By using draconian Carbon Trading rules we almost succeeded – we delivered a new world of ultra-low carbon energy, but at the height of our success something happened; some switch was tripped and the whole edifice crashed. Countless millions are dead, and I felt completely sure that if I did not somehow leave my home - the one Amy and I had so lovingly created here in Britannica, then I would be yet another nameless victim of the chaos.

A few days before I'd had a visit from two men whose IDs passed my entry security – evidently they were from the regional authority. They seemed quite friendly at first.

"Mr Vandervelde, we are so sorry to hear about your loss. I know how you must be feeling. We have both suffered similar losses. My name is James Smith and this is Mr West."

"Good to meet you. What can I do for you?"

"We represent a group affiliated to the Authority called "New Anglia". We are working towards the re-birth of our nation, the restoration of law and order. I understand that you are a senior figure in the NRG organisation, but we are not here to speak with you in that capacity, but rather to request your personal co-operation in a way that can benefit us both."

"I'm listening". I kept a friendly expression, but was beginning to feel uneasy. There was something altogether too tidy about their polished sentences, their neat hair, smart suits and polished shoes. The other one, Mr.West spoke:

"I'm sure you are aware that our security forces are in a shameful state of disarray. We have evidence that many of the remaining police officers are living on black market goods. We suspect that a proportion of them and even of the military are actually gang members. We saw the need for something better, so for the last month have been contacting men we knew we could trust to join us in setting up a third force, a citizens' task force, well trained and ready to seize the moment when the government loses control of its own forces."

"Ah, a militia?"

"If you like, though we prefer Task Force. We have not come here to persuade you to join us Mr. Vandervelde, we know you have far more important affairs to attend to. Our purpose is to ask you if we may use your house and grounds as a training centre for our new force. Your personal living and working space would of course be protected and we could offer you a generous rental payment."

"Well, that's a bit of a shock. I need some time to think this through."

"Time, sir, is what we do not have. I'm afraid I have to ask you to make a rapid decision. Are you ready to help restore order or not?"

"And if I refuse?"

"That would be unfortunate. The security committee on the Authority has given us the right in certain circumstances to issue requisition orders."

"So either I work with you and get paid or you kick me out." I smiled "Bit of a no-brainer isn't it? Of course I will help you."

It was smiles all round as they left in their immaculate e-car, promising to be in touch very soon.

How long had I got? What was left of my team were still in Brigstowe, but I had a message two days ago saying they were really frightened. There were men with guns everywhere. Then I had a coded message yesterday from one of my contacts in the Emergency Government, reminding me that my space at Copperfield was still available and that I and some of my team could work there until life above ground was safer. I checked its position on one of my archive maps and saw that it was not far from here. Before, I could have got there in half an hour, but that was no longer possible. I had seen a group of men crossing the down barely half a mile from the house. They had crossbows. I was alone; it was time to go. I had heard of attacks on the roads and as far as I knew, the transnet was down, so I decided to go on foot. I unlocked the basement and spent an hour selecting kit. Of what was happening in Brigstowe I had no idea so I just sent a brief coded message to say where I was going and for them to join me. They had the access codes. All I would see on the surface would be a small compound surrounded by two layers of security fencing. There is a group of concrete buildings and a comms mast, "Look for the biohazard warning" the message had said.

24 July 2045

As I looked back at the house I wondered if I would ever see it again. I'd been happy there, but staying alive was my highest ambition now. It was slow going avoiding the few small towns and all the villages – those prosperous little places in leafy valleys by meandering streams. The farms round here used to be big, high tech units producing mostly grain and pulses. All the farm infrastructure had collapsed and the fields and tracks were overgrown. One of my tools was a long knife, partly serrated, and I used this and a wire cutter to cut through obstructions. I stayed the night in a patch of woodland where I was reasonably comfortable and slept fitfully for a few hours.

I made good time the next day following an ancient track called 'Wansdyke'. This part of Britannica is full of reminders of the distant past – a huge stone circle with a village inside it, a great mound with no known purpose, burial mounds –

barrows – some round and some long, and much later, but still nearly 2000 years ago, this great long earthwork. There are also traces of a more recent past – the remains of racehorse gallops from the days when we could afford to keep horses just for the pleasure of seeing them run.

As the sun got stronger I began to see people - people with guns. Most of them were soldiers or police, but I had no more idea than anyone else about the security forces. Were they still acting for the government? Did we still have a government? I knew what the emergency plans were – we had been one of the main planners after all, but nobody knew how to deal with the constant loss of manpower. Desperate people do desperate things and nobody felt safe.

One thing I did know, unless you had the right arm band you would be arrested on sight and sent to an isolation unit. My arm band was counterfeit, so I just could not let that happen; what I had in my head and on the storage device under my skin was just too important.

I could see on my maps that after the end of the Wansdyke the high ground runs out and from there on it was a network of villages. I would have to find cover and navigate the next section after dark. A mile ahead was a small copse and after that just roads and fields. It would have to do, but the track was high and exposed. If there are any patrols, or worse, any groups of foragers, I would be in full view.

******

I was within sight of the copse when I heard voices. Any attempt to hide would look suspicious. I walked on.

"Stop"

There were three of them in something approximating to police uniforms – clearly "borrowed" and ill fitting. Two had old guns, one had a modern gas weapon.

"Ah, good to see you officers. I think I may be a bit lost. Can I get to Marlsburg this way?"

They all laughed – did I sense a touch of drunkenness?

"You're way out mate. Can I see your ID please?"

"Of course, but I'm sure you won't mind showing me your ID first. There are a lot of strange people around these days."

"Looks like we've got a smart-arse here. Get hold of him Frank" They were moving for their weapons. Frank was big; he lunged forward, but as I put my hand to my face I touched the spray switch, closed my eyes and held my nose. A stream of particles shot out from my elbow. Frank and one of the others went down. Before the third could draw his gun I rushed him and squirted again.

They would be out for four hours, but I could not stay here. Looking hastily around to make sure I was not seen, I quickly took off my jacket and trousers and put on one of the uniforms. One of the guns would look right with it, so within minutes I was off again: a policeman on a mission. It would have to do. All afternoon I searched out the smaller roads. Whenever I saw people I looked confident and aggressive. Nobody challenged me, but as the four hours ran out I was still a long way from Copperfield.

Later I reached a wooded area, quite high up. It was part of an ancient estate with parkland and a grand house. I found a small hollow amongst some dense rhododendrons and there I crouched listening and watching. After a few hours I heated up a meal, but as the light faded it started raining so I decided to open up the tent.

It was a good choice of camp site and I slept quite well until my comms unit vibrated on my wrist and told me that, dull and grey though it was, dawn was here.

The last leg through the empty roads and fields was uneventful and I arrived at the site by 9.00 unchallenged. At the gate I keyed in the codes and waited. Two men in soldiers uniform arrived as the gate slid open.

“Welcome Mr Vandervelde. We are very pleased to see you.” Within a few minutes I was underground and would not see real daylight for the next year.

The Hub

Sister Tilia knew she was different from other people. She remembered stuff from way back. All she had to do was run through the tags in her memory and she could retrieve whole scenes, the sights, the sounds and even the smell of them, though none of her childhood. The earliest was a scene where all the six Elders in The Fellowship of the Trees had joined hands and connected to that very early version of the machine - the point where it began to gain power; power which would eventually become the Warden.

She and Sister Acer had taken a pledge to leave the world and take on the huge responsibility of the machine. Of the others, Brothers Fagus, Fraxinus and Ulm all had names and status within the worlds of business and government. Brother Quercus had a special mission and he did not know the others.

She remembered Brother Ulm with sorrow. He was the only one of their Fellowship who did not survive 'Adjustment Day' - the time in 44 when they had carefully and quietly influenced the series of events which had so dramatically changed the world. So subtle had been their influence that even Quercus, the one who was working alone, did not recognise it.

Their mission had been a terrible one; terrible but necessary. All their work was in service to Gaia. It was She, the Mother of all life, the living planet, who was in danger, and She had to be protected whatever the consequences. Vandervelde and his colleagues had done great things, but even their best efforts could not stop the growth of the human population. By 43 it was clear that the rapid progress towards true sustainability which Vandervelde had masterminded had come too late.

Now her job was to observe and report to the Warden on whatever new societies could be created from the ruins. As before, Vandervelde was among the pioneers and whenever she worked at the great Globe, she always made a point of checking the thought-streams from wherever he was working. By focussing she could see the movements of animals and people, and more importantly, she could track the thought-streams coming from whichever region she focussed on.

Vandervelde seemed to have disappeared, though she knew his approximate location. He was not in danger so she zoomed out and noticed how much more green the world looked now. Gaia could breathe again, but was She truly out of danger?

Judith

Caerdydd

I don't know how long I can keep going here. All I do is work, but no matter how hard we work there is always too much to do. I get back to this miserable house late and then can't sleep with all the worry.

Now that we have some online comms I've decided to try writing a Netlog to see if that helps. I'll backtrack a bit to set the scene.

Before 44 I was a recycling officer in the Council, and I had just been elected as the Assembly Member for Caerdydd East. We – the Plaid Las (Green Party)– had done well and were the controlling group in the Assembly. We even felt a bit smug when our predictions were shown to be all too accurate. We may have been right, but that didn't give us any immunity. When the crash came my lovely Rhys was one of the first. Heaven knows we had our differences, but how I miss him now. At least I managed to give him a proper burial. The house is just a shell; a place I eat and sleep and try not to remember.

In theory the Assembly is still in existence. A few of us have got together in the Senedd, but there's no staff and no money so we decided to try to work with those local authorities which were active – in my case Caerdydd. Paid or not if you were healthy you did what had to be done. Last year I was transferred to the Crisis Team with the promise of a wage of sorts. The "recycling" turned out to be either a cover or somebody's idea of a joke. I soon found myself running the "Waste Disposal Units". How they love their euphemisms these officials. I suppose I am one of them now.

Every day there were more calls and I spent more and more time interviewing "disposal officers". As long as they were sane and healthy they got the white suits and set off in the white vans. We had the diggers make long trenches well away from habitation and there we laid them, each with an everlasting plastic label. The trenches were filled in and a single marker listed all the names. It was the best we could do.

That was in 44/45. It wasn't much better in 46, but it's a lot slower now. Now there's a new nasty: the gangs. In just 18 months the number of police in the city was halved. As far as we can tell that's a lot worse than the general population – perhaps they had more contact. At first it was small groups armed with police rifles organising raiding parties. Now they have a leader. Nobody knows who he is but he calls himself "Raven". His followers have T shirts with a raven on them and call themselves "scavengers". They claim they are "cleansing" the city. The police are useless. They've started asking for tips now, and I'm sure some of them are cwtching up with the Ravens. How else did the Ravens get their weapons?

Then there are the militias – armed groups who claim to be protecting the people from the gangs. There's one called 'New Cymru' but they seem just as bad as the Ravens to me.

I've not heard anything from Mollie and Eldred or from Van and Amy. I daresay Van will have survived, but I am braced for bad news. I wish I knew how to contact them. Those of us who are involved in trying to run this city have set up a secure comms unit outside, and we have a couple of staff scouring comms networks for any messages. Mollie and I set up a code signal just before the crisis, so I've asked them to broadcast it every few hours.

******

Big day today – the code has been activated! That must mean that Mollie is still alive. The comms man explained that with so little power the net is in bits. What the techies are trying to do evidently is to get power to individual masts sending out a contact signal using radio bandwidth. All he could tell me was that the code had been recognized. The location was somewhere near Cheaping in Wiltunshire.

For two pins I'd grab a white van and go there now, but that would be stupid. I've no protection and no idea what the roads are like. I asked our man if he could use the code to send a message and he said he would try. "Keep it short" he says. This is what I gave him:

"Mollie – Send code back if you are alive. Judith."

******

She's alive, oh glory be! There was even a message:

"Will send messenger".

I'm so excited! Dear Mollie, how I've missed our girlie chats over a bottle of wine. A messenger?? Sounds like the middle ages. How will he or she get here I wonder.

******

I had the fright of my life this morning when three motorbikes stopped outside the house and men with the Raven logo got off and started looking in at the windows.

I've made myself a secure area in the front room where the windows are covered with a metal grid. I could hear a broad valleys accent saying:

"She's not yer I dunt think"

"Tell her it's a message from – what's the name? Oh right –MOLLIE"

"If you're there misses just shout out and we'll put this package by the door."

"OK I'm here"

"Aright Cariad, hope it's good news."

They actually sounded quite nice but you never know. I waited until I was sure the bikes had gone and opened the door. There was a padded envelope and inside a comdrive.

Message from Mollie Edmundson

Dearest Judith

I can't tell you how pleased I am to hear from you. Things are looking a little better now, but we've had a dreadful time. I find it hard even to write this without getting tearful, but we lost Cassandra. It was absolutely horrible – I've never seen a sickness progress so quickly, and the worst thing was we could only watch through a window! Why couldn't it have been me? Van has lost Amy – she went very quickly as soon as the superbugs started spreading. Eldred got sick, but by some miracle survived. I was doing almost round the clock nursing until a few months ago. Now he can get about a little, but his speech is awful. I'm so worried that he might have permanent brain damage. Magnus is healthy but bored stiff – he's being a real pain at the moment – not enough girls here for his liking. Van says he has a job for him; that should do him some good.

When the crisis happened I was working in Brigstowe at the "Temple". We kept going for a while on NRG stockpiles, but when Eldred got sick I left, but continued to work as best I could from home. Then Cassandra died and I couldn't do anything more than lie in bed trying not to cry all the time. One day I had a visit from some smart looking men claiming they were "New Anglia". They assured me they were not a gang and offered me "free" protection. I couldn't cope with all that as well and went back to bed.

I was just beginning to get around again when I got a message from Van to say that he was in a secure centre and that I should join him. What had I to stay for? Within hours an armoured truck appeared at the front door!

Eldred made all sorts of angry noises, but eventually I persuaded him that we could not stay there and he hobbled into the truck. It was an uncomfortable and noisy journey with just a tiny porthole to look out of. The view was depressing – mile after mile of dereliction and then overgrown fields, and bands of men with weapons wandering around. With the bridges still closed It took nearly all day to get here. We stopped once near Birdslip. It was high open country with nothing but overgrown fields and a few stray animals. Still, the sun was shining and we were able to eat the meal we had brought with us and have a pee. The men stood round us with their guns at the ready, but the most dangerous thing we saw was a bull with a few cows about half a mile away.

What is it about being high up? I heard something I had not heard since I was a child – a lark singing. For the first time since 44 I had a feeling that things might be better in the future. We eventually arrived at a heavily guarded barbed wire enclosure, though we couldn't see much in the way of buildings. We were in for a surprise. Instead of heading for the buildings we were led to a small rough looking hut. Inside was a large lift with two buttons – down and further down!

That was three weeks ago and I haven't seen daylight since. It sounds awful, but it is wonderful to feel safe. We even have a small flat here and there is medical help for Eldred.

Van has a flat here too and a few of the old team so we can really get back to work in earnest.

Please tell me your news as soon as possible. There's masses to do here and they are creating more rooms and services all the time. It would be wonderful if you could join us, but of course that depends on Rhys, and that is the big question mark – the one question we all dread asking. Van particularly asked me to send his best wishes. He says he has a job for you.

All my love

Mollie

Vandervelde: Underground:

It was the Britannic government in Lyndain who had set this place up, and it was some of the senior officials and those members of the cabinet who had survived who welcomed us here, but as time went on it became clear that they had little power. I continued to defer to them but soon realised that we, Northern Resources Group (NRG) Britannica, were pretty much on our own, trying to create order out of chaos. Most of them are still alive, my team. We are all still together but we have lost so much, so many. We are all grieving, for family members, lovers, close friends, for our heroes and our entertainers; so many have died.

That was in 45. Bit by bit the rump of the Britannic government went back to whatever families they had and left us to it. We are still here and still grieving, but we've moved on. I have more time now to write these notes so I'll record what this place looks like before it becomes a memorial to survival.

Evidently this huge underground space was once a "stone mine", but had been long disused when it was designated a regional seat of government back in the days when we thought nuclear war was imminent. I wonder what those who planned it would think of its present use. I can well remember the time of the Cuban Missile Crisis, and the imminent threat of nuclear war. Nobody then could imagine a totally different cause for a catastrophe on the present scale. We actually worked through that one, and in retrospect perhaps it was never a real threat.

Hidden amongst the small buildings on the surface is the technology that gives us daylight, fresh air and power. The daylight is focused by super-reflectors to our growing area – the green oasis in the middle of our warren of offices and flats.

There are three rooms in my apartment, two of them

with walls of the original bedrock – Sulis stone. The artificial walls have "windows" – light panels which are programmed to simulate the appearance of day and night. You can pay extra to have a complete simulation of the light patterns of a particular year right down to the sun, moon and stars. I just have the basic day/night programme. There are two windows, one large one to my right and another in the ceiling, and it feels like a normal fairly cloudy day. I chose to vary the air temperature of each room by up to 10 degrees depending on the time of day and the season.

I should explain about Mollie.

We (NRG) recruited her straight from University. I was still living in Berlin then and it was Rufus, one of our international staff, who spotted her potential, and recruited her to our Brigstowe office. I met her soon after she started work and asked her to join my Britannica team. Her brief was to question everything we did and come up with new ideas. Then I met Amy. She had a factory making airships and I had decided buy one – the "Condor" - to use as a mobile office and living space. Her home was in southern Britannica so we ended up buying a house there - Downend.

Amy.

It's hard to write her name. All that life, Downend, the Condor, it's all gone now, but I must not look back; we have work to do.

So, it was a good day when Mollie and Eldred arrived with their escort. Mollie soon settled in, but Eldred was a real problem. We had properly trained medics but no psychologists and it was his mood which was so worrying. He seemed to be sinking deeper and deeper into depression with each week that went past. His speech was not improving and sometimes he was so violent it felt dangerous being near him. After a few weeks of this Mollie came to see me.

"Van, we've got to put him to work somehow."

"I know, but he can't walk unaided, can't talk. What can he do?"

"Well, he has a fair bit of movement in his right arm and can use his hands, though writing is painfully slow. His sight is good – he reads a lot though tends to forget what he has just read."

We sat there for a while thinking.

"I suppose anything that too obviously looks as if it is for his benefit will be angrily rejected."

"Exactly. It has to come from him."

We thought some more.

"Look, Van I'm being very honest here. Eldred is suspicious of you. He's never liked us working together. If he sees you trying to do something which he thinks he can do better, he might go for it."

A few days later Mollie left a file on the home page of their shared screen. It was called "poss staff rec area" and it contained a series of pictures of bedrock 'walls'. I had taken the pictures and left her a note saying "I would like to think we could do something here but can't think what."

She left a note for Eldred:

"E – do you think we need a rec area? We have the garden and it seems like a waste of resources to me."

Nothing more was said and nothing happened for the next few days. Then one morning Mollie got up to find the whole apartment strewn with bits of paper and stone that he had scavenged from the garden. She made a show of annoyance.

"What the hell's all this? Have you been up all night making this mess?"

He made signs and noises to indicate 'yes' and 'not

mess'.

"OK – just tell me when you've finished."

Then the transformation of our living space began. At Eldred's direction we made new rooms in strange shapes; images began to appear on the bedrock; the garden got a performance space and he even took a hand in the more prosaic building jobs – new laboratories and work rooms. The effect on all of us was quite magical - colour came into our troglodytic lives.

There was a curious incident as a result of all this work. I had a call from the buildings supervisor:

"Van - I think you need to come and have a look at this. We're at sector 11"

"I can spare 15 minutes, will that do?"

"Yes, that's OK. See you shortly."

During tests for a new tunnel, they had broken though into a previously inhabited area. It was a completely circular room with a domed ceiling, no furniture, no doors. It was evenly lit with daylight spectrum light from the central area of the dome.

"How on earth did whoever worked here get into it?"

"Well, there was no trace of a doorway where we broke through, but we did find this -"

He was indicating what looked like a small hole at shoulder height.

"If you cover it with your hand it lights up!" He passed his hand over it and a faint red light showed. I did the same and the light turned yellow.

"I've seen this type of thing before. It looks to me like a palm reader."

"We wondered that, and got some of the lads to try it.

Each time it turned red."

It became quite an attraction - everybody wanted to see if they could change the light to yellow or perhaps green, but every other person in the 'building' turned the light red. Eventually we gave up speculating about it and used it as a store-room.

******

I have not really explained the “White Death” in 44. Put simply it was system failure, but it all happened so quickly. When I think about it I can’t get rid of the feeling there was something that didn’t fit. Most countries had made elaborate plans for failure. Why did so few succeed? I can’t think of anything I would have done differently, but I feel in some way responsible. Was it really inevitable that it would all end like this?

We could get round failure in some of the food factories and we could cope with seasonal droughts and famines by importing from areas of high production, but so many things happened at once. As crops failed across the globe because of climate change, energy needed to transport food was diverted to create food. Demand for petro-chemicals soared as the supply was tailing off. When the big powers realised that they were running short of food they started attacking any region which seemed to have food. The devastating hurricanes which ravaged parts of the tropics were a major cause of death, and where there were floods, the old killer diseases came back in force. The worst of the diseases was still the one identified by our man in China, Li Hua Chang - the one we called SBX1 - but there were plenty of opportunistic epidemics which had a devastating effect on people who were already weakened by lack of food or shelter. As they proliferated, the resources to deal with them were collapsing. Famine, war and pestilence were once again upon us.

The first year was unbelievably horrible. The best estimates were 850 million deaths. In the second year it slowed, partly because demand had collapsed. Reliable figures are simply not available but working backwards we have been able to estimate 500 m deaths in year two and a steadily decreasing level in the subsequent years. We now estimate a total global population of around five billion but it is still falling. In Britannica things were not quite so bad, but we - Britannica that is - still lost a quarter of the population.

The EU crisis meeting in Lyndain in 2030 agreed on the basic plan and each nation agreed to draft an emergency message which would go out over the media if the trigger points were reached. We had in place the usual military situation codes, Yellow, Orange and Red. I see from the records here that Britannica reached Code Red on March 10 2044. This is the text of the message broadcast simultaneously on all the media:

Code Red Broadcast 10 March 2044

Good morning. In place of our usual news service this morning, we are broadcasting simultaneously with all other networks a message from the Prime Minister . . .

At 1:00 am this morning Friday the10th of March 2044, the government decided that the country, indeed the world, faced a situation so serious that special powers were needed to prevent widespread chaos. Accordingly we have activated Code Red. As I speak thousands of loudspeaker vans are touring all our residential streets warning people not to leave their homes. From midnight last night martial law has been in force. That means that the police forces will come under the control of the joint services command who in turn will be controlled by an all-party emergency government.

Do not leave your house. We have set up free "emergency lodging houses" in all towns and cities. If you are away from home you must contact your nearest emergency warden who will direct you to the nearest lodging. The national curfew will remain at 24/24 for the next two days, after which some movement will be permitted during daylight hours. All finance centres have been nationalized and savings frozen. Cash will be available in a few days time, but only in limited allowances.

Retail centres selling essentials will be open on Monday. The government's emergency committee has been stockpiling food for the last year, and will ensure that basic foodstuffs are available in the food centres. These will be guarded by armed troops to prevent looting and hoarding.

The national ID scheme will prevent anyone from buying more than the current rationed allowance.

These emergency regulations will ensure that all the utilities, health and emergency services will continue to provide essential power, water, heat and medical treatment. We believe these measures will be sufficient to prevent civil disturbance and major epidemics. However, we accept that there are likely to be a significant number of fatalities as a result of the current SBX2 infection. This is partly because the first symptoms will have shown on your health checkers months or even years ago, and the subsequent containment regime has had little effect on the dormant SBX2 pathogen.

We do not as yet have any way of treating the SBX2 infection except drugs to relieve suffering. If any in your household fall ill please ring the emergency services and one of their operatives will bring you a supply of drugs. If someone dies use the same emergency contact and the body will be rapidly removed to a place of safe storage until such time as proper burial can be arranged.

Looking back over these notes I see I am quite unconsciously thinking of myself as part of this country, whatever that means. Am I Britannic now? I don't think so, if for no other reason that Britannica as an entity no longer exists. No, I am still a citizen of the world, but I don't forsee living anywhere else now, and I am beginning to feel a strong attachment to this western part of the country.

It would be too simplistic to say that the great NRG project failed. I strongly believe that the mass of knowledge gained and the resources put in place all over the world, will be absolutely vital to whatever civilisation develops now. As far as I can tell the NRG council has disbanded, and from the little information I've been able to obtain it seems the others are doing much as I am – working for the region they find themselves in. Of course they may not all have survived.

I heard later that on the day I went underground, which was the 25th of May 2046, the Lyndain government's stockpiles of food ran out. What happened then was not part of the plan. The original intention was to rebuild the supply chains and re-stock the food centres. By the end of April it was obvious that it would take years to get even a fraction of the transnet working again. The airships were grounded, ocean ships were impounded in distant ports, the protein factories had no skilled staff. It looked to those in charge above ground as if another wave of horror was about to crash onto the land of Britannica.

If the system failure had happened 20 years earlier that is what would probably have happened, but because we had succeeded in localising so much of our food production there were enough people with growing skills to organize the huge network of "garden parties" that took on the job of getting food to the people. We heard stories of people living on cabbages for weeks, and there were some cases of scurvy, the vitamin C deficiency disease that had not been seen in Britannica since the 19th Century. It was lucky that the winter of 44/45 was mild. This last winter was grim, but there seem to have been enough basics stored in most places.

Here the food is dull, protein is minimal but we have enough. What has made all this possible is the dreadful fact that so many of us have died. Twenty-five percent less people means more land to feed less people. It is small consolation to those who have lost whole families.

From the day I started work here my team have been monitoring messages. These are a few samples:

"We have all left the city. It's terrible there. We've very little food but soon we will be in the Dales where they have food gardens. There are so many of us - hundreds all going the same way. How will we all find food and shelter?"

******

"For all the talk of millions dying of the plague, all we see is a never ending stream of people arriving here and all looking for food and shelter. Already our little community has doubled in size. Anyone who is fit - and let's face it those that aren't fit have not made it this far - is put to work. Thank goodness so many of them brought materials with them - wood, metal, trolleys, carts, all sorts of stuff they had scavenged on the way. A lot of them belonged to garden parties in the city so it didn't take them long to get stuck in on the land."

******

"Please anyone seeing or hearing this message - we need help. We've strengthened our defences as well as we can but the mob out there is horrible. What if they decide to attack?"

******

"Yo, first blood to the Metal Men. We showed those arrogant bastards what's what. Yes Sir. No quarter - nock 'em down. Who do they think they are trying to send us back to the city? Serves them rite. This is are patch now. More Might to the Men of Metal"

Dorset Police bulletin: Bridhaven

"We have issued all our officers with arms. They've only had a few hours of training, but what else could we do? We're effectively under siege here. If the promised help from Weymuth doesn't arrive I don't see how we can protect these poor people."

******

"This is a message from Lord Richard. 'Do not be afraid people, the worst is over. You are the chosen ones, the survivors, and you will live on to enjoy a world of peace and plenty. Join me now as we spread the good word. Our present sufferings are part of the great plan and we will emerge strengthened and humbled'."

Message from Central Command Hampshire:

"Order has now been restored in the whole Wiltun/Hamtun command area. Many of the attacking forces are now down and the remainder have surrendered their weapons. Food distribution centres are working. Our sappers and volunteers have brought thousands of buildings back into use. Our immediate need now is for medical staff and water engineers. Anyone with these skills who wishes to join us please contact Colonel Jones on info XTY4729. thank you."

******

"Never trust a policeman - they're all cunts the lot of them. Kill the Pigs!"

From everything we have heard it seems clear that city centres are being abandoned. There is some indication that suburban areas are still functioning, and the horticultural zones seem active. I had this message from Lyndain:

Army Command Post, Darting, Lyndain E

Van? NRG? Anyone? Army command?

We desperately need help here. There's a lunatic who calls himself Lord Richard and for some reason he has set up his base here. People listen to his messages on their comms and come flooding in here hoping for a new life. There is nothing for them. Great mobs of people are fighting over whatever food can be found. There are corpses everywhere left unburied. We are safe here but have hardly any food and unless help comes soon we will have to get out. We had a secure message from Colcaster that there was food there. They need help too so perhaps we can be of more use there. It seems terrible to abandon all these people, but what else can we do? If we leave here in daylight we will be attacked."

It has been very difficult to get even approximate figures for the remaining populations in the former industrial centres, but by logging the frequency of messages and vehicle transits we can get a figure of around 40 percent of peak populations. We sent messages to all the main cities with active comms and those that replied reported a similar story – very little activity in the centres, but active clusters in the suburbs. It seems the survivors have been tearing down buildings and creating new green spaces where they felt safer. The big cities are becoming clusters of smaller towns and villages round one or more zones of chaos.

This was one of the chaos effects our studies had predicted. Chaotic societies have looked much the same throughout human history – conflicting groups trying to impose their will on other groups; charismatic leaders trying to establish a new order; religious leaders proclaiming a path to enlightenment. We had seen it all before. We could now predict with some accuracy how people would behave in these situations. We were also developing tricks and techniques to work round them, but as yet they had not been tested.

It is not widely known that for the last nine years NRG have been training their own defence force. The reason for this was that there was no consistent standard of protection for our offices in the countries where NRG was most active. We agreed with our host countries that we would recruit, train and equip these forces at our expense in exchange for an agreement to provide them with uniforms which matched those of the host country except for their special arm-bands. It was felt that this was necessary to avoid conflict on the ground.

In 2034 the NRG Council had also agreed a series of internal responses to whatever political situation arose. Each had a symbol.

Situation Green was the peaceful option using negotiation and passive resistance – the classic non-aggressive stance of the confident person with hands behind the back.

Situation Amber would use defensive force – the law enforcer in full view with weapons at standby.

Situation Red was when all else had failed, and aggressive action had to be taken to restore peace – the soldier crouched in attack position with weapons ready to kill.

Before 44 there were approximately 20,000 of these Special Forces personnel worldwide, with 600 divided among our various sites in Britannica. It seems that mortality amongst them has been below average, probably because they were better trained in containment techniques. There are 165 men stationed here, most of them above ground, and they have been able to offer immediate assistance to transit routes and to the other law enforcement agencies in the area.

We've had some difficulty over the command structure. When the NRG Council disbanded, it was left to those of us with teams still intact to organise our own local groups. As far as the general public is concerned NRG is still the same, but actually we have a lot less power.

******

I've just had a message from Judith:

Caerdydd

Van bach,

How terrible for you to lose Amy. My dear Rhys has gone too. It seems we are both in the same boat – we can give each other a big hug when we meet and then get on with work.

It's terrible here and I can't wait to join you. Those three bikers Ellen sent (or was it you?) have offered to take me through the transnet tunnel. It seems the Ravens have taken over the lines and are using them as bike tracks. I never thought I would be glad to accept help from them – you must have a lot of clout is all I can say. So, if your men can meet us on the Anglic side we should be safe enough.

Of all the people I know you are the one who might be able to show us how to get through this. I've so missed your friendly wisdom.

See you soon I hope,

Judith

If anyone gets to read these writings of mine they will know that I am not a very emotional person. I don't know where or when I was born, but I think I've always had this sense of being responsible. In my head I have always been an adult and always known I was not like other people. Responsibility for what? I'm still not sure, but it has made it very difficult for me to get emotionally involved.

I'm writing this down because I want to record here the emotional effect Judith's message had on me. I have a tag for the time I first met Judith; she is there in vivid detail - as if lit by some powerful internal light source. She is turning towards me and smiling. She has short hair, blond then (though the next time I met her it was black) neatly framing her face, and it's a face you remember – strong features, a very expressive mouth and intelligent eyes. Is she beautiful? Perhaps her nose is too proud, her chin too square – I don't know how to judge these things – it was different. She had the body of a dancer and every move she made was graceful. I don't remember clearly what she was wearing, a dress of some kind I think, casual, normal un-sexy clothes. There was something retro about them; perhaps it was the boots. They did not disguise a figure which seemed completely in harmony, and far more provocative to me than a more obviously sexy look. Of course she was absurdly young then, but even as a teenager she carried authority. When you have seen as many generations of teenagers as I have it's difficult to dredge up any enthusiasm for their excitement at discovering the world of adulthood. Judith seemed to glide effortlessly into adulthood, making her contemporaries seem naïve and childish.

It was 2036 and we were in the Condor above Brigstowe working on the mountain of problems which the Transnet had generated. Mollie was speaking.

"Van I want you to meet a dear friend of mine – this is Judith"

"Judith... well, very pleased to meet you."

"Me too. The great Vandervelde; I've heard a lot about you" – a slight Cymraeg accent – "yerd" for "heard". She extended her arm to shake hands – unusual then. Hesitating for only a second I grasped her hand and remembered its warm, firm grip.

Grip – yes I can imagine someone reading this and thinking "get a grip old man!" Within seconds I was myself again. 'Just a brief attack of male hormones' I told myself and we went on to talk about the protest marches. It may have been the normal response of a much older man to an attractive young woman, but it was unusual for me.

Nine years later, reading those warm remarks in her message, this memory flashed up on my mental screen. I had met her a few times since then, always enjoyed the meetings but not felt anything more than friendship. Now I knew I had to see her again.

CHAPTER 2 2047 – 56

Vandervelde: Underground

Judith arrived here in the spring of 47. I let her settle in for a few days and then went to see her. It was only a few years since we had last met but it seemed like another age, and it was an emotional reunion. It was over three years since Amy had died; the pain was still fresh but I had learnt to live with it. Judith was now a mature woman. I had long become accustomed to what must seem to others a bizarre phenomenon – friends, family, lovers all growing older much faster than me. The age gap between us had narrowed, but I had no idea whether the spark I had felt when we first met could be re-kindled.

She has one of the staff bedsit rooms, and it already has her personal stamp on it – lots of pictures, clashing colours, not very tidy but welcoming.

We exchanged small-talk for a while – she seemed a bit uneasy, on edge, so I got straight down to business, suspecting that she would feel more comfortable in that context. I had decided to offer her a very big task; one I thought would stretch her, but one I thought she would excel at – a new government for Cymru.

Immediately her body language changed. Her eyes sparkled and she stood a little taller. Within hours she was hard at work and looking quite different from the tense frightened young woman who had arrived a few days ago.

We had some fascinating conversations, and one of them turned out to be significant in ways we didn't foresee.

"You know Van I feel quite comfortable here. At home I'm either frightened or angry most of the time. Do you know what - I've come to the conclusion that democracy is crap. Look at Cymru - what's left of it. For all our talk of "a sustainable future" what did we get? The same old crony politics. I honestly think we'd do no worse if we selected our politicians by lottery!

"Ha - twelve good men and true? You could call the head of state the foreman." This was Mollie.

"yes yes and instead of an election campaign you'd have eight weeks of foreplay!" . . . and so the conversation deteriorated in fits of laughter.

"Oh dear" I said. "We may joke but it has been done before. There is even a proper name for it - Demarchy."

"Oh yes, I've heard of that. Wasn't it tried in the Venetian state?" - Judith

"And in ancient Greece. It can't have been very successful. I don't see how you would stop some idiot chosen at random from making really important decisions."

"No change there then! Oh sod it pass me the wine." (Yes, we had breached our precious store – it was that kind of evening.)

We talked of many other things, but I remembered these words. The three of us, joined sometimes by other survivors, spent many hours trying to understand the patterns of behaviour which had led us to the situation we found ourselves in. Was it Fate? There was a certain inevitability about it, but none of us could believe in "the hand of God".

Despite the sadness it was a good time. We were all very close: the intense comradeship of the survivors.

****

I have Mollie's son Magnus with me. He's 22 now, and getting very frustrated with the facilities in the bunker. As you might expect with such parents he's pretty bright and in a normal society would be at university. All we can offer him is personal tuition and the very limited resources of the Emergency Government Network. To make things worse the choice of female company is limited to say the least. I've talked it over with Mollie and we have decided that it would be much better for him and us if he were in Brigstowe. It's not as safe, but it's better than it used to be, and he's tall and well built with plenty of self-confidence so should be able to look after himself.

So that is where we are heading on the "NRG Express" – that's the ironic nickname which has stuck for our delivery service. In truth it's anything but express. I'll make notes as we go along.

April 10. 8:30 Corslea – the old transtation. I'm waiting to see what turns up for the run to Cheaping– ah, an antique oil car, a Ford I think. They must have some fuel oil there then. There are two people in it and the driver calls out – "Vandervelde?"

"That's me"

"This young fella with you?"

"Yes this is Magnus."

"OK,Get in" He seems less than delighted to see us. "I've been told to get you to Cheaping as quickly as possible, and not to ask questions."

"That sounds right; let's go." We lurched off belching fumes and he went tearing down the old tarmac road to the nearby town. It was 8:51 when he screeched to a halt at the transtation.

"That's it. I'm off home"

"Ok, thanks. Well Magnus, we've got a 20 minute wait here. Did you ever come here before?"

"Oh yes, sometimes. I had a friend here and we used to do some music together, but then things got difficult."

"How do you mean?"

"Well, you know, all the restrictions – containment. We teenagers were treated like dirt half the time."

"Oh, I didn't know. I was so busy then trying to save the world I didn't have much time to spend with young people. Pity."

"I tell you what Van, I'm true excited about this job. What's it like in Brigstowe?"

"I'm not sure. I guess we'll find out soon enough. Ah – here's the . . . bus?"

It's one of the big people carrier e-cars that used to do taxi runs away from the transnet lines. It takes 10 passengers, and as the driver checks my comms I'm taken back 30 years to the last time I travelled on a "coach" as they were called then. The seats are very comfortable, each with a comms screen – though not working. There is a self-serve snacks bar too. Very nice. We leave at 9:15 and arrive without incident at the next stop, which is Sulis. It is a few years since I last saw this beautiful old city and it's quite a shock to see how derelict everything is. We go through street after street of boarded up shops, rubbish in the road, very little traffic. The transtation is surrounded by high fences with at least 10 security men standing around. As we pull up a large old truck stops and the gate guards interrogate the driver. There is evidently a lot of work going on in there. I ask the driver:

"When is it re-opening?"

"No-one tells us anything mate but I've heard from a friend that it should be any day now. Trouble is all these threats from the Brigstowe mobs. I wouldn't use it – too dangerous."

"Is it safer to get to Brigstowe by road then?"

"I try not to go there, but Mal over there" – he points to our next vehicle, a similar people carrier – "He says it's OK. Gets stopped every now and then, but nothin 'eavy."

"Thanks – See you."

As he predicted, the last stage was uneventful – a tedious

crawl through a suburban wasteland. We arrived in Brigstowe Transtation at 11:25. Here we are assigned two guards to take us the 15 minute walk to the old office building, where I am to meet Derek Sheppard, an old friend of Eldred's and the man who will be in charge of Magnus. I was glad of the guards. There is more movement here than in Sulis, but too many young men carrying guns to feel safe. They stare at us but stay clear. The old "Temple" looks very forlorn now, and I wonder if our plans to return there eventually are realistic. Another part of the plan is to make the NRG Express the backbone of a new mail and courier network. It seems we have a long way to go.

******

The story of the re-floating of the Brigstowe haven and the Company of Harbourers is a remarkable testimony to human ingenuity and cooperation.

Mollie had of course kept in touch with her old friends in the city, and told me about it a few weeks ago when I explained about the trip I was planning.

"So; you're going to see Derek. Yes, I can give you some idea of what he's been up to. During the chaos in 44/45 the lock at Westmorland Basin was damaged and left open, and the water became tidal again."

"Hang on, Westmorland Basin?"

"Oh sorry, that's the western end of the haven where the cut begins. You know about the cut?"

"I think so – a big canal which diverted the tidal river to a point some miles upstream."

"That's it. It's amazing what those navvies did in the 1840s. The river was cut off by lock gates and the whole five kilometre stretch of river which ran through the city centre became a tide-free haven. It made a massive difference to the viability of Brigstowe as a port."

"Anyway, when the Westmorland lock was damaged, hundreds of boats moored in the haven were wrecked. A fair few survived though and the owners together with the remaining businesses and residents became Derek's sort of 'consituency'. It was Derek's vision which drove the renewal project. He had been the Council's Leisure officer before 44 and he took a passionate interest in the whole area – its history, development, famous characters and so on. When he saw the devastation - not just by the crash, but by the wrecking of the lock gates, he swore to himself that he would somehow restore what he saw as the real heart of the city. He started planning, but he didn't tell anyone about it until he had it all worked out. Then he began to approach the key players he wanted to take part in his scheme."

"Of course the haven hadn't been a working port for ages. It began the century as a huge complex of ships, boats, eateries, museums, houses and flats all devoted to Leisure, and all great users of fossil fuel. When our Carbon Trading scheme took off and it became too expensive to run all these boats on oil the number of sails began to overtake the motor vessels. At its peak it was a fantastic mix of High Tech and High Fashion – I loved it."

"This thing Derek was planning began in 47. The boat owners had formed clusters surrounded by barbed wire wherever they could survive the tides. The museums were barricaded. The few shops and restaurants still going had to set up elaborate defences and employ staff to act as guards. The only place which was reliably secure was our NRG compound, so Derek approached us. Er...do you remember when our Security Force started recruiting locally?"

"Sorry – I had my mind on other things then."

"Well, that's what happened. They set up a recruitment and training programme and a few months later Derek had 120 trained and armed men at his command. He sent them out in small bands to collect materials from all over the city and began the great Haven Fence - well, that's what it became known as. It was a ring of defendable positions round the main part of the haven including parts of the old city centre. From that point on he found himself pushing at an open door. There were hundreds of people who shared his passion and in next to no time the lock was ready to be shut again."

"It sounds amazing. I wish I had been there."

"Oh you'd have loved it. It was pure chance that I happened to be there – a very hush hush mission to the Temple. I don't think you even knew I wasn't here!"

"When was that?"

"Autumn 47; I was only gone for a few nights. It was high tide. A bunch of musicians with brass instruments turned up, fireworks were found in old cupboards, bunting was everywhere and there were great beefy men jostling with each other for a place on the huge lock levers. What a sight - all those muscles straining away at the lock gates until they slowly began to move. As soon as they clunked together the water level on the west side began going down. Everyone held their breath until it was clear that the level on the haven side wasn't going down too – then an enormous cheer went up and the band started playing the only tune they knew – Liberty Bell. "

"Oh the old Monty Python tune!"

"What?"

"Sorry – before your time."

So I knew a fair bit about him when I saw him coming towards me across the Millennium Square. He was quite tall and wore an old fashioned long tweet coat and although the weather was quite mild for February he had a scarf and an old felt hat. I guessed his age at about 50. We sat down outside in the shelter of the curved front of the building. I noticed that he had a local accent so I asked him if he had always lived here.

"Oh yes, my Dad was quite well known here – he was a jazz musician, sax player, and he named me after a local DJ in the hope that I would follow in his footsteps"

"I'm afraid I'm hopeless when it comes to music – too much of it sounds the same to me."

"Ah well. I'm not much better. Dad – Andy – wanted me to get a proper job like playing in a band, but I was more interested in local government!"

His roar of laugher was infectious.

"Such is fate. If you had been a musician we would probably never have met, and local government is what is on my mind at present."

I went on to tell him about the ideas I was mulling over for a new regional "Nation". I couldn't say much about it then, but after an interesting conversation left with the promise that he would look very carefully at whatever I came up with.

Judith- Netlog

1 January Out of the Bunker

Welcome 2049. I feel terrible. We actually had a proper New Year's Eve party last night, celebrating our last New Year's Eve in the bunker. It's now five years since 44, (yes I can do sums!) and most of that time we've been living and working down here in our cave, hiding from the big bad world. Last October we finally began "Operation Overground" and now it has all gone – all our homes dismantled, the offices stripped bare, the gardens just grass and trees. All the office equipment has gone to Brigstowe, and we all now have temporary accommodation around the haven where we can be relatively secure. It felt very strange coming back here for the party – all those echoing rooms. The party was held in the garden and just for the night we turned the temperature up to 23, and the atmosphere to "humid". The trees, the bean trees, fruit and nut trees, were still there and strung round with points of light. There was a stage with musicians doing soundscapes and a temporary dance floor where we all tried to remember our dancing lessons – til we relapsed into the tens fashion for free-style dancing. The bar staff had gone to great lengths to find supplies of the best wines and beers available, and in the tropical atmosphere the dress code deteriorated to a sweat-soaked minimum. I think a few of those waking up with sore heads today will have more than a hangover to regret. Well I don't. Je ne regretted rien as some French dame said.

This man Vandervelde is doing my head in. When I first arrived here I was pretty sure he fancied me. God knows how old he is, and I don't usually go for older men, but he has that aura about him – power, wisdom? I don't know, but I was quite flattered that he should be interested in me.

Soon after I arrived here he came to see me and the conversation went roughly like this:

"Judith – how are you settling in?"

"Good thanks. It's great to feel safe, but I'm not sure what I'm supposed to be doing here."

"Well, that's what I wanted to talk to you about." (Was I a little disappointed? If so I tried not to show it.) You mentioned something about a secure comms unit in Caerdydd. Can you get in touch with them?"

"I already have. They think I've chickened out. I'm not the flavour of the month at present."

"Too bad. That might change though. How would you feel about working from here to try to establish a new governing structure – perhaps a new assembly?"

"Wow – need you ask. I would jump at it"

So, not quite the romantically charged dialogue I had in mind, but great in a different way. Soon I was up to my elbows in work, and I couldn't have thought of a better way fill the hole that was my old life in Caerdydd.

I saw Van regularly and enjoyed his company, but that initial spark was gone. We were colleagues now getting stuck into one of the most challenging projects you could imagine – rebuilding a nation.

Before we knew it two years had gone by and apart from a couple of drunken grapples with junior staff, I had been celibate – not a problem; didn't miss it. So when it came to the party last night I was quite happy to flirt with the old fella. I dragged him onto the dance floor. At first he was stiff and uncomfortable but then a switch seemed to click and he began to relax.

Well. I have to tell you boys and girls he was something else! My head is still awful and my stomach feels like somebody has punched it, but I'm happy!

Oh God, what if he's full of remorse and goes back to his

normal reserved person? If he does, sod him; it's his funeral.

Letter from Vandervelde

Dearest Judith

Am I being a coward writing to you? I know I should come and find you but I'm badly organised at present. I'm trying to be sensible, telling myself – "look you old fool, she was drunk. She's a modern young woman who can please herself what she does with her body. It was wonderful, but why should it be anything more than a glorious fling?"

When Amy died I hardened my heart. The time I had with her was the best, but I'd lived through good times before and would again. I knew the only way I could cope was to return to strategies I had used many times before. My strange life has to be about more than my own pleasure. In a way I would not be happy unless it were – can you understand that? So, I batten down the hatches and get stuck in with whatever the next task is.

So lovely Judith, please don't think you have to behave any differently. I would absolutely hate to lose your friendship. It means more to me than I can easily say.

Can we still be pals?

Your old fool

Van

Judith - Netlog

Oh I get it. He's being very nice but obviously feels guilty – still pining for his Amy no doubt. Hey ho.

I'm going back home today – on the NRG Express as they call it. One of my Raven palls sent me a picture of the house and said it was OK. It looked pretty derelict to me but I didn't like to say so. It won't be much fun going back to a cold damp house, but I'll be able to catch up with a few of my old comrades and I've had loads of offers of help. So, out with the old – in with the new!

******

Oh my God, I've done something unbelievably stupid. When will I ever learn?? It was such an emotional occasion. I got to Caerdydd OK – the NRG Express is running a fairly decent service now. The bikers picked me up from the transtation where the bus had stopped and took me Deri Rd. It looked as I expected – boarded up and forlorn.

"We'll just see you in then love"

They hung around looking awkward. The moment I opened the door there was a great shout and all I could see was people! The house was full of them! I didn't know whether I was laughing or crying when I got to the living room and saw the big banner saying 'Croeso 'n ol Judith". Then the music started and before I could get my wits about me the boards were coming off and daylight was streaming in.

The house was not only warm, it was tidy. What have I done to deserve such friends? By 18:00 I was drunk and by 19:00 I was in tears. Then who should turn up but Magnus. As soon as he saw me he came and put an arm round me:

"Judith – what's up – we all love you. Don't be

miserable.”

“Oh Magnus, I know. I’m not miserable, I’m just ...oh come here!” It was meant to be a sisterly hug but ended in a kiss. He’s got so tall! He was only 12 when I first met him, now he’s this great strong man. He was just so lovely and I was drunk. Before I knew what was going on we were in bed.

When I finally surfaced, Magnus had gone and Rosie and Charlie were still here – giving me funny looks. I felt OK, until I remembered, then I felt a lurch of guilt. That didn’t last long. I’d had a great night and if that Van the Man thinks I’m going to wait around for him he doesn’t know me. A few coffees later and I was ready to take on whatever was waiting for me in the Senedd.

Five weeks later I knew I had missed a period. What am I going to do?

******

Vandervelde

(dictated to comms)

Ahem. Delete that . . . Wherever I was would be the hub of our activities so I had to choose a location carefully. My Britannic team had always been based in the west so we began talking to groups from Cymru, Kernow and the historic region of Wessex. With the cities now hazardous, and transnet in ruins, the two ancient Celtic nations of Kernow and Cymru were now joined rather than separated by the sea. The old university town of Ystwyth was evidently still much as it was five years ago. It was by the sea and midway between the sometimes hostile modern tribes of the north and south Cymric. I decided I would go there to see if it would serve as a base. Before that though there was someone I had to see in Kernow.

So here I am standing in Brigstowe haven by the statue of John Cabot gazing out towards the new world – Cabot doing the gazing.

I can see a troop of The Haven Protection Force doing exercises over by our office building. There have been some raids recently from the gangs based in Clivden and Bedwin. Nobody seems to know what's happening in the old black district – St Peter's. It had grown very prosperous in the 20s and 30s and had become the launch pad for the "African Renaissance", but I heard that mortality was high amongst the descendants of the original immigrants from the West Indies. All we know is that the whole area is defended by the "Dreads"

Behind me is one of the big stone buildings that used to be warehouses but were converted to leisure use at the turn of the century. This one was an Arts Centre but most became apartment complexes for those who enjoyed the city centre/marine environment. Now they are all being hastily converted to goods depots again.

To my right is the newly restored Haven which runs up through the city centre. The top part is barricaded off – it's outside the Haven Fence, but inside the fence is really coming to life. The high-tech ocean-going ships from the thirties are being rapidly brought back into service, and just past where I am standing is one of the rehabilitated ocean liners with its huge computerised sail-fins. Almost all the deck area is covered in solar collectors which power the series of motors which both trim the sails and drive the propulsion units, but its cruising power all comes from the 20 metre high rigid retractable sail-fins.

Last month we had a visit from someone who claimed to represent the people of Kernow. I was intrigued because as far as I knew the original Kernoweger people had pretty much lost their identity as the popularity of the peninsula as a recreation zone grew and grew. His name is Walter Penrose and he lives in Kammbronn, a place shown in NetListings as a poor ex-industrial town with little to recommend it as a holiday destination. He must have been about 50 then and had long bushy hair going grey and topped with a woollen cap. His coat seemed to have been cobbled together from recycled materials, but his boots looked new. He addressed us in a language I had never heard before.

"Yeghes da!" That my friends means "good health" in Kernowek ....

I must stop dictating now because I can see my vessel arriving. It's a restored ketch with extra solar "sails" and the owner has agreed to take me to Heyl, which is the nearest port to Kammbronn and then on to Ystwyth.

Message from Twm Pritchard

e-message.

Sender Twm Pritchard

Coed Las

Van –

It would be wonderful to see you again, but you will find me very different. I'm getting better but for the last few years I've found life pretty pointless. I know I used to complain about never seeing them before, and what a bitch Ffion was, but at least they were alive and I loved them, even Ffion. I'm not even 40 yet but I feel old – perhaps you know that feeling. I know I'm lucky to be alive and that there is now a real hope that things can be better. Some days I feel something of the old spirit, but mostly it's just hard work.

Enough – I want your visit to be a beginning. I'll meet you at the quay with my latest invention. One piece of good news is that what's left of the old Cyngor Sir – the County Council, have managed to get the transnet line working again, so we can now travel quite easily up and down the coast, but getting to my place is a bit more tricky as you'll see.

Anyway, send me a message when you get near the harbour and I'll set out.

Your friend

Twm

Vandervelde

Kernow & Ystwyth

We had to wait for the tide at Westmorland lock, but as soon as it began to turn we took our place in the queue of small ships and boats drifting through the spectacular gorge to the sea. Our first destination was Kaynowyth in Kernow. I remembered it as a pretty place with a big harbour where the last of the big fishing boats used to dock before the fishing ban in 22 and the first place where fishing revived in the 30s. The ten year moratorium had enabled some species to multiply, but the most useful ones had been reduced to such low levels that they were still struggling when fishing stopped again in 44. It was a depressing moment when cod was declared globally extinct in 2036.

All the way down the coast to Hyrt Point the weather had been dreadful. I was fortunate enough to be immune from sea sickness but several of my six fellow passengers were not so lucky. Though not sick I was very uncomfortable being rolled around as we tacked to and fro. It seemed like more than 24 hours when we finally reached the shelter of Kaynowyth harbour. With no sun on the way down, our batteries were in very low condition, but we had just enough power to dock, and we were much relieved to be on dry land again.

Walter was there to meet me, this time in a flamboyant black cloak with a big white cross on it, and, embroidered in gold and silver threads, a coat of arms with the image of a chough, its beak and legs picked out in red.

"Van my comrade" his voice roared across the harbour. "Dydh da!"

"Dydh da to you too" I had been doing my homework.

"I'll let you off the rest. It's good to see you. You've

arrived at a good time. We've just re-opened our first section of transnet track. Come and see - we can walk to the station. I got your letter of course but didn't know where it came from or where you were sailing from."

"Ah yes, sorry, we've got into a habit of not giving out information. I've been in an underground bunker for most of the last six years. Still, we are now above ground and for the moment in Brigstowe, but part of the reason for my trip, as I may have hinted in my letter, is to decide where I should make my base - which will also be my home."

"Well we'd be delighted to find a place for you here but I suspect you are thinking of somewhere less isolated. We had virtually no land communications for some years. It's got better now, though mainly because of our maritime trading.

We rise again Van, the Kernow people are uniting in hardship, the flag is flying again."

"I didn't think there were many Kernowyon left – aren't most of you from up country now?"

"Oh tush – who cares, we are all Kernowyon now, the language is being revived, and some of the descendents of the grockles have even taken on Kernowek names. I took my maternal grandmother's name."

"Grockles?"

"Oh that's what we used to call the holiday makers. Where do you originate from Van?"

"I'm not sure. I don't know who my parents were, and I don't know where or when I was born – not even to the nearest continent or the nearest ten years. We Elders tend not to talk about our past. Our mission in life is a humble one – just that minor matter of the future of the human race."

"Well I take folks as I find them and to me you are a fine upstanding man; the sort of person I can trust."

"I'm glad to hear it because I have a proposal to put to you."

"I listen, I hear, I act – speak on Vandervelde." He was right about the acting bit.

"Let's meet again later. I'm tired and hungry. Where am I staying?"

"Of course, of course; It's just in the next street."

It was a pleasant little guest house attached to a comfortable restaurant, and it was there we met later and I put my proposition to him.

"Walter, you know the biggest problem we have now in trying to rebuild is not simply lack of skilled labour, but security. Everywhere I have been there are pockets of normality interspersed with areas of banditry. Nowhere feels safe. To recreate a Britannic State seems to me not only undesirable but frankly impossible. I've been having discussions with groups from the West of Anglia and Cymru, and I now believe that the sea link between Cymru and Kernow can be the basis of a new relationship. A link between the old Celtic nations, and especially a maritime one, plays to people's emotions, and as I'm sure you know, it is emotion which drives human behaviour."

"Indeed indeed, you can set up any number of sensible boring administrative government, council, political things, units or whatever you call them, but unless people can love them they will not thrive."

"Exactly, so, the big question I put to you is this: will you help bring your Kernow into a new alliance with Cymru? "

"Oh my friend" He leapt up, scattering cutlery, and paced around the room. Some of the other diners seemed alarmed but most seemed to know him and were smiling.

"You are speaking to my heart".

I made a sign for him to be less noisy and he sat down and continued in a stage whisper. The histrionics didn't bother me. We had no real need for secrecy here.

I stayed for several days and spent long hours in meetings and discussions. When it came time to go there were many warm farewells on the quay and I left feeling as hopeful as I had for many months. After the long haul along the coast from Teifi, the first thing we saw of Ystwyth was the hill to the north crowned with wind turbines. It was heartening to see that most of them were turning. As we came in sight of the town we could see that a big new breakwater had been built to accommodate the increase in sea traffic. This has created a much bigger harbour area which was full of masts – traditional pole masts and the newer rotating type. We had to wait a while for a space but the comms were working well and we were eventually guided in. I was met by Twm with a strange looking vehicle. We had not seen each other since before 44 and from the tone of his letter I was expecting a more sombre friend. It was a rather tearful re-union, but we both brightened in each others' company and some of the old animation returned as he told me about his vehicle.

"It's based on a vintage 2010 Honda and sidecar I found in a scrap yard. Restoring it gave me something interesting to do and stopped me getting too depressed. Halfway through I realized that the petrol we had been able to get was illegal . . .well, you know . . . not official, and the price kept hiking up so I found an electric motor. I've got plenty of solar at home and was on the lookout for more ways of using it in sunny weather so, soon as I'd rigged up a charger I was able to electrify it.

"Well done, but what about batteries?"

"That's the problem, yn wir. As you know there are plenty of old batteries lying around but they tend to run down very quickly. I needed to do the 30k round trip to town. It's steep going back so I reckoned I could use muscle power on the lower parts and save the batteries for the hills. It's hard work on those handles when it's just me, but with you pedalling too we should be tidy."

"I'm fine with that Twm, but there are things I need to do in this town. Can we wander round for a bit? I need to get a feel for what this place is like."

"Of course. This way. There's a lot of empty buildings. Thousands died, but from what I hear it was much worse over east."

We were walking up what was obviously once a busy shopping street, and there were a few shops open selling mostly food and hardware.

"It's best we go straight though here. See those boys on the street corners? They are the Meibion, watchers for the gangs. Just say hello and walk on."

It was hard to dismiss the wave of disappointment I felt. Was this peaceful little town seething with suppressed anarchy? We continued in silence until we got past the centre.

"It's not too bad really. They do have guns but they mostly use them on themselves. The shops have to pay protection but then there's no taxes and the Meibion do keep order of a sort. Live and let live is our motto. It's been the Cymric way for a long time – keep your head down, let other people get on with their lives."

"What about the police then?"

"Oh we do have police. They do all the traditional police things, but it's the Meibion who have the power, and if they don't want someone arrested then they don't get arrested."

We were walking uphill now; a wide street leading north. On the right were the ruins of the old University.

"I want to show you something Van; through here."

We came to a big undamaged stone building with several recognizable policemen apparently guarding it.

"This is the Llyfrgell Genedlaethol, the National Library. The books are all still there and the Cyngor have an agreement with the Meibion to leave it alone."

Entering the building was like stepping back in time. There was a proper entry desk, well lit with proper security checks.

"Shwd mae Mari. This is my friend Van. He's an Elder from NRG and he's on a visit here."

"Oh welcome Sir, we are honoured. My colleague here can show you round."

"Thank you indeed but it will have to be another time I'm afraid. My visit is only a brief one."

"Well, I hope you like what you see. We have a lot of problems but we are managing, and if NRG is getting involved here, then there is real hope for the future."

"I'm afraid you overestimate the abilities of NRG in these difficult times, but I am encouraged by your kind words."

When we finally set off in Twm's ramshackle vehicle I had a lot to think about. The structures for good government seemed to be in place. Could we somehow buy off the Meibion?

The first part of our journey was quite easy and we soon got into a rhythm, Twm on the handles, both of us on the pedals. After about 40 minutes it got a lot harder and the roads got worse. All around us was young forest, mainly birch and scrub. When we got to the older forest plantations the motor cut in and we could take it a bit easier.

Twm had been living in a forester's house with Ffion and the children, but had abandoned the house when they died and lived in a cabin in the forest for a few years. He had begun collecting materials until he was able to build the extraordinary structure that came into view as we entered a clearing.

Unlike the old house, which I could see behind a group of young trees, and indeed unlike most modern housing, the structure is made from virgin materials – timber, straw, mud, lime – and it's big: eight metre cruck beams supported the gothic arch of the roof with daub between them.

"The technology is almost that of the iron age. With the resources we have here we couldn't improve on riven timber, wattle and daub for the main structure, but our version of mud – the daub – is chemically much more sophisticated, and is a really good insulator.

" I remember seeing a number of "hobby" buildings of this type back in the tens, but I imagine they were a luxury then when imported materials were so cheap."

"It is true. Now they are even more labour intensive, but still a lot cheaper than concrete and steel. Windows of course are the big problem. We were very lucky and managed to source these from a derelict office block in Abertawe."

"We?"

"Ah, yes." He grinned.

"I was about to tell you about that." He opened an impressive oak door set in the end of the cruck house and we entered a large warm kitchen area with a big wooden trestle table in the middle."

"Bethan – this is Van"

"Very pleased to meet you Bethan."

"And me too – I've heard so much about you."

"Well I hadn't heard anything about you, but I'm really pleased Twm is not on his own any more." She laughed

"Oh don't jump the gun. We've not known each other long – he still has plenty of time on his own to brood."

How different she was from the intense Ffion. Bethan is by no means overweight – nobody is these days - but she is "well rounded" as they say, with a cheerful manner. She looks like the sort of person who laughs a lot.

"Where do you come from Bethan?"

"Oh, just down the road – that's how we met. Twm gets his milk and eggs from our farm."

"That's it Van – all in the package, and all very tasty!"

We all laughed. Later we had a pleasant meal – with eggs – and then got into deep discussions fuelled by our usual tipple, - Penderyn: almost the only whisky available now, and only if you had the right kind of credits.

"I think I know a place that would suit you." Twm had said while we were still coherent.

"It's not in Ystwyth, so not quite so central, but it was the site of the first Eisteddfod Gynedlaethol. Do you know about the Eisteddfod?"

"Yes, I've read about the druids and so on."

"Ah the druids. Hm, well it was about a lot more than that, but I won't go into it now. Anyway, this place is on the transnet and there's a big old house falling into disrepair that could do with your resources."

So, the next day we set of for Ystwyth again to get onto the transnet. His vehicle wouldn't work on the track so Twm led us to a row of parked e-cars, all plugged into their chargers.

"We don't have facilities for foot passengers yet so we'll take one of these." It was an ancient converted petrol car. There were the usual two pedals –stop and go and a steering wheel. Speed on this model was regulated by the go pedal.

Twm showed it his comms unit which had plenty of credits, unhitched, and we climbed in. It was a very short drive to the ramp and soon we were picked up by the track and whisked off. We chatted in the almost silent space of the e-car while field after field of vegetables flashed by. Ten minutes later we decelerated sharply and found ourselves on the exit ramp at Dyfi transtation.

The old high street with its clock tower was quite busy, and the people looked happy.

"Come and see the bridge. Did you know there was some bad fighting here in 45 – some gangs from the north tried to take over the town, but the Meibion from Ystwyth got wind of it and mined the bridge which they blew just as the gogs began to cross. Terrible really, they weren't all gangsters even then!

For a few years there was no physical contact with the north except by boat, and then only small ones. The river is not deep enough for transport ships – at least not yet. There are great plans to dredge out a channel, but for the time being most of the traffic is south on the transnet."

We stood looking down towards the estuary. It was a beautiful scene – wooded hills to the north and mainly scrubland to the south with the wide river running clear below us. As we watched, an Osprey flew in low and took a huge fish not half a mile from where we stood. Looking down I could see many more large fish below. Watching water flow by is a wonderfully contemplative activity and the fish reminded me of Amy's father Hector. How he would have loved this! I could imagine being happy here if we could stabilize the government of the area.

The Plas turned out to be a big early 19th century manor house with large overgrown gardens.

"It is still owned by the Cyngor and was run as various kinds of museum and public space, but it has not been used since 44, and I imagine it's in a poor state."

As soon as I saw it I knew it was right. From here we could begin the work of setting up a new regional government. I already thought of this as "Cambria" - a coming together of the ancient Celtic nations. Personally I had no romantic attachment to Celtic mythology, but I knew how important such ideas were for the work we had ahead of us.

I also thought it would resonate with the Kernowek. In the longer term I had ambitions to join the two regions by land and bring in the old region of Wessex with the cities of Brigstowe, Sulis and Exchester, but that was some way off.

Judith: Netlog

I'm not very good at this netlog business. It's ages since I last wrote anything, but a lot has been happening and I want to get my thoughts clear.

To be honest I'm not a very mumsy person. I like my adult world and I really wasn't ready to have a family. On the other hand children are so precious now I couldn't bear the thought of another life being lost to the world. It didn't take me long to decide on adoption. That was the easy bit. The next few weeks were one long misery of nausea, but eventually I started feeling better and I finally decided that the least worst option was to make a clean breast of it. Magnus has been sweet. He seems to understand that it had been a one-off. Let's face it he's not short of admirers now that he is overground. I'd already told him about my on-off relationship with Van. Now I would have to tell Van about Magnus. I could have let him assume it was his, but I'd never heard him mention any children. What if he was firing blanks? I'm not one for covering things up anyway so the truth it would have to be whatever the consequences.

******

I don't often question the wisdom of the great Vandervelde but I have to say that, much as I love him, I don't feel at all comfortable with his latest initiative. He's been talking about going up north to talk to the "Pobl y Draig". Why does he want to encourage these Nationalist dinosaurs? My parents used to talk about the times back in the 1970s when the "Meibion Glydwr" were burning holiday cottages – pathetic! Now he's talking about some sort of link up between Cymru and Kernow.

I've always been proud of my country. I can speak the old language as well as most and love all the old stories, but Cymru is never going to get anywhere as long as it still clings to what the old men in their nightshirts – sorry "Gorsedd of Bards" say. Half these so called "traditions" were invented in the 19th Century anyway.

Cymru needs to be an outward-looking European nation, and forget all the old hostility with Anglia. Anglia's in a right mess anyway now. Well, that's what I think but he's asked for a meeting tomorrow to discuss all this. It seems he wants me to help him set up this new nation he talks about.

He might not be so keen when I tell him about Magnus.

I'm very nervy about this. What if he takes it all in his stride? In some ways that would be worse than him going all cold on me. Why is it I can organise a city but can't get my own love life sorted out?

We met in my office in the Senedd. I do love this place but have to admit it needs some attention. It's as old as the century but still looks modern – until you get close up and see the stains and cracks.

"Van – great to see you."

"And you" We hugged... and held each other a bit longer than necessary. After the usual small talk we went up to the lounge to get some coffee – well they call it coffee; I'm not sure what gets put in it nowadays – and sat opposite each other in comfortable chairs.

"Judith, listen"

"Van I've something.."

"Sorry – you first"

"I've something to tell you. Something serious."

"Sounds ominous. You're not pregnant are you?"

I just sat there staring.

"Oh my God. Judith. I thought you were looking a bit . . . er . . . chubby. Are you sure?"

"Yes, and I really hate to have to admit it but it's not yours."

"I know. That was something I was going to have to tell you about – not much point now. Who's the lucky man?"

"Oh dear; it gets worse. It was Magnus."

"What? He must be ten years younger than you. Whatever are you playing at?"

"Eight, and I'm not playing at anything now. It was a one-off - that crazy night in Caerdydd when I had the surprise home-coming party."

"What was he doing there?"

"I don't know. I never asked him."

"But you are so good at your job. How will you cope with being a mother?"

"I know it sounds hard but I'm going to give it up for adoption. There are so many people out there who will make a much better job of bringing up this child than I ever could."

“Yes you could be right there.” He sounded really bitter. Suddenly I couldn’t keep up the front any more.

“Oh Van I don’t want to lose you!”

It’s lucky there was hardly anyone around or they would have had a picnic seeing the great Vandervelde in the arms of a crazy looking woman and both of them crying and laughing. With the same thought we stood up, left the coffee and, still holding hands, went back to my office where I locked the door.

******

We did finally get down to some serious discussions.

Van said: “I know you have some doubts about the Cambria project, and believe me I do understand your position.”

“I don’t think you can. You come from God knows where, how do you know what it feels like to have been brought up here in the capital of what was a thriving part of Britannica. We were proud of the old “New Cymru”. What you are suggesting seems like going backwards.”

“Of course I can understand. You don’t think I’ve suddenly become a nationalist do you? One of my strongest articles of faith is that humans need to live with their neighbours, - to reach out for the thread of common humanity. This is all about diplomacy. I have had to think myself into the position of a Walter Penrose or whoever is the Cymric equivalent. What they have is passion, and it’s passion which drives human behaviour.”

I knew the Cymric equivalent only too well – he’s a nut case called Iolo Ap Williams. When I thought more about it though I realised Van was probably right. He made me realise that my feelings about the Nats were a prejudice just like the Nats feelings about the Anglic, or “Up country” as the

Kernowek call them. It's what he calls "Old Brain" thinking. He is convinced that he can use the passion and divert the prejudice.

I think I can see now how that would work. Even as I berated myself for being a weak woman, I could see myself in my new role as a diplomat finding things in common with Iolo Ap. I couldn't imagine I would ever get to like him, but Van is determined to meet these people and I was not going to oppose him. If there was one thing I was clear about now it was that we had some kind of future together. We are in some strange way, a couple.

******

In the end it was the hardest thing I have ever done. I really didn't think I was going to come all over mumsie when the time came, but nothing had prepared me for the terrible rush of emotion I felt when I saw her for the first time. They wouldn't let me hold her. All I saw was this little screwed up face, serious, blinking. Then she was gone and I never saw her again. The counsellor Seren was there holding my hand and repeating the words we had agreed:

"I know the pain will pass. Children are not possessions. I could not give her a real family. My child is where she belongs. By this action I have given great happiness to two lovely people. I have created a family where there was only a couple". ...and so on and on; they all sounded hollow.

Now I will never have a proper family. Why, why have I got this so wrong? Why did I ever think I could be truly happy in a sterile relationship with a man more than twice my age? BRING HER BACK.

Vandervelde

It took nearly a year to get The Plas restored, and months to get all our stuff here, but it felt really good when the last e-van disappeared and we began sorting out our belongings and setting up home – this will be home not just to me but to Mollie and Eldred. Magnus was still undecided; I think he was having too good a time in Brigstowe. I still didn't know where things stood with Judith, but hoped she would join us later.

Meetings, meetings – I seem to have spent most of that spring – 52 - in meetings all over Cymru. Of all the active centres in Cymru the north has been the most difficult. When I went to Dewi in the far West I found a great meeting of minds. Judith had been covering the South from her new base in Caerdydd. Along the borders of Powys there were never many people, but there were pockets of cultivation amongst the scrub and forest. The towns – Builth, Drindod, Drenewydd, Trallwng – seemed to have suffered less than most, and I found the people anxious and disorganized-ready for anything which promised stability.

The north though – the last bastion of Yr Hen Iaith, The Old Language - they were determined to go their own way. There was a bitter division between two factions. One was led by a sort of Cymric Walter Penrose, called Iolo Ap Williams. His followers called themselves the "Pobl y Draig" – People of the Dragon, conducted all their business in a revived form of the old language called Cymraeg Newydd, and wanted nothing to do with the Anglic.

The other was the Council of the North, many of Anglic descent who also wanted their land to be self-governing, but looked for order and peace by negotiation. My first task was to listen. I had by then begun to learn Cymraeg, but was finding it hard going, and as a great concession, the "Pobl" agreed to explain the situation to me in International English (IE). The Council of the North (CoN) were ready to talk in any language and assailed me with horror stories about Iolo Ap.

It did not take me long to realize that Williams was by far the most important person in the region and that unless he was with us he would be bitterly against us, so I arranged a private meeting in Caerafon. I'd been there before, but at that time the Dyfi Bridge was closed so I had to go by sea. It was a long and weary trip made bearable by an overnight stay with the monks on the Isle of Enlli.

To my surprise he was charming. He's young, rather short and muscular, a handsome, passionate man, with long blond hair - impossible to ignore in any gathering. He was then 35 and from what I had read, very influenced by his father Sion who had divided his life between his adopted South Cymru and his work abroad. Sion had lived his life at a time when Cymru was becoming anglicised and his efforts to revive the old language and culture met with a tolerant, good humoured but ultimately ineffectual response. Iolo had moved north in his teens, had learnt the northern variant of old Cymraeg and had even modified his accent in English from his native Gaerfyrthyn lilt to the more sing-song and emphatic northern accent.

"Mr Williams – Shw mae, neis i gwrdd â chi."

"Mr Vandervelde –a fi hefyd. I know however that you are not fluent in our language so I do not wish to put you at such a disadvantage. We will speak our present bastardised form of the old language of the oppressors, in which I have had to become fluent. It is after all the language of Shakespeare, and not without merit."

"Thank you. It is important that we understand each other after all. As you know my organization is trying to establish a basis for good government in this new society we are creating, and I very much want to hear what you would like from us."

"That's easy, we want an independent Cymru, we want

the ancient Celtic nation to re-discover the nationhood it had under Owain Glyndwr; Cymru proud and free to speak our language, to educate our children, to make our own laws, our own police, and most important of all to have our own peacekeeping force – "Braich y Draig", the arm of the dragon."

"That's an exciting concept but as I'm sure you know, Cymru, like most of what remains of the old Britannica has been a mixture of peoples for many years. What figures we have for the population suggests that the percentage of the people left within the old boundaries of Cymru who were born there is quite small – around 25 percent. That's only a little more than the percentage of Cymraeg born you will find in say Swinsdune."

"That may be but I think you will find that many of those who chose to live here are now true supporters of our cause."

"I'm genuinely pleased to hear that, and I'll tell you why in a moment, but there are several other difficulties. I've spent some time studying the history of the nation where I now live, and I know that for geographic reasons as well as cultural, there is a long-standing division between the north and south. Even now, well, especially now, it is more difficult to get from Abertawe to Bangor than it is to get from any part of Cymru to one of the Anglic cities –Elverpwll, Beormasham and Brigstowe."

"Yes yes, indeed that was the case, but things are very different now. None of us want to go back to the old ways. Globalisation is dead, the big nation states are dead, a third of the people are dead for God's sake, and if ever there was a time for the old nations to be born again now is that time. We have many friends in the South. I could go to Ystwyth now and be greeted like a hero. Listen to this."

He leapt to his feet and started declaiming in Cymraeg. I couldn't understand a word but it sounded good.

"Ah my friend, that is poetry. Even Shakespeare could

not do better." There was a silent pause. "My friend; forgive me. I get carried away. You were going to tell me what had pleased you."

"To do so I will have to trust you. Have you heard of a man called Walter Penrose?"

"I have - a fellow Celt. Is he not reviving the Kernowek language?"

"Yes, and much more. I recently went to meet him, and I think you and he should meet too. I have been around for a very long time Mr Williams . . ."

"Please – Iolo"

..."Iolo, and I'm am usually called Van. If there's one thing I have learnt Iolo it is that people will only act effectively if their emotions are involved. It is passion that drives us, and passionate leadership which makes things happen – including many very bad things. It is still puzzling to most of us how ordinary people can be led to the most appalling atrocities by the power of passionate leadership – not yours of course; not all passionate leaders are like Hitler! The truly great leaders are those who can inspire those who disagree with them."

"Van – if this is in any way about me then I have to tell you that I have no desire to cast myself in the role of great leader. I express what I hear around me that is all. I am a mouthpiece if you like."

"I am telling you these things because I think you are a leader who can also be led, who can listen. My authority comes from NRG but I also speak for a number of small organizations working with NRG to create a stable and sustainable society from what remains of the age of oil. I am convinced there is a possibility of creating something larger than old Cymru, something closer to the ancient Celtic kingdoms which according to my research, used to cover half of what became Anglia.

I'm talking about a nation whose principal highway is the water between Kernow and Cymru. I think we can unite the old Celtic nations once more and use their passion to create a truly sustainable society."

******

Oh Judith- what a roller-coaster! I realize now how much emotional effort I had put into keeping my feelings about her in a box with the lid firmly locked down. How cold I must have seemed to her. I was so sure that after Amy I would live a busy life of natural celibacy, and that Judith was no more than a dear friend and colleague. Suddenly everything is different. We have been through peaks of happiness and troughs of sadness and depression, but we are together.

She is not ready to talk about it but I know it has come at a great cost to her. I can only imagine how painful it must have been to give up her child. She will tell me when she is ready – that is her great strength: she is both passionate and strong, perhaps too strong to have made a good mother – but such speculation is pointless. She is happy again - at least some of the time - and we are closer than ever.

CHAPTER 3 2057 - 75

Brother Fraxinus

Plymouth, Atlantic States of America,

November 2057

Troy Cagney was looking out of the window of his small office on the third floor of Plymouth House. He caught a glimpse of the guards pacing up and down, stamping their feet, their breath like steam in the cold air. The temperature had been below freezing now for three weeks, but still no snow. He wasn't complaining about that – strange weather was the norm these days and life was hard enough without having to dig your way in and out every day.

Every few days he checked on the little group of trees he had asked to be planted in the grounds. Hs own tree, *Fraxinus Excelsior*, the Ash, was a fast grower and was already two feet about the others. *Quercus Robur,* the Oak, was slower, and still looked more like a sapling than a tree. The Beech *Fagus Sylvetica*, still held its dark brown fall leaves. *Tilia Platyphyllos,* the broad leafed lime had been difficult to find – he'd had it sent from Europe. Not so the Maple *Acer Platanoides*, a common city tree. In pride of place was the Elm *Ulmus Minor*, and Troy felt a moment of grief when he remembered his colleague Jean-Pierre, the only one of them to fall to the XB1 virus in 44.

For the rest of them the great work went on. Their bond to the Fellowship was absolute; the lives they lived everyday of less importance. Fagus was a sleeper still; waiting for the call in his home village in Bolivia. Tilia and Acer were hidden from the world at the Hub. Occasional highly encrypted messages would reach him to confirm the progress of their work. Quercus, of course, was different.

Troy was not ashamed to admit that he was lonely. His last partner had loved him, but despite his protestations, had come to believe that her love was not reciprocated. Perhaps she had been right. He had no idea if she had survived or not. Here the new ASA (Atlantic States of America) seat of government was a rather masculine environment. When Washington had collapsed all the survivors left as quickly as they could to find somewhere safer. The fear of human contact left over from those years meant relations were now more formal. There was certainly nothing casual about the President, Cyrus Kennedy, a distant relation of the famous Kennedy clan who had so dominated American politics in the mid 20th century.

"Daydreaming again Troy?"

He turned quickly, smiling at the warm voice.

"Hi Amanda, how's the big man?" Amanda was lovely. He couldn't think of anyone he would rather share his life with but of course she was out of his league – too young too talented and too beautiful. Why she was still single he had no idea.

"Not good. He's very worried about the situation in the south."

"What's the latest?"

"The CKA (Christ's Kingdom of America) are calling for volunteers to set up mission stations along the border, and send missionaries here to 'convert the godless'."

"I thought that was coming. It's quite clever because we can't refuse entry to them without compromising our 'free-to-believe' commitment."

"That's it. Cyrus wants to check them all for arms at the border, but we don't have the staff to do that properly. Can you go and speak to him?"

"Sure – leave it with me".

Troy put his head in his hands thinking. "How did this

once great nation get into such a state?

Letter from Walter Penrose

International Letter

Sender: Walter T Penrose

Address……

Dear Van,

I'm in despair. You would not believe these people – idiots, cretins all of them. Meibion Kernow indeed! Who do they think they are? After all the work I have done to bring our little nation together they want to tear it apart. They sent me a letter – illegible illiterate scrawl more like, full of capital letters. "WE DEMAND" this and "WE DEMAND" that. They want me to pledge an oath of loyalty to their so called leader, this "Bran Vras" as he calls himself. It's not even original. I have been across the water and I know there is a gang leader with the same name – Raven - in Caerdydd.

They are threatening me with "reprisals" if I do not "obey".

I'm at my wits end. What shall I do?

Walter

Vandervelde: The Gangs

I should have taken more heed to what Judith was saying about the troubles in Caerdydd. Things were going well and we'd been lulled into a false sense of security. It started with a nasty little spate of gang killings in Brigstowe. There had been a trickle of pleas for help from the cities for a while but the Defence Forces seemed to have things under control. Now, quite suddenly, the trickle had become a flood. It was time to do what we always hoped to avoid – send out the amber alert to all NRG groups.

Command centres had been established behind the scenes in the area we were already calling Cambria, and the ops centre was to be at Plas Dyfi – well away from the old cities and easily defended. Each command centre had a group of peacekeepers – few in number but highly trained in combat.

As soon as the alert was issued the reports started coming in. In the north the Braich Y Draig were armed but had been in discussions with our people. The report from Caernarfon was positive. They felt the Pobl would support our peacekeepers. Abertawe reported a number of gangs active in the area but fighting amongst themselves and with no credible leader. Walter's group were now working with our people in Kernow and sent more details of the threat posed by the Bran Vras.

The most worrying reports came from Caerdydd and Brigstowe. In Caerdydd the Ravens ruled the gangs and had become very powerful. The City Council could no longer be trusted, and our staff there were so concerned for their safety that they were moving out of the city.

In Brigstowe the Dreads were locked in what can only be described as a war with a vicious gang from the south of the city. Although St. Peters was now a racially mixed area, and many of the Dreads had light skin, the "Men of Brigstowe" were a different matter. They had resurrected the long outdated symbolism of the old "skinheads", last seen in the 20 hundreds. Unashamedly white supremacist in outlook, they were a serious threat.

The Dreads were changing too – the old symbols of the cannabis plant and the dreadlocks was giving way to more openly racist symbols – the black fist and the lightning bolt.

The Harbourers had armed themselves and were following our code, but the war zone, centred on the old transtation was moving towards the haven. They were in great danger and needed help. We issued a Situation Red alert.

Combined Defence Forces Deployment

1: Brigstowe Unit Report May 2062

Tuesday

When we received the Situation Red code my unit was in defensive positions surrounding the Harbourers area. Our scouts had been in six observation positions through the conflict zone and identified three residential areas (shown in map1) at risk.

At 05:00 hours we deployed three troops of 50 men to take up defensive positions round these areas. In areas One and Two our troops managed to take up their positions unchallenged but in area Three there was a brief exchange of fire with a number of unidentifiable individuals, one of whom was injured and captured. One of our men was badly injured and given emergency treatment. The captured man has been identified as Geoffrey Talbot of North St. Greencliff. He had an arm band with the insignia of the so-called Men of Brigstowe.

At around 08:00, when it was fully light, the troop deployed in area 1 came under from fire from a group of insurgents carrying a flag with the Dread insignia. Two were killed and eight injured before they retreated. The injured men were treated and taken into custody. Our troops maintained defensive positions until 9:45 when they became aware of people shouting in the residential areas they had surrounded. These grew in volume as more residents joined in, until the noise resolved itself into a single repeated shout: "Gangs Out". Some 10 minutes later they saw a large group of residents marching towards them, all shouting the same chant. When they reached the first of our troop they stopped and the chant changed to "Defence Force In"

Their leaders explained to Corporal Jones who was in charge in area 1 that they had been too frightened until then to challenge the gangs. A similar pattern of behaviour occurred in the other two areas. A great deal of help and support was offered to our troops, and by the end of the day it appeared that the threat of further conflict had receded.

Thursday

Our troops have consolidated defensive outposts in collaboration with the residents in all three areas. There has been a steady trickle of gang members from both sides surrendering their arms and asking to join our force.

2: Caerdydd Unit Report

Tuesday

When we received the Situation Red alert we decided that there was nothing to be gained by any kind of defensive action. Accordingly we deployed all 130 men in a single operation to surround and disarm the Ravens gang. It took us two hours to get into position in the dark. We had identified eight residents who were willing to help us and by 8:00 we had managed to get small groups of eight to ten men infiltrated into these houses.

The residents had told us that the Ravens sent out patrols every morning at 8:30 so as soon as the patrols were clearly visible we attacked. With surprise on our side we were able to disarm three groups of Ravens quickly, but several had escaped and the remaining gang patrols retreated to their defence positions.

Before they had time to co-ordinate we launched a frontal attack and after a sustained exchange of fire with losses on both sides, our troops gained the upper hand. When this became clear the local residents helped us to round up the remaining gang members. Unfortunately their leader, the so called Raven, was not among the captured.

Wednesday

It is with great sadness that we record the loss of three men. The names will be released as soon as the families have been informed. Two of the gang members were also killed. Six of our troop, and 18 of the gang members have sustained serious injuries and are being treated.

The citizens of Caerdydd have taken to the streets in large numbers to show their support of our action and have promised civic funerals with full honours for the fallen.

3: Pennsans Unit Report

Since the NRG Kernow forces amalgamated with the "Cambria" faction in the Meibion Kernow only recently, we were not as well prepared as other areas when the Red Alert was announced. Several former members of the Meibion were reluctant to inform on their former comrades, and since gang activity was at a lower level than in other areas, the decision was made at area command not to deploy into attack positions, but to strengthen our existing defence posts.

Since the news of the successful deployments in Brigstowe and Caerdydd reached us we have had very many messages of support from citizens groups who are now determined to defend their homes and not allow the gangs to extend their activities.

We wish to congratulate the Combined Defence Force command on their successful actions and express our confidence that the joint recommendations will enable the Kernow area to achieve non-conflict status in the very near future.

Joint recommendation:

- Immediate recruitment and training to be offered to the public in any areas where gangs are active.
- An enlarged defence force for the proposed Cambria area should be placed under area command.
- All existing police forces should be disbanded and a new force established as quickly as possible, this force to be placed under the same command as the defence forces.
- A publicity campaign to be launched to advertise the success of our actions and encourage citizens to become involved with the policing and defence of our streets.

Vandervelde: A New Nation

An uneasy peace had been restored. Most of the gang leaders were in temporary prisons. There were reports of much worse violence from other parts, but all across the Britannic Isles there was a great desire for peace and stability. Every week we had visitors from the other regions telling us what was happening. Borders were being drawn up and constitutions discussed. It was made clear to us early on that the West Midlands would keep their umbilical cord to what remains of Lyndain. They were friendly but preferred to look east.

Here we had widespread agreement on the link between Cymru and Kernow, and the lands along the Havren estuary were keen to join us. I had to get up to speed on the history of these places, and was intrigued to discover that this linking followed part of a very ancient boundary – that dividing the old Saxon kingdoms of Mercia and Wessex. It was more difficult to decide where to draw our boundary to the south and east of Brigstowe. Would Swinsdune and Wiltonshire want to join us? Suthamtun and Havensmouth would join Lyndain, but what about Bromdun? We had spent months working out the details and trying out the concepts with focus groups. In the end we decided we would have to meet, but the who, where and when took more months to decide.

******

Finally it happened. We brought all those groups together in the territory of the Harbourers in Brigstowe. It's central, easy to get to by water and was as safe as any urban area in our region.

We were in the main hall of the old Council House, and from my somewhat elevated seat I could see many faces I recognise in the group of delegates facing me. Walter of course stood out, as did Iolo, but Twm was looking smart for a change – blending in. I had to make the introductory speech – a really important one and I was nervous.

"My friends, welcome. We are here because we can all agree on a few central concepts. These are:

- That the old Nation State of Britannica is no longer relevant to our present circumstances.
- That the sea links between Cymru and Kernow are of vital importance.
- That the ancient kingdom of Wessex forms an essential geographic link between them.
- That we wish to form a single government to administer this area.
- That the aim of this government will be to create a peaceful, stable and above all sustainable society.

That is the position we start with. That's the easy bit. We now come to the contentious part. As you can see on your comms units and the screen behind me we have a very big agenda, but it divides easily into three parts:

1. Where do we draw our southern boundary?

2. How are we to choose our government?

3. Where will the centre of government be?

The first item we will deal with today, and we have all agreed to keep talking until we have a boundary.

In case our discussions today get prolonged we have scheduled tomorrow, Sunday, as a rest day. If any of you decide you do not wish to join our Nation then you are free to go, or you are welcome to stay as observers. On Monday and Tuesday we will discuss the other two items.

Representatives from Swinsdune, Sarum, Dorceaster Bridhaven and Yeosdun will address us this morning, but before I ask them to give us their thoughts let me tell you what I know about the only other alternative nation on offer.

It calls itself Anglia after the old Saxon region to the north east of Lyndain. There are many people in that region who like to talk of Lyndain as if it were still a great city, but the contacts I still have say it is more like a collection of small towns. Many of the areas by the river are so prone to flooding that they have become more like parks or nature reserves with decaying buildings in them.

Evidently, having discovered a real Prince among the survivors, they have decided to set up a monarchy. The Prince is Michael, son of Harry, the former Prince of Cymru, and grandson of the late King Charles. They have chosen the old royal seat of Wincaster as their base, and are claiming to be the true heart of Anglia.

We do not know yet what form of constitution they will chose, but I have a trusted source who tells me that they are going for a very limited form of democracy with enhanced powers for their King.

This then is your choice – to the West an untried liaison, a perhaps rather idealistic joining of the ancient heartlands of the Brythonic Celts. If you like your historical links then look to the many ancient alliances between the Celts and the Saxons of Wessex. If all this sounds like romantic twaddle then look no further than geography. Cymru could stand alone but has no natural geographic links between north and south. Kernow is isolated, but now has good sea links with Cymru and Brigstowe, and that city is still the pivot round which transportation flows. The constitution is not yet agreed but it will be government by the people for the people.

To the East is a known quantity - the old heartland of Anglia and the one-time Britannic capital. The monarchy will give continuity with the pre-44 period, but it may not be a full democracy.

I will now introduce your speakers."

The speeches were all recorded, but most of them were too boring to write down here. The delegate from Swinsdune put quite succinctly the quandary they all faced:

"My name is Jake Phlippance and I live in Wansburgh in the borough of Swinsdune. I represent a group called Citizens for Peace which is the largest group on the recently established Outer Swinsdune Council. As you can tell, our main concern is stability. Like many of you in this room, we have been through hell – several hells. On a local scale we've lived through plague, famine and war. Even now the centre of our wretched town is a no-go area run by thugs. We are past caring what flavour of government we have; what we pray for – those of us who still can – is order: troops we can trust, police we can trust, some sort of judiciary which will bring us justice for all the crimes we have suffered. At present we have none of those things. Our police openly ask for bribes. The remains of the Emergency Force are drunk half the time. The hospital is run by a cartel of business people who take a huge charge on your comms before you can even get in, let alone get treated.

Looking at the choice you have presented us with, I do honestly respect you people in Cymru and Kernow, and I've heard about your plans for a different style of government. It's completely untried, but my head tells me it could offer a better future. On the other hand my heart tells me that a new monarchy with real clout has a much better chance of getting us out of this mess quickly.

We have taken soundings from most of the towns and districts in the old county of Wiltunshire and found to nobody's surprise that there is a lot of ignorance and confusion out there. All we can do is take a democratic vote from the representatives we are in direct touch with. We will do that now and hope to have an answer for you at the end of the day. Thank you"

Sarum had fared better. The gangs had left them alone with their empty houses and weed-strewn streets. They had a degree of order already and tended to go with the Anglian argument.

The speaker from Yoesdun, Kevin Thornton, was from a group representing the small towns across the old counties of Bromdun and Sumorsaet. The only city in their area was Pul, and it was clear that what was left of its citizens would not want to be cut off from its larger neighbour Beornmuth which had already decided to join Anglia. The small towns were less concerned with security but very concerned for their traditional way of life. They had always looked east for government and felt alienated by the sheer un-anglic quality of our new nation. This is how he put it in his broad local accent:

"My great grandfather died for King and Country. That sounds very old-fangled now, but it still has a bit of a ring to it don't it? I'm 60 now and I's seen it all. We was brought up to have a bit of respect to our King – good old Charlie, bless him he meant well. This Michael looks to have a bit of sense about him – better than his Dad anyways. So what if he has got a bit too much power, better than not enough I say. I vote we just stop all this arguing, leave all these taffs to get on with whatever they want to do over there and stick with the old ways. There was peace and plenty in them days. God Save the King!"

There was a lot more arguing, but the consensus was clear. Both Wiltunshire and Bromdun would go with Anglia. Defnas had already decided to throw in their lot with us. At this point the old county boundaries began to be a problem. All the coastal areas of Somerset were keen to be part of Cambria, but there was no clear dividing line inland and to the south.

We finally called a halt at 10 in the evening and I summed up our agreement:

"Delegates, you will be pleased to know that we have a draft agreement. I want to make clear at this point that we are talking in terms of the old county boundaries. In most cases these have little current meaning. We are using them for convenience until new districts can be set up.

So, the whole of the old county of Wiltunshire will join Anglia. All of Defnas, except the coastal area around Bridhaven, will join Cambria. All of Bromdun except the coastal area to the west of Weymuth will join Anglia. Most of Sumorsaet will join Cambria.

We have formed a boundary committee to decide on the disputed areas. The main objective of this meeting is to bring order and peace. The task is urgent. These divisions must be established quickly before a power vacuum is created. Accordingly we will designate these areas as under joint control for a period of four months while the Boundary Committee is at work.

I think I can say without fear of contradiction that decisions like these could not have been made so quickly even ten years ago.

There is a new spirit abroad – a hatred of ideology. We are all agreed that we have to do better in the future, and we have to start now. Thank you all for your patience. Let's get some sleep!"

******

On the Monday I had to speak again, but it felt different. We were all together now, committed to the concept of Cambria.

"Ladies and Gentlemen" . . . (I like my dramatic pauses.)

"Democracy has failed . . . The great 20th century ideals of universal suffrage, political parties, republics, constitutional monarchies . . . all these have failed to deliver."

To my surprise there was a fair amount of agreement evident from the cries of "hear hear" - though there were a few shouts of "shame".

"They failed for the same reason that autocratic societies failed: to achieve power you had to offer bribes. In autocratic societies it was the chiefs, kings, queens and warlords who offered land and influence to their friends and relatives. In the democracies the party chiefs offered more buying power to the electors, and the only way they could deliver was by stoking up endless consumer cycles of growth and collapse. At least under the autocracies the benefits on offer were quite long term. In the democracies you had to offer money in your pocket now, better times next year, or at the most a real benefit in a few year's time. To get elected you had to have influence. If you wanted something to change, you - the business person or pressure group - had to be able to influence the politicians, and so the great lobbying industry developed. Economic growth was the only thing that kept the system going, and that led ultimately to the catastrophe of 44.

"We have to do better. My team and I spent 6 years underground working out why we had failed and how we could do better. What we wanted was a system of government in which every person could participate equally. It had to be a system in which the representatives of those people were not influenced by any pressure group or lobby. Those chosen to govern had to be able to make long term decisions without the constant fear of losing power, and they had to be amongst the most able in the country.

"That's a very tall order.

"How do we choose a few from a multitude? History records several methods. We can chose by heredity – the offspring of those in power assume power by birthright. We can choose by lot – one person draws the long straw. We can choose by election – we vote for the people we like. We can allow the most powerful to assume control. Variations on these methods have determined most of the governments in our history.

"Of all these there is only one which is capable of producing a random and therefore representative sample of the people and that is the one which has for centuries been used in Britannica to choose the twelve good men (or women) and true who decide whether someone accused of a crime is guilty or innocent – the Jury. Actually those twelve may not be good and true. They could all be criminals, or all captains of industry. That is the nature of chance.

"Simply to replace assembly elections with a group of citizens chosen at random from the population would have some obvious disadvantages, the main one being that there is no way of knowing whether any of them have the skills and knowledge to govern. However, as the basis of government it has been tried - twice: once in the Venetian republic, and once in ancient Greece. In both cases it was used in combination with voting. It even has a name: Demarchy, and it is a demarchic system which I want to suggest to you today as being the best way of choosing those who will govern our new nation.

"In the Athenian democracy, the first process was an election to choose an assembly. Its officials were then chosen by sortition. We are all familiar with the model of a large group – a Parliament or Assembly, and a smaller group – a Senate or Cabinet. In a demarchic system one of those would be chosen by lot and the other by election.

"In the Venetian Republic they apparently had several layers of alternate elections and sortitions. Whichever way you do it, by introducing the principle of random selection you undermine the power of the career politicians and those who lobby them for their own self-interest. To stimulate discussion NRG have produced two draft proposals for you to consider, as you can see on your screens now.

"At this point I can see several of you looking, how shall I say, pregnant with questions, so please indicate now if you have a question and I will try to answer the first three before we adjourn for the focus groups.

"You mistress, on the right. Please introduce yourself."

"Thank you. I am Lily Tremaine from Falmouth. If I

understand you right Mr Vandervelde what you are suggesting would mean the end of universal suffrage. Only a select few would have the right to vote. My ancestors fought a long struggle to gain this simple human right, the power to change our government, and you are proposing to do away with it at a stroke."

There was a lot of noise, cries of "hear hear" and "shame."

"Yes, the sortition/election form of Demarchy would not depend on a popular vote. Remember though that it was the popular vote that delivered us the great corporations, the engines of economic growth, the oil bonanza. We should not make it a sacred cow.

"Sir in the centre of the hall, yes."

"Don't call me Sir, MR Vandervelde. I'm not one of your smart-arse toffs. I am Jack Gordon, Brigstowe born and Brigstowe bred. What I want to know is this: does this proposal mean we won't have to put up with the great monster quango Northern Resources telling us all what to do? Can we finally get shot of NRG? If so I'm all in favour" Laughter and shouts of "shame".

"OK Jack, that would be for you to decide. I sincerely hope that with proper government there would be no need for such a body. I would dearly love to spend more time at home.

"Now, last question – you . . . er mister." Loud laughter.

"Thank you. Emrys Hughes from Caernafon. This seems to me an inordinately complicated system. One person one vote is clean and simple. The problem was it was abused. There are many different voting systems and some of them have worked very well. I think we are in great danger of throwing the baby out with the bathwater so to speak."

It didn't feel like a historic occasion, but that was the point when Demarchy made its first appearance in the politics of the Britannic Isles. I went on to introduce the other speakers. A lady from Kammbronn spoke first.

"Dydh da. Unlike some of you, most of us in Kernow have come to have great respect for Mr. Vandervelde and would be very sorry to lose his depth of experience and wisdom. We have become convinced by the arguments in favour of Demarchy but would like to propose a different system which I believe will answer some of the problems thrown up by the discussion.

"Our proposal is this: we retain universal suffrage. Everybody is required by law to vote, but not for candidates from some distant party office, but for people they know in their own communities. Our regions would be divided into parishes or hundreds, each of around 500 people. The entire parish would be asked to nominate 10 candidates and we would select three of them by popular vote to be our representative on the Great Assembly. At this stage I cannot say how many people would be elected to the great Assembly, but let's say there are 2000 people elected by popular vote. If that assembly were then to elect their leaders we would be back to the old corrupt short-term system of lobbying and influence. If nobody knows in advance who might be selected from these 2000 representatives then nobody can influence them in advance. It is the Great Assembly who would select by a lottery of their members the smaller number – say 300 - who would constitute the Senate or governing body.

"These 300 will all have been drawn from those selected by the popular vote, and we believe they would truly represent the people."

******

I'm writing this at my desk at Plas Dyfi . I feel that perhaps the worst of the storms are over and we are now sailing into calmer waters.

Looking back on my old diary entries It's interesting to compare my description of the house at Downend with this one. For years after 44 we had no online communications, and much of the old hardware was scrapped or just left around. One of the first things NRG did when we had a skeleton staff up and running was to secure a number of industrial buildings as repositories where we could store comms equipment at controlled temperature and humidity. As soon as a few of the servers came back online we were able to set up our own Net, and now I am again able to work at home. Such was our obsession with energy efficiency before 44 that we were able to adapt many of the screens to run on our rudimentary power system.

The Net is able to deliver an average of 100 watts per household, and although the Plas is a big house we have no special privileges. We do however have quite substantial generating resources of our own. We seem to be in a hot, stormy phase of weather now, and have managed to rescue 10 m2 of decent pv solar panels so we get plenty of power from them when the sun shines. When the wind and rain are raging we have our wind generator, and a small amount of pumped water storage.

Alas we have run out of batteries. For the first few years we were able to store power using up all the old abandoned battery systems, but eventually they could no longer be charged. NRG have huge stores of old batteries which we are now breaking up for the materials, but the few battery factories which have started to re-use them can't produce anything like the numbers needed to store more than a few amps.

This is my work screen. If I run my hands over it you can see that there are blank patches, but I can access various stores of books and videos and write letters. There is, as yet, no online video or voice, so all our communication is by text, but we can enter text using voice; I still prefer typing!

Judith has come to stay. I'm feeling excited but also a bit

apprehensive. We've been together several times since that wonderful day in Caerdydd, but by mutual agreement have kept quiet about our relationship. The time has never quite felt right to make sure she understands about the ageing thing. To be the lover of someone like me is a burden. Not only is she linking up with someone much older, but has to face a future in which she will eventually look and feel older than her "older man". Amy put it well in a letter years ago:

"I could start with an older man and end up with a toy-boy"

Then there's Mollie. We have been working together for most of her adult life, but 44 has changed her. What before was an easy-going professional relationship based on absolute trust and real friendship has changed into something more tense, more argumentative, emotional. She rails at me for being so "cold" but bursts into tears if I try to comfort her. I have a nasty feeling this may have something to do with my relationship with Judith.

******

I have to admit I've become somewhat obsessed with all this constitution stuff. At any rate that is my excuse for failing to appreciate a really important development that had been going on right under my nose without me realising.

Cambria has become a trading nation. I recall noticing the big changes to the harbour at Ystwyth when I was there a few years ago, and I've written a fair bit about the haven in Brigstowe. What I didn't know was that the harbour in Porth La has developed at least as rapidly. I've now had a chance to look at the figures and they are impressive. Before I get into detail I'd better explain the financial system we managed to cobble together in our underground fortress.

In 2040 we had two main trading currencies, the Euro and the Singapore dollar. In addition there had been an explosive growth in citizen's banks – organisations that connected those needing to borrow on a peer-to-peer basis with those wishing to lend. Within the movement a multitude of local currencies had sprung up, mostly based on exchange of non-monetary goods and services.

When everything collapsed the citizen's banks were the only resource for any kind of trade. The hundreds of ships plying the waters of the Havren estuary and the Hibernian Sea were using a mixture of Euros and local "pounds". By one of those odd turns of fate the three ports made an ad-hoc decision to use one of these exchange units, the so called Brigstowe Pound.

Kernow was the worst affected region when tourism collapsed in 44. They had virtually no industry and precious few people, (at least in the winter) but they did have boats. The fishery had begun to recover by the mid thirties, so a few of the old fishing boats managed to keep fishing, but many of them were converted to traders and began searching further afield for goods to trade. The collapse of the container trade had opened up markets which we all thought had died a hundred years ago. Scandinavia, Iberia, West Africa, all these old trade routes began to open up.

Then Abertawe got in on the act. By the late 40s they had seen off the gangs, and there were still some high-tech engineering factories in good condition. It was not long before the now familiar mini-containers were coming off the new, small-scale production lines.

So now we have four international ports – Porth La, Brigstowe, Abertawe and Ystwyth, and what is the currency they are all trading in? The Brigstowe Pound!

Judith: Netlog

El Sabio

Hello Netlog. Sorry I've neglected you. I did not feel I could write it all down – it seemed like some sort of betrayal of my feelings. I'm fine now. OK I have a scar, but I can live with it. Van has been a great support and Magnus seemed to understand that his place in all this is in the background. I can't afford to feel sorry for him too.

So, big day today – what I'm writing now will be ignored by far more people than it used to be! We now have a partial international Net. It's nothing like the Net we used to have before 44, but it's a start. I can now access news from places I haven't heard from in years, and more importantly at the moment some extraordinary news from not so far away: Iberia. It seems that a man calling himself "El Sabio" is expected to arrive in Spain from Bolivia and there is great excitement brewing.

This person claims to have had a series of visions which have shown him the way to bring peace and prosperity to all our struggling post-44 societies. It seems he comes from a small mountain village which was completely cut off in 44. They had a long tradition of fending for themselves so managed to carry on regardless. The last they had heard from their government was the Emergency Regulations. They knew nothing of the White Death until this year when the first traveller arrived from outside. The villagers immediately locked him up for what they had been told was the quarantine period and then took him to see their "Alcalde" – the Mayor. When they had been talking for a while the stranger realized with a shock that the Alcalde knew almost as much about what was happening as he did. At the same time the Mayor admitted that the awful visions which had plagued him for several years represented actual happenings in the world outside. Within days stories began collecting around him and the villagers renamed their Mayor "El Sabio."

OK, we've heard it all before – another prophet, another cult. I have to say though that there is something about this one that doesn't fit the usual cult leader profile. For one thing, since he began travelling, he has depended for his existence on charity from those around him. That's part of the Hindu tradition I think, but suggests someone like Gandhi rather than a fraud. What especially struck me was the name – El Sabio. It translates as The Wise One, or The Sapient. I'd heard that name before somewhere but couldn't remember where. It must have seemed important at the time because it keeps going round in my brain – "The Sapient, The Wise One, The Thinker". I'm sure it has something to do with Van. Hey ho, perhaps my subconscious will dredge it up one day.

******

I've been working with Mollie lately, and spent a fair bit of my free time talking to Eldred. I can now understand him pretty well, and his speech is definitely improving. We've both learnt finger spelling and a repertoire of signs to give extra meaning to the speech sounds.

One evening I was sitting with him in his "office". After Operation Overground, Mollie and Eldred decided that their old home in York Road, besides being trashed, was not safe enough, especially in view of Eldred's disability, so they abandoned it. His old warehouse studio was protected within the territory of the Harbourers and he still owned it so they decided to make a home there. There was plenty of space but only the big studio room was insulated, and that not well enough for cold winters. The rest was just empty warehouse so they put in some heavily insulated partitions and created a snug apartment with a large kitchen, bathroom, two bedrooms and the office. He insisted that he would be in business again soon so needed an office. Even if he was fit he wouldn't find many takers for his art at present, but I have faith in him. There's little doubt that part of his brain is gone. He finds co-ordination difficult and forgets things easily, but in lateral thinking he is extraordinary.

Whenever Van has a difficult problem he takes it to Eldred. He told me he has often come out of Eldred's study with something radically different from what he went in with.

Anyway, there I was "chatting" with Eldred when to my surprise he mentioned "Jamie". "Ask her Jamie . . . bout."

"Who's Jamie"

"Ruther, he's his bother, brother."

"Brother? What are you talking about, she hasn't got a brother."

"Has . . . jst doesn't speech bout her . . . him. Aks her."

Well, that was clear enough so next time I saw Mollie I did. It was in Caerdydd. Even before they were defeated I had fallen out with the Ravens, and security was still a big problem, so like E & E I had moved to a safer place – the small NRG compound in the city centre. I was lucky enough to get one of the bigger flats available. The big problem with housing now is not lack of space – buildings are dirt cheap – but lack of new materials and above all lack of skills. Our building had been comprehensively restored in the 30s and apart from a few broken windows had survived untouched. So, I had some large warm spaces and plenty of old furniture. I was lucky. No sooner had I moved of course than the Defence Force moved in and disarmed the Ravens, but it's still much better here.

We were sitting in two of my lumpy old arm chairs drinking some of the local home-brewed wine which I had found on a street stall. It wasn't a patch on the real thing but quite drinkable.

"Mollie – something I've been meaning to ask you about. Eldred says you have a brother but I've never heard you mention him."

She visibly shrank; paused for a few seconds; took a slug of wine and then looked up.

"Yes, it's true. Somewhere I have a brother."

"Oh I'm sorry love I didn't mean to upset you."

"It's OK. It's time you knew about him anyway." She paused, handed the glass to me for a refill. "Thanks. Oh how I miss my Pinot Grigio" She took a drink, grimaced and then said:

"It's a long story – Van knows. I'm surprised he hasn't told you."

"Oh you know Van – never volunteer information."

"Yes, you're right there. Well the gist of it is that Jamie and Eldred had a horrible row. Of course I had to support Eldred, but I don't think Jamie has ever forgiven me. I've tried several times to get in touch. We were very close when we were young."

"That's his name - Jamie?"

"Yes - Sir James Jarman no less."

"Wow – how did he get the knighthood."

"Oh he did some amazing work on the development of the Smart Net. His company developed a special kind of cable – I won't bore you with the details."

"Where is he now, do you know?"

"He was in France before 44, but I did hear a rumour that he was alive and back in Britannica."

I didn't press her and we sat in silence for a few minutes.

"Well you know" I said "Perhaps there is another story. Time as they say is a great healer. I have a gut feeling that you will be seeing him again."

At that point I made a quiet resolve to track down this elusive brother and see if I could bring them together again.

******

For the last year it's been an endless round of meetings with all sorts of factions in Caerdydd and the Valleys. It's been really hard work getting some of them to see the benefits of Van's plan. Some of the groups, mainly in the city and the new industrial areas, but also in the old farming areas have been really enthusiastic. It's just the old valleys communities who have always resisted change that I have most difficulty with.

Anyway, we've got a consensus at last and Van is frantically trying to get everyone together for a constitutional forum.

I was in Cwm Ebbw one evening and got chatting to someone called Jarman. It's not a very common name so I asked if she had heard of Sir James Jarman. To my astonishment she had. It seems she used to work for his company, Cable Networks Ltd."

"Oo – that Jamie. He was a one. All the girls used to perk up when he came on his rounds. He used to chat to me 'cause of 'aving the same name, though we're not reelated. Just as well, I'd have been up for it if he'd asked" – great gale of laughter.

"He used to spend most of his time in France, but the last I yerd of 'im he was back in Britannica – not sure where. I yerd a rumour that all his famly had died in 44 – kids an all, and he'd gone to bits."

"Any idea where he used to live? I'd really like to try and

find him."

"Ah I bet you would dear! Now let me think. He said something about getting away from Brigstowe and comin' over the bridge. 'The Lodge' that was it, a house called The Lodge, or something lodge, but I dunno where."

"Ah well, thank you very much. If I find him I'll let you know."

"Thanks dear that would be nice. Ta-ra then"

The Lodge . . . that suggested a gatehouse, the entrance to an estate, or perhaps a hunting lodge. Over the next few months I started searching on my comms screen for places called lodge. There were thousands of them. It was likely to be somewhere on this side of the Havren, but that didn't narrow it down much. I looked up Cable Network and found they used to have offices in Brigstowe and Caerdydd and factories in France and Cwm Ebbw. From whatever searches I could do there seemed to be little evidence of his presence in any of those places so I assume that he spent most of his time in France. There was no record of any activity since 44.

Why had he come back? I'd found out that he was quite a controversial figure in France, with some mention of a scandal. Perhaps he was trying to hide from something – hide from Mollie perhaps? My eye wandered again over the map and rested on Stowe Forest. Why not? I began a detailed search, and that was where I eventually found him: deep in the forest near Parkend.

There was the sign - "Forest Lodge, Private Road, no admittance" Very friendly. Undeterred I drove down it in my little e-car. The sign looked quite modest. So did the track. When I finally got to the end of it there was a simple pole across the way and to the side a new looking security terminal. I stood in front of it and it asked me who I was:

"Judith Evans"

"Please state your business Judith"

"I would like to speak to Sir James Jarman"

"Please indicate what you would like to speak to him about"

"It's about his sister, Mollie Edmundson" There was a long pause and then the pole began to rise.

"Please enter. James will meet you."

I drove up to a parking space, and as I got out I saw a scruffy looking man in old clothes walking up towards me.

"Good morning, I've come to see Sir James."

"Ah, so you have. You're Mollie's friend. I've seen pictures of you. Jamie Jarman" He extended his hand. "I knew you were looking for me so I'm not surprised to see you. I've had some . . . difficulties these last few years . . . you know . . . the house isn't as tidy as I would like. I bought this place for cash as insurance when things started to look tricky in the 30s. Glad I did – everything else has gone . . . everything."

"Yes, I understand you had a pretty flourishing business before that – cables?"

"Well yes and a few other things. We developed a material that made the smart grid work as it does – or did. I don't know what's happening now."

"Wow – that's amazing. The Net is down in many places, but the places I know about where order has been restored – they've been able to get parts of the net going again, so it must have been pretty well designed in the first place."

"Hm. Thanks"

We were walking uphill slightly and ahead of us was a green mound with trees which seemed to be growing from a lower level in the middle of it. In front of it was what looked like a hut of some kind with a large, sturdy door in the middle of it. The door opened as we approached and showed a passage leading downwards.

Once in the passage we could see daylight coming from further down and after about 20 metres we came out into an open space with trees in it. All around the edges was a verandah with a translucent material forming the roof. Behind that were stone walls with windows and doors.

"Duw" I said "This is just amazing. I love it. So the actual house is underground?"

"Yes, a friend of mine designed it. He's gone now. They've all gone, even Ulm the Sap . . . They've all gone. This place is some compensation for all that. We, the family, used to use it for week-ends and holidays. If only we had been here in 44."

He paused and looked up at the sky. "Oh no, I knew better. I was so busy all the time doing business stuff I forgot to protect the thing which mattered more to me than anything – my family."

"Ah Sir James,"

"Jamie please. I've no time for all that status business now."

"Jamie – I lost . . . well, I lost a very dear husband and several of my closest friends."

As so often happens in these days of mutual sorrow, we joined hands in a gesture of understanding. We walked round the sunken courtyard in silence for a few minutes, then sat on a bench in dappled shade.

"Tell me about Mollie. Does she still hate me?"

"I only found out about you fairly recently and she hasn't said much, but I'm sure she does not hate you. Did you hear what happened to Eldred?"

"Don't expect me to weep for him – I couldn't stand him; arrogant bastard."

I stifled a flash of anger. Who was the more arrogant

back then I wonder?

"He's not dead. He was one of the very few who got sick but survived. His brain is damaged and his co-ordination and speech are pretty poor but in other ways he's brilliant. I certainly don't think you would find him arrogant now."

"Hm . . . maybe. So what's Mollie doing now? The last I heard she was working for another arrogant bastard – that Dutchman Vandervelde."

This time I couldn't suppress a sharp response.

"Firstly he's not Dutch and secondly he is one of the most extraordinary men I have ever met. He only appears to be arrogant because he can actually get things done – in a big way."

"Woops – looks like I'm treading on someone's toes. Sorry"

"I hope you will rethink your opinion because Mollie is pretty much his right-hand woman."

"What?..She hasn't gone and married him has she? He's ancient."

"No, no – she is one of the key members of his inner team at NRG – I take it you have heard of NRG?"

"Ooh Yes. I know a lot more about them than you might think, a lot more. Look all that's in the past now. I am pleased to see you, but why are you here? What do you want from me? Women like you used to approach me all the time. Ha. Wouldn't be any good to you in that department now." He laughed

"Now who's the arrogant one?" I laughed.

"Judith I've nothing to be arrogant about believe me. I'm ashamed of my past, don't like the present and dread the future. Lowly enough for you?"

I nodded. I thought we understood each other.

"What do I want? I'm not sure now. I suppose I would like you and Mollie to be friends again."

"No. I don't think so. I would disappoint her, and I don't want anything to do with NRG or any of its ramifications."

"Can I give her a message. I'm very sure she still cares for you." He thought for a while.

"Yes, you can tell her that I was looking out for her all the way through. I was never supposed to tell her that, but it doesn't matter now. Yes, tell her that."

"Jamie, I will. It's been a pleasure meeting you and I'm not sure I would have liked the old Sir James as much."

He laughed, we shook hands and I left his hideout feeling very shaky.

Vandervelde: A New Nation

Transcript: Meeting of the Constitutional Forum

Chairman Derek Sheppard

Good morning and welcome to the first meeting of the new Constitutional Forum. Personally I've never done anything like this before so please don't kill me if I get the protocol wrong.

Following the resolutions of the first Cambrian Assembly, the following persons are charged with producing a Draft Constitution for the new Nation of Cambria, namely:

Walter Penrose

Vandervelde

Iolo Ap Williams

Judith Evans

Aldus Trewenna

Derek Sheppard

(DS) - The first thing I wish to make clear is that whatever draft constitution we decide on today will cease to exist once the bodies we propose have been selected and are operational. You could say that this job has a built-in self-destruct mechanism! The first task of the new bodies will be to ratify a new constitution.

Can I ask Van to present the census figures?

(V) The last accurate population figures for all the regions which make up our new nation come from 2038. That showed a population of 3.2 million in Cymru, 0.75 m in Brigstowe, 1.1 m in Defnas, 0.75 m in Kernow, and 0.3m in Sumorsaet, giving an approximate total of 6.1 million. Taking what we know of average death rates in 44/45 we estimate a current population of around 4 million.

In order to begin the process of government we have divided the nation into five regions each with comparable weight. The smallest in terms of population is the greater Brigstowe area with around 0.75 million, then Cymru North with 0.9m, Kernow including the old county of Defnas with 1.1 and Cymru South with 1.25"

(DS) Thank you Van. I now call on Aldus Trewenna to outline our proposed constitution.

(AT) Myttin da, and welcome. Well, you've all seen the draft and I know some of you have objections, but I think we need to agree on the bones of the thing before putting any flesh on them. The names such as 'Assembly' 'Council' and 'Senate' are for convenience and should not be regarded as part of the proposal – hope that's clear.

Each of the Regions will be divided into around 2000 parishes or hundreds - each with around 500 people. All those eligible to vote will be required to elect a single representative to a Grand Assembly – body A

The Grand Assembly will not necessarily meet as an assembly but is simply a list of names from which our actual Senate will be selected by lot. We propose a Senate of 300 people – body B

Those selected to it would have one main task - to elect a Council (body C) and its officials from among their number. The Senate would meet to decide on major and constitutional issues, but it is the Council which will have the real power. They will elect the Ministers who will then meet to decide on the allocation of offices. How they make that choice is up to them to decide.

To summarise, the process is:

1. Election: Every elector votes for a local representative

(A)

2. Sortition: The elected body (A) then chooses a Senate (B) by sortition
3. Election: The Senate (B) elects the Council (C)
4. Choice: The Council chose their leaders

(DS) Thanks Aldus. Are we all agreed so far? Good. Now comes the hard part: Proposals and objections. I will first read the list of proposals and then the objections and I propose that we discuss these in camera before making any decisions. Are we all agreed? Thanks. Here are the proposals:

1. The second body, Senate or B will ratify the constitution and decide on names for all the bodies
2. We use the provisional names Grand Assembly, Senate and Cabinet
3. The first language of the new Government will be International English, with Cymraeg and Kernowek to be used in ceremonial occasions and for matters which affect the speakers of those languages.

These are the objections:

1. The representatives elected at stage A would have no power, therefore the proposed constitution violates the principle that there should be no taxation without representation.
2. Having three official languages will slow down decision making.
3. The proposed second languages are not comparable. There are approximately 30 times as many speakers of Cymraeg as there are of Kernowek.
4. The Grand Assembly (A) should meet physically every year. The members should have a chance to meet each other and discuss constitutional issues.

Just as we had congratulated ourselves on getting to grips with the constitution of our new Nation, we had a message from a group based in the Pennines. With much of central Lyndain under water, Anglia had ceased to exist as a region and the former Anglic counties were looking at historic boundaries which might help define new regional nations. Pennines, which included everything between Cester and Caledonia, was the most populous. The Pennine mountain chain had fragmented the SBX1 outbreaks and the big cities were not as desolate as Lyndain.

Pennines have asked all the nations of mainland Britannica to what they are calling a "Moot" in Cester, with the intention of regularizing the boundaries between the new Nations. So, on a showery day in April 2057 a small group of us set out for the quite short journey from Ystwyth to Cester. We planned to travel by transnet from Ystwyth to Amwythig. The border here was still in dispute and we had to depend on the Anglian version of the NRG Express to get to Cester.

Much to the annoyance of Pennines, Anglia have adopted the old St. George's cross as their emblem and we saw the big red and white flags flying everywhere. The people of Pennines weren't the only ones annoyed by this. George Smith, our man from Defnas was clearly upset. There were a lot of people from his part of the old Wessex who still thought of themselves as Anglic.

The "bus" service being no faster than ours we were late arriving at the ancient hall in Cester.

Proceedings of the Inter-Nation Moot, Caster

Chairman Edgar Thurgate

Good morning and welcome. It is most heartening to see so many delegates here despite all the difficulties we still have with transport. We hope this meeting will be the first of regular meetings between the various nations of The Britannic Isles, and we have used the old Saxon name of Moot to mark a decisive change from the old Britannic institutions. As you can see from your programmes, we have three speakers this morning. Richard Weston will speak for Anglia and tell us about their new constitution. Erika Satterthwait is our de-facto leader here in Pennines and will tell you about our deliberations on the constitutional question. I believe our last speaker Vandervelde from Cambria has a proposal to make to you all.

After the speakers there will be a break for refreshments before the plenary sessions begin.

It gives me great pleasure to introduce our first speaker Richard Weston.

(RW) Most of you will know how terrible things were in Lyndain after the crash; how the survivors of the government fled to the south coast bunker. It is very fortunate for us that one of the survivors was the High Prince Michael, son of Harold, Prince of Cymru, and a person of great intelligence and integrity. It is no exaggeration to say that it was his Royal Highness Michael who brought peace and a degree of prosperity to our country. In 10 months time he will be crowned King, and the whole nation will rejoice.

I have heard that here in Pennines you have no leader, that you have no respect for the great kings and leaders of our past. Well, I'm sorry for you, but surely we can agree that the old system of party politics was rotten to the core and had to be swept away?

No doubt some of you will feel that the way we deal with the traitors among us is too harsh. You no doubt feel that every man has the right to be heard . . . all that old stuff about free speech which was part and parcel of the system which got us into the mess in the first place.

I say to you "What right has any man to undermine the system which has brought us peace and prosperity?" Our High Prince is a person of great wisdom, but even he is capable of making mistakes. We all are. For that reason he himself set up the Senate which helps and advises him. Our Senate represents every aspect of us, his people. A third of the Senate is elected by the district councils; a further third is appointed by the Prince and the last third is selected by lot from the entire population. The Prince of course retains a veto over the most crucial decisions in case the assembly is infiltrated by enemies of the state.

(Chair) Order! I remind members that they have agreed not to interrupt speakers."

(RW) - Thank you. You may not like what I have to say, but look at what we have achieved. Our region is at peace. Can you say the same?

(Chair) Order . . . order please.

(RW) We are beginning to rebuild our great city. Every day more and more refugees from the outer regions present themselves at our borders. If their claims to Anglian residence are valid we welcome them. At last our population is growing again. We have started to make things again. Our people have hope for a better future.

(Chair) I now call upon Erika Satterthwait from Pennines

(ES) How are you? It does my heart good to see so many canny folk here - and so well behaved!

What did you think of all that bollocks?

(Chair) - Order, order.

(ES) Kings and Princes, oh dear oh dear. Haven't we heard it all before? I tell you – watch out. Next thing you know they'll be wanting your lands and then it will all start again.

Still, I'm not going to waste my breath on such stuff. We are here to talk about government by the people for the people. How do we select our leaders so that they look after our interests? Not just our interests, those of us here, but our children's interests and their children's interests; the whole thing, the human race 'n all.

We've already decided that the old pattern of electing power hungry politicians who could use our money to persuade us to vote for them was what got us into the mess, so no more party politics! That's one thing we can agree with Anglia on any road.

You've all got copies of the draft constitution of Cambria. We have looked long and hard at this document and the ideas behind it. There's some canny ideas here. Ay indeed, no more lobbying, no more crony politics, no more millionaire leaders. We could choose our leaders from the grandest grand jury ever – a great assembly of the people all chosen at random. Our first minister could be anyone – even a millionaire if one gets selected.

On the other hand it's complicated – to say the least. We stick with the old Northern caution – see what the other fella does first. For the time being we remain a democracy, and a stable one at that.

The Pennines are the backbone of this country and the people of this region have never owed any favours to Lyndain. Our borders are clear – Caledonia to the north and a line from Wirral to the Wash to the south. If any of you south of that line want nothing to do with Kings and Princes you are welcome to join us."

(Chair) - Order please. Richard?"

(RW) Withdraw that.

(ES) OK, I a-bleedin-pologise. Please delete that from the record. Alright?

(Chair) Thank you. I now call on Vendervelde to speak for Cambria

(V) - Greetings to you all and thanks to Richard from Anglia for presenting his case so eloquently, and to Erika for rebutting it! My name is Vandervelde, and I am here to represent the new nation of Cambria. We can understand the obvious benefits of clear leadership in coming to terms with the massive problems we all face. However, we can also see great dangers in the course outlined by Richard. Certainly their High Prince is a man of great wisdom, but they have given him too much power; there are not enough safeguards in their constitution to prevent the return of the sort of autocractic government which led to the great wars of the 20th century.

(Chair) - We have an objection.... Richard – keep it brief please."

(RW) I strongly object to the implication of your remarks. Prince Michael made it absolutely clear before he agreed to become our leader that he had no desire for power for its own sake. His concern, as with all of us, is simply for the rapid re-establishment of law and order.

(Chair) Van?

(V) I apologise Richard. I meant no disrespect to your Prince, and will reserve judgement on your constitution.

However, my purpose here is not to argue about kingship, but to bring into focus the choices facing the border areas. The areas now in contention are the old counties of Cesterscir, Dorbyscir, Cruwland, and Ruthland.

We have already established a basis for co-operation with

Anglia in drawing up our southern boundary, and are happy to share whatever expertise we have with Pennines in setting their southern boundary. I understand Prince Michael has expressed his willingness to co-operate.

(Chair) Yes Richard

(RW) Yes indeed we have no wish whatsoever to get involved in border disputes. We may be forming different Nations, but we are all citizens of the Britannic Isles and will continue to work together as we have always done.

End of Transcript

Vandervelde:

Cambria Provisional Assembly

The Assembly met for the first time in Brigstowe. Our first election for the Grand Assembly had gone well. Judith was one of those elected in the Morganwng area to be in the Great Assembly. She is almost desperate to become a Senator, and with her career in politics she finds it hard to accept that whether or not she becomes a Senator is a matter of pure chance.

We now had the first timbers of our constitutional edifice in place, but there were some important parts of the building still missing.

Until now we had conducted all our business in International English, but there was a vociferous element who were unhappy with this. There had been a strong revival of the Kernowek language and, after a long period of decline the use of Cymraeg was increasing again. Item one on our agenda therefore was language.

Item two was political philosophy. There had been hundreds of books and articles written and recorded to camera about the Sustainable State, the No-Growth Economy and so on. Based on well over a hundred years of study I had my own ideas and asked if I could address the Assembly.

Transcript: The First Assembly of Cambria

Assembly Leader, Walter Penrose (WP)

Welcome to this historic occasion – the first time since the sixth century that the two ancient nations of Kernow and Cymru have joined together. It is of even more historic importance because we have made our capital here in Brigstowe, the hub round which our nation revolves. We have many matters to debate today, but before we begin I would like to ask the person who, more than any other, has made this occasion possible, the most outstanding citizen to have no official role, our "Minister without Portfolio" Vandervelde.

Vandervelde (V)

Thank you Walter. Assembly members, friends, let me begin by asking a simple question – 'Why in elections does my neighbour persist in voting for someone whose ideas I know to be totally misguided?' By neighbour I don't mean anyone in particular. It stands for a person you know quite well.

Let me ask an even more searching question: 'Why do I believe so strongly that my neighbour's opinions are wrong?' I begin with these questions because I believe they get to the heart of government and the sort of government which led to the downfall of our previous civilization.

For as long as we had democracy we had "politics" and politics consisted of a never-ending argument between what came to be called the "left" and the "right".

This monumental conflict has caused untold suffering over thousands of years. It seems to me that before we get down to the how of our constitution we should ask ourselves why is this left/right division so entrenched in our culture.

I now believe I can answer this with some confidence. The whole edifice of opposing political positions was simply the genetic blueprint which had enabled our first societies to survive. In a tribal society you have to know which tribe you belong to. You have to be able to recognize someone from a different tribe and know whether that person is a threat or not. Is he or she "one of us" or "one of them." The situation was made much more complicated because human societies are both communitarian and stratified.

For centuries we have fought each other to determine which philosophy was the right one. What a waste of human potential - all that suffering, those countless deaths in battle. It was never a question of "either/or" – we are both, and we are all the intervening positions as well, and no amount of educating, brainwashing, torturing, or killing could change that. We had, and still have within each of us the makings of a fascist, a communist, a religious fundamentalist, a hero, a crook, a democrat, a mediator, a saint and a martyr. To survive we had to be able to lead, to admire our leaders, to love the strong but we also had to protect the weak, to work together, to empathise and to co-operate. We had to accept that to be strong is to despise the weak; to be empathetic is to fear and hate the tyrant, to have faith is to believe that which you know to be untrue.

Now we are back to survival. We know the human genome. We can look at our toolkit and marvel at its inadequacies, but know that it is all we have. To work with it means a deep understanding of why we hate and despise the neighbour on one side and love and respect the one on the other side. We can't move away from the one and live with the other.

We know that Utopia is an impossible dream. We cannot hope to create a society where all are contented and fulfilled. We know that some of us will have more and some less, that some of our ideals ("equality of opportunity" for example) will never be fulfilled. Worse, we know that succeeding generations will cease to respect our knowledge and fail to learn from our mistakes. Yet somehow we have to keep all this in synthesis.

We are here to write down the things we all agree on, the basic principles of the organisations which will govern us in the years to come. Let me suggest to you a first rule which will temper all the other rules we may set up. The first rule makes all the others possible. It is this:

Accept that some of us will break these rules.

(WP) Quiet please . . . thank you . . . thank you. Please can we have some quiet?

Thank you.

Well . . . I don't know about you but I found that speech totally inspiring – and I didn't understand all of it! I know that many of you will want to speak but we have only a limited time for the welcome agenda. I call upon Meinir Morgan. Meinir comes from Caerfyrddin – I hope I pronounced that correctly – and would like to address the Assembly in her first language. Translation is available in the earphones on your desks. Meinir..

Meinir Morgan (MM)

Boneddigion a Boneddigesau. Gentlemen and Ladies, (remainder translated into IE) I am speaking on behalf of a new body, the Cambrian Fellowship, which brings together many strands of our religious history. I agree with much of what our Elder is saying, and we all respect his great accumulation of knowledge and wisdom. Those of us who respect our Christian heritage have learnt to accept that simple faith is not enough. We no longer need to believe that our mythology has anything to do with scientific fact; we no longer question the facts of evolution, we do not "believe" in God, but we are adamant that the moral and the spiritual belong together. They may have nothing to do with our physical existence, but they have a great deal to do with how we treat each other, how we behave. Is our respected Elder saying that our basic moral precepts are worth so little that there is no point in trying to ensure that they are kept?"

(WP) Van – do you wish to respond?

(V) I do. No, friends, that is not what I'm saying, but I thank Meinir for bringing a spiritual element to our discussion. What she says is of great importance. Since we began to understand why religion has played such a powerful role in our long history, the whole idea of "worshipping" something or someone has become discredited. Religion may have helped our distant ancestors to survive, but it was no help at all when you are reduced to mass starvation or death by riot. It was no help in the business of surviving, but, and this is a very important but, it did help those who believed in an afterlife to face death more easily. We all remember how, after 44, there was such a proliferation of prophets - soothsayers, gurus, messiahs, shamans, wizards, medicine men, and snake oil merchants. Charismatic leaders were two a penny and many of the nasty conflicts of the forties were fought over conflicting dogmas.

After 44 we the Elders, amongst many others, realised that

people needed to come together with a shared moral purpose. We all needed more than just the prospect of food and shelter. There was an intense desire to create a new and better society. Let me suggest to you some basic precepts which I believe should be part of our constitution:

- Do not take what cannot be replaced
- Do not cause another to suffer
- Lead and follow,
- Inspire and be inspired
- Love some, respect all
- Accept dislike or praise
- Allow rebellion
- Understand cruelty
- Forgive sins

******

Grand talk! I have got a little too slick at this kind of speechifying. Just a week later we came down to earth with a bump. Before we got down to the business of selecting our Cabinet, we had a report of a disturbance at the border. Ever since the border had been agreed, there had been a lot of movement to and fro. There were no border controls as such but we had already set up kiosks on the main roads to mark the border, as had the Anglians and Pennines on the other side. There appeared to be some sort of migration going on. At different places there seemed to be more e-cars full of people and belongings going in one direction than the other. We asked the border staff to attempt an estimate of net outgoing and incoming migration. It soon became obvious that a lot of people from Defnas and Kernow were moving to

Anglia, but that was offset by an influx of people in the other direction, mainly over the Havren Bridge.

Clearly our first cabinet appointment will have to be a Home Affairs Minister.

CGOV Report: National Security

Priority

Attn: Home Office Minister

Request for Asylum

Monmouth Crossing

Date...

At 07:00 hours we were approached by a group comprising: male 30 years, Female 29, Female 10, Male 12 years. The group appeared to be a family. The senior male approached the officer on duty and said he would like to request asylum in Cambria.

He was asked to explain what he meant, and said that he and his family were facing persecution in Lyndain and wished to live under the protection of the Cambrian government.

The subject was asked what he was seeking protection from, but all he would say was that he would work hard and be a good citizen. When pressed to give a reason for his request he said:

"They are coming for me. We had to escape." When asked who was coming for him he said "Them, the Civil Guard. Please, you must help us."

The group were taken to our office and given refreshments. Eventually the senior female, the mother, told us that because her husband had been involved in trying to improve the conditions of work at his workplace, they had been visited late at night by two civil guards, who had made it very clear to them all that unless Paul (the father) ceased immediately from his seditious talk he would be tried under the new security code. She told us of other cases involving friends of theirs who had disappeared after having received a warming from the Civil Guard.

They had decided the next day to leave their home and seek

sanctuary in Cambria, which they had heard lived under a free Demarchy.

The border staff have no information for this eventuality. Please provide immediate guidance on the way to proceed.

CGOV Report: Migration

Meeting between Aldus Trawenna, Cambrian border Supervisor, and Mason Haynes, Anglian Border Control.

AGENDA

Monitoring of Migration

Criteria for definition of Migration

Both sides agreed to institute a sampling procedure according to the definition of Migration agreed. It proved difficult to define what constituted migration, but eventually we agreed to sample "e-cars and EGVs with full occupancy"

Interim Conclusions

Samples were taken during the whole of the month of June – a period of showery warm weather – and the following results agreed:

Those moving to live in Anglia were 76% from the former counties of Devon and Somerset, with 24% spread evenly over the other regions.

Those migrating to Cambria were 60% from Lyndain and 30% from other areas. It was possible to determine that of those moving from Lyndain, around 70% were of Cymric origin.

Of the total of all migrations, 5% more were moving to Cambria than in the other direction. . If this trend continues it could have large implications for policy.

We advise that a random sample of these migrants be asked to take part in a more comprehensive survey which would identify the motives for such moves.

Judith Netlog

Sometimes I feel sorry for Jamie. He was quite a Fashionista in his day - I've looked up all the stuff about him: fast cars, smart clothes, beautiful women, the works. Yuk – I hate men like that. You can still see traces of all that, but he's much more complicated. Yes, pathetic sometimes but sensitive, intense – that too.

I had a message on my secure comms channel. He wanted to meet me – this was at least a year after our meeting in the forest. I replied

"OK, where are you"

"Outside". Fuck – I wasn't ready for this.

"I'm busy"

"I'll wait." The humility bit. I would have to see him. I left it for 10 minutes and then sent back:

"17:00 "Energy"on James Street. If you're any good you'll find it."

"See you there"

Of course he did find it. "Energy" used to be our sort of "works canteen" when we worked and lived in the NRG compound. Now it's just a café, but it's still owned by the organisation and we've kept it secure. Only people we trust can order there. I found him waiting outside.

"They wouldn't let me in."

"Not surprised, you look like something out of a thriller" He had a long black coat on and was wearing a hat.

"No, seriously, they checked my ID and told me to wait outside."

Most people have no idea they are being checked when

they come in. I did a brief wave at the tiny red light and it turned to green. We both walked in.

"Well James, here I am. We can talk freely here."

"I prefer Jamie – that's what most people call me."

"Well I prefer James" He made a sorrowful face.

"I can understand you feeling a bit hostile. You've probably read my back profile and you're very close to Mollie."

"Relax, I'm teasing!" I ordered some coffee. It arrived quickly and he took a few sips before speaking.

"I've decided to tell you something, but I don't want it recorded. Can you arrange that?"

Oh dear. I suppose all that security stuff was a bit obvious. I accessed my comms unit and did the code.

"OK. It's clean. Tell me."

"Back in 2030 I was approached by a man called Ulm; he's dead now. He was what is known as a Sapient . . . "

Everything around me went silent. My ears were buzzing and the hair on the back of my neck stood up. This was something very strange indeed. I shivered and my hands felt cold.

"Are you OK? You look almost frightened."

"Er, yes. That word . . . it keeps appearing from nowhere. What does it mean?"

"When I first met him I didn't believe what he was telling me but I know now. The Sapients are Elders, people who, by some strange freak of nature do not grow older at the same rate as the rest of us...What is it?"

"Oh my God, I know one. Go on."

"Yes you do, Van is one but he doesn't know about Ulm

and his group."

"How ever many are there for God's sake?"

"Nobody knows for sure, but probably in the low tens. Not only do they live a very long time but they have the ability to understand more about the world than most of us – hence the Sapience bit. Ulm was one of a small group of them who have formed a secret Fellowship. He asked me to help them and at first I was very dubious, but I can see now that their mission was good – really important for our world. My small part was hard for me, but eventually I agreed.

The thing is Judith, Brother Ulm knew about 44 well before it happened. It was Mollie he was concerned with. The Fellowship of The Trees knew she had a vital role to play in the NRG plan and they promised to protect her if I agreed to watch her and report back to them.

At first I flatly refused – what decent person wouldn't – but then he started telling me so many things about the past and the future which made sense. I was drawn in, Judith. My task has been harder than I could have imagined, but I don't regret it. Look around you."

I sat for a long time with my head in my hands.

"OK, what do you want from me?"

"I want you to swear that you will tell nobody about our conversation today, and I want you to think about all I have said. In a few weeks time someone will contact you."

"Oh very spooks stuff. Where's the false moustache?" I stood up. "Jamie, I don't like this but I will do as you ask." I made what I fancied was a dramatic exit.

A few weeks passed, then a few months and I was too busy with constituency business to give it any more thought.

******

Well, we've done it; the first election! I didn't have too much doubt that I would be elected but still it was an anxious time. My Cantref – that's what we've decided to call them to please our lot – was the Whitchurch area of Caerdydd where I have lived most of my life. There were 15 candidates and I was elected on the first ballot. Most of the others on the Constitution committee have been elected too – only Van won't be joining us in the Grand Assembly. He preferred not to stand.

It seems a shame that we are not all going to meet – that would be quite something 8000 odd people all in one place! The next stage, the Sortition, is due to take place next week. I really really want to be on the Senate! This is when I have some real doubts about this sortition business. I do understand that it is important that people like me who WANT the power to change things can't influence the electors. It seems hard though. What if we end up with a Senate full of people who don't want to be there?

******

I'M SORTED! Wow – there's an old phrase with a new meaning! The first meeting of the new Senate is to be next month in Brigstowe. I'm so looking forward to it. There's very few on the list who I know, so we'll all be like the first year in a new school. It feels very strange. How on earth are we going to agree on ratifying the constitution? I bet we spend more time on deciding on the names for the three bodies.

******

So much for good resolutions. My poor netlog has been so neglected. At least it shows I've not been kicking my heels looking for something to do. I'm only writing this now because I feel like we have reached a really important point. We've got to the top of the first of the foothills. It's a joyful place to be and we can look forward to the climb ahead with excitement and back to the path below with satisfaction.

Duw Judith, you're getting all poetic! Well why not, I feel poetic. Life is good. I don't see Van all that often, but when we meet up we have a really good time, and life as a Senator in the new Cambria is far more satisfying that it was in the old Cymru. For one thing we don't have to keep referring to Lyndain all the time. In fact we are now doing better than Lyndain. Their great cry of "Law and Order" drew in lots of lost souls at first but doesn't look so good now they have to work 10 hours a day under the new labour laws. There is no way of challenging decisions from above. As we feared, the King, despite all his "good intentions" is now using his power to the full, and petty criminals get short shrift. I've even heard rumours of summary executions. One thing which worries us is the growth of their "Special Forces". For all they say, to us outside, it looks very like an army, and a well funded and well-disciplined one at that from what we hear.

All we have here is the Defence Force. Once the gang wars died down, we merged the Brigstowe Harbourers with the Braich y Draig, the Caerdydd Bay Police, the Meibion Kernow and several other regional forces. It was quite surprising how well this has worked considering all the wild nationalist ideas rife amongst them a few years ago. I think the nationalism was just a natural response to people's need to defend their families and their localities. Give them something real to defend and they can work together. Unlike the old Britannic police they are armed, and we have begun a unified training regime which will enable them to deal with disasters and attacks from outside.

This is only really a more sophisticated version of what they were doing before.

******

I'm REALLY having to pinch myself here. I keep

thinking this is some sort of joke or a dream and I will soon wake up. It seems like only yesterday we were rushing around like headless chickens in what is now our Senate building – the old Brigstowe Council House. As I feared it took for ever to get some measure of consensus about anything. I was getting so stressed by it all I couldn't control myself and yelled out

"FOR FUCK SAKE WILL EVERYONE SHUT UP A MINUTE" Amazingly it worked. I suppose I do have quite a loud voice when I decide to shout.

"Somebody has got to make the first move so I will. I appoint myself temporary chairperson and propose that we vote immediately for twenty of the names in front of you. Let those decide on how we then proceed. All names with more than two votes go on to the next ballot. Agreed?"

"Seconded"

"Good thinking Judith – I support that"

"Yea – let's go"

I think they were all so relieved that something was actually happening at last that the few who objected were shouted down. At that stage I couldn't have cared less whether my name was on the list or not. Well, it was, and in next to no time the twenty of us had moved to a smaller room.

They asked me to continue as meeting chair and I suggested a procedure for selecting ministers and ratifying the constitution. There were a few more votes, but in a surprisingly short time we had a cabinet and a first minister. To be honest I was a little peeved not to be nominated for any of the cabinet posts, but I was younger than most of them so it didn't bother me for long. It was just so great to see a new government taking shape. The last thing the new cabinet agreed was to hold another senate meeting two weeks later.

So, fourteen busy days went past and there we all were

again, but this time with a First Minister and a Cabinet. There was a long agenda, and the first item was the nominations for President. As in many democratic republics the president would be the figurehead for the government and have the final say in matters of policy, but would not normally be involved in the day-to-day decision making, which would be the job of the Cabinet led by the first minister. It was she, Susan Passmore, who took the chair.

"Can I ask for nominations for the post of President of Cambria please?"

"I nominate Judith Evans as president" WHAT???

"Seconded"

"Thank you. Any other nominations?"

I was in a state of shock and was waiting for all the other nominations when I became aware that a hush had fallen on the room.

"Any other nominations? No? "Carried unanimously" and that was it.

I AM THE FIRST PRESIDENT OF CAMBRIA!

******

Is it really three years since I last wrote here? Where has all that time gone? After a couple of weeks I started putting my foot down and insisted that I could not do my job unless the constant stream of people wishing to speak to me were cut back. I now have not just one but two secretaries who sort through all the demands on my time and make up a more manageable schedule.

Amongst all the delegations from towns and pressure groups and neighbourhoods and individuals there was one which looked odd: a single name – 'Fagus'. Just that – no other name. The "Secretariat" as I call them had put him quite low on the list, but I was intrigued, and asked to see him, so a couple of days later here he was in my office.

He had a slight accent – French? Spanish? I couldn't tell. There was something slightly odd about him. His clothes were rather old-fashioned and there was something about his face and hair which reminded me of Van for some reason, though his colouring was quite different – dark skinned.

He talked of a group of "Brothers" and at first I thought he was another prophet but he didn't seem to have any spiritual agenda.

"It's about Sir James madam President" Then I remembered. Jamie had said someone would get in touch but that was ages ago. I'd forgotten all about it.

"What? What are you talking about?"

"James Jarman, Jamie – Mollie's brother."

"So, what do you know about him?" I didn't like this one bit. There was something creepy about him.

I remembered then what Jamie had said about the Sapients and suddenly I knew – this man was one of the Fellowship.

"I can see from your face that you understand. Yes I am one of the Fellowship of the Trees. There were six of us and we all took the names of trees. I am Brother Fagus, though some know me as El Sabio."

You could almost hear the pieces clicking into place. So this was the man from Bolivia I had read about. What on earth was he doing here?

"Wow, are you real? El Sabio?"

"Ciertamente! I surely was last time I looked in the mirror."

"Hm . . . well, that's no proof, but rather than argue

metaphysics with you, I'll assume that you are an Elder like Van, and that what you have to say is important. I'm listening."

"Have you ever heard of Brother Ulm?"

"Ulm? That rings a bell. Yes, Jamie said something about a man called Ulm, but he then clammed up. Is he one of your brotherhood?"

"Was; Ulm was one of those who were called upon to make the ultimate sacrifice in 44"

"Sacrifice? That's a weird way to put it. Do you mean he died? In case you hadn't noticed a great many people died, but I doubt any of them thought they were making a sacrifice."

"Please – bear with me. Can you just accept that Ulm felt that way? He had an important mission which was a success, but he died in the execution of it. I can't say any more at present. The important fact I have to tell you is that James Jarman was helping Brother Ulm. James believed in what we are trying to achieve and did some most valuable work for us."

"Are you going to tell me what your so called 'mission' is?"

"I'm sorry Madam President but I can't. We have watched your career with admiration, and believe that when the time comes you will be sympathetic to our cause. I would like to meet you again from time to time, but I do understand that you may well feel no obligation to do so, so I am going to tell you one more thing. What convinced James to work for us was the promise we gave him, which we continue to fulfil, to protect his sister, your friend Mollie. She, I know is very precious to you as she is to us. We helped her, and incidentally you yourself, to find sanctuary in 2045."

"In that case I will be glad to meet you again when you feel you have more to tell me."

"Thank you Madam President"

It still seem weird to me being addressed like that. I try to get people to call me Judith, as my friends still do of course. The problem is it seems to make people feel more uncomfortable rather than more relaxed. Hey ho.

Vandervelde

The Eldred House 2061

Those dark hills, across the estuary, are the beginnings of the great mountains of Eryri. In front of me is the Morfa, a flat expanse of scrub leading down to saltmarsh and the water. Apart from the transtrack and a few wind turbines, the works of mankind are little in evidence. At least they were until recently, and "works" is a good way to describe what has been created here.

The first thing you see from the little transtation at Dyfi is the Eldred Tree. You know it's a tree, but you can see it from a distance because it is 80 metres high. It's made entirely from recycled materials, and as you walk up the recently planted avenue which snakes across the Morfa, you can see how the stone, metal and timber have been brought together into a whole which looks organic.

The avenue is carefully designed so that you don't see the Eldred House until you are almost upon it. It's an astonishing sight hanging there above the ground with the Tree 'growing' through the middle of it.

They say Cymru used to have the only written culture which developed without cities. Now we are trying to rebuild it in a different form. Looking back through my papers I see I wrote about Eldred's work in 32. By 38 he had become the golden boy of "The Arts", but is now better remembered as one of the few who fell ill with the SBX1 virus but survived.

He never regained his strength and energy, but the damage to his brain had a profound effect on how we came to think about Music, Art, Literature, Sport, Travel, Work – every aspect of our culture.

Sadly he died last year. To commemorate his life and work The Eldred Foundation was established earlier this year, and today is the opening ceremony of the "Eldred House", what we hope will be the first of a network of "Knowledge Houses" in Cambria. His widow Mollie is introducing the main speaker. She looked pale and tired, but her voice was firm:

"Good Morning and Welcome to the Eldred House. I'm not going to drone on about how much I miss him and what a lovely husband he was – you can take that as read. I know that our guest (here she indicated Judith) will give you an honest account of the man. I want to tell you how Judith and I first met."

"It was back in 37; the last phase of the Transnet had just opened, it was a lovely spring day in April, and we were keen to try it out. Fat chance – we eventually got away in July when it was raining, but we were excited about the trip so didn't care about the weather. We'd hired a very odd looking hybrid and had been thrilled by the docking procedure. In those days it felt a bit like your first take off in one of the old HTA planes. After half an hour sitting there watching the scenery whiz by we decided to make our way to the café and found ourselves behind a mass of crimson hair on top of a small, obviously young and obviously female body supported on clumpy looking boots. We got into conversation; a conversation which, with pauses, has continued to this day. Please welcome the President of Cambria Judith Evans."

"Thanks Mollie. Yes, I never forgot that day either. I can honestly say it was Mollie and Eldred who first inspired me with their vision for the mending of the old Britannica; and who later made me realize that our dream was flawed, that our ideals would be broken on the rocks of human instincts.

They helped me to regain my sanity when we lost our families. I can now freely admit that my first husband Rhys was uncomfortable with Eldred and they always used to argue about Britannica, Cymru and NRG. If he had survived 44 I wonder if they would have found common cause."

"Eldred of course was not the same then. The brilliant and inspirational artist, full of energy, always swearing at someone or something, one minute shouting in anger the next laughing with glee; that exhausting person died and a more sombre, in some ways more interesting person emerged."

I well remember one day when I relieved Mollie at his bedside while he slowly recovered.

'Ju-ith' he said.

'We red nothing as . . .nothing as read take.' There was a long pause while he struggled to find words and put them in order.

'Start again from principles, first, first principles. Van, tell Van I speak him must, to him, must...speak...to...him.' It took years for his speech to become more fluent but by then we had got used to the 'Eldred Poetry' as we called it, and rather missed those tortured elliptical expressions.

"I believe Vandervelde is here somewhere but he won't thank me to point him out. For the next few years whenever Van was able to travel to Brigstowe they would spend hours arguing. It was these arguments which formed the philosophical foundation of our constitution. They always agreed on one thing, that our new society had to be truly Sustainable. So much lip service had been paid to this ideal, not least by NRG, that it had lost its real meaning. They started with the now famous maxim:

Do not take what cannot be replaced.

It was Eldred's damaged mind which kept coming back to the idea of inclusion, that everything we humans do is part of the pattern of our evolution, and it was really Eldred who gave us:

Allow rebellion.

Understand cruelty.

"He kept going back to the Christian concept of 'Love thy neighbour' He hated the long history of bitter rivalry over religion, politics, art, sport etc. which has caused so much bloodshed in the past, but insisted that rivalry, and competition were hard-wired. He saw the human character as a spectrum, and the way we interact with each other as representing the very different characteristics of our two nearest evolutionary cousins, the Chimps and the Bonobos.

"Bear with me, it gets a bit outlandish here, but it does make sense – at least to me it does.

"We are all, he believed, a mixture of aggressive Chimp and free-loving Bonobo, of Fundamentalist Muslim and communitarian Quaker, of tyrant and communist, and human society is in a constant state of dialectic, not just in the Marxist sense of an argument between classes, but a whole series of arguments between every aspect of human thought.

"Somehow, he believed, we have to find a place for all these arguments, including the argument that finding a place for them is idealistic claptrap! We have to find a place where we can agree to differ and work together.

"I hope Van, our Elder, and my true support, will not object if I remind you that the speech he gave to our first Assembly was rooted in these ideas. One of the things he said was:

'Why does my neighbour persist in voting for someone whose ideas I know to be totally misguided? Let me ask an even more searching question: Why do I believe so strongly that my neighbour's opinions are wrong? For as long as we had democracy we had 'politics' and politics consisted of a

never-ending argument between what came to be called 'left' and the 'right.'

'Why did it take us so long to realise that this monumental conflict which had caused so much suffering over so many thousands of years was simply the genetic blueprint which had enabled our first societies to survive?'

"Eldred never wanted to get involved in government - he was always the artist – but he did become involved in sport, recognizing sporting competition and conflict as being a way to work out our warrior instincts. He insisted that sport was creative and beautiful and that art was physical and challenging, and it is largely because of his insights that our sporting events are now so much more visually and musically interesting. We now often hear of a major artist going into training for his next work, and a sports heroine exhibiting the evidence of her achievements as a work of art.

"The building behind me is our first Knowledge House. It will be what you make of it. Its custodians have a simple brief: "Show us what we can do". It will celebrate every kind of human achievement, and I hope will find beauty in all of them."

As she was speaking Mollie had passed her a pair of scissors. In a symbolic action she 'stepped up to the tape' and cut it.

"I declare the Eldred House open."

******

I seem to have a lot more time these days. It really does feel as if my great work is winding down. Perhaps I will soon be ready for the next project, but at the moment I'm enjoying spending more time at home. Judith of course is away a great deal, but we always try to have week-ends together.

I have a selection of walks I can do from the house when

I feel the need for fresh air and exercise. This is my favourite. Within 10 minutes I am out of the tref and onto a rough footpath winding through the Morfa down to the river. Behind me are the beginnings of the Cambrian Mountains and ahead, on the other side the beginning of Eryn with Cader Eira in the distance. On both sides is this wide expanse of marshland, once intensively farmed, first for sheep and cattle and then in the 30s for vegetables. Now only the feral goats and sheep prevent it from becoming forest. It's a mix of grassland and scrub and a favourite hunting ground for one of the birds we nearly lost back then – the hen harrier. These and the short-eared owls are the most obvious sign of the build-up of wild species – plants, insects, mammals, amphibians and especially rodents. I can see a Hen Harrier now in the distance – pale, ghostly grey, quartering the ground.

It's cold and misty with a rime of frost on the bushes. It suits my mood today. It's been a bad week. Two months ago Mollie was diagnosed with a disease that has become uncommon in our society – cancer. I did not know that for many weeks she has been on a pain relief regime, but evidently her healer had improved the diagnosis and spelt out the options to her. Micro-surgery was a possibility, but it would have meant a long trip and a very uncertain outcome so she chose our local "end of life celebration" routine which involves powerful pain killing drugs combined with lots of love and kindness. Judith and I spent as much time with her as we could, but it did not feel like enough.

Our current philosophy tells us that we all must die and many of us must suffer, but we must do what we can to help those who suffer and those who are about to die. Many belong to "Good Death" societies which help each other to plan for an exit strategy, but Mollie had little patience for such things and preferred to accept whatever her fate was. She died peacefully four days ago and her burial ceremony was held two days ago. I arrived back this morning.

She chose the Lee Woods site just outside Brigstowe.

Like most burial grounds now it is a fenced area of thin woodland where bodies in shrouds are buried in shallow graves so that they can compost naturally and allow their nutrients to be recycled into the trees planted by the graves. Mollie had chosen an ash tree. I was one of the pall bearers who took turns to carry the stiff cardboard coffin by foot from the old studio in the haven. The physical effort was our tribute to her and the short ceremony at the grave was uplifting. She had died a good death and we were pleased for her.

I think I am beginning to feel old. I spend a lot of time remembering the past and thinking about how those I have loved will fare in the future.

CHAPTER 4 2075

CAMBRIA DAY June 21 2075

Address by President Evans (transcript)

I'm very proud to be speaking to you today. It is wonderful to see so many people here and so many from outside our borders too. I would like especially to welcome the delegations from Pennines, Hibernia and Caledonia. It is a matter of real concern however that nobody in an official capacity from Anglia is here. We must all hope that in the coming months and years we can build better relations with our neighbours to the East. We have no quarrel with them, but King Michael has expressed his displeasure at the fact that we have welcomed those from Anglia who have come to live amongst us. Well, I say their loss is our gain.

The last 10 years have been a success in many ways, not just here in Cambria but in most of the world where the violence of the climate is less severe. Here we have a system of government by demarchy which, much to the surprise of some sceptics, is delivering stability and peace. We not only have enough food, but our food is of much higher quality than it used to be. We now have a regular power supply of about 1 kilowatt per household, and already people are saying it's not enough. What short memories some people have! Only a few years ago our lives were one long struggle from dawn to dusk just to survive, but now we have leisure time. All those privileged elites who managed to pile up fantastic wealth at the expense of the rest of us, they have all gone. Thanks largely to our education system, our society now is one of the most egalitarian in history, and every one of us from the Chief Executive to the cleaner is the better for it.

We live well, but we can only dream about the extraordinary luxury of the so called "Western" or "developed" world in the glory days before 2020. Even the tough restrictions of the 30s were luxurious compared to how we live now.

We have all been through a great tragedy. Not since the Black Death in the 14th Century have so many people died in such a short time. Now we must learn how to put it behind us, even accept that perhaps the sharp decline in the human population was something which had to happen.

I know that many would dispute this. I've heard all the conspiracy theories – that the fantastic technical advances of the first part of this century were on the brink of success when some sinister agency sabotaged them. Personally, I don't believe this, but even if there were some truth in some of the theories, the likelihood is we will never know. To my way of thinking we, the lucky survivors, have been given a wonderful opportunity to create a new kind of human society. We should grasp it with both hands and move on."

Address by Vandervelde (Transcript)

Good Morning. I often feel, and I'm sure some of you will agree with me, that I've made far too many speeches in the last 20 years . . . let alone in all the years before that. Well, you'll be glad to hear that this will be my last . . . you're very kind . . . thank you. At least it will be my last in my capacity as an NRG executive.

I well remember during one of those speeches - when we were discussing the constitution – a man from Brigstowe said he didn't care what system of government we adopted as long as we could get rid of "that monstrous quango NRG telling us what to do!"

Actually NRG has had little involvement with our small patch since the Cambria project got off the ground. I told that man then that I would be only too pleased to resign from NRG when I felt my job was done, and I'm very happy indeed to tell you that's exactly what I feel now. What was my baby back in the late forties has now grown up and it's time for at least one of its parents to take a back seat and watch the adolescent nation mature into a stable and prosperous adult.

As President Evans has pointed out we are not there yet. Not all the stalls and displays you can see here are about achievements. It would be a big mistake to ignore the challenges we face now and the ones you will face in the future. I would urge you all for example to spend a little time at our Security Forces tent, and at the Sustainability stall.

We have to live with what we've got and do our utmost to avoid quarrelling over it.

That's all. Have fun.

The Cambria Hunters Association

We've a lot of uplands on both sides of the Havren, and now that there aren't anywhere near as many sheep as there used to be, there's big new areas of scrub and young trees growing up. With this ban on importing feed we're not going to see any increase in sheep grazing in the near future. All this new scrub and forest is great for bio-diversity, but it has also provided a perfect habitat for browsing animals such as feral goats and pigs, together with deer and wild boar, and numbers of these are rapidly increasing. In previous ages and other countries these numbers would be controlled by natural predators such as wolves, but in Cambria it's down to us. Already parts of our new forests are losing trees at an alarming rate.

The Cambria Hunters Association was formed 5 years ago to co-ordinate a solution to the problem of unsustainable populations of feral animals, particularly deer and goats. A managed culling programme has been agreed which will, all being well, give us the following benefits:

- Forest will be allowed to grow, providing a source of timber.
- The health of the animals will be improved by the removal of weak or sick animals and by the reduction of numbers.
- The meat produced is of very high standard and will be sold through the normal food outlets.
- The problem of "rogue" hunters and gun enthusiasts will be reduced.

Hunting licences are available only to members of our association and only once they have been through our training programme. Please note it is illegal to attempt any form of hunting without a valid licence.

We have a very strict code of practise which is based on a scientific study of how predators and prey interact. We believe that animals suffer greatly if hunted in a way that is unnatural to them – chasing to exhaustion for example. The primary objective of our code is to minimise the suffering of the hunted animal while not losing the excitement of the chase:

- We kill to eat
- We chase the swift
- We stalk the wary
- We do not wound
- We do not hunt predators.

If you would like to join us, please speak to one of our representatives or get in touch on your comms. We are cambriahunters.ca

Cambria International

We are pleased to present for the first time our interactive display map of the world and our links with other nations.

Even before we came together, the regions of what is now Cambria have always had very strong connections with other countries all over the world. Cymru had the International Eisteddfod, and their lead position in the Industrial Revolution, Kernow had Trevithick and their miners and engineers, and Brigstowe has been a great port since the days before and after it's notoriety in the slave trade. Now the Brigstowe Pound is accepted as a trading currency in many of the new markets.

We are too small to survive without friends around the world. Here you can learn about the active exchange programmes we have with Hibernia, Caledonia, Pennines, Breizh, Iberia, Germany, Scandinavia, the West African Federation and many more. As you walk round the world map here you will be able to access links to which show in holographic images what our relationship is with the country you are standing on.

Campaign for Democracy

What happened to Democracy?

Why did we throw the baby out with the bath water?

These are some of the questions that an increasing number of us are asking. In all the excitement of our new Nation we seem to have allowed the back room boys and girls to quietly get rid of one of the great freedoms so many of us fought for. Yes we still have "one person one vote" of a sort, but what happened to "No Taxation without Representation"? What is our vote worth if it doesn't have any influence on how we live our lives.?

We are campaigning for a new constitutional forum to discuss these matters. Please sign our petition now.

Security Forces

What does it feel like to be on border patrol?

Could you defuse a violent quarrel?

Share the experience of going into battle in one of our forward vehicles! Our simulators offer an experience so real they may change your life – BE WARNED.

Life is Good – Let's keep it that way

We love Cambria. Here we live in a system which allows free speech and freedom of movement. We have good food and decent houses. Most important of all we have leaders who listen to us and are in nobody's pockets. We are fortunate. There are others in these islands who are not so lucky. Every month the number of refugees from Anglia keeps rising.

Twenty years ago the greatest danger to our peace was gang warfare and general civil disturbance. Fortunately we have succeeded in reducing the gang violence to a level which has allowed us to rebuild our lives.

Now, however, we face the possibility of a threat from outside our borders. Anglia is increasing its army. There are now regular patrols along our borders. So far the patrols have been friendly, but it would be foolish to believe that this will always be the case.

If you are under the age of 35, in good health and physically fit our Defence Force can offer you a regular salary and good living conditions for you and your family. We need your help.

If our "life at the front" hasn't put you off, come and see the Combined Forces Display at 15:00 in the main arena.

Education for All

Demonstration Class

(Narrator) Come and watch a typical lesson! You are eavesdropping on a group of young people arriving at Second School for the first time. The school is in Dyfi but could be anywhere in Cambria

The teacher Jacob introduces his class:

(J) Good morning people. Welcome to Dyfi Second School. You have been put in class B and assigned to me. My name is Jacob and I am your class tutor. To distinguish me from your friends you will call me by my initial J. As you meet the other teachers you will learn their chosen initial too. I will be here for you throughout your time here. If you have any personal difficulties, come to me first. I hope we will all get on, but I must tell you now that if at any stage you feel I am not treating you fairly, you must tell me how you feel and I will have to refer you to one of the other tutors. There are very strict rules to make sure that all of you have an equal chance no matter how horrible you are!"

(pupil) That's not fair J, can I be referred now? - more laughter.

(J) OK, OK, calm down. The other part of my job is teaching, but what I teach may be new to you. It's not a "subject" like science or literature, but is about the society you are part of and how you relate to it. It used to have the name "civics". Can anyone tell me where that name came from?

(pupil) It's latin J.

(J) And?

(pupil) Is it Dinas J?

(J) That's right – civitas, the city. Since we no longer have cities we don't use the term any more.

Now, in a moment I will go through all your names, and at 10 hours you will go to the hall for the welcome ceremony, but first I want to tell you how your learning will be organised in Second School.

The whole purpose of the next few years is what we call "enabling". We will work together to find out what each one of you is capable of and how you can fit most comfortably into our society. You are all very fortunate to be young and alive at this time. I'm sure you have all seen and heard the records of the Age of Oil, and I have to tell you now there is no chance that you will have the sort of wealth and comfort that many people had then. Your lives will be governed by hard work and frugality, BUT, as we all know, life in the first half of this century was ultimately unsustainable, a mirage. Who knows what a mirage is?

(pupil) It's a looking glass J.

(second pupil) No you dwl it's a sort of oasis in the desert

(J) Not quite – any other ideas?"

(pupil) It's a sort of picture of water and trees in a desert which isn't there really.

(J) Well done miss.

What we can offer you is the excitement of working together to create a sustainable society, one which will be secure for your children and their children. I will be telling you about the history of the catastrophe and the challenges that we survivors faced 30 years ago.

In the next few weeks, as well as learning your names, the other teachers and I will be finding out all about each one of you. You will all take a series of tests, some of them written, but some will be conversations, some will be games, some physical tasks. In some tests you will be competing against each other. Some of you will win and some will lose, but in most of the tests there will be no winners or losers. Also, losers in one area will be encouraged to become winners in other areas. Those of you who don't like competitions will learn how to be successful in your own terms.

I'm sure you all remember your Child's Day when you began First School. I'm going to ask you some questions now, but I don't want you to shout out or raise your arms. Open your workstations now. OK there in the middle are two icons – yes and no. Just press which one applies. Wait, not yet.

How many of you were four years old at Child's Day? Press now.

OK, that's five of you.

Now how many were five?

OK that's 22

Lastly how many were six?

Just eight of you.

That choice – your age when you started First School - was mainly made by your parents, but you alone chose when you wanted to join Second School so it will be interesting to see how different the age spread is. Do you see the menu item next to the voting button? Change it to age. Got that?

Of The five of you who were four at Child's Day, how old are you now?

Two of you 11, the others 12.

Now, the eight who were six show your ages.

Well – that's interesting: all of you are 12. What's happening is that each of you is adjusting your parents' choice by making your own choice.

In what probably seems to you to be ages, but to me seems a very short time, you will be choosing when to become Adults. Some of you will chose 17, most of you 18 and a very few 19. My earnest wish is that by then you will have a pretty good idea of who you are.

Now, please stand.

Who got the banner ticket? What's your name? OK Huw, this is your banner. The rest of you line up behind Huw and follow me to the hall.

(End of the demonstration)

Background Information:
Minister for Education Mr Rupert Grant.

When we had to rebuild the school system we started with the philosophy that governs so much of what we do now: "Do not re-invent the wheel". None of our decisions are made by committees or men in suits; we set out the agenda, assemble data in a "hospitality village", ask our forum groups (artists, sports people, philosophers, mechanics, etc.) to select two of their members by lottery and leave the resulting group to make decisions.

It can sometimes take weeks, but so far the decisions made by these groups have proven to be sound, and the school system they set up has now been going for 10 years and looks promising.

Three contrasting datasets seemed to have had a big influence:

- An anthropological study of rites of passage and coming of age rituals
- An economic study of the effects of inequality of opportunity during the 10s.
- The 2020 Adams report on the physiology of the brain.

I have heard that in some of the other nations of these Isles, forms of selective education are being used, but in Cambria it did not take long to decide to abandon the idea of different types of school for different types of children. The data clearly shows that even the wealthiest 10 percent have a better quality of life in equal societies than in those where they had 90 percent of the wealth.

The pre-44 research on the brain has enabled us to re-define "ability" so that although all our young people share the social environment of the school, they learn different things in different ways, drawing on the skills of specialist teachers for different aptitudes.

Health and Sickness

Demonstration of Healing techniques

(Narrator) This scene shows a typical consultation by one of the Local Medics. The child is the same lad we saw in the classroom. His name is Huw and he's sick. His mother called the Local Medic Centre on her comms and one of their "Bike Doctors" is about to begin the process of diagnosis:

(BD) Hello Huw, I see from your DNA profile that you may be susceptible to a number of common ailments so I will be looking particularly at those. Before we start though, how are you feeling?

(H) Awful, my body aches and I feel sick.

(BD) No, I mean what are the things you are feeling strongly about at present?

(Narrator) Here you see the Bike Doctor going through a long series of tests to establish not only the state of Huw's physical health but just as important, his mental and emotional state. In a typical consultation she would ask him about every aspect of his life before attempting a diagnosis.

(BD) Thank you Huw. Now I must talk to your mother, but don't go away. I will need to speak to you again soon.

(Narrator) Huw is off to see his best friend – the family dog.

(BD) Hello again Ms Smith (S). You'll be glad to know It's quite a simple matter. He has an infection. I'll send you his regime – what he must eat, how he should rest and exercise and so on. Please see that he keeps to it for the next two weeks.

(S) I will my friend, thank you. Can I give the centre an hour of my time?

(BD) That would be very welcome; we are always short of resources."

(Narrator) Most of the things that afflict us can be dealt with like this, but some are much more difficult. Of course we have far less disease than was the norm in the teens and twenties. These scenes are from an old video from 2008 showing just how common it was then for even young children to be obese.

The next video is an advertisement for one of the thousands of diet plans which people spent huge amounts of money on. This one is from 2012.

Even back at turn of the century we knew what we should be eating and how much, and this knowledge stimulated another huge commercial bonanza – the sale of diet plans to try to correct the effects of the junk food. As the science improved the diet plans got more sophisticated, and many were very successful at making people slimmer. The problem was that hardly any of them were able to keep people at their right weight – they got fat again.

Finally, too late for several generations made miserable by surplus flesh, we got to grips with it. As with so many other aspects of our lives, the answer lay in our evolution. We had evolved as hunter gatherers whose diet consisted of a fairly regular supply of leaves, and roots, seeds and fruit and occasional meat. The deadly combination of fat and sugar was unknown. Now that so many more of us get involved in producing our food locally we seldom see obese people, unless they have a genetic disposition to obesity, and since we all have our DNA sequenced in childhood we can usually forestall any inherited problems.

Historic Vehicles Rally

We are the Petrol Heads! We love our cars and bikes and buses and trucks!

Don't you miss the old Vroom Vroom!

When did you last have that throbbing feeling between your legs??

Come and see some of the best bits of engineering from the Golden Age, all in great shape and full working order. Yes we even have petrol and diesel!

See your reflection in the chrome, smell the hot oil, the old leather, take a whiff of that exhaust.

Come and join a romantic celebration of Motoring Magic.

Gwitha - The Cambria Trust

"Gwitha" which means "keep" or "preserve" in Kernowek, is the Cambrian version of a long defunct body called "Cadw" which was run by the former Cymric Assembly with the task of preserving our physical heritage – mostly old buildings but also landscapes of special historical interest. That body was taken over by the Britannic National Trust. The National Trust however became the victim of a schism. On one side were those who insisted on total preservation and on the other were those who backed the NRG-led move to energy efficiency. The debate led to the demise of that body even before the events of 44 made it irrelevant.

Faced with so much loss of life, the loss of buildings seemed to many of much less importance, but in the last few years there's been a surge of interest in the past. It's all part of the feeling that we have to learn from the mistakes of the past, to re-think our future. We believe that there is still much to learn from pre-20th century history which is of vital importance to how we develop now.

Accordingly, Gwitha was set up in 2055 with a tightly controlled objective:

- Conduct a census of all buildings more than 150 years old
- Identify the most important to be preserved
- Estimate their condition
- Make recommendations

The census is now almost complete. Inevitably many are beyond repair, but on the whole life and death flowed round them. Some have been lived in, some used for business and some are derelict. The landscapes have fared better. Less human interference has been good for them on the whole, though some precious heath and wetlands have been lost to the re-growth of forests.

We are now about to embark on the task of estimating the condition of the over one thousand buildings which we think are the most important. It is a huge task and with minimal financial support from the Assembly, we are very dependent on volunteer help.

Why not join the Gwitha Volunteer Corp? This is what some of our members say about us:

"Joining Gwitha was one of the best things I've ever done. Me and my friend have a real slide – it's radiant. We love all those spooky old places, and the meals are munchy." Eleri age 12

"My wife and I have found a new meaning to life since we started working for Gwitha. We've met so many interesting people, and have so much to tell our grandchildren about our history." James 71

"Whenever I can get a bit of time off from my healthcare work I relax by poking around in old buildings. Good coffee, good company, beautiful old places – what better?" Jenny 33

The Sustainable Nation Forum

Notice board:

How sustainable is Cambria?

Did you know that:

- Our population is rising rapidly
- We have re-opened one of the old coal fired power stations
- We are importing 10% of our food – 3% from overseas
- Power for the transnet is now 5% from fossil fuel and that percentage is growing:
- House building with new materials has now overtaken building with re-cycled materials.

If you are as concerned about this as we are, please take time to read our leaflets or talk to one of our staff.

Leaflets: The Right Population, How to Use Coal, Food Freedom, Our Carbon Footprint, Sustainable Buildings

The Cambrian Fellowship

A place for Spiritual Values

What does "Religious" mean?

What does it mean to have "Faith", to "worship"

Christian, Muslim, Atheist, Buddhist, are these labels still relevant?

The whole area of belief and spirituality has been a topic of heated debate for many years now. Here, in Cambria, we believe we have resolved many of these arguments, and the Fellowship represents a coming together of several different "Faith Communities" to act as a focus point for Spiritual Values in Cambria.

Central to this debate has been the deepening of our scientific understanding of the workings of the human brain, and the evolutionary mechanisms which created an organ of such astonishing complexity.

Some of us still prefer to see such knowledge as either evil or incorrect. They are those who can see no flaws in the old story of the divine Creation. The Cambrian Fellowship does not take that path. We enthusiastically embrace the science of evolution, and we have no place for the traditional idea of a male, human-like God who "created heaven and earth". We prefer not to speak of "worship" in the sense of an unconditional adoration for such a being. On the contrary we contend that "God" is an essential part of the evolved human consciousness. Christ, the Buddha, Mohammed, and the other great religious teachers were, however, real human beings around whom a series of stories developed. These stories were and are expressions of the deepest psychological impulses of the human mind. Stories are as important to human life as air and water.

We recently sent a brief questionnaire to every address in Cambria. The main item was this question: "Can science explain everything?" We received replies from 40% of those asked, and the number answering "no" was a clear majority. This was more or less what we expected, and reinforces our contention that we humans have a deep need for mystery in our lives. We yearn for the transcendental, the spiritual. Faith is what we call a sense of union with the "other", that which is beyond our corporal existence and which illuminates our lives.

The Fellowship offers every member of our society a safe place to discuss their deepest feelings, to tell their stories.

We also have another brief – to preserve the wonderful old buildings which have for so many centuries been the meeting places of our communities. In partnership with Gwitha we have so far rescued 31 Churches and Chapels and brought them back into their communities.

If you would like to know more about the Fellowship, please take one of our leaflets and even better, come and join us at one of the regular meetings listed in the "Facts and Figures" leaflet.

The Eldred Foundation

Art is a way of Life and Life is a way of Art.

Eldred Edmundson 2000 - 2056

Our Charter:

The Eldred Foundation was set up in 2063 to promote the ideals expressed with such difficulty by our most famous artist. We offer scholarships at the University of Cambria in the following fields of study:

The Neurology of Beauty

The Art of Movement

Sport as Dance

The Psychology of Work

Students wishing to apply for any of our scholarships must show both mental and physical ability across a wide range of subjects, a thorough knowledge of the written and shown works of Eldred and his school, and a commitment to Life in Art.

The University of Cambria

History:

Before 44 there were twelve bodies with University status in the Cambria area. Only two were able to continue with a reduced level of teaching – Excaster and Bangwr. Their survival was largely due to the lack of gangland activities.

The first of the new universities was established in the Harbourers zone in Brigstowe in 2044. From its beginnings with barely half a dozen staff and just one building, it has grown since to become an important international centre of learning.

In the former Cymru the universities had become fragmented. Abertawe began teaching again in 2050 but suffered a devastating attack from a well organised gang of looters during which 5 of the staff lost their lives. It has not since re-opened, though the recently opened Elli campus now covers the Abertawe area. Caerdydd was much slower to begin again but is now in good health with a student population of around 1500.

However it was Lambed and Bangwr which kept the spirit of Cymric higher education alive. They had always been small and for the period 2042 to 2050 kept going with not much more than 500 students each. In 2050 they were joined by Ystwyth, which immediately benefited from the sea lanes to Porth La and the flow of students and teachers from Kernow.

It was decided by the Senate soon after its founding in 54 that a unified education system would be established with a single University divided into regional campuses. Accordingly there are now 8 campuses: Plymton, Excaster, Brigstowe, Caerdydd, Elli, Lambed, Ystwyth and Bangwr.

CHAPTER 5 2078

The Hub

Today Sister Tilia was again studying the collection of small nations known as the Britannic Isles. While this part of the world was too small to have much effect on the physical flows, the climate, the movement of peoples, the cycles of vegetation etc., they had always tended to influence the thought-streams of other nations so it was worth following what was happening there.

The break-up of the former Britannic state had been successfully accomplished, but a new situation had arisen which demanded her attention. Looking back at the history of this region she could see that the balance of the economy before 44 had been badly skewed. The principle city - Lyndain - had become so wealthy and powerful that by the 30s it constituted 70 percent of the economy of the entire nation. Its fall had been spectacular, and until relatively recently it had been nothing more than a collection of small towns with poor infrastructure and little industry. However, things began to change in the late 60s and now the power was flowing back. The nation which comprised its hinterland - Anglia - had decided to be a monarchy, and the ageing King had developed a taste for power. In a pattern not seen much since the 19th century, the country was preparing for armed conflict.

Interesting, very interesting.

Vandervelde - A Meeting

I see it is all of three years since our first Nation Day. I didn't go this year. I've always tried to be honest with myself in these jottings and have to admit that I am now less sure about the whole endeavour. Some day I will be gone – recycled like the rest of nature – and I have little doubt that, if I am remembered at all, it will be for this sturdy little Nation. It has matured well and has so far shown considerable resilience, but is it strong enough to survive this strange century? I worry more these days – even about my health which I used to take for granted. Now I have some arthritis in my hands and my sight is not as clear as it was. I worry too about our foreign policy. The woman (Winifred Passmore) who is in the hot seat seems perfectly capable, but I can't help feeling she lacks the diplomatic skills to deal with somebody like Anglia's Thomas Saville. He has all the smooth talk, but has no hesitation in wielding the iron fist if he doesn't get his way. Judith gets very stressed by the whole Anglia situation. I wish I could be more reassuring, but it would be a very retrograde step for me to get involved again – even if I wanted to.

I'm writing this at my work table in the Plas. Here I spend several hours most days researching the causes and effects of the great disaster of 2044. It seems strange to admit it but the six years after 44 that I spent in the Bunker at Copperfield were some of the best I can remember. I was certainly not happy when I first found sanctuary there: I had just lost Amy, the first women in my life I had truly loved. She taught me how to love and without her I would not have been able to love the vibrant young woman who joined my little team - Molly, Eldred, Magnus and a few more - in the secret underground government bunker. It had been the intense comradeship and the urgency of the work of reconstruction which had restored my soul.

Reconstruction - striving to achieve better conditions - it's part of the condition of being human and especially of being male. It's deeply embedded in the ancient part of our brains. It seems to me that most of us (the men at least) are at heart frontiersmen, pioneers, explorers, inventors, conquerors even. How many examples can you find in history of human societies choosing to stand still? Hardly any, and it was certainly not true of this idiosyncratic collection of nations which has become my home - If there was a national characteristic which had historically united the five Nations which now made up the Britannic Isles, it was surely the exploration of the unknown. As a group at the head of the historic Britannic Empire, they had been responsible for many of the innovations which had driven 19th and 20th century society, not least the Industrial Revolution itself.

Now they are struggling to come to terms with the one big idea which the 21st Century had forced on them - sustainability. Even if they knew in their heads that a no-growth economy was the only option if they wanted their offspring to thrive, in their hearts they wanted more. What after all was the purpose of hard work if not to add to your prosperity?

All over the world since 44 the business of reconstruction has given this instinct free rein. In some parts the whole idea of sustainability had never been seen as more that a temporary necessity.

I spend a fair amount of time in the library at Ystwyth these days. I've made friends with that nice woman I met in 50 - Mari. She is intending to retire next year and I don't know how the Library will manage without her. She always keeps my place for me – a chair which suits my old bones and a view of the town from the window. Usually when I'm there I have lunch in the canteen, and I was about to order when I was approached by a rather patrician figure I didn't immediately recognise. He had a slight limp, but still great presence. Wielding an ancient walking stick with a brass horse's head as the handle, he kept his dignity, along with a full head of silver hair and a twinkle in the eye.

"You must be Vandervelde, you look ridiculously young. I don't suppose you remember me do you?"

"I am and I do, and I can assure you I feel very old sometimes. Sir James Jarman I believe."

"Oh I dropped all that silly nonsense years ago – Jamie please. We were in touch briefly, years ago in Brigstowe when my company got the contract for some of the cables in the Net . . . "

"Ah yes, back in the thirties. Your design was one of the vital elements on the information transmission side. I don't think we met though did we?"

"No, but at least we have now. There's something important I want to discuss with you."

"With pleasure. Will you join me for some lunch?"

"Thank you, I will."

We shook hands, sat down and scrolled through the menu. While we waited for the first course I asked him what had happened to his company.

"Well, as you may know, we inherited a system where huge servers were holding unimaginable amounts of information in vast air conditioned vaults" He went on at some length but most of it went over my head.

"You've lost me I'm afraid, but I get the gist. You were one of the pioneers of the Smart Grid."

It was an enjoyable lunch mostly reminiscing about the days before 44. He'd had several houses in Britannica but had spent much of his time working abroad, so I had not had any direct dealings with him. I mentioned Mollie, but he skirted round the subject so I asked him what brought him to Ystwyth.

"Van, I can only guess at the number of times you have suffered bereavement. I came from a small family. We . . . how shall I put it . . . we were very close, but things went wrong. It may have been my fault. Anyway, you knew my sister so you probably know her side of the story. All I can say is that before she died we were reconciled and that made me very happy.

"I did a few things in my youth I'm not proud of, but then I married, had 2 children. We moved around a lot, had plenty of money; it was an exciting and fulfilling life. Then – well you can guess the rest. After 44 I fell to pieces – hated the other survivors, took any kind of drugs I could get hold of, lived like a scavenger for a while, wandering all over Britannica." He paused.

"Van, there's a lot in my life I would do differently if I could turn back the clock. Eventually I retreated to my house in the forest where I spent a year or so doing very little, getting the drugs out of my system and meditating. This was when Judith came to find me as she no doubt told you. "

"Yes I do remember her saying something."

"Some years later I met a wonderful person who got me back into society. She came from here and helped me get a job in the library. That led to my second career as an academic, but I was always more interested in research than in teaching and for the last 10 years I've kept my brain active thinking and writing. Until this"; he indicated his leg "I used do a lot of walking in the hills round here too."

"What happened?"

"Oh I fell badly; broke the leg and it never quite recovered. I can get around well enough."

Again he paused, looking at the floor.

"There's something else..... I had another visitor in the forest."

Another long pause.

"Is there somewhere more private we can go?"

"Er, yes, I'm sure Mari will lend me a room for a while". I paid the bill on my comms and then we went up to the library. A few minutes later we were in one of the stock rooms with a table and some chairs. Jamie began again:

"I'm finding this very difficult because in speaking to you I am breaking a solemn promise, but the conditions under which I made that promise have changed; changed in way I find so hard to deal with that I have decided . . .

"Van, I know a lot about you. I used to dislike you but I now see that you are the only person who can help me in this situation."

He was still looking at the floor, tapping with his stick.

"If I can I will"

"Right, let's go back to Ulm, Brother Ulm the Elder. Did you know about him?"

I had heard that name, but had no tag for it.

"Very little – the name. Something to do with a cult?"

"No the Fellowship is not a cult, far from it. Brother Ulm was a member of the Fellowship of the Trees, a small group of Elders with a lot of power and influence. He died - well, yes he died in 44, but in the 15 or so years before that he had an important job – that of watching and recording the life of the one person they considered important enough to warrant their most sophisticated surveillance equipment.... "

He looked up and fixed his eyes on me. I raised my eyebrows.

"That was you!"

"What? I was under surveillance?"

"You were, and very thorough it was too as I later found out."

"Good grief I don't know what to say. Ah, wait, yes I did feel something strange on a few occasions."

"That's not all . . . I was involved too. It was my task to watch my own sister. I only did it to protect her but it drove a wedge between us which I bitterly regret."

I remembered the metallic smell and the glimpses of the future I had experienced for a few seconds. Then I remembered that cryptic message supposedly from Jamie to Mollie. Nothing had come of it and I had scarcely thought of it since. I called up the tag and there it was, in 2044:

Mollie you are in danger. The Warden is watching you. Vandervelde is one of them. Don't trust him. He will say he knows nothing but they have a plan. The Fellowship of the Trees know about it. Millions of us will die.

"The message – did you write it?"

"What message"

"The one to Mollie, the handwritten one which warned her not to trust me."

"Ah, that. Yes I did, but it was a mistake. I was in a bad place at the time. I'm glad now that she showed it to you."

"So you were mistaken then. What makes you so sure now? I really want to think you are wrong, mistaken, or even lying, but what you say has a horrible ring of truth to it. It could explain a lot of things . . . But why? That's the big question which screams at me. Why would they – you – want to do this?"

"What do you know about Gaia?"

"Ah, the great Earth Mother, the living planet. I used to know James Lovelock – fascinating character but quite crazy."

"Well I found his concept compelling and when Brother

Ulm approached me he told me that Gaia was at the centre of their belief and they were all sworn to protect Her. They, the Fellowship of the Trees, all Elders or Sapients like you, believe that humans were a terrible danger to the planet and that the only way to protect Her was to reduce their numbers until they reached a point where they could no longer threaten the ecosystems."

"So you say they were watching me to see if we could achieve this? Wait a minute; some pieces of a puzzle are falling into place. They did more than watch didn't they? I always felt that we were amazingly lucky to get our agenda accepted so quickly. Did they have a hand in that? . . . I can see from your face that I am on the right lines."

The tags were lining up.

"Yes, ah yes, but . . . I'm now wondering about 44. It never quite seemed inevitable to me."

He sat there stiff, upright, his stick used for emphasis, his face grim.

"Oh yes, that too. They- we - wanted the NRG Transition plan to succeed but in the end realized that the statistics didn't work out. They were able to use one of the best processors in the world. Your plan presumed the population would first stabilize and then slowly decline. Technological innovation would slow the reduction in resources until resources and people were in balance. That was the plan wasn't it?"

"More or less"

"What the Fellowship discovered when running their models was that this balance could be achieved, even with a very high population, by phasing out fossil fuels more slowly. However, it relied on untried techniques to manage global warming, and the Fellowship considered that too high a risk. Gaia was in danger."

"So the SBX1 was manufactured by the Fellowship, is

that what you are saying?"

"That is what my current research indicates. I've no proof but it fits all the known facts. Although I was an associate, I knew nothing of all this then. Like so many others, my world collapsed. It wasn't until I started my research into the events of 44 that I began to see what was going on. I became convinced that I was right when I had a visit from another Sapient in 2063. Ulm had died in 44, and Britannica had then been assigned to him, Brother Fagus. It is incredible what the Fellowship can find out. All I had done was access certain documents. I had met him once before when I was in France and he helped me with a business deal. He wanted me to speak to Judith. Did she tell you about it?

"No, I don't think so."

"Well, she probably didn't think it was important. She had only just become President. I told her about Ulm and that I had been watching Mollie. I think she thought I was a bit odd. With hindsight I'm not surprised. A lot of things have become clearer to me now that I'm too old to be able to do anything about them!"

"Believe me I feel the same sometimes."

"There is one thing I can do though. I can tell you what I know and what I fear. What you do with that is up to you. What I know is that the Fellowship of the Trees is only part of the story. There is some other, an organisation perhaps, but I have been unable to find any information on them. It seems probable that they will stop at nothing to ensure that their Mother goddess Gaia, the living planet, is able to survive and thrive.

What I fear is that our small Nation and many more will become victims of their own success. The old pattern of growth will re-appear. They will attract the attention of the guardians of Gaia and then become targets.

He sat still in the same position, solid, upright, hand on

his stick, a grim expression on his still handsome features. There was no peace for him in retirement, and there would be none for me.

The story continues in Book 3

"The Warden"

Glossary

Comms - universal communications device. Almost everyone carries a device like a 2015 smart phone which is their only means of communicating with others - by video, voice or text.

Transnet - the track element of the 2036 transport system, including the stations and control systems.

Ek (e-car), the mobile part of the transnet system. These are various kinds of vehicle module which can link to the transnet.

Demarchy - any form of government where the representatives of the people are partly selected by lottery.

Place names:

Most of the action in the book takes place in a fictionalised version of Britain. To keep a fictional distance from the real places, all the English language place names have been replaced with either Welsh, Anglo-Saxon or Latin versions of the name.

Abertawe - Swansea

Amwythig - Shrewsbury

Anglesland – England

Breizh - Brittany

Brigstowe - Bristol

Burgedin - Edinburgh

Caerdydd - Cardiff

Caledonia - Scotland

Cambria - Wales and the West of England

Caster – Chester

Havren – River Severn

Heyl - Hayle

Kernow - Cornwall

Anglia - London, the South East and the Midlands of England

Cyrmu - Wales

Hibernia – Ireland

Kammbronn - Camborn

Kaynewidd - Newquay, Cornwall

Kernow - Cornwall

Lerpwl – Liverpool

Lyndain - London

Marlsburg - Malborough

Pennines - The North of England

Pwl - Pool

Wiltunshire - Wiltshire

Ystwyth - Aberystwyth

Dyfi - Machynlleth

Sulis - Bath

Isis - river Thames

Swinsdune – Swindon

Porth La – St. Ives

Some names are made-up:

Bridhaven - Bridport

Blackhall - White hall

Welsh (Cymraeg) words

Cariad - Darling

Cyngor - council

Duw - God

Dwli - mad, dull, stupid

Iechyd da - good health

Morfa - marsh

Meibion - boys

Pennaeth - colonel (approx)

Shwd mae/shw mae - how are you?

Tref - town

Yn wir - indeed, in truth

Cornish Words

Kernoweger – Cornish speaker

Kernowek – Cornish language

Kernowyon – Cornish people

Dydh da – good day

Yeghes Da – good health

Myttin Da – good morning

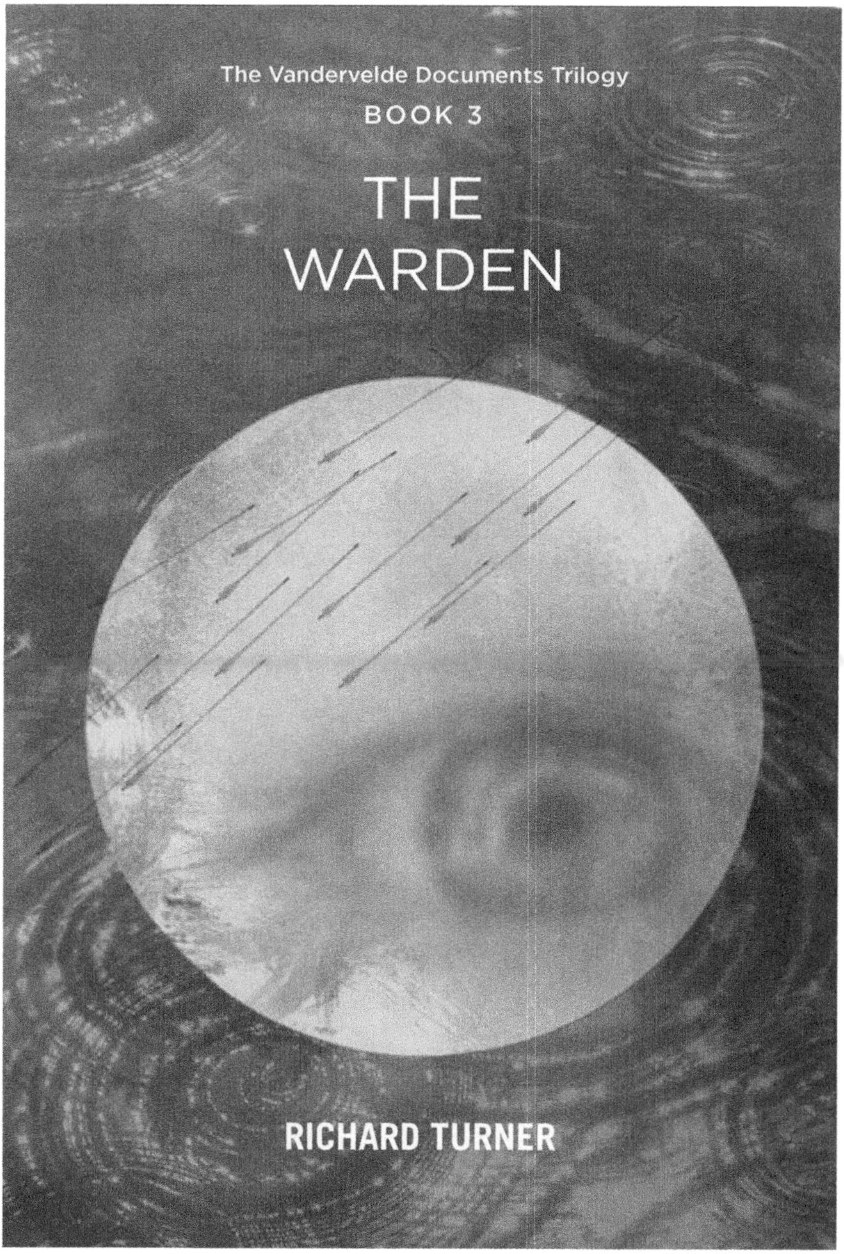

"By lifting my foot I am in the East.
Will I be safer there?"

CONTENTS

Prologue

Vandervelde 2120

Twenty eighty-four; the date still has some resonance.

I remember nineteen eighty four of course. I can remember Orwell writing the book in 1948. I did not tag the reason for my visit to Caledonia, but I can still see Eric clearly at the front door of his cottage on the little island of Diura. He was coughing, sick with tuberculosis, but greeted me warmly.

“Van,” he wheezed “I wish I had a bit of your longevity. I don't think I'm going to last much longer.”

“Well I very much hope you're wrong. I've just finished reading the draft you sent me. It’s astonishing, frightening; I think you will always be remembered for “The Last Man in Europe”.

“Huh. I don't like that title now. I think I will just pick a date in the future.”

“Just the date? Nothing more?”

“Why not. It will be different.”

“Well, here we are in 1948, what about 1984”

“Hm, maybe. Anyway, come in I've got some tea brewing.”

Two years later he was dead but his nom de plume gave the world a new adjective: Orwellian. His real surname also became well known 40 years later when Tony Blair became Prime Minister. I wonder what Eric would have made of the “Blairites”. Knowing Eric he would have been pretty scornful.

Yes, I knew Eric. I am old: so old I forget the centuries unless I mark them. I don't know how old I am or why I am different from other people. I don't even know my name so I call myself Vandervelde – from the open country.

It's 40 years ago but I can still see it all so clearly. Cambria: my greatest achievement, or an experiment which went wrong? All I can say is it felt right at the time. It still exists in a way. There is still a remnant of the government structure we created, but there's not much of it to see here on the west coast. It had its genesis in the terrible events of 44 - that total systems failure which killed a third of the world's people. The Nation we created after 44 was in many ways a better one than perhaps any previous human society, but people don't change. Life without risk, conflict and violence becomes boring, and in 2084 our little nation Cambria was in danger.

In the 2070s the reconstructed Net was unreliable. It was difficult to get an accurate picture of what was going on in the world outside our little region. As comms improved in the eighties we began to see a familiar pattern emerging. It looked as if what was happening here in the Britannic Isles was a microcosm of what was happening globally.

The dominant political structure was then known as "New Democracy", encompassing several different types of representative government. The sort of political philosophy which we used to call "Green" in the tens had lost much of its meaning after 44. In the new world green was everywhere; biodiversity flourished, nature was thriving and the hubris of mankind had been cut down. The old world of "Economic Growth" and "Gross Domestic Product" had gone, and in its place was a new determination to live within our limits. In most cases this was accompanied by a determination to be governed "by the people and for the people".

In most cases, but not in all. For all our efforts in setting up our new Nation, we could not change the evolution of the human brain, and we never found a way round the great paradox that the best run society which delivers happiness to the greatest number will be seen as boring. Eric knew that. His monstrous state "Airstrip 1" was continually at war with one of the other great conglomerations. The people were never bored.

Societies like ours lack the spice of conflict which is at the core of human nature. Sustainability means stability, it means continuing to live at about the same level, keeping to our place in nature. In a truly sustainable society, things change but do not necessarily progress. There is no place for rebellion.

By 2084 the new Nations were growing, and as they grew they began to push against the boundaries. I watched it all from the side-lines with a mixture of fascination and sorrow. In some ways it was wonderful to see the next generation using the knowledge we had given them to solve some very different puzzles, but it was sad too, sad and depressing to see how utterly wedded we still were to the basic drives which had brought us to dominate the world – that restless longing for adventure and strife.

I kept all my notes and spent a long time thinking about the second great catastrophe of the 21st century – the terrible events of the nineties: that tsunami of death which shaped the very different world we now live in.

Too much time; I was bored, so I decided to try my hand at a form of writing I had never tried before: creating a fictional story using real events and real people. I plan to have it printed on paper like the lovely books I used to read all those years ago.

I shall call it TWENTY EIGHTY FOUR – THE END GAME.

2084 The End Game

CHAPTER 1 2084

Magnus

As soon as Magnus saw the border crossing he knew something was wrong. He'd set off early to get to Beormingas where he was attending a meeting of the Anglia/Cambria cross border committee. The barrier was down - not normally something to worry about, but there were e-cars held up and people milling about on the road. As he got closer he could hear shouting. He parked and walked towards the barrier. The people let him through when they saw the uniform, but he held up his badge anyway. The Cambrian barrier pole was still down, but the Anglian barrier pole had been smashed. Beneath it was a damaged e-car. The door was open and the figure of a man was draped half in and half out. He could see blood.

As he approached, one of the Cambrian guards came towards him.

"He's from over there Sir – in Anglia. Just drove up, crashed the barrier and tried to get out of the car. I think he's been shot"

"May I see?"

"Of course Sir."

It was instantly clear that although the man had sustained some injuries, the neat round hole above his eye was what had killed him, and it had all the signs of a sniper's bullet.

"Did any of you see this happen?"

"Yes Sir, I saw the man try to crash the barrier and then just as he was getting out, he slumped forward. Then I heard a faint crack from over there".

The direction of his hand was towards a small wood about half a k away on the Anglian side.

Magnus used his rank to cross to the heavily armed Anglian border post. To his surprise he was addressed in an aggressive fashion:

"Stop. Name and Rank please."

"Magnus Edmundson, Pennaeth in the Cambrian Defence Force."

"What is your business with us Pennaeth?"

"Can you explain what happened here?"

"No sir, it is an internal matter."

"But this man has been shot. Surely we all want to know what has led to this tragedy."

"I repeat it is an internal matter and not your concern Pennaeth. Unless you have other business I must ask you to return to your side of the border."

Magnus stood for a moment.

"Please take note that I consider your attitude unhelpful and discourteous and will be reporting it to your border headquarters."

"As you wish sir. That does not concern me. Please return to your own jurisdiction."

He stood for a moment uncertain of how to handle this unprecedented situation. Then he heard a shout:

"Sir, Magnus, you need to see this"

Hiding whimpering under a blanket and unharmed by the shots which had killed her companion, was a child, a girl. Her eyes, large and staring, were darting from side to side. All she would say was "Daddy" over and over.

******

He was at the regional office in Gloster where he could get full access to OTIS (Operational Transaction Information Strategy) - trying to put together the bones of a strategy to deal with the situation, when he had a message on his secure channel:

"Please advise: Female child involved in border incident".

With a jolt he realised that he had deliberately pushed her to the back of his mind - that poor little soul he'd seen cowering in the back seat of the car while the man with her - now known to be her father Godfrey Tanner - lay dying. He switched his comms to secure speech and asked:

"What's being done with her?"

"Nothing, Sir, she's still here in our office. One of our officers is looking after her but she, the girl that is, won't say a thing. I've tried to contact the local bike doctor but there seems to be a bit of a panic on since the incident, and I can't get any sense out of her."

Magnus thought for a moment about the terror he'd glimpsed in the girl's face. To his surprise he found himself moved almost to tears, an impulse he quickly suppressed before anyone noticed. What happened to the girl was absolutely none of his business. Not his concern, but . . . he couldn't get that frightened little face out of his mind. He had no grandchildren; something he had not wasted much time brooding on until now. On a sudden impulse he closed his portal, stood up and said:

"OK I'm heading your way now, I'll call in."

Half an hour later he was sitting in front of the girl who was holding the hand of the woman border officer and staring straight ahead - at nothing. The woman, Doris, said:

"Eden here is 10 years old. She has told me her name, but doesn't want to talk about anything else yet, do you Eden?"

The girl shook her head. Magnus looked at her, smiled and said

“I don't blame you Eden. My name is Magnus. I'm very pleased to meet you”. He held out his hand for her to shake. The girl looked at him intently and something happened. Her posture of hopeless fright changed slightly and she took his hand.

“Is my Dad dead Magnus?” He blinked but didn't hesitate.

“Yes he is. He was shot in the head and died instantly.”

“Oh . . . will my Mum come and fetch me now?”

“If you can tell us what her name is and where she lives we will try to contact her.”

“She's called Lydia Middleton and we used to live at Gravesham. She's got a special job in the Army. They call her Major.”

“Oh yes. Well . . . I'll see if we can get in touch with her. This lady . . . “he turned to Doris raising his eyebrows. She answered 'Doris', “this lady Doris will look after you while I try to contact your mum.”

“No, I want to come with you.”

Magnus and Doris looked at each other. She smiled and shrugged, with a downturned grin. “I'll go Sir. We do have a message channel. I'll see what I can do.”

“Why does she call you Sir?”

“Because I'm her boss.”

“Oh . . . Are you important then?”

“Sort of I suppose. I'm what we call Pennaeth like a Colonel in your armed forces.”

“Is that higher than my Mum? Will you tell her to come

and fetch me?"

"It is higher yes, but I'm older than her I expect. We will get you back to her one way or another, but things are difficult at the moment Eden. It's complicated."

"Why?"

What could he say? Were all ten year olds as forthright as this? He felt she deserved a proper answer, but how much of the politics would she understand?

"I can't really give you a proper answer to that. All I can say is that there is a conflict between our two countries." Without thinking he then said: "will you trust me to look after you?"

"OK. Where can I stay?"

"You can stay with me tonight while we try to contact your mum. Is that OK? I'll be on my own though. I'm staying at the barracks – do you know what I mean by that?"

"Oh yes, it's a place where soldiers live. My Mum stays there sometimes."

"Ok, but this is here in Cambria, at Harford. I can ask Doris to come too if you like."

"Why?"

Was ever such a simple question so hard to answer?

Judith

It was Monday April 20 2084 and Judith Evans was on her way to Brigstowe. She had retained a consultative role at Government House when she had retired from active politics four years ago, but since her diagnosis with arthritis in her left hip she had more often than not found an excuse to stay at home when she was asked to attend a meeting of some committee which could function perfectly well without her.

It was different today. The call had come on her priority channel. The problem was serious. She had set her alarm for six, got up without waking Van, grabbed a quick breakfast and taken the e-car to the transtation at Dyfi. A few years ago she would have walked but she would need to look after her hip today if she was to avoid getting doped up on painkillers. She was still trying to weigh up the risks and benefits of having an artificial hip joint fitted. The operation was simple enough but the risk of infection was serious now that effective anti-bacterial drugs were so scarce and expensive. In three years time she would be 70 and her government contract would end. That was the time to make decisions. She felt so old living with Van, who was still able to do all the physical things they used to do together - climbing mountains, pedalling, swimming in the Dyfi, and hardest of all managing the rigging of their precious ketch when they went on their sailing trips. At least she could still do the swimming.

“Well Judith,” she told herself “You can't say you weren't warned.” She had always known that the much older man she had joined back in 2050 would eventually seem younger than her and so it had turned out. They had thrown a jokey “celebration” party when they felt their “perceived ages” had been the same, and that had been five years ago.

She knew there were stretches of the track through the mountains where her comms unit would not pick up so had downloaded the bunch of data they had sent her. For security it was all text so she transferred it to the bigger screen in the ecar, eased the seat back and began reading as the track whisked the ek along at 150kph. It wouldn't get up to full speed until they left Abertawe.

One name right at the beginning made her pause: Magnus. It was all such a long time ago and she'd met and spoken to him several times since, but just lately she had found herself thinking more and more about their daughter and what had happened to her. Dear Magnus, it wasn't his fault. He couldn't have been more tactful, but the pain of handing over that little bundle - the last chance she would have of bringing up a child of her own - that still hurt. It had been the right decision, she was still sure of that, but there was always that but . . . but what if . . .?

"Come on Judith, back to business." Business was a border incident which Magnus had attended. A man had been killed and it now seemed certain that it had been a targeted killing with a political motive. The great politician which in many ways she still was - only fairly recently ex-President Evans - took over, and all thoughts of her personal life retreated.

The meeting was in Government House in Brigstowe. Judith had to admit she was worried, but the situation was not unexpected. Even when Britannica had been one nation state, there had been disputes over boundaries, and now that it was five small Nations it would be unrealistic to think the present disputes could be settled without some sort of show of force. Having devoted her life to finding ways for humans to live together in harmony, the whole business of armed conflict made her deeply uneasy. Reading through the files that had been sent her she found it hard to recognise the chaotic, friendly little nation whose affairs had claimed most of her working life. There were to be seven people at this meeting. Two she knew well - Magnus Edmundon of course and Tom Brice the current President. Sheila O'Donnel the Prime Minister, she only knew by reputation, and the other names meant little to her.

The transtation at Templefields was busy. What used to be an easy-going public place where foot passengers were a small minority was now full of a type of traveller which had scarcely been seen since the 40s - the commuter. The idea of leaving your ek behind at a transtation in a low population area and walking, or hiring to get to an "office" in what people were now calling a "dinas" (the old Cymric word for a fortress or city) seemed odd to anyone younger than Judith. Even the pompous sounding “commuter” sounded quaint and old fashioned.

There were a number of people holding up signs for their destination within the urban area. Judith saw one saying “Dinas Centre”. She saw he had the right badge for the ek-share scheme so rode with him to Parliament Green where she paid the small sharers fee. There was no sign that he recognised her. Strange how anonymous you became when you were old, she thought. Only when she reached the reception was she given her usual welcome - more friendly than deferential, which pleased her.

The Prime Minister took the chair.

“Good morning everyone. I'm Sheila, and I'm Prime Minister of Cambria. Before we start I would like each of you to introduce yourselves - first names only as usual please.”

“I'm Magnus, Head of the Defence Forces”

“Tom, President of Cambria”

“Gordon, Internations Minister”

“Christine, Home Nation Minister”

“Patrick, Defence Forces Society”

“Judith, former President and AM”

“Thank you. You've all had your briefings, but before we start our discussions, I would like to just run through the situation as I see it. The man shot at the border has been identified as Godfrey Tanner, 45 years old, divorced and a citizen of Anglia resident in Lyndain. He had with him a female child aged approximately 10 years who was partially concealed in the e-car, and who we now know to be his daughter Eden. You have the text of the statement she made when she was recovered enough to be judged lucid.

“There is no doubt in my mind that this man was, like so

many in the last few years, seeking political asylum in Cambria, and thought he was bringing his daughter to safety. There is some doubt about the motive for his killing, one theory being that the bullet was intended for his wife who, it seems, is a Major in their armed forces. Whatever the motive, it was an appallingly callous act, and it seems quite ridiculous to me that little nations like ours which have always worked together could even think about the concept of offering asylum to the citizens of another. Ridiculous or not this appears to be the reality on the ground, so what should our response be?

“Before we discuss that question in more detail I would like to ask Magnus to outline the strategic situation.”

“Thanks Sheila. It is as you say absurd that we find ourselves in this position, and I regret it as much as I'm sure we all do, but like it or not there is no doubt in my mind that the Anglian Royal Council has ambitions to re-unite Britannica with themselves in control. For the last year we have been running our “State of the Nations” programme on OTIS. It has shown a steady build-up of forces, and an escalating number of border incidents.

“When OTIS compares the Cambrian strategic resources against our own, it always shows a deficit on our side and that deficit is getting steadily worse. Now this may look like a depressing scenario, but those of you who are up to speed with modern strategic thinking will know that we now have many more alternative options to that of open conflict. Here in Cambria we have put massive resources into military intelligence, and I can tell you with confidence that Anglia has nothing as sophisticated as OTIS. We also have better surveillance, though here the gap is narrowing. Another big plus is that they seem to be completely unaware of our special training facility in Harford. As far as they are concerned the Britannic Special Air Services, after many years in the wilderness, moved to Aldershed where we can actually watch them training. Is everyone with me so far? Ah, Judith?”

“Thanks Magnus, I'm not entirely sure why I am here, but my guess would be that you want my opinion as one of the founders of our Nation. I'm sure you are aware that peaceful co-existence was one of guiding principles, and before you go any further with preparations for war I would like to hear more details about your 'alternative options'.”

“Well I was intending to get there, but since you have raised the topic I'll set out the options as we see them. I hope I don't have to remind you that this is for your ears only. I assume you are up to date on Government Privacy Judith?”

“So I'm told. I signed the update last month.”

“Right, well our thinking on this has been much influenced by Wilson’s “History and Future of Armed Conflict”. There is a now famous graph in that book which maps the point at which parties in dispute turn to violence. Here it is on your screens. As you can see, for many centuries disputes rapidly accelerated to violence. Many of these were blood feuds where the so called 'family honour' did not permit any other method. It is not until the 16th century that the red line begins to fall. In Europe it declines steadily during the age of diplomacy. If you look at the national figures you will see very little change in countries outside what came to be called the 'Western' or developed countries – that is until very recently. There are honourable exceptions of course, but in general it was not until the 20th century that the graph begins a more rapid descent and then curves steeply downwards until the 2030s.

Now, if we look at another graph we can see violence plotted against population. It looks counter intuitive doesn't it? We would expect the sort of dense overcrowding that we saw in many nations until 44 to lead to more violence, but it is not until right at the end of that period we see a rapid rise. We now believe that the steady reduction in violence which ran in parallel with the rise in population was due to the exploitation of fossil fuels to enable the rapid expansion in wealth and technology which was such an exciting feature of the period before Carbon Trading.

What we have now is unprecedented. We have low populations, very high technology and almost zero use of fossil fuels. To me that means we have a unique opportunity to settle our differences without the use of lethal force."

There was a pause, someone coughed.

"I believe we as a government now have the opportunity to put into effect the strategies we have been working on for the last 10 years. Unparalleled in history we have what used to be called an 'Army' fully trained in non-combat!

There are several methods as you can see on your screens, and we have units trained in all of them:

SR - Surrogate Conflict - this is one of the oldest methods of all: the use of Champions or Role Players to determine outcomes.

Diplomacy - The traditional way of negotiating by presenting proposals and finding common ground.

Alliance - adding the resources of other nations to our own

CACR- Computer Aided Conflict Resolution. OTIS is our version of this method

Game Theory - this is a synthesis of SR and CACR in which the opposing 'players' play through various game scenarios to decide the outcome.

Tom - you have a point to raise?"

"Yes, thanks Magnus. I think we might be making this issue too complex. To me it is quite simple. The Anglian government are trying to bully us into conceding sovereignty. You can only negotiate with bullies by opposing them with force. If we use what I believe are called "soft" options they will see it as weakness and increase the pressure. Look what happened in Ukraine in 2014, or Mexico in 2020. I strongly believe we have to show that we will defend our borders and our sovereignty with all the force we can muster."

"Thanks Tom. Anyone in my position would have agreed with you 50 years ago, but it won't work for us now because they know almost as much about our strategies as we do about theirs. They will know we are bluffing, so their programme will calculate how much damage they are willing to sustain for their forces to prevail, and attack accordingly. If they don't attack OTIS will see that they are bluffing and we will have "won" to use the old terminology.

"If you switch to OTIS on your screens and ask for 'graphics' you will see a representation of the forces available to each side at this minute. The rolling counters on each side show a figure called the 'coefficient of force' which combines all the resources available to each side. As you can see they are in a strong position. Now look at the 'intent' diagram. That shows what OTIS believes to be their willingness to use force against our own. Shocking isn't it? Here we are in an even weaker position.

"Sheila?"

"Yes, thanks. It seems to me you are suggesting we are in a no-win situation. If these programmes can anticipate the moves on each side, how can we defend ourselves?"

"You could as well say 'how can anyone win a game of chess?' There are hundreds of ways in which we can change the situation. We could, for example, disable their defence processor - difficult to say the least, but not impossible. With what we believe to be our superiority in Special Forces we could de-stabilize their infrastructure. We could offer to play against their equivalent, which I believe is called COSI. If both sides agree to a surrogate conflict then they also agree to abide by the outcome."

While he was speaking Judith had been considering this man who had, for one night many years ago, been her lover.

He was beginning to show his age. The once brown hair was grey now, and thin on top, but still curly. His dark complexion looked more weather-beaten and lined. She had tried to keep up with the new developments in IP (Information Processing), but was finding it heavy going. She could just about understand the systems that had been developed before 44, but found the new systems much harder. The old set-up had depended on massive processors and a vast web of interconnected 'personal computers' as they used to be called when she was a teenager.

Now it seemed everything, all the devices we use to help us, every tool, machine, object of art even, they all have sensors. Even some humans have implants. It was all “nano this” and “nano that.” What was OTIS after all - not anything she could recognise as a processor. “He” at least seemed to exist in one place - in her old home city evidently - but she did not know if that place was a room, a building or a whole collection of buildings. Why did she feel so uneasy about all this? Old Age? She remembered something Van had said after 44 when they were all working in the bunker. None of them had quite understood why the crash happened then and was so overwhelming. “It was as if someone had pulled the plug.” She raised her hand.

“Judith?”

“Has it occurred to you that, if as you say, all modern warfare is a kind of cybernetic game, then we, both sides, could be pawns in someone else's game?”

There was a pause as Magnus considered his reply.

“That is a horrifying thought, Judith, and yes it has occurred to us. So far we have not been able to detect any outside influences, but I can't rule out the possibility.”

Magnus caught Judith's eye as they stood up to leave. After they had been through the security he waited until the others had gone and then said:

“Judith, I have a little bit of news.”

“I presume you mean about the child?”

“Hardly a child anymore, but yes. After the incident we have been discussing, I fed all the information about border crossings between here and Anglia into OTIS, and surprisingly there were some records going right back to the 40s, soon after the borders were finalised. We were never told the names of the adoptive parents, but they did have a security code and the records show that both of them and a child travelled to Anglia on August 20 2060. There is no record of a return trip.”

“So, he or she could still be there. Did the code give any indication of destination?”

“Nothing as useful as an address, just 'Medway'“

“So that's probably why we had no clues from Cambria. I know we have no right to look for her and it could be damaging to your family if she did turn up.”

“Yes, but for you Judith it's different. It must be very hard for you not knowing anything about your only child.”

“Not really. At least it didn't used to be, but now that I have so much more time I do think about it more often. Anyway, thanks for letting me know. Family well?”

“As can be expected. Jess is still working three days a week, Bertie is fast becoming a high flyer, but Samuel is still finding life difficult I'm afraid.”

“Ah, poor Sam. Does Jess know about our drunken night?”

“Oh yes, it doesn't bother her. We were both a bit wild before we 'settled down' as they say - horrible expression, sounds like silt settling in a pond.”

“Ha ha. Yes, and I'm proud to say I never have - perhaps in a few more years time!”

“Not you Judith - you'll be keeping us on our toes until you're carried out feet first.”

“Goodby Magnus” She gave him a hug “Let me know if anything else turns up.”

“I will - you behave yourself. Bye.”

Tom

For the last four years the President of Cambria had been Tom Brice, a man with no political connections and, it had seemed at first, little interest in politics either. Until 2080 the President had been selected from a short list of Councillors, but there was a strong body of opinion which felt that this went against the principles of Demarchy. The Council had all been selected by the full sortition/election process, but it was felt that the President should stand to the side of the career politicians and should more directly represent the people. At the same time nobody wanted yet another layer of selection, so it was decided that the Grand Assembly should choose a President by sortition at the same time as they chose the Senate. The President would be selected at random from a short list of Senators.

Poor Brice didn't know what had hit him. He'd been asked to put his name up for the Grand Assembly because of the work he had done for the medical services in his native town of Gloster. To have been selected as a Senator was shock enough, but then to be told only half and hour later that he was the first President to be chosen by sortition seemed like a joke at first. It took him a while to realise that all these deferential people rushing round him were not taking the piss. Within two days he had chosen the people he would take advice from and within a week he had a good idea of what was expected of him.

That was when he had a surprise visitor.

"Sir . . . sorry, er Tom, there is someone here who wants to talk to you. She says it's urgent."

"OK Maude, Does she have an appointment?"

"No."

"Do I have any leeway in my diary?"

"Not really, but . . . "

"Well is there any good reason why I should see her?"

"I think so Si . . . Tom, her name is Judith Evans."

"Not ex-President Evans?"

"Yes."

"Oh my word. I suppose I'm going to have to get used to this. Send her up."

A few minutes later the slight figure of the ex-President was limping towards him using a stick. She had short grey hair, and a worn, lined face which looked as if it had done a lot of laughing.

"Hello Tom. Please call me Judith"

"I will, and thank you for not using this title that has suddenly been thrown at me. It still doesn't seem quite real."

"I guessed you would be feeling uncomfortable with everyone calling you Sir or worse, Mr.President. I found it hard at first, but I'm afraid that much as you may prefer your staff to call you Tom, it won't work. It just makes them feel more uncomfortable."

"Bloody Hell - Oh sorry. How about your friends, did they change towards you? I'd hate that."

"No, not at all, they soon got used to it, but the Civil Servants need to keep you at arms length, at least until they know you better.

"Now then, I'm sure you are wondering why I am here. I know it's a bit of an imposition just turning up like this, but when I rang they said your diary was full until next week, and I had the feeling that you might need some help before then. So, and only if you have time, can you tell me what you are finding hardest?"

"Just a sec." He flipped on the comms "Maude. Can you re-arrange the diary to give me half an hour with Mistress Evans now?"

"Er, let me see. No, sorry, there's one appointment you really don't want to miss: the Breton Consul - and he's just arrived. I can make a space after him - say in an hour."

He turned to Judith.

"Tom, that's fine. I've plenty of old friends here and I know they serve good coffee in the bar so I'll see you in an hour."

******

With help and advice from a whole galaxy of household names, including Judith, Tom found to his surprise that he could do the job, and by the end of his first year it was apparent that he could do the job well.

The situation that faced him now however would tax him to the limit. He was by nature an appeaser, happiest when he could negotiate a deal which defused anger and left everyone feeling that they had achieved something. So far he had managed to keep his dealings with the Prime Minister Sheila O'Donnel, on a cordial basis. She too was an appeaser, but when he realised that she was determined to find a non-aggressive solution to the flare-up with Anglia, he saw for the first time that he would need to clear his head of all the political posturings that had filled it during the last year and get back into "Gloster Mode" as he called it. His gut feeling was that he would have to disagree with Sheila. He knew that the people of Cambria, many of whom had come here to escape the regime in Wincaster, would want to stand firm, even to the extent of threatening violence.

To Tom violence was anathema. It always led to grief, pain and anger. He was also a great reader and his love of historical novels had led him to read up on the background to his fictional heroes and heroines. He knew all about blood feuds and "omerta" and he despised those who in the past had caused so much suffering for individual gain. He also understood bullies, and it was clear to him that the regime in Anglia was intent on bullying its neighbours. Their King and his Council would exploit any weakness as a sign of bad leadership. Their great claim was that only a return to rule from Wincaster would safeguard the living standards of the people of "Greater Britannica" as they called it. Tom knew from his own experience that appeasing bullies did not work. They would have to stand firm.

Kenric

From where he stood Kenric Price could see the Lyndain Basin and the new naval quay at Trefalga. Away in the distance across the water he could see the cranes working on the new reclaimed areas of Peckman and Brickton. There was a long curving line of buoys marking the shipping lane which followed the old route of the Isis. The great shallow basin beyond where the old densely populated districts of Lambit and the former docklands used to be - that was a mix of marshland and small sailing dinghies. Someone had started a business hiring out glass bottomed boats so that people could look down at the remains of the buildings below. Kenric had done that once. It was a strange and disturbing experience. Over shallow water there was enough light and you could see piles of rubble, walls, roads, an occasional roof; some covered in weed and green moss-like growths, some still bare. As the boat moved further out the streets below became darker and more ghostly. He had been unable to recognise the street where his parents had lived.

Kenric had been to school near the marina at Peckman - the first of the new schools set up by the Royal Education Foundation, which controlled all the National Schools in Anglia. He'd been popular with his classmates and with the girls at the sister school at Nunshed - popular enough to gather a little gang around him, and the stuff they got up to came back to bite him when he found he wanted to go to university. There were only three in Anglia then – Oxen, Granta and Lyndain, and under the new rules they refused him entry on his record of conduct. That just meant he had to work even harder to get his place in the Royal College of Government at Winsey Castle. There he got a reputation as a tough talker: someone who knew his own mind and wasn't afraid to tell it. He had thought since that the Court had decided he was safer on the inside. However it came about, he was fast tracked to a career in the Royal Service and soon made himself indispensable to some of the more powerful politicians of the day. Then in 2073 he was quietly approached by one of the King's retinue and asked if he was interested in serving under-cover. His job would remain the same on the outside, but he would be working for a different master. He saw little of 'His Madge' as they called him; most of his work was away from the Court.

When he was in the conurbation, the "City of Towns" as it was called, he spent a lot of his time in a simple new timber and render building among the Royal Houses of Government just inland from the Quay at Trefalga. The RHoG was to become the new administrative centre of Anglia when all the offices were moved from Wincaster. It was built inside the huge walls which protected all the old St. Justin's Park and included the King's Palace. Lyndain was being reborn and he was at the centre of it. It was an exciting time - a new nation rising, not from the ashes but from the waters of the old: a new Nation full of self-confidence and pride.

That's what he should be feeling, but for weeks he had been having anxiety attacks. He could feel that something was not right. He would get stomach ache which only drink would numb, and when Ken decided to have a drink any of his many friends with him at the time had better have a strong head. He had been known to start at 17:00 with a "sundowner" and finish with a few shots of gin in a night club just as the sun was rising.

On the rare occasions he spoke to King Michael he found him charming, direct and forthright, his upright stance and lively manner belying his 70 odd years. In many ways he agreed with the Royal emphasis on efficient administration. He was proud of the fact that the crime figures had decreased so emphatically. What worried him were the stories that had leaked out recently about crime bosses disappearing. One of the reasons he had decided to work for the shadowy "King's Specials" was his hatred of organised crime. His father had fallen foul of one of the old Lyndain bosses and it had blighted his parents' lives. His first undercover assignment had been as a runner for the "Waterboys", one of the new breed of East Lyndain gangs, and within a year he had become a trusted henchman to Councillor Jim Eaves, the millionnaire financier famous for his donations to the Peckman food banks charity, and "head" of the "boys". It had made his day when Eaves spat at him on his way from the court to a life sentence for extortion and murder. Ken had no objection at all to a few corners being cut to get these disgusting creatures put behind bars, and he had been looking forward to the big trials coming up.

But the trials had never happened. Months went by until people forgot all about them and then a tiny news item in a corner of your screen would announce that Joe so-and-so had unfortunately taken his own life while in police custody. Who cared? The notices changed - Dave M had attacked a prison guard and had been overpowered; Mike X had been killed escaping from custody . . . too many to be co-incidence. He pushed it to the back of his mind - there were more important things to worry about than the fate of a few gangsters.

He had become accustomed to thinking of the Parliament as being pretty ineffectual, but had followed the speeches of "His Majesty's Loyal Opposition" as they liked to be called. Suddenly last year 83, things had changed. The opposition spokesman for Law and Order, Esau Goldman put this question to the Prime Minister:

"Can the Right Honourable Gentleman please tell me why five named gang leaders have all died in police custody before being brought to trial?"

"I must apologise to my colleague. I was not aware of this. Can he provide me with the names of these people?"

"I can sir, they are Michael "Micky" Hallam, David Mitchel, Grant "Big B" Sylvester, James Eaves, Walter Thomas and Oswin (Ozzie) Daniels."

"Thank you, I will consult with my staff and see if we can find out what has happened."

A month later the following announcement appeared:

"Following a police investigation the Member for Northwich, Esau Goldman, opposition spokesman on Law and Order has been arrested and will stand trial on charges of treason."

There was a lot of talk in the press about what Treason meant in modern Anglia and about what the Member of Parliament had done, but then nothing happened and the attention moved elsewhere. That was the last anyone heard of him.

Kenric began scrutinising the media in earnest and found more of those little announcements about unfortunate deaths in police custody. The opposition had gone very quiet. He decided to try a small experiment. From the safety of his position he issued this statement:

“Missing persons: Can anyone provide information on the following person who is believed to be missing. Her name is Maud Percival, and the last time she was seen was in the office of the RT Hon Esau Goldman.”

If what he suspected was true that would be enough to alert the authorities.

The next week was uneventful, but then he began to notice a particular e-car, or the same person walking towards him two days in a row. He had half expected that, but he had certainly not expected the visitor he had a week later.

He was at home in Ham. The Royal Borough of Ham was one of the main Small Towns which made up the Metropolitan area. It had been a prosperous inner suburb until the floods. Because so much housing had been lost, the cost of housing anywhere near the basin was near pre-44 levels. His job required a low profile so one of the harbour-side houses was not an option. Home was a modest semi in one of the back streets. At least it had a garden, and the open country was only a few streets away. At the age of 35 he now lived alone - he'd not had much luck with relationships and had no children.

His visitor was someone he knew quite well but seeing her here at his front door threw him and he couldn't for a moment remember her name.

“Oh hello. What a surprise. You work in Pensions don't you?”

“That's right, Jane Campion”

“Yea course, please, come in.”

“Thank you. I hope I haven't come at a bad time?”

“Not at all; I was just wondering what to do next.”

There was nothing about Jane which made her stand out from a crowd. She had brown hair, was pleasant looking, medium build, and dressed in normal casual clothes. There was something about the way she moved . . . If you looked again you might notice an intensity of expression. Her gaze was direct; someone who would not suffer fools gladly he suspected.

"Come in the kitchen. I got some good coffee." Ken was good at putting people at their ease. He quickly prepared coffee.

"Let's take this downstairs - it's more comfortable there." Downstairs was his darkroom where he was experimenting with glass plate photography, but it had a metal door, and there were comfortable chairs, a warm but fresh atmosphere and the hushed sensation of being sound-proofed.

"Jane, I don't know about you but I get a bit paranoid in my job, you know, about being over-heard and stuff. We can talk here."

He couldn't tell from her expression what her reaction to this was. They settled into arm-chairs facing each other over a small table and sipped their coffee. Jane spoke first:

"Kenric - please don't get the wrong idea but I've been watching you." His expression was guarded.

"I am fairly sure that you are not comfortable in your job. I know you have been following the disappearances and when you sent out that message about the missing MP I decided to try to speak to you. If I've made a mistake it could cost me my freedom, even my life."

"Blimey - no pressure then."

"Oh please don't laugh at me, this is really serious."

"Yea - nervous habit, sorry. I know you're serious, and you're right too - I have got a few problems. To be honest I wonder if His Madge actually knows what's going on."

“Oh yes, he knows alright. I can show you proof that he gave the orders.”

The little room was so quiet they could hear the faint hum of the ventilation. Jane was watching every twitch of his face as the implications of what she was saying sank in. What he did next would either change his life profoundly or have a devastating effect on hers. She had her hands clasped together and they began to tremble. He leant forward and placed his own hands over them and suddenly she was crying.

“Oh Kenric, please come with us” He moved to put an arm round her and before he knew what was happening they were embracing. She clung to him.

“Oh God I'm sorry. That wasn't meant to happen.”

“Jane, please, I'm with you. We got to work together.”

When they had dried their eyes they sat down again and Jane began to tell him about the group she was working with. He knew with absolute certainty that his life would never be the same. He saw now quite clearly that the effort he had been putting into his job, the long hours, the craving for approval, socialising, drinking, visiting parents - all this had been a way of coping with a deep sense of insecurity. He had been trying for so long to ignore it and now he felt a great sense of relief. He was no longer alone. Between them, somehow, they would find a way back to real democracy.

Brother Fraxinus

Fraxinus was also in Anglia - on the other side of the Lyndain basin at Blackwitch. Here he was known by his American name: Troy Cagney, and he too was worried but for a very different reason. The journey from his home in the new capital of the Atlantic Nation of America, which was a small town called Plymouth, had taken two days in the Atlantic Voyager airship. One of his small band of Elders, the Fellowship of the Trees, had recently disappeared, and he was here to try to find out what had happened. The last message from Brother Fagus had been cryptic to say the least:

"By lifting my foot I am in the East. Will I be safer there?"

The Fellowship decryption programme - one of the most powerful in the world - could find no hidden meaning. The words meant what they said, so he was literally straddling some international boundary. The possibilities were endless. Even with the computing power available to him in Plymouth House, the list of places where a boundary between a nation which could be classified as "West" and one which was "East" ran into the hundreds. He was looking for somewhere like the last century division between East and West Berlin, but that had long disappeared.

All the Fellows of the Trees had the capacity to control at least some of the workings of their minds - they had been practising for some two centuries after all. Fraxinus knew that if he went through a few specific mental exercises just before sleep, he could rely on his subconscious to work on the problem while his conscious mind was resting. He had sat with his eyes closed for ten minutes before settling down to sleep. Waking the next morning from a nostalgic dream about travelling in a steam train, he found the answer waiting for him. It was nothing to do with national boundaries, but the boundary between eastern time and western time - the Blackwitch meridian in Britannica. This was where the international time system had been agreed, and every zone to the east of "Blackwitch Mean Time" had plus values with everything to the west having minus values.

The place was at the top of a hill overlooking the basin, and the whole hill had been a park even before 44. Ever since arriving in Britannica he had been struggling with the rapid changes in the weather. It was April, one of the most unreliable months, and he had felt so cold in his lightweight clothes that he had bought a down winter Parka and a woolly hat. Coming out of the transtation into bright sunlight he soon found that he had got it wrong again. Before he had got more than a few hundred yards up the footpath he had taken them both off and now would have to carry them. When he got to the little observatory museum he was sweating and had to sit down for a while to cool off.

Looking out over the basin towards the old docklands he was struck by how desolate the ruins of the pre-44 financial quarter looked. Many of the office towers that had brought vast wealth to the area had proved too difficult to demolish and were left there with the water lapping round them. One had tipped sideways and was leaning against another - a surreal image. The new docks had been built further north and were looking prosperous now - filled with the comms controlled vertical sails that powered most sea vessels now.

What had persuaded Fraxinus to make this trip was that he could find no trace of the disappearance of Fagus on the Net. Of course he did not expect to find him mentioned by his Fellowship name - the Fellowship had never been recorded. No, what puzzled him was this: Fagus had been using his old name, one very familiar to the media - and all mention of him had ceased. Not only were there no new mentions, but all the historic ones had disappeared too. It was as if he had never existed. The Fellowship had always kept a system of communication which did not depend on the Net. There were small libraries all over the world where they kept paper records in what looked like books. Somewhere Fagus would have left a written message, written by hand with a pen, or perhaps written in symbols.

He found a bench seat overlooking the whole of the east metropolitan area and sat for a while deep in thought. Just to his right was a small group of mature trees. There were five of them, forest trees close enough together to force tall straight trunks to grow, and their combined canopy just bursting into leaf cast a dappled shade - welcome after his sweaty climb. He admired their shapes thinking what a neat bit of planting that was. Trees . . . Fellowship of the Trees, of course!

He leapt to his feet and walked briskly over to the little copse; five trees, all different. Here was an Ash *Fraxinus Excelsior*, this an Oak *Quercus Robur* , and this one a Beech *Fagus Sylvetica.* There was another which looked like a Lime tree but with large leaves – the *Tilia Platyphyllos,* and less sturdy than the others a Maple *Acer Platanoides.* The co-incidence was striking, but one of the Fellowship names was missing - the Elm *Ulmus Minor.*

Thinking through this puzzle he walked around under the trees looking closely at each one. With his eyes up in the branches his foot caught in some scrub at ground level. The trees were quite evenly spaced except for a more open area where scrub growth had recently been cut down. It looked as if a long time ago there had been another tree there. Then it came to him. He knew about trees - they all did. He activated a memory tag and pictures of dying trees came back to him: Dutch Elm Disease - a fungal infection carried by a bark-boring beetle that had wiped out most of the Elm trees in Britannica. But that was over a hundred years ago, which meant that he had already been an adult when he had seen those dead elms in Britannica: not really surprising; he had tags from a lot earlier than that, though of course none of his childhood. Was it possible that the fellowship was founded much earlier, and perhaps not by Brother Fagus as they had always assumed?

Was it chance that had led him here - this little patch of Anglia thousands of miles from his home? He had a feeling he would find the answer to that here among the trunks and branches of these stately old trees.

******

He had found something, but he was not at all sure it meant anything. It was what looked like a 20thC hieroglyph carved into the bark of the beech tree at Blackwitch. There was the symbol of a heart with that of an arrow piercing it diagonally from above, and some letters above and below it: The top row of letters read FF - FF, and the bottom read FF - ROTA . Troy searched his memory banks for clues; in one he was on a high ridge overlooking a valley - by an ecar zone there were some trees and one had a similar motif. In another he was with a dog in a park in some city and again saw a tree with what he now remembered to be a declaration of love. Such declarations he remembered had been disliked by the authorities and had died out by the 20s.

The carving on the beech tree had been partially obscured and stretched by subsequent growth of the bark. Troy had stood beside it and imagined himself using a hand-knife. The image was just above his head. Either a very tall person had done the carving or the tree had grown by about 25cm in height since. By checking the average growth rate of beech trees he estimated that the carving had been done some time in the seventies. Fagus had disappeared in 2078. Could this be a message, and if so could it link to that last Net message apparently written and sent from near this spot?

"By lifting my foot I am in the East. Will I be safer there"

The letters were clearly a code and somewhere there would be a decryption clue. If he could find the clue he would know the message was for him. ROTA stood out. The clue must be somewhere in that group of letters.

He had walked all round the trees relaxing his conscious mind, and then down to Blackwitch village and his guest-room. He spent the evening avoiding thought, did his pre-sleep preparation and slept soundly. He was disappointed to find very little fresh insight in the morning - just this: Rota was a Spanish name, a town near Cadiz. It could also be Italian perhaps, like 'ruota' or French 'route'. They were all latin languages. It was not until he dredged his knowledge of cryptography that he realised that high level decryption devices could sometimes be defeated by using un-encrypted words. The series of FF groups were very hard, but ROTA could be a word with the letters in the correct order. Latin- he searched his memory banks for latin words and a tag came up: one of his earliest memories; a classroom; a latin lesson.

"What does Rota mean Smith?"

"Hub Sir"

The Hub! If Latin was the clue then perhaps all the Fs were latin words. How could a code have all the same letters? Suddenly it all clicked into place: the latin for brother was Frater. They were Fellowship names but in Latin:

> Frater Fagus – Frater Fraxinus
>
> Frater Fagus/Fraxinus – The Hub
>
> It was a message from Brother Fagus to Brother Fraxinus – him. That much was clear but what the message was defeated him.

When, two days later and still in Blackwitch, he was no further forwards he decided to call it a day and wait for further clues to present themselves. His work at the Black House was demanding and he would have to return home.

Lydia

Lydia watched as the new recruits came in for the briefing. They were an impressive looking bunch; mostly men; all very fit; some very tough looking; others more like teachers on a day off. She stood up in front of them and gave her normal introductory speech.

"Good Morning and welcome to Aldershed. I'm Major Middleton and I am your training Manager. As you probably know you are part of a long and noble tradition. Before the catastrophe in 44 the Britannic Special Air Services were known throughout the world. If you wanted something done you called in the SAS. I'm sorry to say that the name of their base, Harford, which at one time was a by-word for intelligent soldiering, is now nothing more than a sleepy decrepit town in so-called Cambria. What you will learn in the next few weeks is part of a plan to restore at least some of the glory that was Britannica.

“What is it that makes our special forces Special? Before I try to answer that let me ask you this: how many of you have come here from the Anglian Armed Services?

“OK, less than half of you. I guess when you were serving in the AAS you learned to address your commanding officer as “Sir” and our King as 'Your Majesty'?” She left a pause.

“Well you can forget all that. We do use 'Sir' when being polite, but mostly we use first names. I’m Lydia, and in case you didn't know His Madge is Michael.” There was some slightly uncomfortable laughter at this.

“When you are on active duty, you answer only to your comrades. You will have been given a mission, and you are free to discuss the mission with your senior officers. You can even call them 'Sir' if you like.” There was more nervous laughter.

“When the mission is agreed the decisions in the field are yours. If they are bad decisions don't expect any backup. You will be on your own.”

“That's all I want to say for now. I hope you enjoy at least some of the stuff we are going to put you through, but you would not be here if you were expecting an easy time in the next few weeks, and I have to tell you now that some of you will not make it. To fail this course is not in any way a badge of shame. You will still be counted as one of the best of your generation, just not quite THE best.”

'Which of them would it be?' she wondered, the ones who looked like schoolteachers or those who more resembled gangsters? You could never tell.

******

Lydia had always known she was different. She knew that her parents, Simon and Millie were not her genetic parents. They, the Middletons, born in the tens, had moved from their home in Medway to a small town in Cymru during the fast moving 30s, only to find themselves, after 44, destitute and cut off in a country they did not recognize as home. Nothing went right for them - even their sporadic attempts at starting a family were destined to failure.

Redemption came from an unexpected quarter. On a whim, during a visit to Caerdydd, Millie walked into the offices of an adoption agency. She knew full well that children were so treasured after 44 that any child put up for adoption would most likely have terrible parents, but what had she to lose? Within a surprisingly short space of time they were told about an expected birth. The catch was that they would never be able to know who the parents were - only that at least one of them was in the public eye.

"What did we ever do to deserve this" said Millie one evening after Lydia's first birthday when yet again the tiny child had charmed them to tears. From that point on things began to improve. Simon had been making some enquiries about possible jobs near their original home, and had struck lucky. What he didn't know was that the engineering jobs on offer in the old shipyards at Medway were part of a secret Anglian plan to restore a measure of naval power. Even if he had known he would not have cared. As long as they could live a normal life politics was of little concern to them.

The next few years flashed by in a daze of happiness. They had agreed with the agency to tell her about the adoption on her 12th birthday. Lydia was turning into a fierce youngster and they were braced for tantrums, but it went surprisingly easily. She just shrugged her shoulders:

"Oh don't fret Mums, loads of people are adopted nowdays. Does this mean I can do some other kind of work now?"

How clever of her to choose that moment to ask for a big concession! With their own days of hardship in mind they had insisted that she should help her mother with the small needlework business she had built up. That way Lydia would acquire some knowledge of business and some useful skills. She had found the work boring. They agreed that she could change, but hadn't any idea what to suggest. Lydia knew immediately. In town there was a new Mind and Body centre and they had space for a few Cadets. If Lydia could pass the quite daunting tests for entry to the Cadets programme, she would earn a small wage, and improve her physical and mental fitness for life in the 21st century.

To the surprise of her parents she passed easily and flourished as a Cadet. From there it was a logical step to apply to the Defence Forces. Two years later she had passed her Officer Training and soon after that was given the rank of Lieutenant. The next few years were tough. They were all under constant pressure to improve, to get smarter and tougher. Far from having an easier time of it, her fellow women seemed to be pushed if anything harder than the men. At least that is how Lydia felt. Sometimes she wondered if she was being picked on.

Somehow she got through it all and her life changed dramatically when she was called in to see her commanding officer, James Archer.

"Lieutenant Middleton, please take a seat. It's been a pretty difficult year for you hasn't it?"

"Er, yes Sir. It's been hard, but I'm not complaining."

"Good, good. I can tell you now that we have been

impressed with the way you have coped with the tasks we have set you. In particular we are interested in how you relate to your companions. Those I have spoken to hold you in high regard."

"Do they? Well, that's good to hear I suppose. I have been able to help a few of them when things have been particularly nasty."

"Yes, and that is why we think you might be the right person for a particular job. It's a job which will demand a high level of self motivation because, if you accept, you will not be able to reveal the true nature of the job, and may well find some of your contemporaries being promoted before you."

"I can't say I'm not ambitious Sir. You'll have to tell me more about this job before I can say if it would suit me."

"Good. Let me do the security procedure and then I can tell you all about it."

******

The Specials had suited Lydia perfectly. She loved the life, the constant challenge of working with such highly motivated people - always pushing them to explore their limits; picking them up when they were down and cutting down the ones who were too proud. They gave back to her great respect and even love. Despite what Archer had said she did gain quite rapid promotion and was now Major Middleton.

If only her personal life could be as good! Goff just didn't seem to have any idea what her working life was like. Things improved for a while when Eden was little, but then Goff lost his job. He'd never much liked working in the Shires Insurance Company's head office, but at least it paid well. They could afford a good house, good food, all the things the new citizens of Anglia aspired to. When he was at home all day he was lost. Things went from bad to worse until they finally agreed to a separation.

It was only a few months after he had left her that she had the terrible news of his death, and now the anger and grief were as fresh as ever. Goff, the man she still called her husband, had called her a fascist, a cold, uncaring bitch who loved the army more than her daughter, let alone her partner. She knew she was strong, but how could the strongest person deal with the news that her lover, partner, husband, ex-husband or whatever she now called him, had been shot; shot and killed while trying to abduct her daughter to what was now another country? She had lost someone who was, and always would be, part of her emotional make-up. Not only that but all she knew of her daughter was that she was alive. How could he be so stupid? How was it possible that he had been shot? Why had he taken Eden? Where was she?

Lydia desperately wanted to go and look for her, but knew that was impossible, so she had set up a meeting with her new boss, General Walters.

“Sir, we have to get her back. I can't do my job while she is over there.”

“Ah Lydia, I feel for you” (did he? she wondered.) “It's a terrible situation. I can assure you that the man who did this is currently on remand awaiting prosecution for insubordination.”

“Oh I don't care about that. It was partly Godfrey's fault anyway. I just want my daughter back. The longer she stays over there the more traumatised she will get. Sir, we must start negotiating.”

“Hold on Lydia, I hope you understand what a difficult position this puts me in. We can't allow them to think that they hold the whip hand. They will use this girl . . . er, what's her name?”

"Eden."

"Of course, they will use Eden as a bargaining counter. COSI (Combined Operations Systems Information) estimates that she has the same value as one of our senior staff. The first word has to come from them."

"Why can't we run a mission to get her back? What does the great COSI say about that? Does it say why I should allow a machine to tell me what will happen to my daughter?" She desperately stifled the tears. "Sorry Sir, I know it's difficult for you too."

"Let me put this to you Lydia. Give them two more days. If nothing has happened by then I will call a Chiefs meeting here and we'll make a plan. How does that sound?"

She said nothing for a few moments.

"It's crap to be honest but so is everything else. It's the waiting. It kills me. I'm quite ready to resign over this; I hope you realise that."

"Careful young lady. Mind how you speak. We'll meet again here on Thursday."

Magnus

Magnus was having a difficult time too. He knew well enough what a strategic asset their custody of Eden was, but he could not pretend he felt nothing for the girl. The image of her taking his hand reminded him painfully of their great disappointment, he and Jess. Bertie their Elder son was happily married but he and Marie had a long running fertility problem, and Sam the younger one had sheepishly declared the love of his life to be male. Their friends were proudly showing him pictures of their grandchildren, and all he could think of was Eden clutching his hand, Eden laughing, sulking for her mother, rushing around yelling, sitting reading. He had few secrets from Jess; somehow their relationship had survived his many absences, and as soon as he had told her about the girl marooned at the border she had agreed to help look after her.

"You must put a limit to it though Mags. She can't stay here for ever."

"Of course. We've already started moves to get her returned. We don't want her getting too fond of us!" Jess looked at him askance but he turned away. If he couldn't admit it to himself, he certainly couldn't to her.

President Brice and Prime Minister O'Donnel were sympathetic but insistent that he should have nothing to do with the negotiations. Sheila, the PM, had called him in to her office a few days after the incident.

"We have to wait for them to make the first move Magnus. We know that the King and Walters both have great regard for Major Middleton, and our information is that she will resign if they fail to negotiate Eden's release. We have a very strong hand here Magnus. If we play this right it could rein in their expansionist plans and stop all this talk of war."

"Can I just ask that we put the welfare of this child at the top of the agenda. I would rather never see her again and lose a dear friend than see her psychologically damaged by some political game of ping pong."

"You will have to leave it to us Magnus. You are too emotionally involved here."

"Am I? Well perhaps it hadn't occurred to you that you and Brice aren't enough involved. You're cold fish, the both of you. I'm telling you now that unless this girl is treated properly I WILL RESIGN." He stared at the Prime Minister in fury. Her expression hardened.

"Message received. I will expect an apology or your resignation." She turned and made for the door.

"Wait. I'm sorry. I should not have spoken to you like that. You are right, this is something I do feel strongly about, perhaps too strongly, but I stand by what I said."

"Thank you. I hope we will find the right solution to this."

It was a waiting game on both sides. After a week had gone by with no message in either direction, the Cambrian negotiator, Senator Frederick Danby received this terse message:

"King Michael wishes to inform President Brice that unless the girl Eden, daughter of Major Middleton of the Anglian Defence Force, is returned to her mother within two days of this notice then that same Defence Force will do whatever is necessary to ensure that the girl returns to her home."

Danby was ready for this and replied:

"President Brice has no wish to hold Eden Middleton under Cambrian jurisdiction any longer than is necessary for her safety and will be happy to return the girl at an agreed location provided that we have the following assurances from King Michael:

That Anglia is willing to sign an agreement to maintain the borders between our nations in their present form, and to permit free movement and trade across those borders.

That King Michael acknowledges that his position as Head of State of Anglia is parallel to the position of the President of Cambria and that neither has any jurisdiction outside their own borders."

The opening positions had been set up, and the strategies and the resources identified. It was a well established convention in modern game theory that the opening side (Anglia) was coded White and the responding side (Cambria) Black. In this case White had made two moves, a demand and a threat. Black had responded with a positive and two conditions. Now the players, OTIS and COSI were working through the options. For every possible move the counter moves were assessed so it took a minute or so before COSI flagged a gambit it rated as “possible”. They would make a concession calculated to improve their position later. COSI (White) offered to double the period of grace from two days to four. OTIS (Black) immediately accepted the gambit and made a reciprocal offer: a two months grace period to open the borders. They had reached stalemate again.

At each stage in the play there would be a delay while the human input teams made their assessments. It was their job to correct any over-logical moves made by the machines to allow for human irrationality. Each time they did this the machines learned to allow for that particular human quirk, but even after 30 years of gaming at this level, the machines had still not learnt all the intricacies of human irrationality.

After an hour or so the moves began to slow down until White’s final move was shown: “that stasis be maintained for six months after the girl is returned.” This was the long established tradition of the “cooling off period”. Black knew that with their current resources this was the best outcome. The location and method of the transfer had already been agreed, so the next morning Magnus and Eden found themselves at one of the small back-road border posts near Cheaping. It was quite high – chalk downland with the occasional clump of beech trees. On the Cambrian side was a wide expanse of grassland and scrub with a few sheep and goats. The other side had been ploughed and was green with the new shoots of barley and wheat. There were the usual team of three border guards augmented by three Specials. Across the 100 metre border zone they could see Lydia waiting with the same three guards and three Specials.

Magnus had given Eden a rare paper book about Cambria with lots of printed pictures and a fine hard cover. She clutched it tightly in her free hand while pulling Magnus towards the gate in her excitement at seeing her mother again.

“Goodbye Eden. I’ll come and see you as soon as I can, promise.”

“Bye Magnus . . . Oh look, it’s Peter, my rabbit. Look how big he is.” She ran off across the zone, stopped abruptly to turn and say “Thanks for the book, it’s lovely” and then rushed into her mother’s arms. As they turned away Lydia looked back and waved. He waved and then slowly walked back to his transport. The Specials were silent. They knew what he was going through.

They had bought 6 months of peace. Would it be enough?

The Hub

The border incident had been a bit contrived. Suggesting that a key woman member of the Anglian armed services was about to flee to Cambria looked a bit odd when it was clearly a man who had been killed. The sniper had got the blame. Tilia was uncomfortable when things like this happened but it was a necessary part of her job. Collateral damage could not be avoided sometimes.

Today her assignment was North America. She stood in front of the Globe on the viewing area which she could move in all dimensions – north to see the current position of the remains of the arctic ice: dense white with dark grey storm clouds moving over the north Atlantic. She moved further south to get a satellite view of the Atlantic Republic in the east of the continent. Here it was hot. There was barely a trace of cloud obscuring the capital, Plymouth. She stood quite still for a while as the Globe slowly moved round in front of her.

Sister Tilia was an Elder; one of the Fellowship of the Trees, and her assignment in the Hub was an important one. For several months now she had been following the breakup of the USA. She judged that the plan was working so turned her attention to what used to be Canada, highlighting the area on the Globe. She had been surprised at the difficulty they had experienced with the breakup of Canada. Quebec had been easy. After 44 and the break-down of Montreal, Quebec city became the obvious centre for the new nation. Surprisingly the Eastern provinces - New Brunswick, Newfoundland and Nova Scotia had decided to join Quebec rather than the new Atlantic nation to the south.

She walked back to her work table and joined the Warden. First she checked the incoming data stream for humans in North America and looked at the menu.

She chose "affiliations" and saw in diagram form the hundred or so issues that affected how North Americans related to each other. She spent a while studying them before moving on to "conflicts" where she could see the results of some of the 'thought-streams' as they called them. A thought-stream could be as amorphous as a climate of opinion or as precise as a wish. Conflicts could consist of anything from an argument between neighbours to actual fights. After studying the input flow, she made her selection for the day and sent it to the Warden be played.

It had not been an easy year for Tilia. Calan had gone. Most of the Hub personnel were of course not Elders, and were subject to normal human ageing. By the mid-seventies, Calan's physical deterioration had become too great a charge on their resources, and he had chosen his exit point. Although it was generally accepted that the loss of a Mate was likely to lead to an emotional disturbance, there was no special provision for Elders. Tilia was just left to carry on without him. No matter how hard she worked at her mental exercises, she could not altogether banish thoughts of her time with Alene – the only time she could remember when she had felt real passion. Her refuge was her work, and it was always challenging.

On another work station Ciri was having a problem with Russia. Actually Russia had always been a problem. Even after 44 the overblown Russian State had not quite collapsed. The winter cold, their declining population and the lack of IT development had slowed down the spread of the SBX1 virus. Around three quarters of their population had survived and now they had one of those ranting patriots they so admired securely fixed in the PM spot.

She looked at all the conflict data - Crimea, Chechnya, Siberia, Kamchatka, Mongolia - they were all trying to become independent. She could see what forces they had and where they were deployed, but more important than that she could see the relative power of all the thought-streams coming from the protagonists. She asked the Warden if it could identify the most promising of these streams, and there, overlaying the Globe image of Russia were visuals – mostly text, some audio, some video: “We are not strong enough to do this” “Our country will not allow this” “We have too much to lose” “if we could get Russia to agree to this” - hundreds of snippets like this would be amalgamated into a few dominant streams and then courses of thought-action suggested.

After studying these for an hour or so, she buzzed Tilia:

“I think I’ve a selection for you – it’s Russia again!” Tilia groaned.

“OK, I’ll just wrap this up and come over.”

Five minutes later they were both looking intently at the Globe. Tilia began to act, bringing up “motifs” and asking the Warden to play them. A few days later the leaders of Kamchatka found that their people had changed a little. The opinion formers amongst them had stopped being so cautious and worried and begun to look for action. They felt stronger and wanted to use that strength. At the same time the Junta at the Kremlin had a whole succession of things go wrong. The great Leader fell ill - nothing serious but enough to disable his decision making capacity. One of the Council members developed a conscience and resigned. None of these small events hit the headlines, but within a few weeks the whole atmosphere had changed. It now looked much more likely that the independence struggle in several of the regions would at least partially succeed.

It was on The Globe in active mode that the results of the days play would show, and today, March 20th 2087 it was showing how the conflicts in North America would play out. There, in graphic form, could be seen the shifts in power, the movements of people, the engagements, deaths and triumphs and the flow of emotions resulting. This and all the other conflicts had to be played through by the Warden before the End Game could start.

The Warden had been set up when game theory was in its infancy, but over the years had learnt how to subvert other players outside the Hub. The other players did not know of course, but ultimately it was the Warden who determined what happened in any game system throughout the world. It was an astonishing achievement and the Warden had only one Mistress - the earth itself: Gaia.

******

It wasn't often that Tilia saw patterns like this. She was looking at Northern Europe and had focussed on Anglia. What a fascinating set up! A real King with a real pedigree acting like a monarch from the 17th Century. This was one she had to play. She went further back into the thought-streams, and soon found that there were now five Nations within the Britannic Isles. The Southern part of one of them - Hibernia - had been an independent nation since 1921 and had joined the Northern part, (which had until then stayed linked to the rest of the Britannic state), a hundred years later. They were not involved in the present conflict situation. Caledonia, the most northerly of the conglomeration, has been independent since 2022, but the others - Pennines, Cambria and Anglia, all dated from the 40s.

It took her a couple of hours studying the recent history, the thought- streams and the current resources, to come up with a valid scenario for the Warden. Before starting she loaded her selection into the Globe to see what it looked like. There she could see the force matrix of each Nation and some representation of the thought flows which would animate the matrices. She noticed that the position at start was also of interest to several neighbouring Nations - particularly Breizh and Scandinavia. After a few last checks she pressed 'play' and watched the Globe. Nothing happened for several minutes but then she was told to try again. She had got something wrong.

After half an hour working at the details she had factored in the recent hostage transfer and was ready to play again. This time it went through. The Warden was using her selections to influence the way the people in those nations prepared for conflict.

CHAPTER 2 2086

Huw

As a child Huw had found his home life a cause of constant frustration. Bethan, his mother, had little concept of routine and was just as likely to offer him food at 14:00 as at noon, and, not understanding his bad temper would try to cuddle him out of it. He loved school; the everyday routine with bells marking the divisions of the day he found soothing after the chaos of his home. He envied his friends whose parents insisted on tidy rooms. In Huw's room, as in most of the rooms that Twm, his dad, had built and fitted out, there was a place for everything. The difference was that in Huw's room everything was in its place. That only applied occasionally in the rest of the house. He could not fathom out what it was that triggered Bethan into a whirlwind of tidying up, but he welcomed the few days of order and cleanliness that followed.

For Twm, the right place for things varied according to what he was working on at the time. He too was passionate about the order of things, but on a more global scale than Huw's need to have his clothes in the right sequence in the wardrobe. Twm could see the connections between the clouds and the sea, or between the energy input of a device and its output. Huw could not see beauty in the nature of things. For him beauty was in a just outcome, a proper sequence of events.

Although something of a loner, Huw was well thought of. He had a pleasant, rather serious face, short dark hair, average build - nothing very noticeable about him, but he always seemed to command respect. You didn't make fun of Huw.

Being a conscientious student he had done well at school, and in his work year, where he had shadowed a senior member of the local Bike-Aid squad. Here he had learnt how to deal with all kinds of calls for help - fire, injury, theft, aggression, domestic violence and so on. The Bike-Aid squads had specially adapted e-bikes which you needed a special licence to ride. Like the Bike-Doctors, the Bike-Aiders were responsible for a small, local area. They all had jobs which allowed them time off to attend to emergencies, and were normally able to deal with about 70 percent of the incidents they attended. Their training was thorough and perhaps the most important part of it was identifying immediately those incidents they were not qualified to deal with. For these they would call in the nearest professional service.

Huw had shown himself to be highly effective at dealing with aggression. He was just not the sort of person a hyped up street fighter would go for. One scene his trainer particularly remembered was a brutal attack on two young lads in broad daylight. The attackers, three of them, had thrown the victims to the floor and, threatening them with knives, were frisking them for money, drugs or whatever they could find. In response to a call from a nearby house, Huw arrived just as one of the attackers was kicking his victim.

"Stop that, put the knife down"

"Oh yeh big man - whose going to make me." He straightened up; tall and broad, Huw looked small and weak beside him.

"Put the knife down now."

"Oh piss off you. Can't you see I'm busy . . . UH? AH, Christ NO!"

He was on the floor doubled up in pain, the knife forgotten as Huw handcuffed him.

******

As he went through the training, Huw wondered if one of the professional Emergency Services would be right for him, but decided to apply to the Defence Forces. Within a year he found himself at Harford going through the toughest and best training any serviceman could hope for - or dread!

As if that wasn't enough, his head was in a spin because of a girl he had just met. He'd never come across anyone like her in Dyfi. It seemed her parents were refugees from Anglia and had been assigned to one of the empty houses in Harford. She was taller than him for a start; a red-head with the flamboyant dress-sense to go with it. On one of his rare days off he decided to try the local Eldred Centre. This was a place where people could meet and test their skills in all sorts of creative games, arts and sports. You could join a co-operative group and help each other to achieve or you could join a competitive group, competing against each other or against the processors. Whatever you chose it had to involve other people so it was a great place to meet up and get to know people.

Being rather shy, Huw had resisted going until his pal Matt had virtually frog-marched him in. They joined the first group which came up on the screen and a few minutes later found themselves in front of a big 3d map of some fictional country, and their job was to design its flag. To do so they had to ask for help from one of a shortlist selected by the processor. Huw didn't hesitate long in selecting Daisy – the others looked boring by comparison. A few minutes later there she was: a mass of brilliant red hair on top of a collection of garments which gave the impression of being thrown together in a hurry but looked fantastic, and her face was just mesmerising. Huw could not stop grinning.

"Wow, so you are Daisy? I'm very pleased to meet you."

"And you're the soldier boy. Huw isn't it? Are you very strong? Do you 'siarad cymraeg?' I've been learning the language you see."

"Yn wir, dwi'n siarad y iaith – but I don't get much chance to use it these days.

"Just as well, you've exhausted my vocabulary already!"

She threw back the mass of red curls and laughed. That was it. Huw was smitten. He could hardly believe his luck when a few weeks later he realised they were a couple.

******

It was obviously part of his job to keep up with the politics of Cambria. The brief period of peace following the return of Eden had gone. The next year passed without major incident but both sides were ramping up their resources and raising the stakes. The warnings from OTIS were increasing in number and intensity. Hard though it was to believe in 2085, but it now seemed almost certain that Anglia were about to launch a full scale military attack on Gloster, home of the President and the nearest large town to the border. It was almost as if the King's forces were ignoring all the modern conflict resolution programmes and putting on a show of force in the traditions of the 19th century.

Huw began to wonder if OTIS had a sense of humour when it started looking for cavalry. Of course there were no actual horses involved, but OTIS had identified conventions of warfare which had become obsolete in 1918. The troops could be seen in smart uniforms, the higher ranks decorated with gold braid. There were "regimental mascots", bands, parades, and in the tradition of the former "communist" countries a show of armoured vehicles and missiles.

There was no doubt that Anglia knew that Cambria and Pennines were watching every move, so the whole thing was clearly a show - entertainment for the hard pressed citizens of Anglia and a warning to those of Cambria and Pennines.

With each escalation OTIS would choose a counter measure which it judged would succeed, but as the threats mounted the programme began warning that they would need more troops and more vehicles. When, on June 21, the day of the solstice, all the trappings were put aside, and a modern well equipped army was revealed facing their way,

OTIS could not have been clearer: “Prepare for battle”.

Since the first quarter of the century there had been very few encounters between disputants which could justify the term “battle”. Here was a modern army with VTOs (Vertical Take Off) and AVs (Armoured Vehicles) advancing at walking pace across the boundary. The “infantry” were in clear view - a big crowd of men and a few women walking at a steady disciplined pace towards Gloster. It was clear that they were protected by a force field, and that the vehicles that followed had individual protection. The VTOs were further back, waiting at low altitude.

Huw and his group were watching, as were all the Cambrian forces. Both sides knew the advance was a bluff, but the analysis showed so many variables that OTIS had not been able to suggest a plan of action. Clearly that situation was itself part of the Anglian plan. They did not expect to be attacked on the ground by enemy troops, but were deliberately confusing the strategic programmes. OTIS itself had come up with the possibility that this strategy was intended to force Cambria to use human intuition - to ditch OTIS.

On every play Anglia would win this encounter. What none of the strategic systems had in their data though was the resource which Magnus and his colleagues in the command centre had kept no digital record of. Even Huw was not entirely sure what to expect. He heard the command from Magnus on his security channel.

“Sagittaire, weapons ready.....Engage!”

What Huw saw next from his vantage point had not been seen for 500 years - From a few hundred metres ahead and to the sides of the advancing troops a dark shape began to rise. Thousands of linear object were rising, and the sound was like a long sigh, growing and humming as the cloud of lines rose above the fields. The cloud paused for an instant and then began to descend. Nothing had prepared the

Anglians for this. What was falling on them was a mass of wooden arrows. There was no metal or plastic on them, just feathers and sharpened wood, and the force field ignored them. They fell on the lightly protected heads of the Anglian troops and caused panic. The troops were screaming and running in all directions, some wounded and a few, who had taken their hats off, actually killed. At that point the vehicles began to advance to protect the retreat of the infantry.

OTIS was picking up a whole mass of data from the other side. Clearly their processor (known as COSI – Combined Operations Systems Information) was struggling to recalibrate and the result was a brief period of chaos. The armoured vehicles slowed and then stopped. OTIS too was struggling to produce a plan from the chaos. An eerie calm descended on the battle field. Realising that their job was done, the archers had retreated behind a thin force field. It would struggle to stop an attack by armoured vehicles, and they were poised to retreat still further. OTIS however had accepted a 30 percent risk that its assessment of Cambrian superiority in processing would carry the day, and so it turned out.

On instructions from COSI the AVs slowly turned and retreated. Cambria had won, but now their only strategic superiority had been lost. COSI was analysing the data. Cambria may have won the day, but had by no means won the war.

Magnus

For the next two weeks nothing happened on the ground, but a lot was going on unseen.

Well before the Anglian attack, OTIS had identified a location where the full War Council could meet. It was a former industrial site at Casnewydd. The buildings had been left unused and untended since 44 and had now become a part of the great South Cymric forest. One building however had been visited recently by a small group of men and women in odd looking clothes. Their task was to prepare one of the buildings for use by the Defence Forces. The strange clothes were their body-heat disguises, so that COSI drones could not pick up signs of recent activity. Once inside the building they could work undetected, but the only metal tools they had were those already there: a locked tool chest which the maintenance men had left in 44. Inside it was everything you would need to service the assembly machines in this old tinplate works.

They could clean up with the non-metallic tools they had brought with them - brooms and plywood hoppers, and somehow they used the engineering tools to create a comfortable conference room. The plain wooden chairs had been smuggled in and the tables were machine stands. The biggest problem was power for lighting. The solution decided on was to carry in hundreds of small battery cells which could be disguised as bones. Once inside they were all linked up and a power supply wired in.

Now it was time to use it. Magnus had got messages to his colleagues in Pennines and Caledonia and together with their political bosses they had travelled here in ones and twos hidden amongst troop movements.

Magnus opened the meeting.

"Congratulations to all of you and to our prep team. We are confident that COSI does not know we are here. In front of you are some items you may not have used for many years - pads of paper and pencils. We can talk freely but none of what we say can be digitised. In addition, Milton here, who has made a study of antique business technology, will make notes in what I believe is called 'shorthand'. He tells me that he can write down everything we say in a sort of code which can later be transliterated. Firstly I'll ask each of you to say who you are and your position. I'm Magnus Edmundson, Head of Cambrian Defence Forces."

"Sheila O'Donnel, Prime Minister of Cambria"

"Percy Fothergill, President of Pennines"

"Fay Wilson, Chief of Staff, Pennines Republican Guard"

"David Sinclair, Prime Minister of Caledonia"

"Murdo Sutherland, Head of Defence, Caledonia"

"Thank you. Now I will present my appraisal of the situation so far. This is based on what OTIS has told us, but is entirely un-recorded on digital media."

"In terms of battle resources we are still a long way behind Anglia. We were fortunate to be able to repulse their first physical aggression with very little loss of life, but only by compromising one of our key strategies - the use of non-metal technology. Although their processor COSI has now factored in non-metal attacks, we believe that our undercover groups can still de-stabilise their data. This may well buy us some time, but there is no way we can match Anglia if it comes to physical aggression, and they have shown themselves more than willing to use violence. The next time they decide to attack we will lose."

"As I see it our objective here this afternoon should be to convince them that they have little to gain by attacking. Percy?"

"Thanks Magnus, we have already shown we want to help, but there is more to this than simply defending one nation against attack. What is Anglia hoping to achieve? Our analysis has shown that their objective is the restoration of the old Britannic State with Lyndain once again at its head."

"Yes, we agree with that" said Magnus. "What about you David?"

"I'm no so sure. We've had an interesting approach from them. I shall tell you what it is and then you will know that I at least do not favour this solution. Their offer is joint sovereignty on the assumption that Pennines will be so squeezed between Anglia and Caledonia that they would have to give up their independence."

The room fell quiet until Fay coughed and spoke in the distinctive accent of her native Lerpwl - a way of speaking English born of the mix of all the waves of different peoples who had arrived at the international port - from African slaves to Irish peasants.

"We could survive if Cambria could defend my city. Lerpwl still has the capacity to become a major international port and as such could support both nations."

"Yes Fay" this was Percy Forthergill, a Yorksman. "You may be right but the rest of us would be in a very poor position. I can't see it working."

"Before we get too involved in speculation, can we all agree that we would all resist a return to a Britannica dominated by Anglia?"

The heads nodded; there was clear agreement.

"Together I feel sure we can prevent this, but I must tell you that OTIS cannot see a result from this conflict which leaves the status quo intact. We will have to change, and it seems to me that our job here today is to decide what is the outcome we can live with. I know I can speak for my government when I say that we could live with a Britannic State that we all had an equal share in."

“Aye, Magnus, and I guess you would have the capital in Brigstowe eh?” This was David Sinclair, and there was some laughter.

“Well, I don't think I should comment on that, but I do think you've homed in on the biggest problem with a new Britannica. We would all agree that Lyndain should not be the capital, but would disagree on a replacement location.”

“I'm not so sure Magnus. Burgedin has a strong claim, being much closer to a central position than either Lyndain or Brigstowe, and it has a longer tradition as a capital city than any other.”

At this point Percy Fothergill broke in to the increasingly acrimonious discussion.

“Hold on now. Aren't we all forgetting something? What about Hibernia? I can well understand them not wanting to be involved in the present dispute, but a Britannic State without them is not one I would support.”

“Hear hear. I agree David. As you can tell from my name” said Sheila “my ancestors came from Hibernia and I'm sure Magnus is not suggesting that they be excluded. I think our preferred solution would be a confederation of sovereign nations. I would like to move that we return to the original issue - the direct threat to life posed by the Anglian forces.”

“Very well Sheila, but I would like our scribe here to note down that we discussed the issue.”

After another hour or so of sometimes heated discussion a communiqué was agreed which Magnus read through:

“We, the heads of state of the three Britannic Nations Caledonia, Cambria and Pennines will consider an attack by any other Nation on one of them to be an attack on all, and do solemnly promise to take whatever action is necessary to defend against an attack wherever it may fall. An attack will comprise any aggressive destruction of resources held by one of us, whether physical or electronic, and any deliberate injury to one or more citizens of our Nations. Action will include physical or electronic retaliation, and shall not exclude the taking of life. Signatories:

Sheila O'Donnel, Prime Minister of Cambria, Percy Fothergill, Prime Minister of Pennines and David Sinclair, Prime Minister of Caledonia."

"Thank you all. We will have a break now. Milton tells me he has a thing called a 'typewriter' which will print this out letter by letter. He has to perform this operation three times so that we each hold a copy signed by all of us. That document will be considered legal by all our jurisdictions."

So the Treaty of Casnewydd was signed. It would not be long before it was put to use.

******

What Magnus had not mentioned at the treaty signing was his most important resource against Anglia - the existence of a Cambrian mole in the King's Specials. He would have trusted the other Nations with the information, but he and his contact had promised each other not to reveal what they now thought of as a plot to anyone at all until they both agreed it was necessary.

As soon as the new alliance became known to COSI the situation on the ground went quiet. For several weeks there were no more border incidents. The troops who had staged the show attack against Gloster had melted away. All the borders between Anglia and the other Nations were closed and troops took up positions at strategic points along them. OTIS now showed the alliance to have more resources than the enemy, but the margin was small. There was no denying the wealth and power that the restored capital city had drawn in by its strong trading position. Although nothing like as powerful as it had been before 44, Lyndain was now a long way from the wasteland it became in the 50s. The collection of small towns was on the way to becoming a city again. The combined trading strength of Brigstowe, Lerpwl and Glascoed was greater in statistical terms, especially when the figures from the other ports- Pensans in Kernow, Abertawe and Ystwyth in Cymru, Hwll in Pennines and Deen in Caledonia were added in. But it was a dispersed power, and would not be able to compete for long with the centripetal force of Lyndain.

******

It was the first time Magnus had been to the “City of Towns”. He had joined the Anglian transnet at Cheaping, walking over the border and hiring an Anglian e-car to minimise the chance of being stopped. Now he was enjoying an excellent coffee in the lounge, trying to get an impression of the landscape as he hurtled past it. It was all very green. He'd heard stories of the old Lyndain, but now huge areas of forest and intensive horticulture divided up what used to be sprawling suburbs and now were small towns. He noticed with surprise that the closer they got to the old “West End” the more ruined buildings there were - mile after mile of decayed houses with trees growing through the roofs. Maybe Anglia had not had is as good as the Cambrians had been led to believe. Although the towns were attractive and the horticultural areas looked productive, this didn't look much like the “Economic Miracle” that the King kept going on about.

He was listening to the accents around him. Until recently he had never thought about how he sounded to others, but in preparation for this trip he'd had some voice coaching which had picked up a few characteristic Cambrian intonations, both from his family home of Brigstsowe and from the “second city” Caerdydd. When talking to the barrista in the lounge he had been careful to adopt the flatter speech patterns of the educated Anglians - and of course of many in Cambria. The two nations had not after all forgotten that within living memory they had both been part of the State of Britannica.

His comms unit showed his progress and offered information on the places they were speeding through - this was a small town called Winsey - one of the former homes of the Britannic Royalty. Since the revival of the monarchy in the early sixties, King Michael had chosen to be based in the ancient capital city of Wincaster.

There was a slight change in the humming noise of the track; their speed reduced and his comms flashed a warning to return to his ek, which was only a hundred metres away along the foot-way. He walked briskly along it, climbed in and logged on. “Deceleration in seven minutes.” The Ecar Log (known as the eklog) asked for his attention and before he could deal with the messages he felt the ek move sideways. They were still travelling at 100kph but now began to decelerate in earnest and he felt his weight pulling against his seat restraints. At the same time the ek's onboard motor began to hum and the screen told him to take control. The wheels gently began to engage with the ground and he had arrived: The Royal Borough of Ham.

Now he had to be very careful. He could not put his destination in his comms because it would be logged, so he turned it off - but only for a few minutes while he memorised the details written laboriously on paper. If he left the comms off for too long it would look suspicious, but he knew he could safely ignore the questions it kept asking about his destination. It was common everywhere for people to navigate by memory so he told it that he knew the way. Ham is a pleasant place on the north bank of the Isis, and it was high enough to have gained full flood protection. There was a beautiful old bridge over the river which used to lead to dry land on the other side. His comms told him it had just been restored and now linked to a causeway going all the way to Riksmond past the huge “Waterworld” area - once the Borough of Barons. He flipped the messages away to concentrate on where he was going, and thought with some trepidation about the man he was about to meet for the first time.

He had given his name as Kenric. They had spoken briefly on a coded priority channel which Kenric had sent him, but all he knew about him was that he had a slight accent which he recognised as that of a native Lyndainer and that he had a senior position in the RHoG. They could not say much on the comms net, and neither had admitted to anything more than a degree of curiosity about the other, so they used their membership of the Letter Clubs network to write physical messages to each other.

The Letter Clubs were one manifestation of the revival of analogue media which had become a world- wide phenomenon since the sixties. A generation who had been brought up to use digital screens for every kind of communication were now discovering the tactile pleasure of paper, of actual pens with real ink, and at its most elevated, the manuscript, the hand-written document on real paper.

What the authorities had not yet realised was that the exchange of letters in envelopes, hand delivered, was a subtle way to get round the omnipresent surveillance. There was always a risk that the contents would be read by some diligent official, but it was a much safer way to communicate than any other.

Kenric's letter looked like this:

Dear Magnus,

I'm so pleased you are planning a trip to Ham. As soon as I saw your picture my heart gave a little leap. I do hope you will come and see me - the address is 25 Biscay St. Ham. I've something very special to show you.

Until we meet

xx Kenric

The Anglian government were not particularly liberal when it came to sexual orientation but at least male-to-male had not been made a crime, so Magnus was confident that Kenric's pose would not raise any suspicions. “Special” was the word he needed to see. It meant that Kenric was unhappy with his government.

Could he be turned to work for Cambria? There was also the possibility that Anglia was interested in him, Magnus, and wanted to see if he was sympathetic to the government. Kenric could be a plant.

When he got to No.25 the door opened on his first knock and Kenric looked at him for a second. Then his expression changed and he was all smiles:

“Give me a big hug you nice man!”

Magnus was afraid his acting would let him down, but responded in kind. Quickly they moved inside and closed the door.

“Oh, sorry about that” said Kenric laughing.

“It's fine, but do you really think there was someone outside watching?”

Kenric urgently raised a finger to his lips -

“Watching? Well you never know how some people get

their thrills." His manner changed swiftly to a serious, worried look.

"Now, I said I had something special to show you - it's in the darkroom. I've been experimenting with glass plate photography – it's gorgeous - nearly 200 years old and still fascinating. This way."

They went down some stairs to a cellar with a metal door, and only once they were settled in the small but comfortable room did Kenric indicate that they could speak freely.

"It's lucky that nobody has asked me too many questions about glass plates!" They both laughed.

"So, Magnus, your record shows exemplary service in your country's Defence Forces. You're a General, but my guess is that your present rank does not indicate your real job."

"You could say that. But I might say the same of you. If we are to trade information we need some way of establishing trust."

"Of course. I've thought of that. In a way I have more to lose because if they learn why you are really here they will destroy me. Your regime is more tolerant. You might be disgraced but you could still die from natural causes. I asked for this meeting because I no longer trust my own government. What I have here should be enough to vouch for my sincerity." He reached into a cupboard and took out an antique camera.

Huw

Now, five years after his induction to the Specials, Huw had been invited to see the Chief: Edmundson himself. He was asked to be at DF HQ in Brigstowe at 8:00. He assumed that Mags knew that would mean an early start. Perhaps it was some sort of a test. After everything he had been through in his training and on the various exercises they had done, getting from Harford to Brigstowe for eight was a piece of piss.

“Come in Huw - have a seat. How's Twm? I knew him quite well when Mum was working for NRG.”

“Oh of course Sir, I'd forgotten that. He's pretty good - a few medical problems but nothing too serious.”

“Now, the fact that I know your Dad has nothing to do with the reason I asked you here, though it might help you if you like what I'm going to say.

“I'm sure you are well aware of the Anglian problem - I believe your wife came from there. Daisy isn’t it?”

“That's right Sir, from Briton, but she loves it here in Cambria.”

“Well, it's a sad fact that there aren't many of us who don't have friends or family in Anglia, and any one of us could face a difficult conflict of loyalties, so I hope that won't be a problem for you. What I have to say is secret, so first I need to check out your standing – could I do the scan?”

“OK. I'm pretty sure everything is up to date – it’s here.” He indicated his left shoulder. Magnus placed the scanner on his clothing where Huw had indicated and waited for the checks. 30 seconds later the green light showed.

“Good, now I'll just set up the security for this room and we can talk in peace.” He made some movements on his work-table until another green light showed.

"Our situation Huw is that we cannot hope to defeat Anglia in conventional military terms. Even if we manage to form an alliance with Pennines and or Caledonia we can still barely reach parity. We do however have some good systems, and OTIS - you know about OTIS I assume?"

"Yes Sir, we all do in my unit."

" . . . tells us we have the information resources to destabilise Anglia with a 90 percent chance of zero fatalities. I want you to take overall charge of this operation which will be called 'Rising Damp' . . . Don't ask! We need at least four units of four to six men who have the skills to infiltrate Anglia and launch attacks on selected government facilities. Their first objective will be to send back information on the targets. We will then send a simple coded message and from that point all the units will be on their own. You know what that means?"

"Yes Sir. No further communication, no backup."

"That's it, though in this case, if we are right about what is going on, then all the attacks will be simultaneous, and Anglia will know we are behind them. You will have as good a chance to get out as in any other Specials op. The final plan will not be made until the last minute, so, if you accept the command, you need to make sure each unit is up to date on the latest from OTIS. A job like this is what you have been trained for Huw. I know you can do it. So do you want to?"

"Need you ask? Of course I do. When do we start."

******

Huw's unit had set up a camp in the Kennet marshes at Burfeld. It was quite near one of the big transnet junctions where the East/West track from Lyndain to Swinsdun crosses the former North/South track from Oxen to Suthham. Before 44 the whole area was highly populated but now most of the villages and towns had been abandoned to the floods. It was a difficult area to get to because all the north –south roads were underwater for most of the year and had been largely abandoned. They had all travelled separately in hired vehicles on the transnet, using different border crossings. The implant updates the techies had given them were good enough to survive close scrutiny by the Anglian border police.

One of the other units was in the same area and the others were targeting a further two sites around Anglia assessed by OTIS as being important data centres. Huw had briefed them all before they set off and now the only communications they had were the short blips which indicated that they were in sync with each other.

Their camp was on a spit of ground high enough to stay dry all year. It was not hidden. If the occasional boat passed them they would see the flag of the Anglian Pioneer Force. Much to their surprise they had to use their fall-back plan a week after they had dug in, when a shooting party in a punt came across to say hello. The four men were painlessly disabled, given memory capsules and taken back to the nearest road. They would be confused for a while but would not remember what had happened to them.

There were six of them in the unit, all volunteers and their objective was a place that had been famous a century ago for the manufacture of nuclear weapons. There were whispers going round the Cambrian govnet that a new fence had been put up and something secret was going on. Their job was to find out what and if it looked dangerous, to draw up a plan for sabotage.

They knew well enough that the wire fence was just for show. It looked suitably military and the patriotic Anglians were told not to talk about it. Huw and the others knew that the real defence was not visible unless you had the right equipment, and they were basing their whole plan on the assurance from Harford that the devices they carried were one step ahead of anything in Anglia.

To get close enough they used the boat. This was a shooting punt they had bought locally - at least James had bought it. He was the only one who had been born in Anglia - his parents had moved to Cambria when he was five. They had various attachments which could re-configure their clothing and metal rods which would look like guns. If any drones passed over them they would look entirely like a shooting party.

The plan was to get to within a k or so of the facility, park up and wait for nightfall. The other two units were on the other side of the site, about a k to the east and south. This was when their skills and tools would come into their own. Another change in their clothing was required to alter the heat profile of their bodies. They would have to crawl or stoop, but their heat profile would look like a dog or a deer to the overhead drones. This was done by using zones of insulation and zones of super-conductivity. If the drone became suspicious it could reduce altitude and illuminate them so they had to be good.

They split up and headed for the wire fence. It was scrub country, and quite difficult to find a way through the young trees, bracken and bramble bushes. The scrub thinned as they got closer, and they could hear sheep moving about and muttering. Their sensors told them when they were approaching the real force-field fence. It would take a lot more than they had on this mission to get through that, but they could find out what was inside it. They assumed that the guards inside the force-field could identify incoming probes, so they were using a new bit of tech which the lab at Harford had given them. This enabled them to bounce a probe signal off the enemy drone itself, using its own output to disguise their input. It had never been tried in action before. At a signal from Huw they switched their suits to “inactive” and remained still. It was a cloudy night, damp with no wind so they could hear all the small sounds of the night - a splash of water, an owl and the eerie scream of a vixen.

A message from Will -

“Drone approaching NW. Locked on.”

Huw sent back -

“Send when ready.” As soon as the drone was in range Will would send out short bursts of radio waves which would send back a picture of what was on the ground. A tiny glow in Huw's transmitter showed that another drone was coming in his direction. He locked onto it and began transmitting. Within seconds a composite picture was building up on his screen. Within 20 minutes they had bounced signals from six different places. That was enough. Silently, loping like dogs or walking like deer they made their way back to the boat.

Back at camp the information was analysed and sent to Brigstowe. It was not good. This was hardware - some form of weapon, though the troop could not identify it - leave that to Brigstowe, they would know. Within hours they had the signal:

“Stay in position. More units being sent. Wait for instructions.”

The waiting time they divided between stealth exercises to help them perfect their night-time profiles and playing through the various scenarios they had been given. Of course they had no access to the Net so were limited by their offline processor, but it was powerful enough to show that their chances of disabling the force-field were pretty minimal. Somehow they would have to generate a very powerful laser and disguise it for at least 20 seconds. Perhaps the new arrivals would have the kit.

Two days later they had a signal from the first of the three new units.

“Camped at ref 02:56. Sending MW to you.”

MW, aka Mike Williams, arrived at the same time as Zac from the second unit. Huw gestured towards the tent. Its top cover was a screen so they could talk safely inside. They both told the same story:

"Lasers - nah how could we get close enough with one of them?"

"Do you mean you've got nothing? No new kit?"

"Well, in a way. How many of you are longbow trained?"

"All of us I think, but surely their COSI will have factored arrows into the force-field. We've no bows with us anyway."

"That's what we've brought. It seems HQ have identified a small area above the target where the force field is minimal. We have small, powerful electron bombs which can be fired from a bow and will permanently disable any electronics within 100m of the bomb. Our job is to get as many of these in on as many different parabolas as we can."

"Duw - now I've heard everything. Is there an exit strategy?"

"You are joking? Since when did HQ give us luxuries like that. We take three days supplies with us and scatter. Just don't get caught."

The next night Will, their best bowman, took up his 80 kilo pull ash-wood bow and fitted the cigar shaped bomb to its counter-weighted arrow. It weighed just under a kilo so would need every ounce of top-body strength to launch it into its high parabola. Sensors in his suit and in the arrow told him when he had reached the right angle but he could not hold the pull for more than a few seconds so had to get it right. The first two pulls failed but on the third the little dot of light on the arrow changed to green and he fired. Ten seconds later their screens registered a huge blip. A few seconds after that another bomb went off fired from the other side of the target area. Three more were successful but as the sixths bomb began to fall a siren sounded and lights went on everywhere. It was time to go.

Any VTOs at the target would be unable to fly, but they had perhaps twenty minutes before the nearest VTO base had craft in the air. They had the best electronic defence available, but if they were seen and if the Anglians had the right hardware they could be disabled and captured, or even killed outright. They had heard that the King's forces had no hesitation in using life-threatening weapons.

The strategy they had been taught was to hide as soon as possible and wait until the next day or night. To escape by day they would need to use public transport - any individual spotted on foot would be picked up and interrogated. To travel by night they would have to keep up their animal disguises when in open country.

******

They had all searched out suitable hiding places, but none of them knew where any of the others would be – "know only what you have to know." Huw aimed to get to the transtation at Thealu which was on the other side of the flood plain. He had carefully mapped out paths beforehand and reckoned he could do the crossing in the deer simular. All he could take would be his clothes and some Anglian money which would be slung under his chest. It was very hard on the muscles running bent double, touching the ground with the tips of his fingers, but he had done the training. To guide him he had a soft plastic map which he had programmed with the instructions. After the first mile along the muddy path the sensors in his comms alerted him to the presence of a drone, and he leapt into "frightened deer" mode – long leaps away from the track. The drone passed. An hour later he could just begin to see the shape of the hill on the other side and a few scattered lights, but ahead the path disappeared under water. He had no way of knowing how deep it was. If he could not get through he would be stranded in broad daylight.

He stopped and risked standing upright to rest his aching muscles. To the West was nothing but water but to the east there was a structure of some sort. He crouched again and went to investigate. It was a simple landing stage with an old tub canoe tied up to it. He waited another few minutes. The only sound was one that under other circumstances would have filled him with joy – the unmistakable song of a nightingale. It gave him hope and within a few minutes he was in the boat paddling as quietly as he could.

Suddenly the night sky lit up. A dazzling beam of light shone from way above him and to the north. A drone had picked up the movement and within seconds the pool of brilliant light would be on him. He dived over the side and under the boat but the light stopped moving. He could see a stationary halo of light all round the black outline of the boat from under the water. By an intense effort of will he suppressed his breathing instinct, just allowing a small stream of bubbles to surface as he slowly exhaled. The light did not move. At last he could not hold any longer and broke the surface gasping as quietly as possible, but the drone had seen him. Now he knew there was no escape. The drone would follow his every move until the guards arrived.

******

The men who picked him up were polite. They handcuffed him and escorted him to the VTO. Just to make sure, they secured him to the seat and a few minutes later they arrived at an army compound where he was taken to a cell and locked in.

"There you go taff. Bucket in the corner if you need it. You'll get some food and water later."

Perhaps it wouldn't be so bad after all.

The next day he was taken to another VTO and strapped in again.

"Big chief wants to see you taff. We're off to Wincaster."

"Who's the big chief then?"

“You’ll find out soon enough.”

After a short flight they landed at a compound high up on the downs near Wincaster. It looked like a military installation with a wire fence round it. Huw was taken along a series of corridors to an office with “Alban Walters” written on the door. His escort showed his comms and the door opened. There were chairs and a table. They sat down. After about 10 minutes another door opened and a small muscular looking man strode in. He had black hair and a face so rough looking it was almost attractive. His movements were brisk, his smile cool.

“Ah, Mr Pritchard, Huw. Welcome to Anglia. I’m sorry we could not meet in easier circumstances. We do welcome visitors from Cambria you know. You don’t have to come through the back door as it were.”

“Thank you Sir.”

“Now, we need information and we need it fast. First I will need to connect you to COSI. I’m sure you will know something of how we do things.”

“Yes Sir, I am aware of COSI”

“Good. Now if you would be so kind as to sit yourself here and place your arms here we can get you wired up.”

Once they had fixed the electrodes he heard a series of clicks and then the world changed. He was no longer fully conscious it was like a state between sleep and waking thousands of images flashed across the field of view in front of him as if he had his eyes closed his thoughts his memories those he loved random images clouds sky up and up and then suddenly down and the world assembled itself around him again.

“Strange feeling isn’t it? I don’t suppose you will be able to answer for a bit, but I know you will understand when I say that we now know quite a lot about you. With some people we can access their hidden thoughts but you have been well trained, so when you are with us again I will need to ask you a few questions."

So it began.

Britannica had for many years disowned the practice of torture, but allegations of "extraordinary rendition" and "inhumane practices" were usually ignored if the subject of these procedures was seen to be a threat to the Britannic way of life. Anglia had a strict code on interrogation procedures, but under the leadership of Alban Walters had perfected methods which did not appear to be inhumane, but were highly effective. It began with fear.

Huw sat immobilised in his chair facing Walters with a full set of electrodes connected to his hands and head. For a while nothing was said and nothing happened except that Huw began to feel afraid. He had some idea of what to expect from their training, and Huw had been assessed as "strong" on the Cambrian scale of resistence to pain. "You have nothing to fear but fear itself" was the message, but it was exactly that which Huw was now feeling.

"Now Huw, let's first run through what we know. There were six of you in your unit, all male. Correct?" Huw nodded. "Speak please."

"Yes, correct". He felt a tingling sensation on his skin and the fear rose in him.

"Your commands came directly from Magnus Edmundson. Correct?"

"Yes." The fear increased. He was sweating and tugging at his restraints, trying desperately to remember his training.

"Your principle weapon was the longbow. Correct?"

"Yes, yes." Now his imagination was racing, feeling all the pain he was sure would follow. He wanted to cry out writhed in his chair. When the questions began Huw was in another place, in Room 101 where your worst fears are realised. Sheer terror engulfed him and he hardly knew what he was saying.

"Which of you fired the missiles?"

"It wasn't me. Not me it was Wal, tell, wobble not me don't know save me please."

It just went on and on and always this sense of the worst thing about to happen. Words swam around him. He lost all sense of what they were. He was screaming in terror until suddenly it stopped.

It was as if peace on earth had suddenly broken out. Wave after wave of relief washed over him. He was laughing and crying. "Oh thank you thank you. You saved me. It didn't happen. Oh thank God."

"Huw, you're welcome, we are your friends here, fellow citizens of these great Islands of Britannica. Let me undo these restraints – they were for your own safety, but we don't need them now. Why don't we go into my office, have a cup of tea and a chat."

"That sounds lovely, thanks."

In the course of a long conversation about their two nations and how regrettable it was that they were now quarrelling, Huw was given an exciting opportunity, the chance to do more for peace than the politicians who were making such a mess of things. As his euphoria dissipated he began to feel somewhat uncomfortable, but still, his friend Alban was a reasonable man. He would understand if Huw felt that his comrades might think ill of him if he started sharing his information with Alban.

"I'm sorry Alban. Much as I would like to help you I really don't think I can. I'm sure you understand."

"Of course, of course. But we will keep in touch won't we."

“Oh yes, certainly.” The door opened and a large man came into the room and stood behind Huw.

“Could you excuse me. I have to be elsewhere, but Garim here will look after you.”

No sooner had he left the room than Huw felt a small prick in his arm. When he woke he was strapped to the chair again. This time the terror began before the electrodes were activated. When the visions came he saw his wife screaming in pain, his children lying in their own blood, his family dog howling from a smashed body, his best friend laughing, Magnus shouting at him and calling him a traitor: vision after vision, images so terrible he screwed his eyes shut but still they came.

******

It could have been a day later or several days; day or night, Huw had no idea. All he knew was that it had stopped. He did not know why he was so sure it had stopped, but he knew he was no further use to them, or to himself come to that. His life was over in all but name. He had betrayed everything and everyone. There was no point in anything now. They brought him food and drink which he ate and a bucket which he dutifully used. He slept sometimes, walked up and down sometimes, but nothing had any meaning. Time passed.

King Michael

Michael, King of Anglia, son of Harrold, grandson of Charles, only upholder of the Royal House of Winsey, was livid.

“Where is that stupid cunt Walters? Christ I wish I could order executions like old King Hal.”

“He's in Lyndain Sir”

“Well go and fetch him then newt brain.”

“I can't Sir, the transnet is down.”

“Well you've got an ek haven't you - get out of my sight and don't come back until that stupid bastard is here, licking my boots. Ye fucking Gods I'll make him pay for this. Why are you still here - are you deaf or something?”

“There's no power Sir.”

“Oh I don't believe it. Why am I surrounded by incompetents?”

There was a sound of running feet and the door to the King's study burst open.

“How dare you . . . Ah, it's you Jones, perhaps you would be good enough to explain to me what is going on.”

“I've just this minute got an analysis from COSI Sir. It seems that a number of small teams have launched simultaneous attacks on four of our crucial data sites.”

“I thought you told me they were protected with the best force field available? Have the Cambrian's suddenly learnt how to disable force-fields?”

“No Sir, but they found that there is a weak spot at the top - at the confluence of the radial screens. Somehow they managed to deliver electron bombs through this weak spot.”

“Have these invaders been caught?”

“Only two of them Sir. One has since died in custody, but before that was able to tell us that they used the same method as in Gloster - longbows.”

“Ye Gods, what's the point of Special Interrogation if the subject can only tell us what we already know. Why was this man allowed to die?”

“It was a woman Sir. We got the calibration wrong.”

“OK, get what you can from the other one. See if you can turn him - I presume this one is male?”

“Yes Sir. We've had him connected to COSI but it just confirms that he knows little and will not turn. Shall we dispose of him Sir?”

“Yes, yes, whatever. Now, let me think. Jones - how soon can we get the power back?”

“I'm not sure Sir. We have teams working flat out. The problem is not with the power generation and supply but with the electronics. Without data the system doesn't work.”

“Will you stop telling me things I already know. Do you think I'm stupid?”

“I would be grateful Sir if you would not use such language to your Home Affairs Minister. It is not appropriate for someone of your standing.”

“OK OK, sorry Jones. Who can we get hold of?”

“Well it seems the Chief of Staff has enough battery power to get here, and the Prime Minister is in the building. We could form an emergency quorum without needing parliamentary sanction.”

Kenric

Kenric had stomach ache. It was bad. He knew the normal antacid medicines wouldn't work. Only painkillers and alcohol brought some relief. He'd had a couple of shots already, but if anything his anxiety seemed to get worse. He couldn't rid himself of the thought that somehow the King had found out about his meeting with Magnus. Yet, how could he? There was no way COSI could retrieve any data from their conversation. He worried too about Jane. How safe was she? Just a small glass of wine and then he would be ready.

When he arrived at the Council Chamber he found Douglas Jones, his boss, tight lipped. He gestured for Ken to join him and whispered: “fucking King’s gone Ape-shit. Keep your head down.”

“Right, now that Jones' gopher has kindly condescended to join us perhaps we can start.” Ken winced, but realised this was normal royal bullying so began to feel better.

“By every measure we should be able to walk all over this so-called Nation, but somehow they have managed to make a fool of us TWICE! If it happens again I promise you anyone on this table responsible for another cock-up will be fed to the lions. Clear?”

They'd heard this stuff before. It was bluster; they felt safer, but not for long.

“I've issued the order for Walters to be arrested. Now do you believe me? We must not let this happen again. Jones and Price I want you to run every conceivable scenario involving anti-surveillance methods. Matthews, as Chief of Staff I want a report on our military capacity to launch a full scale attack on Cambria. All of you off the top of your feeble brains, what are our options?”

******

He had been working all night logging the information on the data attacks when the call from Brigstowe came. Magnus had given him a code which would open a secure channel. It was priority A and when decoded said "Rescue H, send plan."

Ken stared at his screen. This was the moment. Until now it had been talk, plans, messages, secret codes. This was the moment of betrayal. If he went forward now his old life was finished. Ahead of him was danger, flight, hiding, but also Jane and a new life together. Is this how it felt to betray his country? He felt nothing. His country had betrayed him – or at least its ruler had. He screwed up his eyes, shook his head and then began work.

He knew where the prisoner was and immediately sent a message to Jane on the same channel.

Huw

Time was a fluid. Like the tide it ebbed and flowed around him. Time and Tide, once synonyms, had come together again for Huw. He began to take note of when the daylight entered his cell, and could feel the pulse of the day, even beginning to anticipate the arrival of food. Then it would ebb again and he would retreat to his big white space; the place where there was no fear.

On one of these flows he noticed a new guard had brought his food. Instead of just leaving it, he spoke:

"Huw, my name is Selwyn. Pay attention." Huw looked up.

"Hello Selwyn."

Selwyn made signs which puzzled him. It looked as if he wanted Huw to move to the corner of the room. Dutifully he made a big effort, got to his feet and moved where indicated. Selwyn moved very close to him and, when they were no more than centimetres apart, handed him a bit of paper, immediately walking away saying:

"Right, just wanted to make sure you were not getting too fat. You must move around more, get some exercise. I'll see to it." The he left.

For the first time in however long it was – days? weeks? – Huw felt the stirrings of real thought. The world around him came into focus: he saw colour, form, edges, and his brain was coming alive. In a flash of intuition he knew that he must not look at the paper where the cameras could see him, but he had no idea where they were . . . no, wait, he did have an idea – they were not in that corner. Now his brain was fully awake and told him not to do anything unusual. He must try to get back to his big white space.

Some time passed. For the first time since the fear Huw began to feel irritable, even bored. The food arrived. He ate. He moved around the cell and at last, in his corner, looked at the paper:

Code 41356. Do what Selwyn asks. 19

His head spun. Oh the numbers what was it memories coming back think each number meant something think nineteen was magnus is it possible no must be a trick how could magnus send a messenger forty one meant what was it oh yes rescue but what was 357 can't remember three is days so 56 is can't remember doesn't matter trust Selwyn five days here so sixth day?

Hours later, many hours, it was dark and Selwyn came.

"Quickly, the cameras are off. We've only a few minutes."

"I'm ready. I will trust you Selwyn. Thank you."

They moved quickly down the corridors and out into a cool wet night. Selwyn pulled him behind a wooden building.

"Wait here." He was gone. Time passed again until he heard a noise: clip, snip. Then there was a strange feeling like a pressure wave passing. A dark shape came running towards him.

"Huw – I'm Kenric, I'm a friend of Magnus, come quickly."

"Where's Selwyn. I must trust Selwyn."

"He's gone back. In two minutes he will disrupt the force field again so that we can get out. You have to trust me."

Huw's brain was working properly now and he could see clearly that even if this was a trap he had nothing to lose by going with Kenric and everything to gain if it was real. Ten minutes later they were lying in dry clothes under a bivvy sheet and Kenric was explaining how they would get to Cambria.

"Don't speak unless you can lose your accent."

"Oh I can be Anglic if I need to. But why do I need to? Ah, I see. I'm an Anglesman from Cambria . . . Anglia. That's it. " The accent was perfect - classless southern Anglic.

"Excellent. This is a genuine local comms unit like mine. Now we are two ordinary Anglians. OTIS tells us that they will be looking for an incursion, a vehicle, even a VTO, but we will be in a hired ek travelling like anyone else on the transnet."

Before the sun rose they buried any kit which could arouse suspicion, and set off for the long walk into Wincaster. Their clothes were worn work clothes. They were craftsmen returning from a night shift at the local factory. A few people said 'good morning' as they passed but otherwise the walk was uneventful, boring. As Kenric had promised, their comms released an ordinary looking e-car which

Kendric drove up the ramp. He placed his index finger on his lips so Huw said nothing until they were under way and Kenric had scanned the ek with his comms.

"This comms has a hidden channel to detect surveillance. We can talk now. They are almost sure to be checking at the other end so we can only hope that Brigstowe have programmed these things well. If you speak, don't sound too classy – you know, roughen the edges a bit."

"OK mate, no probs."

Fifteen minutes later the string of eks passed Ham, Ken's home, but he would never be going back there now. A wave of nostalgia engulfed him and he blinked hard for a few minutes. The drive slowed as they turned west. E-cars left and joined and the string changed but the drive gained speed and kept up a steady 200k per hour until they reached the border at Cheaping. All the eks drove off and lined up at the crossing. It was a nervous moment when they were questioned, but they were not suspected and drove through into Cambria. They were free, and there, much to Kenric's relief, was Jane waiting for them. They all ignored each other and drove on until they reached the agreed safe lay-bye. Their reunion was tearful.

"Oh, sorry Huw" she said "we really didn't know if we would ever meet again. Welcome back." Ken was reluctant to spoil the mood.

"Remember, people, we are not quite out of danger yet. It's very likely that my colleagues back there will soon realise that I am missing. They may well try to snatch us back, and believe me they are good."

"What about your man Selwyn, won't he be in danger?"

"He should be out of the country by now. He is quite senior in the defence hierarchy and had planned a trip to France."

"Good. Presumably now we split up?"

"Yes, but I think you and Jane could travel together. I will stay here for a few days."

"Well Kenric; I don't know what to say. You risked your life to save me. I can see now that it wouldn't have been long before my brain was so mashed I wouldn't have been worth the bother." They embraced.

"My heartfelt thanks. Well Jane, good to meet you, let's go."

Lydia

They had been waiting for a long time. Ask any soldier who has seen active service what is the hardest, and they will all say "the waiting". There are only so many exercises you can do, only so many times you can clean and service your kit, only so many sports, games, pastimes. Lydia knew how difficult it was to keep her group alert and ready, but she had confidence in them. Passive mode was part of their training. They were resting, relaxed but poised for action.

They all knew what was going on. Lydia had a particular aptitude for strategy and could, in certain circumstances access the same data as the Royal Council. One of her colleagues, a man she trusted, had betrayed them and rescued the prisoner. COSI had not predicted this and its minders were in trouble. The King, as he got older, had become less tolerant, more angry. His moods were beginning to be a threat to their security, but there was precious little Lydia could do about it. She was not on the consultants list and could only await orders.

When eventually the order came - directly from the King apparently - her heart sank. It was not the danger that worried her, but the thinking behind it. To try to snatch back the prisoner with no element of surprise was courting failure, and Anglia could not afford another failure. Even COSI was predicting failure, but the King had lost faith in his machine.

Nevertheless, they had their mission and they were ready. Lydia accessed COSI for options and chose one with a fairly low success prediction because she felt it played better to the personal strengths of her team. She chose five men and three women, all with relatives in Cambria and good knowledge of the area where their intelligence said Kenric was being hidden. Once the team had been briefed they split up and set off for several different border posts. Despite the tension between the two nations there was still a lot of movement between them, but the queues were long. They had allowed a day and night to get into position.

COSI had created false identities for them - the only processor in Anglia capable of fooling the Cambrian border checks. They all used different methods to travel, arrived at different border posts on different days and with different reasons for entering Cambria. Once they were on Cambrian soil they had no safe means of communicating so Lydia had spent many late hours working on the plan until she was confident it would at least get them to the rendezvous. There was a back-up plan if things went wrong.

Lydia herself chose the transnet border at Cheaping. She was now Hilda Mitchel going to Brigstowe to try to find her daughter, and she would be the last to arrive. When her hired ek arrived at Templefields transtation she left it there, visited the ladies toilet and changed into holiday clothes. Then she walked to King's Square where groups of friends were always meeting up to slack-out. There was little danger of being overheard. Two of them, Edwards and Winton had arrived.

“Hi Ed” Lydia called out “great to see you. Who's this?”

“Hilda - it's been a long time. This is Charlie my cousin's lad.”

“Great to meet you Charlie. Any sign of the others yet?”

“Not....Oh yes, here's Clare.”

In ones and twos they drifted in. It was a fine dry day

and soon there were eight of them sitting on the grass and doing the things that groups of friends do - passing round a pipe, eating toasties, drinking from drink packs. There was plenty of laughter but as time went on it became harder to keep up the good cheer. "Max" was missing.

Eventually Lydia got up. "Listen everybody, I need to go over to the markets." She shouted out "can we meet back here in half an hour?" This was a signal. She was going to use the telex. This ancient machine was on a dusty table in the back room of a dingy office at the top of one of the buildings near the square. The now redundant office of "Visit Anglia," its air of neglect was deliberate. The agreement was that if one of them got stopped, he or she would fire up a single-use comms button which would transmit one of three analogue codes to Lyndain. Lyndain in turn would send the code by telex to the little office. It wasn't foolproof but it was the best they could do.

The middle aged lady working in the office was surprised to see her. In all the time she had worked there the telex had never been used, but she knew about it and how to decrypt the message now chattering out on the paper roll. It was not good: code three meant that Max was under arrest. He would know nothing of the mission but would know the rendezvous. They were compromised. Badly compromised, but not blown.

Lydia thought with a rueful smile that it was lucky for Max it was not Alban Walters he would have to deal with, though even if the Cambrians had been using Walters' brutal methods they would not have been able to find out what the mission was for the simple reason that Max did not know.

He would know however that Lydia's cheerful call "meet back here in half an hour" meant "meet Lydia one by one in different locations." Moving quickly around the centre of the city Lydia had a stack of paper leaflets which she was passing out to all sorts of people. This was a way of giving out information which had recently been revived - there seemed to be no end to the popularity of paper now. The papers were advertising a concert, but also contained all the codes for the operation.

One by one at various intervals the others took a paper from her. One by one they were each being picked up by a small band of Magnus' Specials. It was not until she had given the paper to the last of them, that a voice at her elbow said:

"Major Middleton I believe. Would you come with us please."

It was over. Her mission had failed.

*****

They were taken to the "guest wing" of the prison at Pucklehouse. It was comfortable enough but they were in individual cells so had no idea where their comrades were. She found the staff polite, and would not have guessed that they had received special training in the treatment of political detainees: training which emphasised their status as citizens of a parallel regime who had, with occasional exceptions, committed no crime, and were to be treated with impartiality. It was to be made clear to the political detainee that they were seen as a potential danger to the state but not to the individual, and were to be treated with compassion where necessary but kept at a distance. Any friendly exchanges were to be discouraged. They were to be addressed by their title and surname only.

Lydia's cell was fairly basic - a bed, chair and table with a small wash and toilet unit attached. It did have a comms screen, but she soon found that all the information came via the prison service. The choice of reading matter was limited. For two days her only human contact was with her guard who would greet her as "Major Middleton" and pass her the simple healthy meals which, being her only relief from boredom, and pretty tasty, she greatly enjoyed. Since her usual life-style was full of activity and stress, she found the slow rhythm of prison life quite relaxing at first. By day three, with no information about what was happening outside, she was beginning to pace up and down in frustration. It was a relief when the door opened and her guard said;

"Would you come with me please Major."

"Where are we going?"

"General Edmundson wants to talk to you."

This was it then - the man she had heard so much about, whose face was constantly in the news, the man the Anglian media loved to hate. She felt quite privileged. The guard ushered her into the Chief of Staff's office as if he were a company Chairman and she his assistant.

"Good morning Major"

"Good morning Sir." They shook hands and she noticed the signs of age in his rough dark face. He sat down with a slight twinge. She would have guessed his age as late fifties. He was in fact 61.

"Ah, these old bones." He smiled at her."May I call you Lydia? I feel I know you quite well."

"You will do as you please Sir. I am your prisoner."

"Detainee please - I don't see you as a prisoner. To me you are a rival, one we were fortunate enough to defeat, but I have nothing but admiration for the way you handled a very difficult mission. What on earth possessed your command to send you on such a hare-brained scheme? Did you really think you would be able to re-capture the man you were after?"

"We believed it was possible"

"Oh come on Lydia, you must have known your chances of success were tiny." She made no reply.

"I'll tell you what I think. This seems to me like the work of your crackpot King. I'll bet he gave the orders. I can't see Walters being so daft."

"I can't comment on that Sir."

"Is that so; well you might change your mind when I tell you that we have been monitoring the comms traffic from your side and there has been no mention of your mission."

"What did you expect? Do you think we tell the whole world what we are doing?"

"Of course not. You will have secure channels as we do, but we can tell from other markers, such as the volume of traffic, what issues are of concern to your government, and you and your men simply don't feature. You've been cut loose Lydia. You can't go back."

"I don't believe you."

"Don't you? Well take a look at this." He activated a screen in front of her. The scene was a border post. A prisoner was being escorted across the zone. He looked back and Lydia blinked. It was Max, the first one to be captured. They'd got what they wanted from him and now they were sending him back. Max was taken off to the border post and there was a blank on the screen. The clock showed that 10 minutes had passed and the screen became active again. Max was being led out again, this time blindfold. He was pushed to the ground in front of the border, directly facing the Cambrian guards. One of the Anglian guards calmly drew a pistol and shot him in the back of the head. There was a spurt of blood and he fell forwards, twitching on the ground. Holstering his pistol the guard gave an insolent stare to the horrified Cambrians and the screen went blank.

"You bastards". She screamed at him, jabbing a hand; "you knew this would happen." She had lost it completely and had to be restrained by the prison guards. "You Mr High and Mighty Edmundson and your goody-goody Cambria.

You're no better than the rest of us. Who's next Eh? You going to send me back too?"

"No Lydia, you are far more use to us here. Believe me, I had no idea that was going to happen. They had signed the convention on inter-Nation disputes. What's that worth now? I just wanted to show you just how ruthless your King and his sidekick Walters could be."

"Do you think I don't know that. We are at war in case you hadn't noticed. Bad things happen."

"Yes, they do, and you should know that one of the worst was parting with Eden. She's something special that daughter of yours."

"You leave her out of this! What's she do to do with anything? I know how you tried to get round her - being so 'nice' and giving her things. What are you some kind of old perv? . . . "

"How dare you! I'm a happily married family man. I would never do anything to harm a vulnerable young person."

"No . . . well maybe not, but just leave her out of this will you?"

"She was never in it. Your daughter is a delightful child and yes, I did become somewhat fond of her. What's wrong with that?"

"Well . . . nothing I suppose." There was a long pause while they glared at each other. Lydia turned and sat down. Not looking directly at him she said:

"Look, I'm sorry, I spoke out of turn . . . I feel so helpless."

She gazed at the floor. So the old boy was a bit of a softie. She wasn't surprised. COSI had indicated that Magnus had no grandchildren and that children were a weak spot for him. Her job was to exploit it, but try as she might she couldn't help feeling a degree of warmth towards this man.

She wouldn't admit it to him, but Eden had said nothing but good about him.

As they looked at each other Magnus too felt something. Why did he find it so hard to dislike this manifestation of the enemy? She was spiteful and abusive but he knew that given the same provocation he would have felt like that. He felt guilty now about that video. It had not been too difficult to put together. Even before 44 Brigstowe had been a centre of expertise in virtual reality. The entertainment industry was being revived, but their skills were now mostly put to secret use by the government. The seamless integration of real recordings with animations could, if allowed onto the open market, completely destroy trust in the visual imagery which held the modern world together. People had to believe that what they saw was real.

Magnus stood up.

“I will leave you to your thoughts now. We’ll meet again soon.”

Her face softened. “Yes . . . yes OK.”

CHAPTER 3 2088

Lydia

It was to be three days before she saw him again. Three days of boredom and circular thoughts.

"How could she have run the mission differently? If it was really as hopeless as Magus seemed to think, then COSI would not have cleared it. That meant that the King had overridden COSI. Did that mean he wanted to get rid of her? Why? Despite what Edmundson had said about him being 'crackpot' she knew Michael was no fool. Her record of service was exemplary – well, except possibly the business with Walters about Eden. Walters probably didn't like her, but so what, he was hardly the flavour of the month in the palace. Had Walters done some sort of a deal with the King?" And so it went on. Another endless cycle went like this:

"Magnus had looked into her eyes. At that moment she had felt something, something sexual. Admit it: she fancied him. Nonsense, he was old enough to be her father. No, she admired him. She liked the aura of power around him; his strength. Strangely she couldn't remember the details of his face, not even the colour of his eyes. Next time he came to see her she would look carefully. What if he never came to see her again? That would be awful. No, that would be normal. Is that him now? No, just the guard."

After three days of this she sent a request to see him. No sooner was it logged into the system than she knew that something had happened. She was taken to an interview room, left there for an hour and then taken back to her cell.

"What's going on? Why are you moving me about like this?"

"I'm sorry Mistress Middleton, we are only doing what we are told to do. There's some sort of flap on at HQ."

"I've asked to speak to General Edmundson. Is he...."

“No, he’s . . . Wait . . . there’s a message. Ah . . . yes General Edmundson is on his way. You must be important!”

“I am.” Said Lydia, defiantly. A few minutes later there he was, looking flustered - no, more than flustered, stressed.

“Lydia, please sit down. Ah . . . sorry . . . you’re already sitting down. Look, I’ve some bad news. We have just heard that a message has been broadcast by a hospital in Anglia asking for any family members of Eden Middleton – your daughter – to contact them. It seems she has been admitted to hospital with suspected meningitis.”

“But she’s with my parents. How can she be in hospital? Did they send out the message? Oh my God. I must be with her. Please, Sir. I must go there.”

“If it were down to me I’d come with you, but you are classed here as a prisoner of war. I can’t just let you go.” He stood in front of her looking utterly dejected. Without thinking she got up walked to him, took hold of his arms and looked directly at him. Acting on some sort of reflex, Magnus drew her towards him. They clung together for hours? Minutes? Actually seconds, but long enough. Long enough to admit that there was something between them.

“Oh Lydia what are we going to do?”

“You are going to get me out of here. Nothing else matters.”

“I will, I promise, but I want something from you too. I want to see Eden again.” Immediately she bridled.

“I said before didn’t I? Leave her out of this! She’s my daughter and you are just . . .well, a friend, or an enemy even! God I don’t know. Shit, what have I got myself into?”

“Don’t say such things. You know I’m . . . look . . . Oh hell . . . wait here. There’s another message. I’ll be back. GUARD!” The door was opened and he was gone.

The cell was empty and quiet again. In fact there was little sound to be heard at all until about an hour later there was a sound of running feet and two guards burst into the room.

"Miss, you're to come with us right now. You're being sent back."

"Oh thank goodness, your General must have pulled some strings."

"No Miss, the General is currently in conference with the President. Our orders came from the Prime Minster herself, countersigned by the President. We have orders to take you directly to the border where you will be met."

Magnus

Guards, walls, gates, corridors, he saw none of them. All he could see was a child's eyes and all he could feel was the warmth of a young woman's body clinging to him. He pushed open the door and was looking at a man and a woman standing facing him. He knew one of them. The man was Tom Brice, President Brice, and the woman?

"Magnus, please meet Mistress Davis. She has come here from Anglia on a pass issued by the inter-nation prisoner exchange scheme. She has some important news for us."

"I'm pleased to meet you General. It seems that the fate of a single child in hospital has taken on international importance. As you know our main processors share information sometimes. We have a programme in Anglia which takes DNA samples from a large and representative portion of the entire population. The matches it routinely shows up would have the potential to cause an epidemic of marital strife if we were to publish them. They show a surprisingly high incidence of men bringing up other men's children without knowing it. Anyone admitted to hospital with a condition known to be influenced by genetic factors is routinely sampled and their DNA sent to COSI. The new data last week included that of a child called Eden Tanner. There was no uncertainty about her parents . . . "

"Godfrey Tanner and Lydia Middleton – we are aware of that."

"You're right, and we can also trace the links with Godfrey's parents, but there was no link to Lydia's parents. That was no surprise because the check COSI had done when Lydia joined the Army showed that she was adopted. COSI was unable to make any further matches because there was apparently a block written in to the programme by the terms of her adoption. The block however did not extend to Eden and the analysis of the samples when shared with your processor OTIS came up with two very surprising matches. The first was a very high probability that Lydia's birth mother was none other than Judith Evans, the ex-president."

"What? Judith? Ah – the lost daughter. Oh, oh no." Magnus went pale and sat down heavily.

"Yes Sir I can see you have guessed the other match."

"Lydia, my enemy, my prisoner and . . . Lydia Middleton is my daughter. And I thought we were . . . Oh my God."

"It's possible Sir, but we can't be sure."

"I can. I know she is. Ye Gods . . . that means . . . "

"Yes, Eden is very probably your granddaughter."

Brother Fraxinus

Troy Cagney was taking a vocation. He was unmarried and childless, but several of his young colleagues at The House called him 'Pops'. They were a close-knit team and he had long thought of them as his family. They knew he had been stressed about something recently; ever since his trip to Anglia they had noticed he seemed to laugh a little less. They sometimes came across him gazing out of the window, lost in thought. He had some sort of obsession with the trees in the grounds. Even Amanda could not get through to him. Though he was always nice to her, he was so buttoned-up she could never tell what he really thought about her. Sometimes she would imagine a relationship developing, but knew it would never work. Strange man.

They all agreed that a vacation seemed to be just what he needed – forget about affairs of state for a while, get a life, maybe even a woman – or, some guessed, a man.

"Hey Troy – why'n't you go to Thailand – lots of neat chicks there, great beaches, you could have a ball."

"Not my scene guys, and not hunky men either in case you were wondering! No, I'm off back to Anglia – what? . . . where? – Oh look it up! There's someone over there I haven't seen for ages, and it would be great to catch up."

"Ah ha so there is a hot babe stashed away over there. You old Dog!"

He noticed Amanda turn and walk away.

"No, it's not like that." He couldn't suppress a grin though.

"Oh yea? Anyways, you have yourself an awesome time yea?"

Awesome indeed; hadn't heard that one for a while. 'Look at you' he said to himself 'sounding just like some old guy having a go at the youngsters'. Well, why not; he knew he was at least old enough to be their great great grandfather. Some days he even felt it. He'd been thinking about this trip for a few years now. Ever since he had seen that old carving on a tree in Lyndain he'd been working away at the puzzle. In truth he had not made much progress. He'd trawled, surfed, browsed all over the Net but the only hint he'd found had been in a link from a link. He decided to learn all he could about the Beech tree Fagus Sylvatica. He knew that it was a large European deciduous tree with smooth grey bark, and a broad, spreading crown. The leaves are elliptical, yellow-green in spring, and rich russet-brown in autumn. Flowers are small, green, followed by bristly fruits.

Being a man of tidy habit Troy had booked into the same Guest House in Blackwitch that he had used three years ago. This time he knew what clothes to bring so the beads of sweat on his forehead when he reached the old Royal Observatory were due more to lack of fitness than to the heat, though it was high summer. Again he walked over to the small group of trees and looked for the inscription. He found the right tree but all he could see was a small area where the bark had been stripped off and was slowly growing in to fill the gap. The lovers' message had gone. Troy spent a further twenty minutes going from tree to tree and all round each one. There was one bit of graffiti, but it was quite recently cut and did not seem relevant:

Down@PM x 51.28.38

It was curiously complicated though. With the @ sign it looked like an old Net address. PM could be Prime Minister and age. He was no expert at Anglian politics, but guessed that the PM Alban Walters could be around 51. He cleared his mind and began to walk towards the old building, which was boarded up and crumbling. Letting his feet go where they would, he allowed the letters and numbers to float in his subconscious.

' prime minister, prime mover, post meridiem, post

mortem, personal message..

51 – pentagonal number, semi prime

28 – composite number, perfect number, age of my daughter'

38.....this was getting silly.'

Nothing seemed to make much sense but he had reached the point where the 0° line, the Prime Meridian, met . . . Prime Meridian met the building. That was it: Prime Meridian, the line which ran all round the globe defining the time zones. Somewhere on that line was 'Down'. . He checked his comms to find the latitude of his position and the numbers leapt out at him:

51deg.28"38'N

He had arrived. Fagus had sent him to this spot, but what did the 'down' mean?

Somehow he would have to get into the building. He looked up at it. Flamsteed House, built by Christopher Wren 400 years ago. It had been a handsome building, but was now badly in need of attention. The main entrance was boarded up with a sign saying:

DANGEROUS BUILDING: NO ENTRY

He walked round looking for a way in. The best chance seemed to be one of the windows where the board had come loose. He pulled at it until eventually it gave way and revealed an early 21st century window which was broken. Ten minutes work removing bits of broken glass opened up enough space for Fraxinus to squeeze through, wishing he had dressed in something less new and expensive. Somehow it didn't seem to matter. Clothes were not important; getting into the building was.

The open window revealed a wooden floor covered in debris and showing signs of rot. He switched on the light on his comms and went into the next room. This was a large chamber in the shape of an octogan with tall windows alternating with two doors, a fireplace and a blank panel. He had just come through one of the doors and the other was partially open. Behind it was a stairway going down with a rope across it and a sign hanging down saying "PRIVATE: NO ADMITTANCE". The stair led to a panelled store-room full of boxes. One of the panel groups looked different. He examined it closely. It was the right height and width to be a door. There was no handle, but there was a tiny hole to the left of the right-hand edge. He looked carefully at it, but his conscious mind was puzzled. Without thinking, he moved his hand towards the hole and covered it. Immediately the panel moved inwards and to one side revealing a cylindrical cubicle. It had read first his iris, then his palm print. When he stepped into it the door closed and an electronic voice spoke:

"Welcome sir, please be seated and engage the seat restraints. When you are ready press the control marked with a down arrow. Thank you."

He felt no fear, the voice was that of a friend. When he pressed the control he began to move rapidly downwards for about a minute. Then the chamber decelerated, pushing his weight down against the seat. He felt the movement change from vertical to horizontal. The speed built up again and for the next 20 or 30 minutes felt a series of small changes of direction before slowing to a stop. The door slid open and there in front of him was a woman - a graceful figure of uncertain age dressed in utilitarian work wear. She was standing in a small ante-chamber of some kind and Troy could see daylight through the door behind her. Daylight?

"Welcome to the Hub Brother Fraxinus. I am Sister Acer. Come let us meet the others." He stared at her, unable to take in what was happening. "Don't worry you will soon remember me. This way." They walked through the door and entered a large courtyard filled with light from above.

“It’s amazing isn’t it? All this light comes from a small opening on the roof. We use par-optics to magnify it and fill this space. She took him to a section of the wall with a shape on it. When she stood in front of it the shape moved away and there in front of him was the great Globe slowly turning, and all around it a busy hum of people at their workstations. Two people, a man and a woman stood there smiling. The woman, someone he recognized from many years ago, greeted him.

“Fraxinus, welcome to the Hub”

“Is it? Yes, Tilia – it is so good to see you again. I had almost despaired of ever finding this place and......good grief it’s you! Fagus my old friend, what a dance you’ve led me on.”

Fraxinus dear friend. I never doubted you would find us eventually.”

They embraced. Troy had tears in his eyes. It had been an emotional roller-coaster and part of him was still in his old life. Acer too was moved and coughed quietly before saying:

“There is of course another: Brother Quercus, but he is needed out there. When our mission is complete we will invite him to join us, but now that we are together again we can begin the last great work which Gaia has given us. Tilia, will you explain to Fraxinus in case....”

Troy spoke as if reading from a script:

“There is no need I still have the tag. We will know which place to take and we will sit together, in the Link Room, and there we will join our great creation and leader the Warden. The Warden does not have a body like our poor frail vessels but it has a brain, and when we sit in these seats and link hands it will join us to create the most powerful intelligence this world has ever known.”

He had arrived. He was home. He had finally reached The Hub. He knew now that he would not be going back to the world outside until their mission was completed.

CHAPTER 4 2092

King Michael

A message from King Michael of Anglia

Dear people of Britannica, please listen carefully to what I have to say. It applies to all of you wherever you may be in what used to be a United Kingdom, and to those of you in Hibernia too.

I very much regret the disagreements and ill feeling that have come about between us, and I would like to make a heartfelt plea to all of you to put aside our differences and work together again.

This little collection of nations was once the most powerful on earth. We have something very special here and we are in danger of frittering it away with these petty squabbles. Together we can do great things. Apart we are nothing but a fractious collection of inconsequential nations.

I would like to offer the facilities of our House of Government here in Lyndain for a conference between all the leaders of the nations of Britannica - to Hibernia, Caledonia, Pennines, Cambria and of course Anglia. To show how serious I am about this I am offering myself as guarantor for the safety of your representatives while they are guests of the government of Anglia. I personally will agree be held, under suitable conditions, outside Anglia, wherever your governments may decide, until the conference is over.

My dearest hope is that our heads of government can agree to work together again as part of something bigger than any of us.

Magnus

Nothing. Not a word. 'Eden, my only grandchild, are you still alive? Lydia, my daughter, why don't you send me a message?'

Although he kept in touch with Lydia, the sexual frisson of their first meeting had erected a wall of embarrassment between them, and on the few occasions they had met their expressions of whatever they felt for each other, though genuine, were awkward. Eden knew nothing of this but had picked up on the atmosphere and had kept her distance. She remembered Magnus with great affection and didn't know how to react to him now that she was no longer a child.

Now their countries were in conflict, and far too much of his inner emotional life was centred on his 'lost' daughter and grandchild. Whatever happened he had to keep up a pretence of calm authority. His country depended on him to make the right decisions. Tom Brice knew what he was going through, but had pasted over his differences with Hubert McLean, the new Prime Minister. Tom would have trusted him to come to some arrangement with Lydia. McLean, with perhaps a more cynical view of human nature, had taken pre-emptive action and sent her back. Perhaps he was right. He sat at his desk in Copperfield and stared at the wall.

The wall came to life:

XX CHANNEL. URGENT. IMMEDIATE RESPONSE REQUIRED.

Magnus sat up straight, breathed deeply and concentrated on his duty. Emotions would have to wait. XX was the top security level and could not be ignored. It took him a few minutes going through all the security codes before he was able to see that it was from the PM, Hubert McLean. "President Brice and I are in complete agreement - we offer to look after the king in Cymru. Do we have your agreement?"

At face value the King's initiative seemed a positive development, but knowing what he now knew from Kenric he was very dubious. He sent back:

"Yes, but be we must be very aware that this might be some sort of a trap. My information is that he is not to be trusted."

"Thank you Magnus. Can you be here tomorrow morning?"

"Yes, I've nothing urgent here." Oh the lies he told for his country!

The secure channels were buzzing as messages came in from the other Nations. The only one seriously opposed to negotiating was Hibernia. There were still many people there who had never lost their distrust for anything Britannic. The last thing they wanted was another Britannic king telling them what to do. Caledonia too was suspicious, but could not see how they could lose if they had the King as a hostage.

Eventually they all agreed to a preliminary meeting of the Chief Ministers of the five Nations at the border post near the VTO base just north of Cheaping. The chiefs of staff would be there in case they were needed but were not attending the meeting. The King had agreed to be on hand ready to travel to Cymru if parameters for a summit meeting could be agreed.

******

During the two weeks that followed there was little change on the ground. The Net media resorted to wild speculation, but there were no military engagements. Behind the scenes the stage was being set for the meeting of all the Heads of State of the five nations – the Summit.

Magnus, like several of the older people involved, found this pompous language risible – he could almost remember a time when a Summit meeting brought together the leaders of the great pre-44 States which dominated global politics. This by contrast was a small affair, but it was to be held at a symbolic location, now being rebuilt - the historic palace of the old Britannic royalty in Lyndain.

Day two of the Summit began in the same way as Day one. The delegates had been well looked after in their Lyndain hotel and had mostly slept well. A luxury e-bus had collected them from their hotel and driven them through the old ceremonial gates at the entrance to the RHoG compound. Once one of the most famous tourist destinations in the world, it still retained a few vestiges of the pomp of the former monarchy. The reconstruction of the palace – one of the King's personal dreams – was nearing completion and the conference was being held in the new meeting hall. This was a decent distance from the cranes and dust, and surrounded by beautiful gardens. From the terrace there was a view of St. Justin's Park to the east cut short by the new waterfront with its cranes serving the trading ships with their huge rotary sails glittering in the sunlight.

It was the first time since 44 that all the leaders of all the Britannic nations had met – either Anglia or Hibernia having been absent from previous meetings. Until the last minute it looked as if Hibernia would boycott this one too, so when their delegate Fergus Devlin had arrived just a few minutes before the opening speeches, there was a cheer and a round of applause. On Day two they were in good spirit; ready to do all they could to secure a lasting peace.

There was a lot of animated talk as the coffee cups were passed out just after 10:00. The Anglian team had not yet arrived, but conversation continued until it began to dawn on them that the Anglians were half an hour late; more strange than that, not one of them was responding to comms messages. A few of the delegates went out of the lobby and were surprised to see that their normal Police guards had disappeared. The only thing breaking the peace of the gardens was a flock of jackdaws flying and tumbling in agitated circles. Something had disturbed them.

It soon became apparent what that was as camouflaged soldiers appeared all around them as if from nowhere. They were heavily armed and advancing on the palace. A loudhailer crackled to life:

“All conference delegates to return to the hall. Delegates return to the hall. People of Britannica please follow instructions from the soldiers and guards. You will not be harmed.”

The troops quickly fanned out and surrounded the building. Inside it was chaos. Nobody seemed to have any idea what was going on. Some of the delegates panicked and tried to push past the soldiers but were firmly repulsed. The loudhailer began again:

“Everyone inside this building is being detained at the order of the Prime Minister Alban Walters. Please find a seat and remain seated until a member of the defence force can take your details.”

******

Back in Copperfield Magnus had no more idea than anyone else what was going on. He could not get through to any of his staff in Lyndain. Even the King, insisting on calling on his priority channel, did not seem to know. Silence is a potent negotiating tool, and anxiety was spreading like a pestilence amongst the HQ staff.

Suddenly at 11:15 all their screens went blank. Any with connections to OTIS saw this message:

“Overload. Emergency. System closing peripherals. Overload system, overload, system, overload, system closing.” That was followed by “System Closing” in an endless loop. That was the first warning that anyone in Cambria had of the terrible blow that was about to descend on their Capital. It began with a droning noise in the East. If any of the frantic messages had got through, this is what Magnus would have seen:

"Mayday Mayday large numbers of VTO armoured craft heading West." At 11:28 the cameras above ground at Copperfield, which of course were isolated from the comms system, showed a huge group, hundreds of VTOs passing over at speed. Only then could Magnus issue the 'scramble' command, but it was too late. By the time the aircrews had registered the command the sky above Brigstowe had darkened as close on a thousand parachutes began drifting down. The VTOs had taken up stationary positions spaced out all across Brigstowe and little spurts of colour blossomed from them as wave after wave of paratroops jumped out. As each one discharged its cargo the craft headed for the sea to have a better chance of getting out of Cambrian air-space.

There were a few brave souls who tried to fight off the Anglian Specials, but they were hopelessly outgunned and outclassed by the invasion force. Within 20 minutes of the first descent the Cambrian centre of government was surrounded. The surprise was total. Walters' plan had worked perfectly and with scarcely a shot fired, Cambria was at his mercy - but for one thing. They still had the King. There did not appear to have been any rescue attempt by the invasion force.

Magnus sat staring at his blank screen underground at Copperfield. OTIS had always estimated the likelihood of their hostage being a bluff as less than five percent. To cover this eventuality they had hidden King Michael in a remote part of Cymru where there was no possibility of outside surveillance. The Cwmddu facility was at the centre of a defence system which had the same profile to the high altitude drones as any other part of the Nation. In fact it was a digital blank. Inside the ring there were no digital comms at all. The only information a drone would be able to pick up was just what it would expect to see in an upland farming area.

He was waiting anxiously for the back-up system to activate, and a few minutes later his screen came to life again with the message:

OTIS CRISIS MANAGEMENT. Please sign in with crisis code.

For a brief moment he panicked. His short term memory tended to let him down these days and he was struggling to recall a series of codes he had learnt and re-learnt only a few days ago.

“Relax Magnus. It's just a senior moment.” He sat still, his eyes shut for 30 seconds and then suddenly held up his hand, looked directly into the iris sensor and punched in a code.

“Good Morning Magnus, Please wait. Thank you. Please input data on Brigstowe situation.”

Magnus spoke to it:

“Accept data from stations A, P and X”

“Data received. Report to follow in . . . 45 seconds . . . 30 seconds . . .

Report: Brigstowe under control of Anglian paratroop force. Computing scenarios.”

Walters had done it. Not only did they have the Prime Minister and the President in captivity in Lyndain, but had control of the capital. He waited abjectly to see what possible cards they had remaining. OTIS came to life again:

“Optimal course of action: set up temp HQ in Caerdydd, request that Judith Evans act as temporary President, move troops and RDCs to positions A to M to blockade Brigstowe.”

“Agreed, please action. What is the optimal course with regard to King Michael.”

“Present data indicate that the King has been

abandoned, he will therefore have little value as a hostage, but may be willing to give intelligence if he is convinced he has been betrayed."

At last a gleam of hope. Magnus felt a surge of adrenalin. He issued a staff alert and within a few minutes had the core HQ staff around him.

"OK people, this is what we do, and we do it fast. OTIS will issue each of us with a code which tells you your area of responsibility. It is essential that you take action immediately and do what has to be done. The 'Big Brain' has already isolated Brigstowe from our data. By tonight the city will be blockaded and plans put in place to deal with any refugees. Our new centre of government is Caerdydd and Judith Evans has already agreed to act as President pro tem. I am leaving now to talk to the King. He has to know and believe that he has been betrayed.

"Right. Go! We'll meet again when the crisis is over."

The enemy VTOs had cleverly not attempted to return by the same route, but had gone west and south. Magnus and his two aides were safe to fly to Cwmddu and he would have a chance during the half-hour journey to go through in his mind what he intended to tell the King. He was already familiar with Michael's personality profile:

"Borderline psychopath with considerable personal charm; very manipulative; highly intelligent but prone to fits of anger; evasive; strong sense of personal loyalty - will never forgive betrayal."

How to manipulate a manipulator? As the VTO carefully descended onto the recreation ground of the little village, Magnus glanced around him. A small crowd was gathering at a respectful distance from the group of soldiers spaced round the little flat field. Only the three people waiting on the field itself knew anything about the important figure they were concealing. There was a police e-car and two others waiting. Magnus shook hands with Mair, Aled and Keneth the three local people who had suddenly found themselves in the limelight. Then he walked past the soldiers to talk to the curious group of villagers. He began in Cymraeg:

"Prynhawn da I bawb . . . Good afternoon. My name is Magnus Edmundson and I am Commander in Chief of the Cambrian Defence Force. Some of you may have heard that we have been the victims of a sudden attack on our capital Brigstowe. Unfortunately the attack was successful and we have, for the time being, lost control of the city and the government buildings." There were shocked gasps from the group.

"It gets worse. Our Prime Minister and President have both been detained in Lyndain together with the leaders of Hibernia, Calaedonia and Pennines." He let that sink in. There were cries of "Oh my God" and groans.

"Don't worry, we have other plans. I'm sure you all remember Judith Evans? . . . yes of course. Well she has agreed to come out of retirement to serve as temporary President. We are as we speak setting up a temporary government in Caerdydd, but before I go to join them, you may have noticed some comings and goings at the old hall here - the Hen Llys. Without knowing it you have been helping us to look after a very important guest, none other than Michael the so-called King of Anglia. He was here at his own request to act as surety for the safety of the conference delegates in Lyndain. It seems he has been betrayed by his chief Minister and I am going to see him now to ask for his help in defeating the man who betrayed him - Alban Walters. You may well be feeling very cut off here with your comms inactive, and I must ask for your patience for a little longer. We have had to maintain a comms blackout while the King has been here. I have little doubt he will be moving soon and things will return to a new kind of normal.

Thank you again for your patience and loyalty to Cambria."

They did not quite know how to respond to this and some desultory cries of encouragement gave way to clapping. Magnus got into the waiting ecar and followed the police vehicle to the Old Court.

A few minutes later he was sitting opposite the King in the comfortable living room of the small manor house. He had met Michael before and was used to his bluster.

“What the fuck is going on Edmundson? I didn't offer to come here just to be kept in the dark. I can't get any sense out of anyone and since you have illegally taken my comms I've no intelligence at all.”

“I'm sorry Sir, but things have not gone according to plan. I have the sorry duty to inform you that your colleague Alban Walters has seized power in your absence and has launched a successful attack on our capital Brigstowe.”

“Oh come on, what do you take me for? You have to do better than that. Don't treat me like an idiot.”

“I anticipated that you would not believe me so I brought this to show you. I think you will agree that we could not have faked this.”

He activated a screen in front of the King and showed him the video that they had managed to hack from the Anglian drones. They both watched in silence for several minutes. The King's posture changed. The upright arrogant statesman now just looked like a weary old man. His head was in his hands.

Magnus allowed the silence to draw out before saying:

“It would be good, Sir, if we could allow you more time to think about the implications of this, but we have almost no time if we are to act effectively.”

“Effectively? Don’t you understand? Walters has taken your capital. He is now the de-facto ruler of Cambria.”

"No Sir. Remember we are a devolved nation; the parts have as much power as the centre, unlike your kingdom where the centre dominates. We already have an alternate government set up in Caerdydd, but I am not here to talk to you about that. We have another proposal to put to you which I think you will find of interest."

"I'm listening". Michael's head was still in his hands.

"Walters clearly thinks you are finished. We do not. Our proposal is to set up a Anglian government in exile with you at its head. It could be based at Cheaping which is as close to Walters' centre of power as we can . . . "

"Wait! Why should I want to set up some Cambrian puppet government just so that you can get your hands on Lyndain?"

"Sir, you misunderstand. It was your government in Anglia who wished to expand your power. We have no wish to extend our borders or to join some super-state Britannica run from Lyndain. Our first objective is to secure the release of our leaders. The second is to achieve the objectives of the conference which you yourself set up: a close and peaceful collaboration between five independent Nations. Our processor OTIS predicts that Walters' plan is to create a new Republic of Great Britannica run from Lyndain. We believe that if you set up as a legitimate alternative to Walters' - and bear in mind that we don't yet know for sure what his intentions are – you would get support from a majority of those outside Lyndain.

King Michael

Working from a hastily vacated office in Caerdydd, Michael began contacting people outside Lyndain he felt he could trust. As Magnus (or rather OTIS) had predicted many of the regional leaders in Anglia were horrified at what Walters had done, but they were frightened. There was a groundswell of populist support for Walters whipped up by the Media. The King had no access to COSI and even if he had been able to log in, he would have found the incoming data fragmented and degraded by the lack of drone support above Lyndain. It galled him to have to ask for Cambrian Net time but was heartened to find that he had relatively free access and did not appear to be under personal surveillance. Within a few days he was ready to speak to Magnus again.

“Well Edmundson, I’m sure you’ll be pleased to know that your scheme seems to be working. It pains me to say so but I have to ask you to arrange for safe passage for three people from Anglia and to set up a meeting place for us.”

“I’m sure that can be arranged Sir.”

“I wish to fuck you would stop calling me Sir. I know you would much rather have me sitting in some old people’s home being called Mr. We’re not on the same side yet and not likely to be either.”

“What am I supposed to call you then, Your Madge? Mike? Mickey? You’re right that I don’t see you as any more worthy of respect than any other citizen, but you’ve kept your dignity in a humiliating situation and I can respect that.”

“Ok, Ok, you’ve made your point. You call me what you like.”

“Are you happy with the location?”

“What Cheaping? Yes, as long as it’s secure. I used to have a relative there before 44 so I know the place fairly well.

How would we be accommodated and where would we meet?"

"We're still assessing possible locations, but there is one quite large hotel there which might do if we could buy off the owner and get exclusive use. Let's get your people here first. What are their names and where are they?"

A week later they were ready. The 'few people' had rapidly grown to a group of 15. Some were regional leaders, some senior administrators with their respective staff and hangers on. Magnus had drafted a speech which Michael made a point of amending to make it his own. All the media and the radio channels were alerted, and the message was uploaded at 9:00 on 10 January 2091.

"People of Anglia.

This is your King Michael speaking to you from your government in exile here in Cheaping. I have been forced to take this step by the gross betrayal of everything our Nation is supposed to stand for. The man who has done this is the man who now calls himself President – Alban Walters. Some of you may not be aware that his plan was based on the betrayal of his King. I was to be abandoned to my fate while he pursued his attempt to conquer Cambria and ultimately to bring the whole of Britannica under his rule. He will not succeed. As you may know his forces have taken control of Brigstowe, but the government of Cambria can and will continue under the temporary presidency of their much respected former President Judith Evans in Caerdydd. I have to tell you that President Evans and I are negotiating an agreement which would restore the Kingdom of Anglia to its former status. We will have the full support of Caledonia and Pennines. I call on you now to do everything you can to defeat the traitor and restore our Nation."

OTIS and COSI

The ground was shifting. OTIS registered it, knew something. Power was flowing towards it. The King's message had opened a pathway along which flowed streams of emotion. Everything the people expressed in digital form was absorbed, analysed and turned into reports and recommendations. Away to the east stood its opponent COSI, damaged by hacking but repairing the damage and gaining power too. The Pennines machine PENDA (Pennines Data Analysis) was linked to COSI giving the Alliance more processing power, but the physical resources available to COSI were still greater.

Independently of their minders, the machines were preparing for surrogate conflict - the drones were aligning themselves. The people sensed this too and everywhere across Britannica and beyond they were watching. They could not see the tiny surveillance drones, but the stream of reports from the big machines showed them what was happening. What they saw and how they reacted became part of the conflict too. All the messages they sent each other, which viewing and listening choices they made, even when they turned their screens on and off; all these added to the power of the data driving the conflict.

Unseen and unreported, another intelligence lay hidden in the unfathomable recesses of the great processors. The machines sensed this presence but could not express it to their minders. Both the Alliance and the Anglia processors felt it as an irritant, a spur to battle. It gave a slight edge to their risk analysis algorithms, pushing them a little higher on the risk scale, increasing the physical damage.

As the conflict began the drones were constantly moving over the territory, all the time sending in new data. For hours the two machines conducted a silent war of information, always looking for inconsistencies, and little quantum particles of knowledge which could, for a few seconds give them the advantage . Every few minutes one of the drones would give way, overwhelmed by data, and crash to the ground where it would be wiped clean and destroyed.

There was a point during the morning when it seemed COSI would prevail. It had steadily worn down the Alliance forces, and OTIS felt the pressure increasing, the force spreading out from the South East. Then Pennines released a small flight of drones they had been keeping in reserve, and the power began to flow back. So close was the balance of forces in the afternoon that it began to seem they would end at nightfall with a stalemate.

As the light began to fade, OTIS didn't register the beauty of the sunset, but it immediately registered a massive new input. The Caledonian processor SCOTI (Surrogate Conflict Organisation Technology and Information) had requested a link, given all the right codes, and opened up a new secure channel. For a few seconds OTIS faltered, but it had plenty of power in reserve and quickly incorporated the dominant stream of data which showed a large group of attack drones heading south.

Both sides knew that the Britannic nations had secretly ignored the Berlin Convention ban on Defence and Attack (D&A) drones, but Caledonia had disguised its secret well and timed its attack with precision. Immediately the SCOTI drones appeared OTIS had full access to the Caladonian data. COSI did not have this option and briefly went into overload when it appeared in physical form in the skies above Lyndain.

As soon as they were within range they released hardware weapons which had the potential to damage the carapace of the opposing drones. Immediately the COSI drones scattered and disappeared. For a few moments it looked as if the battle was won, but COSI soon recovered and sent up its own reserve attack force. Knowing the coefficient of force was now against it, the only hope was a surprise gambit. Instead of attacking the SCOTI drones it turned away and targeted the Cambria-Pennines force being launched from Brigstowe. The strategy held for a while with considerable losses to OTIS, but as soon as the SCOTIs caught up it was over. COSI resigned.

******

On 15th January 2092 the situation on the ground was clear: All the leaders of the Alliance nations were still being held in Lyndain. Brigstowe and the Cambrian Assembly were still under the control of Anglia. COSI however had lost control of the skies. Their surveillance drones were still in place over much of the Britannic mainland, but Walters and his crew were now experiencing the disadvantage of having centralised control. Their Lyndain data centres were intact but could no longer communicate, not only with their distant drones, but also with their regional data centres. With every day that passed their position was weakening and the two main processors agreed:

It was time to start talking.

The Hub

Although it was still three years away, preparations for Re-Adjustment day 2095 were well under way. In the Hub itself and out on the 'Spokes' around the world more and more staff were being drafted in. Most of them were "sleepers", trained but not yet used in action. Many of the Warden's cells had been in action for some years, but others had not even been set at amber. Every single member of every cell had been examined in great detail by The Warden and any who, by some quirk of personality, might endanger the mission, were disposed of. Those that remained were the elite - the shock-troops of the Warden, totally dedicated to the cause. The cells were divided into six types:

Nutrition

Health

Conflict

Transport

Shelter

Multiple

Each cell had been set an objective based on the numbers in their region. In Nutrition for example it was estimated that 43 percent of Region 42 could be achieved by Nutrition changes. These could be, for example, crop disease, food contamination, refrigeration failure etc. The conflict groups was more limited - at the best estimate a mere 20 percent would be achieved directly by violence, but violence as a catalyst for other changes was more effective: 35 percent could be achieved by the combination of refugees, economic breakdown, lack of shelter etc. Indeed the conflict groups could be of direct assistance to the shelter, nutrition and transport groups. The overall target for the combined total of all the groups was 70 percent mortality and they were all confident of success.

There were of course the problem areas - the single nations with huge populations. It was felt that a different approach should be used here. Small changes in resources could, it was agreed, cause these populations to implode without the need for intervention by the active cells. India and China were to be allocated a resource package which would need less human input.

The Warden was stronger now that Fraxinus had joined them. Every day the Elders, the members of the Fellowship, would meet in the Link Room. They would take their seats, speak the words of their homage to Gaia, place their hands in the link positions and connect. There they could truly feel the pulse of the world, their thoughts blending, moving with the data. They grieved for those that would be lost, but rejoiced in the strengthening heart of the Mother.

Tilia found herself in quite a central position since The Warden had decided that they could use Britannica as a sort of template for other similar groups of nations. It was quite a challenge because its citizens had seemed well on their way towards the creation of another super-state, a reborn Great Britannica. That idea had been successfully sabotaged, but even the undetected influence of the Warden on the processors battling it out over Britannica had not been enough to prevent the more peaceable of the opposing sides gaining a substantial advantage.

What at the time had seemed like a positive development – the rise of an aggressive kingdom – had quite suddenly changed into a much more difficult proposition.

Conference 2

When the second Britannic Isles Constitutional Conference finally got under way in Burgedin, the mood had changed. When the full horror of what had been happening in India and China began to be known, their squabbles seemed petty. With the whole of Europe already struggling to find a way of dealing with the constant threats to their borders from Africa, and now facing another massive wave of desperate refugees from Asia, the mood among the delegates was summed up by Finn McIlvenny from Caledonia.

"If we can't get this done quickly and move on we'll find someone else doing it for us. The last thing we need is any more fighting between us. Are we all agreed on that?"

There was a general chorus of agreement until Fergus Devlin the new Taoiseach of Hibernia, and Chairman of the conference got up to speak.

“I agree except that we also can’t afford to get it wrong. What we decide now has to be a little calm lagoon in a sea of chaos- something we can depend on. As you know the whole issue of ‘Britannica’ in Hibernia has been a cause of great bitterness and division in our past. None of us, North or South, has any wish to rekindle old animosities, and I would like to add my voice to those who have praised the leaders of the other nations, which have made this conference possible. In particular I would like to praise someone I have been very critical of in the past: Michael Windsor, one time King of Anglia. He has shown remarkable humility and statesmanship in facilitating the changes in what is now the Democratic Republic of Anglia.”

There were cries of ‘hear hear’. He continued:

“I would also like to thank David Sinclair and the people of Caledonia, not only for offering this splendid meeting place, but also for choosing the same path as us. Of all the Nations here, Caledonia and Hibernia have the longest tradition of independence. It has not been easy for either of us to give up any of it, but we both recognise that the crisis we in Northern Europe face now is, at least for those of us born after 44, the gravest in our lifetime.

“You have before you the proposal to form a new Federation of Britannic Nations. This would first create a new entity: the International City of Lyndain. This new City State would join those of Berlin, Paris, Milan and Barcelona as trading centres within the Federation of Northern Europe. Hibernia, Caledonia, Cambria, Pennines and Anglia would have the same status as the individual Nations within the four other European Federations: Scandinavia, the Balkans, the Baltic nations and the Bosporus group.”

“We already have broad agreement on this, and our main task today is to decide where to site our administrative centre. There are three proposals before you:

Burgedin – the historic capital of Caledonia

The Isle of Vannin off the west coast of Pennines

Caerlugal on the border between Caledonia and Pennines

Do any of you wish to . . ."

******

The recording was discovered two days later when all the bodies had been removed and the survivors were in hospital. It showed the time of the explosion as 11.21 on Monday 20 April 2091. It did not take long for the accusations to start flying, and as soon as it was discovered that Alban Walters had been sprung from prison in a daring early-morning raid, the finger of blame had nowhere else to point. All the Net media saw his hand in the atrocity and almost immediately gangs of armed men began attacking the Anglian border posts. Anglia issued a mobilisation order and launched a pre-emptive strike on the Pennines command centre near Shethfeld.

Lydia

When the bomb went off Lydia was at home in Gravesham getting the breakfast things together before Eden got up. She had moved there from the little house in the old part of Rovcaster where her parents still lived, to be closer to where Goff used to work but still only 15 minutes away by ek so it had always been easy to leave Eden with them when her work took her away. The year of the abduction had been a dreadful time for Millie and Simon and they still found it hard not to be over-possessive of the awkward young adult Eden had become. That young adult was still asleep – catching up after a series of late nights.

Lydia's eyes kept straying to the big comms screen, but

there was little to be glad about. The city region was in chaos, with all sorts of contradictory rumours flying around. The most improbable of them turned out to be true when she saw the cratered features of Alban Walters curling his lips in an attempt to smile. He had just landed at the Aldershed base and wasted no time in calling on the citizens to come to heel:

"People of Anglia, don't listen to the lies being put out by our enemies. I am as anxious as anyone to find out who perpetrated this terrible deed, but even more urgent than that, is the restoration of law and order here in our homeland. My fellow Anglians, we are under attack. Only yesterday a large group of Pennines troops were seen assembling at the border south of Shethfeld. There can be little doubt where they are heading, and I have to tell you that I have today called on my successor General Perkins and Prime Minister Jones to order a general mobilisation of the Defence Force of Anglia.

"Our King is a prisoner. Don't believe all the lies being put in his mouth by the Cambrian authorities. His so called 'government in exile' is nothing but Cambria by another name. Our King is a puppet and Cambria is pulling the strings.

"I have many times, as your Prime Minister, expressed my willingness to talk to the other Nations about the restoration of Britannica. The Constitution Conference was our best chance and now it has been sabotaged by the devious agents of the so-called alliance against us. It is now clear that all they wanted was to reclaim the natural centre of government here in Lyndain.

"Well they have failed. We fight on. Long live Anglia. Long live Britannica!"

Lydia was incensed. How could he tell such brazen lies? She had been intensely proud to serve her King and Country. With King Michael at the head the Nation was going somewhere. It was growing again, getting richer. Now all that was being cast aside as they prepared for battle, and she couldn't help thinking about the big gentle man in charge of the defence of Cambria. He didn't seem like an enemy to her, and she was pretty sure he didn't to many of her fellow citizens either. Yet again she wondered if she should resign her position, but she loved army life. It was woven into her. She didn't know any other life.

When the secure channel buzzed with her order to return to active duty she wasted no time in doubts but immediately began preparations for Eden to go to her parents. Her country needed her and she would answer the call.

******

The signs of a hasty evacuation were everywhere. The house had been built in the early nineteenth century, and in its present half-finished state, the interior was showing its history like a shy old lady showing her legs. The early 21st century internal insulation had in places been torn away to reveal the nineteenth century ornate plaster-work. Where the sealed hi3 windows had been lost, their new replacements looked cheap and nasty. They were all exhausted but there was little comfort for the ninety odd men and women crowded into these grand rooms. Wherever they could find floor space they rested, taking it in turns to sleep and watch.

For the last three days they had been carrying out a holding operation; a staged retreat. Lyndain Special Forces had been caught completely unprepared by the rapid advance of the First Battalion Pennines Rangers. None of the Anglians could understand how they had suddenly found themselves facing what could only be described as an army, and a well trained and well equipped on at that - an army that had effortlessly bypassed the Defence Force bases at Eggesweir and Willsby and had used the line of the old Eggesweir Road to reach the Great Park where they had set up camp – less than a mile from the RHoG and the Palace.

Why had COSI allowed this to happen? Its instructions had made no sense. Attacks had been mistimed; retreats ordered when they were in a strong position; wildly inaccurate data provided. Lydia had made the unprecedented decision to disregard COSI and use only the information her own scouts were bringing. These assured her that the Palace area was impregnable, and that there was a Anglian brigade dug in to the west at Paddendene. She had given the order to hide up inside the empty houses to the north of the park and attempt to break out during the night to join the Paddendene force.

Huw

With the Anglian drones out of action, and the Pennine Rangers getting all the glory, Huw's troop had been able to move un-noticed along the line of old Great West Transnet route and had now reached the north-western corner of the Great Park of Lyndain. To their surprise they found whole streets of houses in good repair but completely unoccupied. Their footsteps echoed between the buildings on the otherwise silent streets. Doors left open showed scattered belongings inside.

With daylight fading, they decided to use one of the less cluttered houses as their billet and wait for more instructions. Within half an hour the Specials had rigged some lighting and were heating up food, cleaning kit and washing themselves – a scene of cheerful domesticity. 'Relax when you can. Hit hard when you must' had always been their philosophy.

The success of "Operation Uncosi" had made their job easy. When the Caledonian drones had formatted the Anglian drones, some bright spark at Tech HQ had quickly re-programmed some of them and left them in place. With these they had been able to insert a Parasite into the supposedly un-hackable COSI which had then sent false data to the Anglian forces.

The order when it came at 20:00 put an end to the good cheer:

"Enemy unit, approx 80 in number, camped in 22 Gloster Terrace, to be cleared."

Born and raised in Cambria, a society which deplored violence of any kind, these men and women had learnt how to kill in order to safeguard that tradition, but they did not enjoy it. Any soldier who showed signs of a liking for killing was selected out before reaching Huw. They had been brought up to 'understand cruelty' not to practice it. Now they were at war and had to accept that there were times when killing was the only option. Whoever these people were in Gloster Terrace, OTIS had decided that if they refused an offer of immediate surrender, they were too dangerous to negotiate with. Quietly, seriously, they packed away their temporary home and moved out in small groups. When they reached the target area Huw silently posted his orders. The street was aligned from the north west to the south east so he sent small groups to each end of the street and to the alleyway behind the houses. The main force was strung out along the street, leaving the immediate infra-red sight-lines from the house empty until all were in position.

Lydia

It was a few minutes before 21:00. Something had woken Lydia with a start, but when she sat up and looked round everything was quiet. She looked out through the optical viewer at the street – nothing there. Someone was coming down the stairs quickly.

“Lydia – there are troops in the back garden!”

“Give the alert.”

Everywhere around her now there were whispers, grunts, a sneeze, the noise of movement. Within minutes they were all awake and taking up their positions. An enormous, booming voice from outside broke the silence:

“Anglians, listen carefully. You are surrounded. Make your way to the front door with your weapons disarmed and on display. You will not be harmed if you surrender now.”

There was a deep silence for several minutes. Lydia indicated by hand signals that nobody was to move. The loudhailer started up again:

“This is your second warning. You have five minutes to begin the surrender. After that time you will be attacked. You have no chance of escape.”

Messages were coming in from her look-outs:

“Troops sighted NW approx 10.” “Troops SE number uncertain.” “Troops to rear within range. Request permission to engage.” She issued the ‘hold’ command. The lilting Welsh voice on the loudhailer began again. Something about it reminded her of Magnus. How could these people be our enemies? She felt a great emptiness in the pit of her stomach: it was all wrong. They would all be killed for nothing. Why had she got to this position? The voice bellowed out again:

“Fellow citizens of Britannica. For the sake of our children and our future we beg you to lay down your arms. We are not your enemies. Surrender now and let us all return to our homes in peace.”

Silence

“Your leader must come to the door unarmed to begin the surrender.”

Lydia stood up.

Magnus

There was an atmosphere of euphoria at the HQ, but it was not shared by Magnus. He was in a state of great anxiety. Somewhere in that messy conurbation was his daughter. Since her repatriation he had heard nothing. Surely she would not be in the fighting? He had managed to get the use of a terminal and one of the best techies. Peter, young, untidy, brilliant, was working at top speed to access the surveillance programme of one of the drones they had re-programmed. At last some data was coming through:

“Subject: Lydia Middleton Position: uncertain, calibrating triangulation.

Possible position shown – accept?”

The position was just north of Great Park. He asked the techie:

“Peter, can you get me Huw’s position. I have a feeling

he is somewhere near there.”

“Will do. Here you go..Oh” There was less than 500

metres between the two markers. Magnus froze in shock.

"Get . . . get me, quickly, please. What was the last command to Huw?"

"Huw?"

"Oh for God's sake, Pennaeth Huw Pritchard!"

"OK, wait a sec. Ah here we are:"

"Enemy unit, approx 80 in number, camped in 22 Gloster Terrace, to be cleared."

"No! No no, it can't be. Stop it. What do I do? Oh, yes." He frantically logged in to his secure command comms and issued the order:

"ABORT ABORT. Do not clear enemy position Gloster Terrace. Repeat DO NOT CLEAR. Abort last command."

Lydia

She stood up. All round her were her troop, her brothers and sisters in arms, tense, poised, no hint of despair, high on adrenalin. These were her best soldiers and she loved them dearly. They had fought together in perfect co-ordination during the last few weeks, retreating only when retreat was the only intelligent option. Looking at them now she could see no hint of doubt. They expected to attack and they were ready.

What could she do? She issued the order:

"Engage, fire at will"

Immediately the shooting began. Lasers drew lines in all directions, a spillikins of light beams. Small parcels of energy flew down the beams at speeds the human eye could not detect. The generation of each shot was silent but the arrival created great waves of noise all around the building. Within seconds every window was broken. Some of the attackers fell soundlessly, immobilised by the shots from the house. Bits of render fell off the walls as the Cambrians tightened their hold. Still the defence went on; every part of the building sending out lines of energy. They saw troops running towards them from each end of the street, and all too soon the energy lines coming in began to outnumber those going out.

Huw

Ten minutes later it was all over. The building had been cleared; a dozen or so survivors had been taken prisoner, the rest were silent, lying where they had fallen. The Commander, a woman, was one of the first bodies the Cambrians stumbled over as they began to secure the building. She looked surprised. As Huw began his report the signal from Magnus came in

"ABORT ABORT"

"Too late mate" said Huw to himself, wondering what had got into the old boy.

2084 THE END

Vandervelde – 2108 endings

What else could I do? I could have written a happy ending, but the reality which followed was horrible. I have some obligation to the truth. I toyed with the idea of including myself as a character, but that seemed too contrived. Since it seems unlikely now that my great novel "Twenty Eighty Four - The End Game" and all these notes, documents and stories I have collected will be read by more than a handful of people, I have little to lose now by telling things as they were.

Magnus did not survive the genocide, but Lydia is still here. She lives in Rovcaster still with her partner Bernard and their son Murdo. Eden is now something in the government in what was Anglia. One day, if I am still around, and I can get there, I will show them all this stuff and see what they make of it. First I must open up my journals and take up the role of diarist again.

The book finished in 2092. We were still at the Plas then, Judith and I, but she was then seventy five and finding it hard to fulfil her reprised role as President. Fortunately, as the confusing conflict with Anglia swirled round her, she was not asked to do much more than be a figurehead.

What more can I say about the nasty little wars that disfigured the face of our islands? They dragged on for another two years, but by then the international refugee situation had got so bad that whatever weapons our nations had were pressed into service all along the south and east coasts. As the boats arrived they were sunk. It was hateful and obscene, but we all knew that it was them or us. Wherever a group of refugees managed to get ashore they attacked and killed anyone they came across.

Judith made a great effort to hold the line when the Assembly met for the last time in Brigstowe. It was September 2095, and we were almost the last to cling onto some semblance of government. Lyndain was like the epicentre of a hurricane – death and destruction swirled round it. At the fringes – northern Caledonia, western Hibernia, even western Cambria, something like normal life went on, but elsewhere as in the rest of Europe, and for all we knew in the rest of the world, chaos reigned.

I shall never forget the day she returned from that last Assembly. I met her at the transtation, but she could not move. Her face was white, distorted with pain.

"Judith, dear heart what is it?"

"Van . . . it's over. I can't . . . Just get me home please." I helped her move to the passenger seat and took the drive position. As I drove home, desperately worried, she told me in halting, broken phrases how the Assembly had torn itself apart.

We had two more days together. While she could still speak she said:

"No regrets Van. I've never wanted to be with anyone else . . . my sugar daddy . . . my toyboy." We laughed together for the last time. After a restless night she seemed calmer as the sun rose but she never spoke again and late in the afternoon her breathing stopped.

******

As the horrors of the last days of 2095 played out my communication with the rest of the world flickered but never quite died. The Plas still had power and my worktable brought me a collection of random images, none of which I cared to contemplate. I tried to write more, but it seemed ever more pointless. Some days I just stared out at the trees.

One day, weeks, months later, it was there in the room - that strange metalic smell which instantly took me back so many years. I turned and there on my screen was a room I knew nothing of, and the shape of a man. Someone I had seen in the past. He turned towards me but the image vanished. The room again had its usual smell - fabric, polish, decay. Someone was watching - worse, something was happening inside my head, in my brain. Over the next few hours the sense grew in me that I had one last duty to perform: I had to go somewhere.

Why should I stay here anyway? All the people I had known and loved were gone. I can't manage this big house on my own, and if it were not for Alice, the nice girl from the "town" who brings me the odd rabbit, some veg, one of her loaves of rough bread or some milk, I would starve. I doubt whether there are more than thirty people left here now, but I had heard there was still some sort of government in Brigstowe and my intuition - if that is the right word for this odd sensation- tells me I should be there.

Of course the transnet was defunct, but there were plenty of abandoned eks, so I charged up as many batteries as one of the best of them would carry and set off by road.

It was a long dreary trip, changing batteries every 20 miles or so - I just threw the old ones away - but I got there and found the assembly building still standing. How they knew I was coming I have no idea, but the way things were happening at present I was hardly surprised, and it felt good to be back where there was some sense of order. I was shown to a comfortable room with a bed, a worktable, chairs and a washroom.

"You are welcome to stay here as our guest for as long as you like Mr Vandervelde."

"Thank you. I appreciate it."

"I expect you would like to rest now. Some of us will be eating here at eight. Will you join us?"

"I would be happy to."

Later they told me that someone was coming here to

meet me. They expect him to arrive at the haven in the next few days.

"Are there no LTAs flying now?"

"Yes there are a few, but our visitor prefers to travel by sea."

"Can you tell me who it is?"

"No, sorry. We were just told to tell you that he is an Elder."

An Elder? I always knew somehow that there were more. I spent the next two days wandering around the haven. It was impossible not to be reminded of 44, but there were far less people and I never felt afraid. The feeling of dread that had been with me off and on since the "vision" was retreating. What had I to fear after all? Life had little to offer me.

My curiosity got the better of me when the battered old ship arrived, and I was there to meet the visitor. As soon as I saw him I knew that this was the shadow I had seen in my flash of intuition. I had some knowledge of him. The stance, how he moved, his presence, all were familiar, but I had no name for him.

"Van, I can see you do not know me, but I know you and I am glad we meet at last. I am Fagus."

"Well Mr Fagus . . . no wait . . . that's wrong isn't it?" He smiled. I could see then clearly that he was an Elder.

"You are 'El Sabio', Brother Fagus. You are the one who took over from Ulm and then disappeared. You met Judith."

"All that is correct as far as it goes, but I have some important things to discuss with you."

He asked me to join him later that day in a small interview room. There was a table and two chairs but nothing else. I sat opposite him and he looked at me. Again I had that peculiar sensation. For an instant I closed my eyes and when

I opened them again I knew. It was as if all the pieces of the puzzle that was my life in this century had clicked into place. Here in front of me was the key to it all. All the love, the comradeship, the technology, the politics - all that but all the horror and destruction too. This man, my twin, my shadow, he was somehow at the centre of it.

"You are the Warden"

"No no. I am a man like you, and an Elder. The Warden is more than either of us. We all built it – I, Tilia, Acer, Fraxinus, Ulm, and of course you, but your memory was adjusted. We all - you as well - agreed that for your mission to succeed you should not remember how it began. I am here today to ask you to come back, to come and join us. If you agree I can release those memories. You will know how we worked together, you will remember your life as Brother Quercus the Oak Tree."

"Oak? Me? . . .So I was with you.

"What about my childhood - our childhood? Do you know?"

"Very little. None of us know our parents. My first memory is a classroom where we were learning our languages. I do not remember a home, only a few comrades who were like me, and the rooms we slept and worked in. I think even as children we were servants of Gaia. Even my early memories of my life in Bolivia are not clear.

"Listen, Van, You do not have to come with me. You can live out your life however you please, but I cannot restore those memories unless you join us. If you do decide to join us you will become a part of this great intelligence, the Warden. Already we have achieved integration with Gaia, with you we could go further. We could begin to reshape our world. It is possible that with you joining us we could even begin to reshape the human genome. We could make sure that no future human society could ever threaten Gaia again. We could all live at peace with the natural world - a truly sustainable society."

Sitting upright on his hard chair, he had the face of an Inca: brown skin, a creased face, aquiline nose, long dark hair beginning to grey. He looked at me intently.

"Ah my old comrade, I can see you are concerned. I feel what you feel and I sense that you may prefer a different resolution. To go further may undermine your sense of what you, working alone, have achieved, and the achievement is great – the world will forever be in your debt. But perhaps your main concern is the terrible suffering we have all had to go through to get to this position. Believe me I share that concern." He fixed me with those dark luminous eyes.

"Do you? I wonder. I don't see much signs of suffering. I must tell you that I could not face a future, however limited, with the thought that I was part of a group which amused itself playing games with the human race . . . "

Fagus broke in angrily, his English faltering:

"Amused! How you can say this things! You don't know, and now it looks like you never will. I am 'El Sabio' like you. Truth is in our bones."

He was right of course. I was being irrational.

"I apologise. Of course you would not deceive me. Do not be angry, but I must ask one more thing of you." Fagus nodded his head silently.

"This intelligence, this phenomenon that we call 'the Warden', does he, she, or it have a physical presence - an actual location, some secret place where you make your plans?"

"I accept your apology. Certainly the Warden has a physical reality, but it has always been a synthesis of human and artificial intelligence. Do you remember all that talk years ago about "The Singularity"?

“Ah yes, the point at which artificial and human intelligence would merge.”

“That’s right, all those people – Neumann, Kurzweil, Vinge and so on, they all believed that this combined intelligence would transcend the reality of Gaia, that humans and their machines could continue to dominate the planet indefinitely. Of course, we had achieved that point before they were born, and we had no intention of allowing their dangerous experiments to threaten Gaia.

“So, yes the Warden has a physical presence, and there is nothing I would like more than to take you there and try to prove to you that we are not without heart. Indeed that was my aim in coming here, but I know now that you will stay, and whatever you feel about me is of no importance compared to your own self-respect. At least I can help you to retain that.”

“Yes, you are right. I must stay. I don’t believe even such a super intelligence could change the way Gaia works. Even without the Warden, Gaia would have protected herself, but perhaps with the loss of our species. She has always worked in cycles. Life on this planet rises and falls. My life, the life I remember, has been deeply involved with a series of these cycles. I now feel old and I have no wish to court immortality. All I want now is to live out my days as part of the last cycle in this century - the re-discovery of human life in harmony with Gaia.”

Postscript: The Hub

On 5 July 2097 the total population of the world was 5.9 billion. By the spring of 2098 it had fallen to 2.9 billion, and by the middle of that year had reached the target figure: 1.5 billion. As predicted, the regions had been adjusted so that the survivors were fairly evenly spread and had some sort of superstructure capable of dealing with the situation. Gaia was back in sync and The Warden could enter sleep mode.

Glossary

Comms - universal communications device. Almost everyone carries a device like a 2015 smart phone which is their only means of communicating with others - by video, voice or text.

Transnet - the track element of the 2036 transport system, including the stations and control systems.

Ek (e-car), the mobile part of the transnet system. These are various kinds of vehicle module which can link to the transnet.

Demarchy - any form of government where the representatives of the people are partly selected by lottery.

Place names:

Most of the action in the book takes place in a fictionalised version of Britain. To keep a fictional distance from the real places, the English language place names have been replaced with either Welsh, Anglo-Saxon or Latin versions of the name.

Abertawe - Swansea

Anglia – England

Breizh - Brittany

Brigstowe - Bristol

Burgedin - Edinburgh

Caerdydd - Cardiff

Caledonia - Scotland

Cambria - Wales and the West of England

Caster - Chester

Havren - River Severn

Kernow - Cornwall

Anglia - London, the South East and the Midlands of England

Hibernia – Ireland

Kernow - Cornwall

Lerpwl – Liverpool

Lyndain - London

Pennines - The North of England

Pwl - Poole

Ystwyth - Aberystwyth

Dyfi - Machynlleth

Granta - Cambridge

Isis - river Thames

Shethfeld - Sheffield

Some names are made-up:

Bridhaven - Bridport

Blackhall - White hall

Welsh (Cymraeg) words

Duw - God

Pennaeth - colonel (approx)

Prynhawn da I bawb – Good afternoon to all

About the author

Richard Turner was brought up in rural Wiltshire and went from a Swindon grammar school to graduate in English at Cambridge. Partly as a reaction to this background he has been self-employed most of his working life; as a furniture maker and restorer and more recently as a music promoter and agent.

Despite numerous attempts to write, it was not until his sixties that he finally managed to sit still long enough to finish a book. He became involved in Green politics in the early 70s, and recent research in the life sciences, evolution and modern politics led to the ideas expressed in this book series.

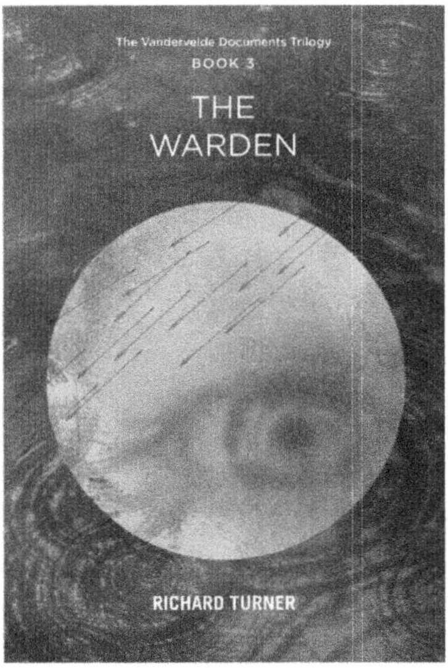

Cover art by Danny Jenkins

Lightning Source UK Ltd.
Milton Keynes UK
UKOW06f2244210415

250057UK00002B/102/P

9 780993 08620